P9-ELN-846

PRAISE FOR THE CHLOE ELLEFSON MYSTERY SERIES

DEATH ON THE PRAIRIE

"Fans of Laura Ingalls Wilder will savor the facts … Ernst does an exceptional job of sharing the kinds of character details that cozy readers relish." —*Booklist*

"A real treat for Little House fans, a fine mystery supplemented by fascinating information on the life and times of Laura Ingalls Wilder." — *Kirkus Reviews*

"The sixth installment of this incredible series … is a super read that sparks the imagination." —*Suspense Magazine*

"As superbly pieced together as a blue-ribbon quilt, *Death on the Prairie* is deft and delightful, and you don't want to miss it!" —Molly MacRae, Lovey Award–winning author of the Haunted Yarn Shop mysteries

"'Die hard fans of Laura Ingalls Wilder' takes on a whole new meaning when Chloe and her sister embark on a 'Laura pilgrimage,' visiting all of the Laura Ingalls Wilder sites, in search of proof that a quilt given to Chloe was indeed made by Laura herself … Fans of Laura and Chloe both will enjoy *Death on the Prairie*. Author Kathleen Ernst spins a delightful tale of intrigue that interweaves facts about Laura's life with fan folklore, and of course, murder. I give this book an enthusiastic two thumbs up!" —Linda Halpin, author of *Quilting with Laura: Patterns Inspired by the Little House on the Prairie Series*

"Suspense, intrigue, trafficking in stolen artifacts, blackmail, murder: they're all here in this fast-paced mystery thriller. Chloe Ellefson set off on a journey to visit all of the Laura Ingalls Wilder sites in search of the truth about a quilt Wilder may have made, and in the process of solving several crimes Chloe learns a lot about the

CALGARY PUBLIC LIBRARY

JAN   2019

beloved children's author and about herself."—John E. Miller, author of *Becoming Laura Ingalls Wilder: The Woman Behind the Legend* and *Laura Ingalls Wilder's Little Town: Where History and Literature Meet*

TRADITION OF DECEIT

"Ernst keeps getting better with each entry in this fascinating series." —*Library Journal*

"Everybody has secrets in this action-filled cozy."—*Publishers Weekly*

"All in all, a very enjoyable reading experience."—*Mystery Scene*

"A page-turner with a clever surprise ending."—G.M. Malliet, Agatha Award-winning author of the St. Just and Max Tudor mystery series

"[A] haunting tale of two murders… This is more than a mystery. It is a plush journey into cultural time and place."—Jill Florence Lackey, PhD, author of *Milwaukee's Old South Side* and *American Ethnic Practices in the Twenty-First Century*

HERITAGE OF DARKNESS

"Chloe's fourth… provides a little mystery, a little romance, and a little more information about Norwegian folk art and tales."—*Kirkus Reviews*

THE LIGHT KEEPER'S LEGACY

"Chloe's third combines a good mystery with some interesting historical information on a niche subject."—*Kirkus Reviews*

"Framed by the history of lighthouses and their keepers and the story of fishery disputes through time, the multiple plots move easily across the intertwined past and present."—*Booklist Online*

"A haunted island makes for fun escape reading. Ernst's third amateur sleuth cozy is just the ticket for lighthouse fans and genealogy buffs. Deftly flipping back and forth in time in alternating chapters, the author builds up two mystery cases and cleverly weaves them back together."—*Library Journal*

"While the mystery elements of this book are very good, what really elevates it are the historical tidbits of the real-life Pottawatomie Lighthouse and the surrounding fishing village."—*Mystery Scene*

"Once again in *The Light Keeper's Legacy* Kathleen Ernst wraps history with mystery in a fresh and compelling read. I ignored food so I could finish this third Chloe Ellefson mystery quickly. I marvel at Kathleen's ability to deepen her series characters while deftly introducing us to a new setting and unique people on an island off the Wisconsin coast. In the fashion of Barbara Kingsolver, Kathleen weaves contemporary conflicts of commercial fishing, environmentalists, sport fisherman and law enforcement into a web of similar conflicts in the 1880s and the two women on neighboring islands still speaking to Chloe that their stories may be remembered. It takes a skilled writer to move back and forth 100 years apart, make us care for the characters in both centuries, give us particular details of lighthouse life and early Wisconsin, not forget Chloe's love interest and have us cheering at the end. A rich and satisfying third novel that makes me ask what all avid readers will: When's the next one! Well done, Kathleen!"—Jane Kirkpatrick, *New York Times* bestselling author

THE HEIRLOOM MURDERS

"Chloe is an appealing character, and Ernst's depiction of work at a living museum lends authenticity and a sense of place to the involving plot."—*St. Paul Pioneer Press*

"Greed, passion, skill, and luck all figure in this surprise-filled outing."—*Publishers Weekly*

"Interesting, well-drawn characters and a complicated plot make this a very satisfying read."—*Mystery Reader*

"Entertainment and edification."—*Mystery Scene*

OLD WORLD MURDER

"*Old World Murder* is strongest in its charming local color and genuine love for Wisconsin's rolling hills, pastures, and woodlands…a delightful distraction for an evening or two."—*New York Journal of Books*

"Clever plot twists and credible characters make this a far from humdrum cozy."—*Publishers Weekly*

"This series debut by an author of children's mysteries rolls out nicely for readers who like a cozy with a dab of antique lore. Jeanne M. Dams fans will like the ethnic background."—*Library Journal*

"Information on how to conduct historical research, background on Norwegian culture, and details about running an outdoor museum frame the engaging story of a woman devastated by a failed romantic relationship whose sleuthing helps her heal."—*Booklist*

"Museum masterpiece."—*Rosebud Book Reviews*

"A real find…5 stars."—*Once Upon a Romance*

"A wonderfully-woven tale that winds in and out of modern and historical Wisconsin with plenty of mysteries—both past and present. In curator Chloe Ellefson, Ernst has created a captivating character with humor, grit, and a tangled history of her own that needs unraveling. Enchanting!"—Sandi Ault, author of the WILD mystery series and recipient of the Mary Higgins Clark Award

"Propulsive and superbly written, this first entry in a dynamite new series from accomplished author Kathleen Ernst seamlessly melds the 1980s and the 19th century. Character-driven, with mystery aplenty, *Old World Murder* is a sensational read. Think Sue Grafton meets Earlene Fowler, with a dash of Elizabeth Peters."—Julia Spencer-Fleming, Anthony, and Agatha Award–winning author of *I Shall Not Want* and *One Was A Soldier*

ALSO BY KATHLEEN ERNST

Nonfiction
Too Afraid to Cry:
Maryland Civilians in the Antietam Campaign
A Settler's Year: Pioneer Life Through the Seasons

Chloe Ellefson Mysteries
Old World Murder
The Heirloom Murders
The Light Keeper's Legacy
Heritage of Darkness
Tradition of Deceit
Death on the Prairie

American Girl Series
Captain of the Ship: A Caroline Classic
Facing the Enemy: A Caroline Classic
Traitor in the Shipyard: A Caroline Mystery
Catch the Wind: My Journey with Caroline
The Smuggler's Secrets: A Caroline Mystery

American Girl Mysteries
Trouble at Fort La Pointe
Whistler in the Dark
Betrayal at Cross Creek
Danger at the Zoo: A Kit Mystery
Secrets in the Hills: A Josefina Mystery
Midnight in Lonesome Hollow: A Kit Mystery
The Runaway Friend: A Kirsten Mystery
Clues in the Shadows: A Molly Mystery

A CHLOE ELLEFSON MYSTERY

a Memory of Muskets

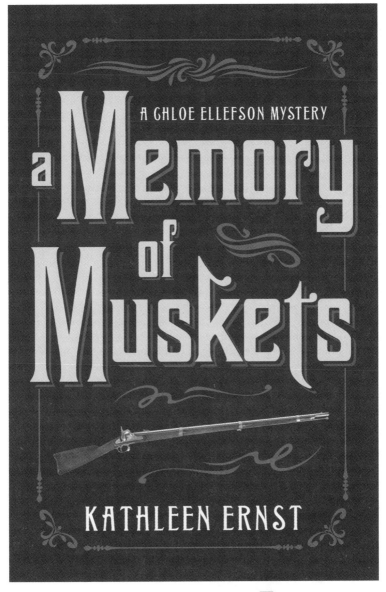

KATHLEEN ERNST

MIDNIGHT INK
WOODBURY, MINNESOTA

A Memory of Muskets: A Chloe Ellefson Mystery © 2016 by Kathleen Ernst. All rights reserved. No part of this book may be used or reproduced in any manner whatsoever, including Internet usage, without written permission from Midnight Ink, except in the case of brief quotations embodied in critical articles and reviews.

This is not an official publication. Some names and designations used in this story are the property of the trademark holder and are used for identification purposes only.

FIRST EDITION
Second Printing, 2016

Book format by Bob Gaul
Cover design by Kevin R. Brown
Cover illustrations by Charlie Griak (and)
                iStockphoto.com/20791980/©Ekaterina Romanova
Editing by Nicole Nugent
Map created by Llewellyn art department
Photos on pages 381–385:
    #1, 2, 6–9 © Wisconsin Veterans Museum;
    #3 © North Wood County Historical Society, Wisconsin;
    #4–5 © Library of Congress

Midnight Ink, an imprint of Llewellyn Worldwide Ltd.

This is a work of fiction. Names, characters, places, and incidents are either the product of the author's imagination or are used fictitiously, and any resemblance to actual persons, living or dead, business establishments, events, or locales is entirely coincidental.

Library of Congress Cataloging-in-Publication Data
Names: Ernst, Kathleen, author.
Title: A memory of muskets : a Chloe Ellefson mystery / Kathleen Ernst.
Description: First edition. | Woodbury, Minnesota : Midnight Ink, [2016] |
  Series: A Chloe Ellefson mystery ; 7
Identifiers: LCCN 2016008350 | ISBN 9780738745152 (softcover)
Subjects: LCSH: Women museum curators—Fiction. |
  Murder—Investigation—Fiction. | Old World Wisconsin (Museum)—Fiction. |
  GSAFD: Mystery fiction.
Classification: LCC PS3605.R77 M46 2016 | DDC 813/.6—
  dc23 LC record available at http://lccn.loc.gov/2016008350

Midnight Ink
Llewellyn Worldwide Ltd.
2143 Wooddale Drive
Woodbury, MN 55125-2989
www.midnightinkbooks.com

Printed in the United States of America

DEDICATION

For Sergeant Gwen Bruckner, Eagle Police Department—
with thanks for your help, advice, and friendship;

and for my reenacting friends—
with thanks for good memories;

and in honor of the immigrants
who sacrificed so much to reach the New World,
only to confront civil war.

Old World Wisconsin is a real historic site in Waukesha County, Wisconsin. I had the pleasure and privilege of working there in the 1980s—just as my protagonist Chloe Ellefson does. My responsibilities included coordinating the site's annual Civil War event; I also was a Civil War reenactor myself. The 9th Wisconsin Infantry Regiment in this story is modeled on the reenactors I knew who participated with respect for those they represented, and who worked hard to create and interpret accurate impressions. The 100th Wisconsin Regiment is complete fabrication, and the plot of *A Memory of Muskets* is completely fictional.

Milwaukee's German Fest has been celebrating German culture and heritage since 1981. *Pommersche Tanzdeel Freistadt* was organized in 1977, in western Ozaukee County, Wisconsin—site of the oldest German settlement in the state. The group preserves folk culture by performing songs and dances from the Pomeranian region.

What is now called the Wisconsin Veterans Museum was known in 1983 as the Grand Army of the Republic (G.A.R.) Museum. I used the contemporary name to minimize confusion.

The Ice Age National Scenic Trail was established in 1980, but visionaries had been working toward that goal for decades, adding sections year by year as resources permitted. Today the 1,200-mile trail is managed by the National Park Service, the Wisconsin Department of Natural Resources, and the Ice Age Trail Alliance.

To learn more, visit:

Old World Wisconsin
  http://oldworldwisconsin.wisconsinhistory.org

German Fest
  http://germanfest.com

Pommersche Tanzdeel Freistadt
  http://www.ptfusa.org

State Historical Society of Wisconsin
  (now the Wisconsin Historical Society)
  http://www.wisconsinhistory.org

Wisconsin Veterans Museum
  http://www.wisvetsmuseum.com

The Kettle Moraine State Forest—Southern Unit
  http://dnr.wi.gov/topic/parks/name/kms/

The Ice Age National Scenic Trail:
  http://www.nps.gov/iatr/index.htm and
  http://www.iceagetrail.org

You'll find photographs of some of the artifacts mentioned in the story on pages 381-385.

You can also find many more photographs, maps, and other resources on my website, www.kathleenernst.com.

CAST OF CHARACTERS

Contemporary Timeline (1983), Old World Wisconsin

Chloe Ellefson—curator of collections

Byron Cooke—curator of interpretation

Ralph Petty—director

Alyssa Greer—interpreter

Jenny and Lee Hawkins—interpreters

Belinda Lansing—Chloe's intern

Kyle Fassbender—interpreter; member,
9th Wisconsin Infantry Regiment

Marv Tenally—security guard

Contemporary Timeline (1983), Village of Eagle, Wisconsin

Roelke McKenna—officer, Police Department

Maggie Geddings—resident

Denise Miller—EMT

Adam Bolitho—EMT

Chief Naborski—chief, Police Department

Marie—clerk, Police Department

Skeet Deardorff—officer, Police Department

Contemporary Timeline (1983), others

Libby—Roelke's cousin

Justin and Dierdre—Libby's kids

Gunter Diederich—founder, 9th Wisconsin Infantry Regiment

Steven Siggelkow—member, 9th Wisconsin Infantry Regiment

Gerald and Marjorie Ostermann—founders,
    100th Wisconsin Infantry Regiment

Mac Ostermann—Gerald and Marjorie's son

Lon Goresko—detective, Waukesha County

Marge Bandacek—deputy sheriff, Waukesha County

Dobry Banik—police officer, Milwaukee Police Department

Sergeant McKulski—head of security, German Fest

Faye—curator of iconography, State Historical Society of Wisconsin

Richard—director, Wisconsin Veterans Museum

Frank Acker—reenactor from Missouri

Historical Timeline (1861–1864, 1879)

Rosina Lauterbach—immigrant from Pomerania, Prussia

Leopold Zuehlsdorff—immigrant and Free Thinker

Klaus Roelke—immigrant farmer

Adolf and Lottie Sperber—Rosina's friends

Franz Sperber—Adolf's brother

Muehlenbergs—neighbors

Old World Wisconsin, 1983

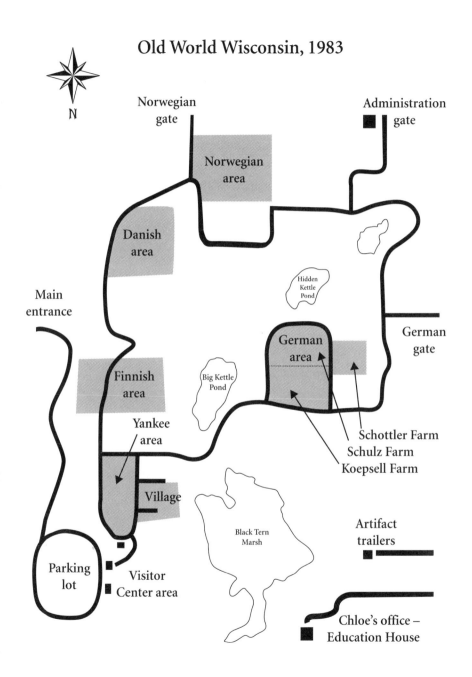

ONE

"I WANT A FIGHT," Ralph Petty said.

Chloe started to protest but remembered just in time that this was not her meeting, not her show. She closed her mouth and tried to look thoughtful.

Byron shifted in his chair. "We have some new ideas."

The historic site director waved one finger—evidently brushing aside pesky new ideas with his whole hand would require too much effort—and peered over his half-glasses at Byron. It was a practiced gesture intended, Chloe was certain, to convey a literal sense of looking down upon ignorant minions. In this case the unworthy were Byron Cooke, Old World Wisconsin's curator of interpretation, and Chloe Ellefson, curator of collections. "Not just a fight. I want a battle."

"Byron's developed some exciting alternatives," she said. "I think—"

"Miss Ellefson, why are you here?" Petty demanded irritably, stroking the tidy beard he'd probably grown to balance his retreating hairline. "This is an interpretive matter."

1

Here was Director Petty's office. Although there was no place Chloe would less rather be, she'd promised Byron moral support. "Yes. But every educational program has implications for the collections, and—"

"Actually," Byron cut in, "Chloe is here because I invited her."

Chloe beamed at Petty. He never knew how to handle that.

"I've never worked with reenactors," Byron continued, "so I asked her to help plan and implement Old World's first Civil War event."

"I'm *always* happy to help a colleague," Chloe assured Petty earnestly.

Petty frowned. He was a misogynistic megalomaniac with a graduate degree in micromanagement. Chloe and he shared a mutual, strong, and barely disguised dislike. He'd already tried to fire her once.

There had been a time when Chloe simply did not care if he raised his metaphorical ax. But now she did care, a whole lot. For reasons both professional and personal, she'd made a commitment to this large living history museum. And she was painfully aware that her desire to stay employed, *here,* surrendered a whole lot of power to Ralph Petty.

Byron leapt into the breach before the stand-off became too pronounced. "We think that a thematic approach might best illuminate our state's experience."

"Thematic?" Petty's expression suggested that someone had hidden a Limburger sandwich under his desk.

"Looking at homefront challenges," Chloe explained. "I'm sure that many people don't know there was a prison camp in Madison. Or we can tell the story of the 1862 panic that swept through Wisconsin when Sioux people clashed with white settlers in Minnesota."

Petty folded his arms. "The 1862 panic is a sensitive topic."

Chloe sighed. Old World was a popular and respected historic site, owned and managed by the State Historical Society of Wisconsin. What better place to explore challenging topics?

"We're proposing an enlistment scenario," Byron said. "Programming could include recruitment rallies, mustering in, learning drill, differing political views among ethnic communities..."

"Women's activities," Chloe added. "Sewing flags, gathering relief supplies, sanitary fairs, shifting gender roles as men left for the front."

"The draft," Byron said.

"The draft *riots*," Chloe said.

"Selling draft insurance," Byron said.

"Buying substitutes," Chloe said.

"I get the point," Petty snapped. "But I don't see why you can't do some of that and still hold a mock battle. Lots of reenactors and a big, bloody fight. *That's* what will sell tickets."

"Well, we don't really know that," Chloe observed, "since this will be our first foray into Civil War programming."

Petty's cheeks were growing ruddy. "*Miss* Ellefson—"

"Ms.," Chloe said for the hundredth time, and instantly regretted it. Petty undoubtedly persisted in the *Miss* stuff because it bugged her, and she'd vowed to stop reacting.

"Since it's already July, it's too late to plan and stage a battle this season," Byron pointed out. "But we can do some limited programming."

"That will give us a chance to make sure any unit involved is able to meet our standards," Chloe added. "I know that's important to *all* of us."

"May I remind you," Petty said, "that there are many kinds of standards. You might not be so lofty, Miss Ellefson, if you received a call every Monday morning from the historic sites' division director, as *I* do. I report attendance and sales numbers, not educational abstractions. Program revenue keeps the gates open. Anyone who *chooses* to invest time and resources in experimental programming does so at his, or her, own peril."

Had Ralph Petty just threatened them? Chloe really thought he had.

Petty twiddled a pen in his fingers. "I doubt if you can entice reenactors to come without offering a battle."

Which shows how little you know about reenacting, Chloe thought. "Look, if we just—"

"I'm finding this conversation *very* helpful," Byron interrupted, making a big show of looking at his watch. "But Chloe and I are meeting representatives from a reenactment unit this afternoon. May we continue our discussion another time?"

"Very well." Petty picked up a stack of papers and tapped the edges against his desk, which seemed to provide a sense of finality. "I expect you to discuss the possibility of a mock battle with the reenactors, Mr. Cooke."

"Absolutely," Byron promised.

He and Chloe made their escape. They left the euphemistically named Administration building—one of the small homes on a remote edge of Old World Wisconsin's 576 acres, acquired by the historical society and forced into makeshift office duty—and headed to Byron's car. Once behind the wheel Byron slammed the door, leaned against the headrest, and closed his eyes.

Chloe slid into the passenger seat and considered her colleague. Byron was a few years younger than she was. He had unkempt brown hair and a tiny goatee, and wore prescription lenses in antique wire frames. As a talented interpreter and a conscientious educator, he struggled to protect the best interests of the interpreters he supervised—a difficult slog when the site director had no experience in the interpretive trenches himself, and no empathy for those who did.

Byron straightened and eyed her bleakly. "Did Petty actually suggest that he'd fire us if we didn't draw a big crowd for our event?" "He did." Chloe exhaled slowly. "Do you have any idea why this particular conversation went so bad, so fast?"

"None."

Damn. "You may not have noticed," she said, "but Ralph Petty really doesn't like me."

"I'd noticed."

"The mood might improve if I don't attend future planning meetings." She looked out the window. Was she backing off to help Byron, or to protect herself? The latter possibility was infuriating. *I need my job*, she thought, *but I will* not *scurry about like a frightened rabbit.*

"We should have gone in *pushing* for a battle," Byron muttered. "Petty would have been preaching the glories of social history in no time." He turned the key in the ignition.

Chloe cranked down the window. The afternoon was all glaring sun and cloudless sky. She was tempted to hang her head out the window dog-like while Byron made the short drive from the Admin building to Old World Wisconsin's main gate. She had second thoughts when he hit the gas. Byron moved, and drove, at speeds clocked at "bat outta hell."

She settled back in the seat. "Try not to let Petty get to you."

"If we're going to do a Civil War event, I want to do it well." He flicked on his blinker and turned onto Old World's entrance drive.

The landscape architects and historians who'd created the massive historic site within the Kettle Moraine State Forest a decade earlier, in the 1970s, had hidden the Visitor Center area from the road. The winding drive forced guests to meander, transitioning from modern life. Trees blocked the sun, and Chloe inhaled the cooler air hungrily.

Byron parked in the lot beneath towering pines. "We're actually early. I just had to get out of Petty's office."

"Fine by me." Now Chloe leaned back and closed her eyes. She'd had a short night. Way too short.

"Up late packing?" Byron asked. "When's moving day?"

"I haven't decided yet." Chloe didn't want to think about moving day. "So. How did you connect with the reenactors we're meeting today?"

"You know Kyle Fassbender, right?"

Chloe thought back to the sessions about collections care she'd provided to the summer interpreters. "College kid? Long curly hair and a big smile?"

"That's him. He belongs to the 9th Wisconsin Infantry Regiment, and he says the group is a good fit for our mission." Byron swiveled to look at her. "But ... is Petty right? Will it take a battle to attract good reenactors?"

"Absolutely not," she said firmly. "We have three—*three*—working farms restored to the 1860s. Trust me, that alone will be a big draw."

"I suppose so."

"And we can prepare a big period dinner as a thank-you for the reenactors' time and contributions." There were a dozen working kitchens among the fifty-plus historic buildings that had been painstakingly moved from rural Wisconsin to the historic site and restored to dates ranging from 1845 to 1915.

"No problem." Byron checked his watch and grabbed a satchel he'd tossed on the back seat. "We should go."

Chloe put one hand on his arm. "Byron, have you ever attended a reenactment?"

"I've seen a few regiments marching in parades."

"Well, here's the thing. Each unit has its own personality. They don't all have the same philosophy, and they don't all get along." That was an understatement, but Chloe figured she'd ease Byron into the wonderful and messy world of Civil War reenacting.

"You're talking about their appearance?" Byron scratched one corner of his mouth. "I saw some guys who had fabulous impressions, and some who … " He searched for a polite description and settled for, " … who didn't."

"That's part of it. The trouble is that sometimes guys who *look* good aren't willing to engage with visitors. Sometimes the best educators wear polyester uniform coats. We need reenactors who look good, know a lot, *and* want to share with visitors."

Byron nodded. "I won't make any commitments today."

Chloe had done quite a bit of reenacting during her college and grad school years. She'd learned a lot, made dear friends, had some amazing experiences. She'd also met a few reenactors who'd gotten involved for all the wrong reasons.

She frowned. Stupid Petty. She really, *really* wanted to pull off a stellar Civil War event.

Maybe she just wanted to prove Ralph Petty wrong, and help stage a nonbattle reenactment that left visitors satisfied, enlightened, and eager to learn more. Or maybe it was because recent life events were forcing her to reevaluate her priorities. She was trying to behave more like a responsible grown-up and less like a gypsy with an overactive imagination and a strong sense of wanderlust.

Whatever the cause, she decided to leave things at that. "Sounds good."

As they walked to the Visitor Center green, Byron gestured toward a man in Union blue near the ticket booth. "There's one of our guys."

Gunter Diederich was stocky, with blond hair and beard, maybe pushing forty. Behind period spectacles, his blue eyes glinted with animation. "So good to meet you!" he exclaimed, offering a firm handshake. "I started the 9th Wisconsin Infantry Regiment reenactment unit six years ago. My great-grandfather fought in the original 9th."

"The 9th was composed primarily of German men, right?" Chloe asked. She'd been boning up.

"It was."

"We have three Civil War–era farms." Byron scratched a mosquito bite on his wrist. "Schulz is German, Kvaale is Norwegian, and Sanford was home to a Yankee family."

"Excellent." Gunter looked happy as a child at the zoo. "That will provide wonderful diversity."

Chloe gave Gunter points for affability and interpretive focus. Now she sized up his impression: battered brogans, wool trousers tucked into heavy wool socks, a dusty sack coat with sergeant's bars on the sleeves. His sweat-stained shirt was an impressive linsey-woolsy repro. He looked good. *Appearance: Check.*

"Are we waiting for one more?" Byron asked.

"Steven Siggelkow—one of my pards—came early to see the site," Gunter said. "His car's in the lot. I'm sure he'll be along."

"Tell me more about your unit," Chloe said. "Do you have a mission statement? Membership requirements?"

"We're open to anyone interested in learning about Wisconsin's Civil War soldiers. Our goals are to honor the memory of those who served, and to portray them as accurately as possible."

"Do your reenactors have to be members of a firearms group? Or a certain political party?"

Byron looked startled, but Gunter merely shook his head. "No. We aren't a militia, and we avoid discussing modern politics."

Check, check. "What kind of experience do you have?"

"We've done everything from big national events—ten, twelve thousand participants—to small living history presentations," Gunter told her. "School programs. A few tacticals, military encampments at historic sites."

Byron shot her a glance: *Sound good to you?* She gave him a tiny smile: *So far, so good.*

Gunter pulled an antique watch from its pocket and opened the case. "Steven's fifteen minutes late."

Everyone looked around. An old barn repurposed as a restaurant stood at one end of the Visitor Center's grassy green, and an old barn repurposed as a gift shop and orientation center crowned the other. Visitors straggled toward the parking lot. One family was picnicking. A young couple was snapping pictures. No other Union volunteers were in sight.

Gunter shrugged. "Let's head out. He'll find us."

They walked into the historic site proper, following a gravel road through the Crossroads Village. Organ music drifted from St. Peter's Church, and a rhythmic *clang* echoed from the blacksmith shop. In the Hafford House yard an elderly woman in a blue plaid bustle dress supervised several children eagerly scrubbing laundry on a washboard. A young woman in a brown dress trimmed with lace walked briskly toward the inn, a basket over one arm.

I should come out on site every single day, Chloe thought wistfully. It was a magical place, one of the few living history museums in the country where it was possible to wander all day and still not see everything. She loved inhaling wood smoke, and the acrid tang of coal from the smith's forge, and the faint floury scent of native grass seed heads baking in the sun. She loved looking out the window of a period kitchen to see garden and field, and prairie or woods beyond. She loved watching the seasons change—loved *feeling* them change, much as Wisconsin's early European and Yankee settlers had. Her responsibilities kept her indoors and behind the scenes all too often.

"Let's visit the German area first," Byron suggested. "The Schulz Farm has been restored to its 1860 appearance."

"It would be *wonderful* if we could spend some time there during the event," Gunter said eagerly. "Did you know that 1983 marks the tricentennial of the first German immigrants to land in America? They settled in Philadelphia."

"Very cool," Chloe agreed.

"What kind of activities do you have in mind?"

Byron and Chloe exchanged a glance. "*Well*," Byron said, "perhaps a recruitment rally, and a reenactment of the draft."

Gunter looked chagrined. "If I'd known that I wouldn't have dressed campaign-style. But we can do early war. Most of the guys have a civilian impression." They left the village and began down a hill. "And we could develop some wonderful vignettes for the guests. Have a few guys go to the German house looking for recruits, that kind of thing. I speak German, and I've been teaching the guys drill commands."

Chloe was liking this guy more and more.

"Maybe invite visitors to muster in too." Gunter rubbed his bearded chin with thumb and forefinger. "Kids love that."

Byron smiled. Chloe could tell that he liked this guy too.

They walked by Big Kettle Pond, a vestige of the last passing glacier, and started up the next hill. "So you're comfortable interacting with the public?" Chloe asked.

"Some of the guys are better at it than others," Gunter conceded. "But when we're drilling or whatever, one person always hangs by the crowd to explain what's going on."

Chloe wiped sweat from her eyes, glad she was wearing chinos and a short-sleeved shirt instead of wool. "Any women members in your unit?" she asked, before she could fall completely in love with the 9th Wisconsin. This was a *very* tricky topic.

"A few. Two have developed excellent farmwoman impressions. Sometimes they come into camp selling vegetables. And they know a lot about relief efforts. We've got several children who are great with period activities too."

Chloe caught Byron's eye: *We can definitely work with these guys.* He nodded.

At the top of the hill the Koepsell Farm, restored to its 1880 glory, emerged from the trees. Byron passed the beautiful farm by, stopping only when they rounded a bend. "There." He pointed. "That's the Schulz Farm."

Although familiar with the view, Chloe felt the spell. The land to their left was forested. Wheat rippled on their right. Beyond the field sat a tidy half-timbered home, and a stable and huge grain barn with thatched roofs. Laundry hung on a line. Oxen browsed in the pasture. It was a bubble moment—when everything looked and sounded and smelled and felt so real that for an instant, just an instant, it felt as if time had truly slipped.

Gunter stood transfixed. "We'd be honored to participate in programming here. This site is first-rate."

"Schulz is very much a German farm," Byron explained. "Unlike the farm we just passed, which is more German-American. In 1860 Charles and Auguste Schulz and their children had only been in Wisconsin for four years."

"The architecture looks European."

"The family came from Pomerania, in Prussia. Trees were scarce there, and the Old Country house design minimized the use of wood. That explains the *fachwerk*."

"Half-timbering," Chloe clarified.

Byron nodded. "A clay-straw mixture was used in between the support beams to conserve wood. Wasting space on grass would have been inconceivable, so we've turned the front yard into a kitchen garden. Wood was plentiful here, but this is the style they knew."

As they began walking again, an interpreter emerged from the back door. The young woman spread her apron and began shooing geese toward the stable. She wore a faded workdress, apron, kerchief—no fancy bustles or hoopskirts out here.

When several geese darted beyond the stable, she hurried after them. She stopped abruptly, half hidden by a cart parked beside a straw pile. Then she turned and ran toward the house, skirt held high, scattering the honking geese. Noticing Byron, Chloe, and Gunter, the girl veered toward them, white petticoat and churning pantalets flashing, trampling wheat. "Byron!" she shrieked. "*Byron!*"

This was not good. Chloe and Byron began to run. When they reached the interpreter—Alyssa, wasn't it?—Chloe grabbed her arm. "What's wrong?"

Alyssa's eyes were huge. Her cheeks were white. She was one of the college kids, a summer hire with only a few weeks' experience. "Behind the stable—I—he was... Oh *God*." Her eyes welled with tears. "A man's hurt really bad."

Chloe and Byron bolted. "Call 911!" Byron yelled over his shoulder at Alyssa. All of the historic homes had hidden emergency phones.

Chloe's skin prickled. *Hurt really bad...* The man might have had a heart attack after walking up German hill, or tripped and fallen against a farm implement. Chloe sent up a silent prayer: Please, please, *please* let him be okay.

Byron beat her to the stable, a two-story structure with an outside walkway on the second story. He ran around the mound of dirty straw—and stopped so abruptly that Chloe ran into him. She steadied herself, looked over his shoulder ... and her heart plummeted like a stone tossed into a kettle pond.

A middle-aged man wearing a Union army uniform lay motionless on his back. The reenactor's head lay at an unnatural angle. His eyes were wide, vacant, staring at the sky. One arm was flung wide.

"Can I help?" Gunter asked behind her.

A vise squeezed Chloe's rib cage as she turned, blocking his view. Gunter shouldn't have to see his pard sprawled on the ground like a broken puppet. "I'm so sorry, but ... I think it's your friend."

Color seeped from Gunter's cheeks, and his eyes went wide. He took one deep breath. "Please. I was an army medic in 'Nam."

Maybe I'm wrong, Chloe thought. Maybe Gunter can still help him. She reluctantly stepped aside.

Gunter paused when he saw the body. Then he crouched and checked the carotid artery. "He's dead." Gunter sat back on his heels. "But this isn't Steven."

Byron's eyebrows shot skyward. "Then ... who is it?"

Gunter shook his head. "I have no idea."

TWO

OFFICER ROELKE MCKENNA KNOCKED on the door of a big old house on the outskirts of Eagle. When a woman appeared he identified himself through the screen. "Are you Maggie Geddings?"

"Yes." Ms. Geddings tucked brown hair behind her ears. "Please, come in."

"Thank you." Roelke stepped inside and glanced around. The house was furnished with antiques. Fancy stuff, mostly. Not the kind of things Chloe liked.

Ms. Geddings did not look particularly at home here. She was barefoot, dressed in cutoff jeans and a pale green t-shirt with spangles around the throat. Roelke knew from the police report that she was twenty-seven, recently divorced.

"Are you here because of what happened last night?" Ms. Geddings asked. "I told Officer Deardorff everything. I heard a weather report about thunderstorms when I was getting ready to go out, so I closed all the windows. When I got home around eleven thirty, one of the kitchen windows was open."

Roelke nodded.

"I went to a neighbor's house and called the police. Officer Deardorff didn't find anyone inside, and we couldn't see any sign of disturbance, but..."

"You did everything right," Roelke assured her. "Have you noticed anything missing today?"

"No, but..." She made a wide gesture. "I inherited this house from my grandparents. I moved in just a few weeks ago, and there's a lot of stuff in this house. I can't swear that nothing was taken."

"We'll keep an eye on your place," Roelke promised. "Don't hesitate to call if anything seems suspicious."

Back in his car he studied the property. The house was set back from the road on a large, wooded lot. Not ideal for a woman living alone.

He was about to call back into service when the radio crackled. "George 220. Respond to a report of serious injury at Old World Wisconsin."

Roelke felt that extra twinge in his belly that came, now, whenever a call came in from the historic site. "Do you know where?" Old World was huge. Not to mention the off-site areas where certain permanent staff members, like the curator of collections, worked.

"The Schulz Farm in the German area."

Roelke backed the squad into the street, considering his mental map of the site grounds. Closest access would be through the staff gate on Highway S. All local first responders had a key.

Once on site he drove with dust billowing and sirens wailing—the last thing he wanted to do was round a bend and collide with a tram loaded with visitors. At the second German farm a young woman in old-time costume stood by the drive, gesturing wildly. "He's behind the stable!" she cried.

15

Roelke pulled in and parked. As he got out of the car he lasered in on one of the bystanders and lifted his eyebrows: *You okay?* Chloe looked stricken, but she nodded.

"What happened?" He directed the question at Chloe and Byron Cooke. Two interpreters stood with them—a young woman and an older woman who also wore a costume. If he wasn't mistaken, the other man hovering nearby wore the uniform of a Civil War soldier.

"Nobody saw it, but a man fell." Chloe pointed to a cart at the far end of the building. "He's back there. Watch out for the goose poop."

Roelke's jaw muscles tightened when he saw the body. Dead of a broken neck, looked like, but he wanted badly to be wrong about that. Crouching, he felt the carotid artery—nothing. He leaned over, wanting to feel a whisper of breath against his cheek—nothing. He watched the victim's chest, hoping it might rise—nothing. It was too late for CPR. The man's eyes were open, vacant, already showing that faint telltale haze over each iris. *Dammit.*

He radioed the EPD clerk. "I'm at Old World Wisconsin with a PNB." Pulseless nonbreather.

"Fire department's on the way," Marie said. "But be advised, the closest county deputies have been diverted to another call." She signed off.

"Is he dead?" That was Chloe, standing well behind him, arms hugged across her chest.

"It's not my place to call it, but … yeah." Roelke heard a siren approaching. "Go out and flag down the fire department, okay?" He wanted to get her away from the body.

Marie radioed again. "Detectives are en route."

"Thanks." Detectives would process the scene. In a situation like this, the death would be considered suspicious until proven otherwise.

"Get somebody to Old World's main gate to question staff and visitors as they leave." All were potential witnesses.

After signing off Roelke eyed the scene, getting his bearings. One long wall of the stable faced east, toward the farmyard. The cart and straw pile blocking the body from general view were at the northeast corner. It *looked* as if the guy had fallen from the stable's second-story exterior walkway, and hit the cart on the way down.

He leaned over the body again, sniffing for intoxicants. No evidence of booze. Heart attack, maybe? The walkway was enclosed by heavy wooden beams, but if the guy had been sitting on the waist-high railing, and passed out or lost his balance … that would have done it.

Roelke carefully slid his hands into the man's pockets. One held a small clay pipe and a cloth sack of tobacco. A little bundle was in another, an old-timey picture wrapped first in a blue-and-white handkerchief embroidered with an elaborate *M*, then protected by a scrap of black canvas.

A pouch on a strap slung over the dead man's shoulder held sacks of rice and cornmeal, a few fresh-dug carrots, and a bit of bedraggled ribbon, pinched and stitched like a flower. No wallet. No ID.

The ambulance arrived, bringing two of Eagle's best paramedics. Roelke had worked with Denise Miller many times. Adam Bolitho, a newer volunteer, had a calming, steady demeanor. Adam was a construction worker, not a big man, but wiry and strong.

Roelke showed Denise and Adam the body. Denise checked for signs of life before sitting back on her heels with a sigh. "I'll call the medical examiner."

"No ID on the victim," Roelke told them, "but he must have been with that other guy in uniform. I'll go find out."

Roelke approached Chloe and her companions just as a church bell pealed mournfully in the distance. He introduced himself to the interpreters and soldier. "Let's go over there." He pointed to the steps behind the house.

He trailed the group away from the stable and pulled his notebook and pencil from a pocket. "I need each of you to tell me your name, address, and why you're here."

Gunter Diederich said he represented the 9th Wisconsin Infantry Regiment. "I'm a Civil War reenactor. But I didn't recognize the man who died."

Great, Roelke thought. That's, just, *great.*

"I wasn't expecting anyone from another reenacting unit," Byron added. "Just Gunter here and one of his friends, Steven Siggelkow."

"Steven was supposed to meet us by the ticket booth," Gunter explained. "His car's in the lot, but he didn't show."

Roelke made a note about Mr. Siggelkow's absence before turning to the tearstained young woman.

"I'm Alyssa Greer," she quavered. "I found him."

The other interpreter draped a comforting arm around Alyssa's shoulders. "My name is Jenny Hawkins," the older woman told Roelke. She had gray hair, kind eyes, and a welcome air of calm. "I was over at Koepsell"—she waved at the big farm beyond the grain field—"when Alyssa called. I'm the lead interpreter in this area."

Roelke looked back at Alyssa. "Please tell me exactly what happened."

"But I don't *know!*" Alyssa twined her fingers together. "My last visitors left so I started closing up. I always start half an hour before we close. Sometimes it takes a while to get the geese in the stable."

"You were here alone?" Chloe asked. She glanced at Roelke and murmured, "Usually two interpreters work Schulz."

"Several people called in sick this morning, so Alyssa was by herself," Jenny explained. "With this heat, attendance has been down."

She pulled a clean handkerchief from her basket—the equivalent of a purse for female interpreters—and handed it to Alyssa.

Alyssa dabbed at her eyes. "A couple of geese ran around the straw pile. I went after them, and there he was, just—just *lying* there. I ran back toward the house to call for help. Then I saw Byron and Chloe coming up the road, and told them first."

Roelke looked from Byron to Chloe. "Do you have any idea how many people came through the museum today?"

They each looked promptly at Alyssa. "I'd say … four hundred," she said.

"We can check the figures," Chloe told Roelke, "but the interpreters get pretty good at estimating attendance."

Four hundred visitors, Roelke thought. Holy toboggans. "Alyssa, had you seen the man before? Did he come through the house?"

"No. I would have remembered, him being in uniform and all."

"I didn't see him either," Jenny said.

Roelke was acutely aware of how big Old World Wisconsin was. "Can you ask the interpreters in the other German houses?"

"They may have already headed down to the Village to punch out," Jenny said. "But I can try."

"A final tram circles through the site to pick up interpreters and any last visitors," Chloe explained as Jenny hurried away. "But the German interpreters often walk back. It's quicker."

Roelke looked around the circle. "The rest of you—please don't leave or go inside. Waukesha County detectives are on their way."

"Detectives?" Alyssa's voice was high and thin.

"It's routine," Roelke assured her. "But they'll want to talk to you." He allowed himself to look at Chloe. "Ms. Ellefson, might I have a moment?"

Chloe followed him toward the pasture, away from the others. Once shielded by the ambulance, he took her hand. "Are you okay?"

"As okay as someone can be after seeing a dead person." She blew out a long breath. "I *hate* it when bad things happen here. Bad things should not happen on the site."

"I know." He rubbed her hand with his thumb, taking in the smooth warmth of her skin, the gentle curves of her knuckles, the so-slender fingers.

But he couldn't forget why he was there. "Are visitors allowed up on that walkway?" He cocked his head toward the stable.

"Definitely not. That's why those boards are over the steps." She pointed to the foot of the exterior stairs, at the southeast corner of the building.

Roelke eyed them thoughtfully. A man could get past the barricade if he really wanted to.

Chloe watched Denise stow a med kit in the ambulance. "What's taking them so long?"

"They're not going to take him. The ME is on the way."

"Oh."

"Chloe—why are *you* here?" The cop part of Roelke's brain knew that although her office was off-site, she could be anywhere on the grounds at any time. But the boyfriend part of his brain wished like crazy that she hadn't been anywhere near this particular farm on this particular afternoon.

"I'm helping Byron plan a Civil War program. We met Gunter Diederich at the Visitor Center, and we walked out here. Alyssa spotted us, and..." She sighed again. "You know the rest."

"Why is Diederich in uniform?" Roelke always tried to be respectful of Chloe's history world, but this seemed extreme. "It's gotta be ninety degrees in the shade. That's just nuts."

"Not if you're really into it. I'm sure Gunter wanted us to see his impression."

"'Impression?' What does that mean?"

"It means … persona. How a reenactor looks and presents himself. Good reenactors can talk at length, in first-person, about themselves. You know, their backstory. Who they were before the war, that sort of thing. Most reenactors spend a lot of time on research. It's a big deal."

"Hunh."

"Maybe the man who fell came out to this farm because he portrays a German farmer. Portrayed." She swallowed hard. "Most visitors don't go near the stable unless we've got baby pigs or lambs or something."

Roelke was dubious. "But why would somebody come here in uniform if he wasn't part of the meeting with you and Byron?"

"It happens." She shrugged. "Occasionally visitors dress up when they tour. Reenactors, kids who are excited about Daniel Boone or Laura Ingalls Wilder. Something like that."

"Well, hunh." Kids in costume he got; the adults, not so much. "The dead man was carrying a handkerchief stitched with the letter *M*. Would that indicate his first name, or last?"

"I can't say for sure, but probably last. Private M." Chloe paused, head tipped toward the road. Her shoulders slumped. "Oh hell."

"What?"

She pulled her hand from his. "I believe Petty is on his way."

Well, Roelke thought, this could be interesting. He'd heard much about, but never met, Ralph Petty.

The site director roared into view on a big red Harley-Davidson Sportster. The motorcycle grumbled to a halt behind the police car. Petty revved the bike, evidently just because he could, before cutting the engine. He removed his helmet and strode over. "What happened?" he demanded of Chloe, ignoring Roelke altogether.

Okay, Roelke thought. I am already pissed off.

Chloe gripped her elbows. "One of the interpreters found a re-enactor on the ground behind the straw pile, just beyond the stable. I'm afraid he's dead."

"Dead?" Petty's eyes widened. "Oh *Christ*. Did an interpreter do something wrong? Could we be in any way liable?"

Roelke was pretty sure that liability had not been foremost in Chloe's mind.

"The interpreter did not do anything wrong," she protested.

Petty scowled. "But if—"

"*Sir.*" Roelke was tired of being ignored, so he stepped in front of Chloe. "I'm Officer McKenna, Eagle Police Department."

The other man finally met Roelke's gaze. "And I'm Ralph Petty, Old World Wisconsin director. I want to see where this happened." He took a step toward the stable.

"I cannot allow you to do that." Roelke clamped one hand on Petty's forearm. "This farm may be a crime scene."

"*Crime* scene? That's absurd." Petty tried to wrench his arm free.

Roelke waited a couple of beats before letting him. In spite of present circumstances, he kinda hoped that Petty would cross the line. Do it, Roelke urged silently, and see what happens. He'd probably get some big-time boyfriend points if he arrested Petty.

Petty disappointed Roelke by giving up his challenge, but he side-stepped and glared at Chloe again. "You said it was an accident."

Roelke inserted himself back into Petty's line of sight. "Any un-attended death is suspicious until proven otherwise. Now I must ask you to—"

"This is *my* site!"

"And until the detectives arrive, this is *my* investigation."

Petty's eyes narrowed. Roelke held his gaze.

Finally the director muttered, "I need to call the Capitol Police," by way of saving face, and walked away.

On the inside, Roelke smiled a tiny smile. Petty was used to intimidating curators and interpreters and volunteers. *He* was used to intimidating wife-beaters, drunks, and drug dealers.

Besides, he didn't like the way Petty treated Chloe. You're Chloe's boss, Roelke told Petty silently, but you are not *my* boss. So watch your step.

THREE

THE DETECTIVES ARRIVED FIFTEEN minutes later. While Roelke was briefing them, a DNR guy showed up, and a part-time Eagle patrolman Marie had called in, and Old World's security guard. Someone from the Capitol Police—who got involved whenever bad things happened on state property—was probably on the way too. Old World Wisconsin was a state-run historic site just outside the Village of Eagle, within the Kettle Moraine State Forest, in Waukesha County. The profusion of responders had surprised Roelke when he'd first moved out from Milwaukee. But generally everyone played nicely together.

Detective Lon Goresko let his partner document the scene while he questioned the Old World employees and Gunter Diederich. Goresko had sandy hair worn in a *Who cares?* style, as if he'd trimmed it himself while watching a Packers game on TV. He came across as a blue-collar guy in a white-collar job, and never looked at ease in his suit. But Roelke knew Goresko was a twenty-year veteran, experienced and capable.

"Officer McKenna." Goresko beckoned him aside. "Can you take Mr. Diederich back to the parking lot? His friend showed up, and I'd like you to talk with him."

"Sure thing." Roelke ushered the reenactor into the squad car. He was eager to talk to the missing friend.

The Visitor Center parking lot was almost empty, but one Union soldier paced beneath the pine trees. Diederich jumped from the squad and gave his friend one of those awkward guy-hugs. "Where have you *been*? You scared the crap out of me!"

"I'm *so* sorry." Steven Siggelkow was a tall man, and older than Diederich—his hair more salt than pepper. His uniform was pretty beat up, so he'd likely been reenacting for a long time.

Roelke introduced himself. "Why did you miss the meeting?"

"I went to the Norwegian area to visit Kyle, and—"

"Kyle?"

"Kyle Fassbender," Siggelkow explained. "He's an interpreter."

Roelke made a note to interview the interpreters working in the Norwegian area.

"He's also a member of our unit," Siggelkow was saying. "He works at the little Norwegian cabin. After visiting him I went to the bigger Norwegian house. The women there were making *krumkakke*."

"I'm surprised you blew off the meeting." Roelke thought Siggelkow seemed anxious, shifting his weight and avoiding eye contact.

"Fresh *krumkakke*!" Siggelkow repeated, as if that should explain everything. If Chloe were there, Roelke thought, she'd probably agree. "I just lost track of time."

"Aren't you wearing a watch?"

Siggelkow looked horrified. "Of course not! But when I realized how late it had gotten, I made haste to get here."

"Did you take a tram?"

Siggelkow looked like he wanted to say *Of course not!* again, but thought better of it. "No, I walked. Unfortunately, the others had left by the time I got here." He cast a guilty look at his comrade, his gray eyes sober. Obviously he'd heard the news.

Roelke waited. Anxious people often couldn't tolerate silence. Sometimes waiting produced more information than a dozen questions.

Siggelkow thrust his hands into his pockets. "I don't know what else I can tell you."

And sometimes waiting accomplished diddly-squat. "That's all, then," Roelke said. "For now." He'd developed a pretty good bullshit detector, but he wasn't sure if Siggelkow was telling the truth—the whole truth—or not.

———

When the ME had departed, Detective Goresko asked Chloe and Byron to accompany him inside the Schulz house. He pointed at the Plexiglas barrier intended to keep guests from entering the bedroom. "How hard is it to remove that?"

"Not hard at all." Byron easily slid the Plexiglas in the doorway from its brackets. The detective walked into the bedroom, took a hard look around, and moved on to the sitting room.

Chloe winced. "Please avoid walking on the carpet. If at all possible."

The detective dutifully stepped from the carpet to a strip of bare floor. "Do you see anything missing? Anything unusual?"

"I don't," Byron said.

Chloe scrutinized the room. "I don't either. It would be pretty easy to tell if something had been stolen. The house is sparsely furnished to reflect the family's status as recent arrivals." Chloe reminded herself that the detective truly did not care about the Schulz family's status in 1860. "Um … so anyway, visitors only have easy access to the workroom and kitchen areas, and the artifacts are arranged accordingly. Visitors have the best experience when they're not forced to spend their entire visit peering over Plexiglas barriers, so when I opened the house last spring—"

Byron elbowed her.

"—I considered artifact placement carefully," Chloe mumbled. "Sorry." It was much more pleasant to talk about furnishing plans than the dead reenactor.

"Not to worry." Detective Goresko walked on. From the front entry he entered the huge, walk-in chimney at the center of the house. The brick walls were dark with many years' accumulated soot, and smoke tainted the air. "Good God. What *is* this?"

"It's a *Schwartz-Küche*," Chloe said. "Black Kitchen."

"Timber was scarce in Pomerania," Byron explained. "A fire built to heat the bake oven could be raked into the fire pit for cooking, and at the same time help smoke meat hung from poles overhead." He pointed. "This structure is one of Old World's architectural treasures. We know of only four Wisconsin houses built with a *Schwartz-Küche*, and this is the only one—"

Chloe elbowed him.

"—that survived," Byron mumbled. "Sorry."

The detective squinted at the space. Chloe couldn't tell if he was looking for evidence or fascinated by the only remaining *Schwartz-Küche* in Wisconsin.

Ralph Petty presented himself, and showed the detective as much courtesy as he'd shown Roelke earlier—as in, none. "Mr. Cooke," Petty barked. "Has that young woman completed an incident form?"

"I'm taking care of it," Byron said blandly.

"Thank you for showing me around," Detective Goresko told Byron and Chloe. "You're free to leave. Mr. Petty? A word?"

Chloe helped Byron take care of final chores: tipping the tin cups upside down to prevent rust, stashing flour in a mouse-proof tin, writing a note about what had happened in the Schulz log—a spiral notebook interpreters used to communicate with each other. The front door was locked from the inside, and they secured the back with a padlock. Jenny and Alyssa were in the farmyard, shooing the geese toward their pen with aprons spread. The birds went with honks of complaint, but they went.

"You're a good boss," Chloe told Byron. She liked how he'd deflected Petty's angst about the incident form.

Byron waved that aside. "Alyssa's had enough stress today without getting any crap from Petty."

Once the geese were corralled and the incident form completed, Chloe was relieved to turn her back on the vehicles and cops and that poor dead man. She headed out with Byron, Alyssa, and Jenny. The walk back to the Visitor Center helped soothe her spirits. The woods and prairie remnants and restored buildings were peaceful. Iridescent dragonflies darted back and forth, and a flock of wild turkeys wandered across the road.

They were approaching the Crossroads Village when another interpreter jogged around the bend. "Jenny!" Lee Hawkins cried. "I heard—oh my God, I'm so sorry." He stopped in front of his wife and cradled her face in his hands. "Are you all right?"

Chloe eyed him, worried he might become the next casualty. Lee was a good decade older than Jenny. He had white hair and a Santa Claus beard, and although Lee wasn't as stout as that famed gentleman of lore, he wasn't in any shape to be trotting about in the heat. His cheeks were flushed, and his shirt damp with sweat.

"I'm fine." Jenny's tone was soothing. "It's—upsetting, but everything is under control."

Lee put his arm around Jenny's shoulders. As they walked on, a little ahead of the rest, Jenny leaned her head against his.

Jenny's going to be okay, Chloe thought. She wished in vain for a handsome young interpreter to provide equal comfort for Alyssa. But when they reached the parking lot, Byron walked Alyssa to her car. He spoke earnestly to her for a moment. Alyssa nodded, swiped her eyes, nodded again. Byron squeezed her shoulder. She summoned a determined smile. Alyssa's going to be okay too, Chloe thought.

Then Chloe and Byron cut through a row of pines to join Roelke in the next bay. He was talking to Gunter and another man in Union blue.

Chloe extended her hand to the stranger and introduced herself. "You must be Steven." He looked rattled, but she couldn't tell if he was embarrassed to have missed the meeting or shaken after being questioned. Roelke could be a bit ... intense.

"I'm sorry our discussion was cut short," Byron told the reenactors. "Gunter? Let's talk again soon."

After the two reenactors had driven away, Roelke surveyed the parking lot. "Just a couple of vehicles left. Since the victim wasn't carrying car keys, I'm hoping one of them belongs to a friend of his."

"I don't think so." Byron scanned the cars. "That one"—he pointed—"is my car. That one"—the arm swiveled—"belongs to the Visitor Center supervisor. She's always last to leave because she has to count money from ticket sales and the gift shop. And that blue sedan"—he pointed again—"belongs to the restaurant manager."

They all looked around, as if hoping another car would materialize. It didn't. "Spooky," Chloe said.

Roelke didn't do spooky. "The man had to get here somehow. Maybe somebody dropped him off."

"But if so, how was he planning to get back home?" Chloe asked.

"His ride should be here, waiting."

"The other gates are all marked No Admittance," Byron pointed out. "Unless we've got bus tours scheduled, they're generally locked."

"The German gate was locked when I arrived," Roelke confirmed. "How about the gate at the Admin building? Someone could have turned in there, right? Driven right onto the site?"

"It's possible," Byron said doubtfully. "But believe me, if someone had driven into one of the exhibit areas, interpreters would have reported it. And if someone parked by the site road, a tram driver would have reported it."

The three looked around the lot one more time. "Spooky," Chloe said again. She just couldn't help it.

"There is a logical explanation," Roelke said patiently. "Goresko's probably set up a grid search already. Unless he needs me to do something else, I'll see if I can find a car hidden off the road." He started toward his vehicle but glanced back at Chloe. "Tell Libby I'm running late, okay?" Libby was his cousin.

"I'll tell her."

Gloomy silence filled the car as Chloe and Byron drove back to the Education House, another small home-turned-office on Old World Wisconsin's periphery. I don't care what Roelke says, Chloe thought. There might be a rational explanation for the anonymous reenactor's appearance—and death—in the heart of the historic site, but they didn't know what it was. And that left *her* with a bad case of the heebie-jeebies.

Chloe gratefully slid into her aging car and got the heck outta Dodge. She'd been looking forward to a pleasant evening, but God only knew when Roelke would be able to get away now. That's the life of a cop, she reminded herself, turning onto Highway 59. And Roelke was a cop to his marrow. At twenty-nine, he was a perpetual advertisement for the police force—neatly trimmed brown hair, strong jaw, and chocolate eyes that could pierce stone when he was focused on a problem. Like he'd been that afternoon.

She smiled a little. It had been interesting to watch Officer Roelke McKenna square off with Director Ralph Petty. Roelke had somehow looked taller, even more broad of shoulder. Petty had just looked pissed and cranky. She'd half expected one of them to unzip, whip his out, and claim dominance the old-fashioned way.

Then her smile faded. Maybe, she thought, I shouldn't have told Roelke about *quite* so many Petty atrocities. Roelke getting mouthy with her boss—or punching him—would not help her keep her job. And she *had* to, now. Moving away was not an option.

Not since she'd said yes to the farm.

Fifteen minutes later, she reached that very place: a century-old farmhouse built of cream-colored bricks. An enormous old tree stood beyond the drive, a glorious remnant of an oak savanna—the once-common border between prairie and woodland. The waving prairie grasses were gone now, and cornfields stretched east of the house. But the yard was nestled into a natural curve on the edge of the state forest, so trees bordered the west and north sides of the property. And although the house had been empty for years, the farm was lovely.

Specifically, it was the Old Roelke Place on Roelke Lane. AKA, Roelke's family farm.

My farm too, Chloe told herself. After Roelke had decided to buy the place, she'd agreed to let her rented house go and move in with him. But honestly, that part still didn't feel real.

Since signing the mortgage papers a few weeks earlier, Roelke had ferried boxes from his apartment. He'd replaced a few rotting boards on the front porch, and secured a loose railing. He'd set up a card table in the kitchen and put new light bulbs in the overhead fixtures. He'd had a new refrigerator installed and a picnic table delivered. His cousin Libby had stashed a big plastic tub of toys for her two kids in the barn. She'd also presented Chloe and Roelke with a small Weber grill. "A farm-warming gift," she'd said with a grin.

Chloe's vague plan had been to bring a carload of stuff over every day. But she'd found herself strangely reluctant to make herself at home here. She'd arranged some pretty stones on the front porch and hung a black-oil sunflower seed feeder near the kitchen window. She'd started reclaiming the vegetable garden from burdock, nettles, and briars. And … that was pretty much it.

Well, I did bring some stuff today, she thought. A box of Fiesta dinnerware. Fiesta had gotten pricey since going out of production a decade earlier, in 1973, but she'd found odds and ends cheap at a garage sale. Libby and the kids were due later for a picnic supper, and Chloe hated using paper plates.

Instead of lugging the dishes inside, she wandered into the farmyard. The *vierkanthof* layout was much like the Schulz Farm's— a square with open corners. The house formed the southern side of the yard. A derelict henhouse and corncrib stood to the east, and the remains of a smokehouse too. A classic multipurpose barn, with weathered red boards above a fieldstone foundation, had been built along the northern edge.

The huge garden Roelke's grandmother had tended was on the yard's west side, marked by rhubarb mounds and sprawls of lacey asparagus. Chloe's friend Dellyn, who supervised Old World's historic garden program, had muscled through one of the beds with a rototiller. Despite the calendar Chloe had planted rows of onions and carrots and lettuce.

She slipped through the sagging gate and smiled at the fragile seedlings. Kneeling, she pulled a few weeds that had stubbornly poked through the straw she and Dellyn had spread between the rows. I do feel at home *here*, Chloe thought. She liked the way the garden smelled, liked the feel of earth against her fingers, liked the miniature emerald rows. It was a start.

Libby could arrive any time, though, so she slapped dirt from her hands and stood. Her contentment faded as she contemplated the only structure anchoring the west side of the farmyard. Constructed in the 1850s, the first Roelke immigrants had presumably lived in the log cabin until the larger house could be built. The cabin was in surprisingly good shape. Roelke's grandma had used it as her potting shed and, Chloe suspected, a haven from the demands of family and farm.

Roelke wanted to make the cabin *Chloe's* special place too. "How about we fix it up and turn it into your private space?" he'd asked, eyes sparkling with pleasure. "For reading, or sewing, or rosemaling—whatever you want."

Chloe loved that idea. There was just one little problem: She hadn't been able to step inside the cabin without getting seriously weirded out.

It was one thing to perceive strong emotions lingering in other old homes. But here, at Roelke's farm—our farm, she reminded herself doggedly—she *had* to get past it. Maybe today, she thought.

Squaring her shoulders, she approached the cabin. She opened the door, stepped inside … and instantly felt what she'd felt before. Something dark vibrated in this musty space. The air felt heavy with unhappiness. Chloe felt an uneasy tremor in her chest.

She stumbled back outside and slammed the door closed behind her. Her hands were trembling, and she shoved them into her pockets. *Shit.*

There was no way around it. This was a sweet cabin, and she was going to have to tell Roelke that one of his ancestors left a whole lot of bad juju inside.

FOUR

WHEN ROELKE PULLED INTO the farm drive, late and hungry, he parked beside a tired Datsun and an even more road-weary Ford Pinto. The two women he loved so much it hurt, Chloe and his cousin Libby, were sitting in lawn chairs behind the house. Justin and Dierdre—Libby's kids, whom he loved just as fiercely—were whacking colorful wooden croquet balls about with abandon.

Roelke gazed at the farm. The scene was pastoral, but nonetheless evoked a disconcerting ache inside his rib cage. He'd been feeling it ever since signing the loan forms, and the weight of owning a whole lot of property settled in. You chose this, he reminded himself, and got out of the truck.

Justin barreled over and wrapped his arms around Roelke's legs. Justin was a smart and sensitive eight-year-old, easily frustrated, sometimes awkward with other kids. Dierdre followed more slowly, dragging a wooden mallet. She was a four-year-old princess, calm and self-possessed. She had a great imagination, could entertain herself, and didn't take it personally when her and Justin's dad stood them up or let them down.

"Guess *what!*" Justin said. "We walked to the springs with Chloe, and she found an *elderberry* bush!"

"Is that good?"

Justin blinked from behind his glasses, as if the depths of Roelke's cluelessness were hard to accept. "You can *eat* them! They're almost ripe."

Dierdre tugged on Roelke's hand. "And guess *what!* Chloe found a bunch of milkweed plants."

"Is that good?"

"Monarch butterflies like them!" Dierdre explained. "Chloe said if we can find a caterpillar we can save it and feed it and watch it turn into a butterfly."

"Cool."

"Come play with us?" Justin begged.

"I will later," Roelke promised. "After I get something to eat." He messed up Justin's hair and kissed Dierdre just behind her plastic tiara before joining the women.

Chloe greeted him with a lingering kiss. This, he thought, is by far the best moment of my day.

Then she put one hand against his cheek. He could tell that she wanted to make sure he was all right. Which was exactly what he wanted to make sure about *her*. It was never pleasant to work on a case involving a dead body, but the incident had been a lot more personal for her. "Are you … " he began.

"Yeah. You?"

"Just tired and frustrated."

"Libby made sangria," Chloe told him. "Want some?"

"I do." Normally he wasn't a sangria kind of guy, but the fruity sweetness sounded perfect after such a scorcher.

She poured him a glass from a sweating pitcher.

"Hey," his cousin said. "Chloe told me what happened. I tried to hold dinner for you but the kids were hungry."

"No problem." He inhaled the lingering, heady scent of grilled salmon and roasted corn. "As long as you saved me some."

"I'll fix you a plate." Libby had everything in hand. She usually did. Libby was a single mom holding financial ends together as a freelance journalist. She looked lean and tanned in black shorts and a sleeveless yellow shirt. She kept her hair cut short and didn't bother to hide the gray strands threading through the chestnut.

"Did you find the dead man's car? Or did whoever drove him to the site show up?"

"Nope."

Chloe's mouth twisted pensively. "I noticed the poor man was carrying a haversack—"

"That black pouch-thing?"

"Right. Was there anything in it?"

"Nothing to tell us who he was, or where he came from." Roelke thought back. "Small sacks of rice and cornmeal, a few carrots. There was also a little ribbon thing. Sort of a—a bunched up corsage."

"A cockade?"

He shrugged. "I guess so. And there was a little photograph in a coat pocket, wrapped in that handkerchief I mentioned."

"Was the photo printed on cardstock?"

"No, on a thin piece of metal."

"A tintype. Very common during the war."

"So, what happens now?" Libby asked.

"Now a detective will spend the evening calling nearby PDs, checking missing person reports. God, I wish we all had computers. One day a search like this will be a whole lot easier." He blew out a long breath. "Meanwhile the ME will check the body for tattoos, birthmarks, scars—any identifying feature."

"I hope you get answers quickly," Chloe added fervently. "That poor man's family and friends need to know what happened."

Roelke tried to study her without being obvious. Ingrid Chloe Ellefson was a beautiful woman, slender but not painfully thin as she'd been a year ago. Her long blond hair was pulled back into a single thick braid. Now that the sun had loosened its grip, tendrils that had been plastered to her skin earlier riffled in the slight breeze. He was looking forward to coming home to her every, single, night.

Libby poured herself another glass of sangria. "Chloe, it's bizarre that you and Byron were meeting reenactors, and that the man who died was a reenactor, but there was no connection."

Chloe stretched out her lovely legs and crossed them at the ankles. "Just a weird coincidence, I guess."

Roelke wasn't so sure, but he decided not to say so.

"How many Civil War reenactors do you suppose there are in Wisconsin?" Libby asked.

Roelke swallowed a forkful of salmon, smoky and flaky and moist. "We don't know if the victim is from Wisconsin," he reminded her.

"There are probably hundreds of Wisconsin reenactors," Chloe said. "And while a lot of units cooperate, some don't. There's a fair amount of bickering within and between units. To put it mildly."

"Bickering about what?"

"The role of women in the hobby is a hot topic." Chloe waved away a fly. "Some units don't permit any women to join, period. Some guys allow women to join their unit if they stick to appropriate civilian impressions and activities. That's what I used to do when I was active in the hobby."

Roelke paused, fork in the air. "You were a reenactor?"

"I was. Before I moved to Europe. Anyway, authenticity is the biggest issue. I've met hardcore authentics who won't hit the field unless the mordant used to dye the thread in their underwear is correct."

Roelke didn't know what mordant was. Given the context, he didn't care.

"Other units have a different focus. Their camps are full of big wall tents and furniture, even modern coolers and things." Chloe drained her glass. "Some reenactors who work hard on their own impression despise anyone who doesn't. There's a derogatory term—'farb'—that describes sloppy reenactors."

Roelke reached for a second piece of corn on the cob. "So much for a happy weekend outing."

Chloe shrugged. "Twenty years ago, when a few reenactments were held to commemorate the Civil War's one hundredth anniversary, guys showed up in blue jeans and plaid flannel shirts. Modern reenactors like Gunter Diederich and Steven Siggelkow probably spent a couple thousand dollars on their impression."

Roelke looked up from the corn he'd been rolling in butter. "Are you kidding me?"

She ticked items off on her fingers. "A high-quality repro rifled musket, a Springfield or an Enfield with correct bayonet, six hundred dollars, maybe more. A good uniform can cost maybe four hundred. Add brogans, undergarments, haversack, canteen, cartridge box, blanket, cookware, shelter half... you get the picture."

Roelke put the corn down and wiped his fingers on a napkin, surprisingly disconcerted. For one thing, he wasn't used to hearing Chloe discuss guns. For another, discovering how much money was involved in Civil War reenacting waved a scarlet warning flag in his brain.

"It may sound excessive," Chloe said, "but most of the reenactors I knew participated with a sense of… well, reverence. Reverence for the suffering and sacrifice of the men and women who struggled and died during the Civil War."

"So you had a dress and everything?" Libby asked. "I'm guessing you were on the high end of the authenticity spectrum."

"I did my best." Chloe stared at the woods beyond the farmyard. "I usually portrayed a farmwoman, or a refugee forced from my home, and tried to help spectators imagine the war's impact on local civilians. I only wore a pretty hoopskirt if a group of us was doing a Sanitary Fair or some social activity at a historic house."

Roelke tried to picture Chloe in a fancy Scarlett O'Hara dress. "Well, hunh."

She smiled. "I don't think I ever pissed off the hardcore guys. But there were always some women who showed up at events in polyester prom gowns and blue eye shadow, that kind of thing. Or women who wanted to sleep in their guy's tent at night. That drove the authentics crazy."

Libby began stacking plates. "That must have bugged you too."

To Roelke's surprise, Chloe shrugged. "It did, but I want people to get interested in history, and there's no single way to facilitate that. Lots of adults come at it romantically—drawn in by *Gone with the Wind*, or the belief that all life in olden times was simple and good. Other people get engaged by collecting antique china, mourning jewelry, whatever. I encourage people in whatever way appeals to them. If they have a positive experience, they'll want to learn more, and then—" She stopped abruptly. "*Sorry.* I've developed a bad habit of pontificating."

Libby waved her apology aside. "I'm not keen on the whole war thing, but I like the way you look at it."

Roelke did too. When he met Chloe, he had no idea what her job was all about. He was making progress. But when things like this Civil War reenacting stuff popped up, he realized he still had a ways to go. What he did get, though, was that Chloe had very special memories of being involved in "the hobby," as she called it. He'd seen it in her eyes, heard it in her voice.

"The guys I met today are particularly interested in portraying German-speaking immigrants during the war." Chloe looked from Libby to Roelke. "The first Roelkes came to Wisconsin in what... the late 1850s?"

Roelke shifted in his chair. When he was a kid his grandparents had told family stories, but honestly, he just hadn't been that interested. "Something like that."

"It would be fun to know," Chloe said. "Did any of your ancestors serve during the Civil War?"

"I think so," Roelke said. "Right, Libby?"

Libby nodded. "Definitely. I don't recall the details, though."

"Wisconsin raised two so-called German regiments," Chloe told them. "I'll check the military records. What was the name of the first Roelke who lived here?"

Roelke had no idea. "Um..."

"Klaus," Libby said. "The story is that after his parents died he immigrated alone, with nothing but the shirt on his back. And I'm pretty sure he and his wife—Rosalinda? Rosina? Something like that—had two sons. I've got a few family heirlooms packed away at home. I'll dig them out."

"Land records, church records, local newspapers—there are lots of ways to approach family history," Chloe said. "I'll see what I can find." She flashed a smile at Roelke.

And suddenly all of the bad stuff—fear of defaulting on his loan, chagrin over not knowing his family history, that niggle of worry that came whenever she talked enthusiastically about things he didn't understand, the unidentified dead man—disappeared like a puff of smoke. As long as Chloe kept smiling at him like that, they'd be okay.

Libby produced a container of brownies and called the kids over. Justin chattered about T-ball and turtles, Chloe asked all the right questions, and Roelke watched the shadows lengthen. Twilight blurred the thistles and peeling paint and missing shingles, which was nice.

Libby smiled at him. "This is good, you know? I wasn't sure, but you and I have a lot of memories here."

"Good memories."

"We still on for the work party on Monday?" she asked.

Roelke nodded. "A friend of mine offered to help." After the ME had left with Private M that afternoon, Adam Bolitho had paused to speak to Roelke. "I heard you're moving to a farmhouse. I've got a pickup, if you need a hand, and I'm good with a paintbrush."

Roelke had been startled by the unexpected offer. Time was, his best friend Rick would have been his go-to guy. But Rick was dead.

Now, Roelke tried to gulp down the sudden salty lump in his throat. "Chloe, did you talk to your sister about moving your furniture?"

"Kari said she and Tryg would be glad to help." Chloe popped a final morsel of brownie in her mouth and licked her fingers in an unknowingly seductive manner that almost made Roelke forget his own name.

Libby announced that she needed to get the kids home. After waving them on their way, Roelke and Chloe tidied up, working side by side in the kitchen for the first time. She washed, and he dried, in companionable silence. Then Chloe asked, "What's that tune?"

"What tune?"

"The one you were humming."

"I wasn't humming."

"You kinda were."

"Really?" He placed a blue plate in the dish drainer. "Hunh."

"It sounded like this." She hummed a few bars—a bit sad, a bit sweet.

And a bit familiar. "That tune has been in my brain," Roelke admitted. "I have no idea where it came from."

"It's pretty." Chloe pulled the rubber plug and swished dirty water down the drain. "It was fun to be here with Libby and the kids, but … geez, what a day."

"Yeah." He did a mental rewind, and remembered something important. Chloe's friend Dellyn lived on the outskirts of town near Maggie Geddings. "Listen, tell Dellyn to keep her windows and doors locked. We had a home intrusion call from the big house kitty-corner across the street."

"Which house? That Queen Anne with the luscious hollyhocks, or the Italianate with the funny addition?"

Roelke sighed. "The white one."

"Okay. I'll call Dellyn."

"There's something else we need to talk about."

"Oh?" She sounded suddenly wary.

"Chloe, it's possible that the guy who died this afternoon fell and broke his neck. Or … "

"Or?"

"*Or* it might not have been an accident."

She sucked in her lower lip. "Did you find something to suggest that?"

"No," he admitted. "The detectives crawled all over the stable, especially the walkway, and didn't find a thing." No drops of blood left by a fleeing assailant. No sign of struggle. "But, maybe he was sitting on the beam and someone pushed him over. It could have been premeditated, or it could have been motive meeting opportunity."

Chloe regarded him soberly. "Sometimes I hate the way your brain works."

"My point is, please don't wander around the site by yourself until we know whether we're looking at murder."

That terrible word seemed to hang between them. After a long pause she slowly exhaled. "It really was a horrible day."

"And I finally met Ralph Petty."

Chloe gave him a sardonic look. "What's your impression?"

"He's an asshole."

"He is indeed. But listen, I'm trying to stay in his good graces." She paused. "Well, I've never actually *been* in Petty's good graces, but I'm trying to stay out of trouble. He may have heard that you and I are together, so try not to piss him off, okay?"

"Sure," Roelke said, but only because he didn't want to talk about Petty any more. Not here. Not now.

"We need to go on a date," Chloe said. "We've been focused so much on the farm, and now that poor man's death … some time out would be good for us. How about a hike on the Ice Age Trail?" The national trail ran through the Kettle Moraine State Forest.

Roelke liked the sound of that, but a mental review of his calendar showed limited prospects. "I think hiking will have to wait until we're settled. Want to come to movie night in Eagle?" He'd started the program the summer before, theorizing that kids watching a movie were kids not getting into trouble. With a few changes this year—like moving inside from the mosquito-plagued village park—he was optimistic that all would go well.

"What's playing?"

"Somebody loaned me a reel of old *Rawhide* episodes."

"Ah. I'll pass."

"It's historical, sort of," he protested. "Libby's bringing Justin."

"I don't like the *Rawhide* theme song."

He blinked. "What's not to like?"

"The lyrics. They're unkind."

"Unkind to *who*?"

"The cattle."

"But—but *Rawhide* is a great show! The episodes are like little morality plays. When Justin and I watch reruns, we always have a good conversation about the choices people made."

"All I'm saying is that a night of *Rawhide* episodes is not for me," Chloe said lightly. "Especially since you'll be on duty."

So much for a date. Roelke searched for a new topic. "Did you decide what color you want to paint the kitchen?"

"I promise to cogitate on it." She grabbed his hand. "Let's visit the Old Oak."

The ancient white oak beyond the drive, she meant. Before getting a graduate degree in museum studies, Chloe had attended forestry school at West Virginia University. She knew a lot about trees, and she'd taken a particular fancy to this one. He'd seen her there before, touching the fissured bark, watching birds, sitting on the shaded ground with her journal.

She tugged him across the drive to stand among the low, gnarled branches, surrounded by the farm, hearing the tiny rustles and whispers of squirrels and bats and whatever other creatures shared it.

Chloe leaned back against him. "This is a Witness Tree."

"A what?"

"Just think what this tree has seen! I bet your ancestors sat under this tree sometimes too."

It had never occurred to Roelke to wonder if his ancestors had sat under this tree.

She sighed. "It must have been so hard for them."

"What?"

"After leaving their homeland, crossing the ocean, trying to start a farm ... the Civil War erupts."

He thought about those first Roelkes—the ones who had walked this land, maybe stood beneath this very tree. Had one of the women stayed in the old cabin alone, or perhaps with kids, while her husband marched off to war?

Well, if anyone could find out stuff like that, it was Chloe. He wrapped his arms around her. "Listen, have you given any thought to how you'd like to fix up the cabin?" Setting up the cabin as her private sanctuary was one of his better ideas, he thought. But he hadn't been able to get her to talk much about it.

She stiffened. "Not really."

He stepped back. "What's going on?"

She was quiet for a long time. "We need to talk about the cabin."

"That's what I'm trying to do."

"I need to tell you something." Chloe took a deep breath. "Roelke, there's something bad in that cabin."

"There's ... what?"

"Something dark is in that cabin."

Roelke heard his grandma singing, saw flats of pansies and squash seedlings. "No there isn't."

"Yeah, there really is." Chloe crossed her arms and grasped her shoulders. "I've tried to go in there several times, Roelke, and I *can't*. Whatever lingers in there is just too strong."

"You mean like … It's like what you've told me about feeling stuff in other places?"

"Yes."

"And you feel something bad in my grandma's cabin?" This did not make sense.

"I'm not saying your grandma left the bad energy behind." She sounded defensive. "It probably goes back further than that."

Roelke felt flummoxed. Chloe had confided months ago that ever since she was a kid, she sometimes perceived the energy, or whatever the hell it was, of strong emotions lingering in old buildings and historic places. Although he didn't get it, he could tell it was real for her.

But … it had never occurred to him that she'd experience something *here*. On the family farm. In his grandma's special place.

"It's not in the house," she added. "Just in the cabin."

"What does it feel like?"

Chloe lifted and dropped her palms. "*Dark*. Maybe … " She sucked in her lower lip, considering. "Maybe hopeless."

"No way." For as long as he could remember, this farm had represented the exact opposite. He'd seen how hopeful his grandparents were each spring as they planned and plowed and planted. When his own parents' disastrous marriage finally ended, the only thing that had given his mom and him and his brother a sense of hope was knowing that the farm would always welcome them in.

"I didn't want to tell you. But I don't know what else to do."

Roelke strode to his truck and grabbed a heavy-duty flashlight. Then he walked to the cabin and opened the door.

Chloe trailed behind. "Roelke, don't do this tonight. I don't want to."

He switched the flashlight on and stepped inside. The cabin was just one room and a loft. The oak logs, originally chinked with mud, had been fortified with mortar over the years. He let the strong white beam sweep the floor, the corners, the plywood tables where his grandma had worked.

"There's nothing to see in here," he called.

"It's not what I see. It's what I feel."

Roelke closed his eyes and tried to catch whatever Chloe had experienced. He waited, and waited some more. He heard crickets and smelled dust. But he didn't feel a damn thing.

Finally he went back outside and flicked off the flashlight. "I don't get it."

"I didn't expect you to. But I assure you, it's very real for me."

Roelke felt like a little boy whose best surprise gift had been rejected. "It was supposed to be your special place!"

"I know, and I love you for that. I'm really sorry. I'll just have to find a corner in the house to call my own."

It took him a moment to summon even a halfway gracious response. "It's a big house. Maybe the little bedroom upstairs."

"That would be nice."

But it wouldn't be nice. Roelke needed Chloe to like the cabin. For reasons best left unexamined, his own personal reasons that had nothing to do with Chloe, he needed her to spend time inside. To fix it up. To be happy there. He hadn't realized how much he'd been counting on that until right this minute.

They stood in the growing gloom for a few minutes longer. Finally Roelke reached for her hand. "Let's go."

They walked back to the drive. They hugged, and kissed, and hugged one more time. Then they got into their separate vehicles. Chloe drove toward the house she rented in La Grange, and he went to his rented flat in Palmyra. Things will be better once we're truly moved in, Roelke told himself.

But the peaceful evening had ended on a sad note. What the hell had Chloe found lingering in the old family cabin? The farm had thrived, grown, stayed in the family for over a century. Why would those old log walls trap something *hopeless*?

FIVE

Rosina pinned her woolen shawl tightly around her shoulders, grasped the *Fair Wind*'s railing, and leaned toward her future. The day felt full of promise. Full of *hope*.

It was almost too much to take in. For the last decade—since she was six years old—her dreams had felt fragile as soap bubbles. But today the sunshine was warm, the breeze was cool, and the air smelled fresh. Sails snapped briskly overhead, but the Atlantic's blue-green swells were gentle. The gleaming three-masted ship was sailing ever away from Prussia, ever toward America. Something so indefinably *good* rose within that her eyes filled with tears.

A hand landed on her arm. "Fraulein?"

"Oh!"

"Forgive me," the man said. "But you were leaning so far over the railing... and I saw you wipe your eyes... I was alarmed."

Heat flooded Rosina's cheeks. "Thank you, but there is no cause for alarm." She squinted up at her would-be rescuer. His blue frock

50

coat looked new, his tan pants and plaid waistcoat clean, his high leather boots shiny. Now that he was assured she was not, in fact, about to throw herself into the sea, Rosina expected him to politely tip his broad-brimmed black hat and take his leave.

Instead, he rested his forearms on the rail and gazed over the water. "You are sad to leave Europe?"

"Oh, *no*. I am overjoyed."

The man turned to look at her. His eyes seemed to take all of their color from the sea. One long strand of dark hair danced against his forehead in the wind. "You are an eager traveler, then? Most immigrants leave much of their heart behind when they board ship."

"I expect most have loved ones to leave their hearts with," she said lightly.

"You do not?"

"My parents died when I was very young. My father's cousin took me in. I … " Rosina considered her words. "I did not weep when presented with the opportunity to immigrate to America."

The man waved toward the small swells moving restlessly to the horizon. "What do you hope for?"

No one had ever asked her such a question before. "Oh, I do so hope for—for *color*."

"For color," the man repeated, fingering his lapels.

Rosina wished she hadn't spoken. Her fellow traveler was perhaps twenty-five years her senior and, judging by speech and attire, no farmer. He could never understand the life she'd lived in Pomerania—all black cotton and gray wool and linen dull as dishwater.

"And what do you see for yourself in America?"

Rosina glanced at him suspiciously, but saw no hint of mockery. "I see possibility."

"Then you are wise beyond your years."

Rosina bundled up the compliment and tucked it away for safekeeping.

"For most, the first year or two in America are hard beyond imagining. But for those who truly desire to start fresh, America is *full* of possibility."

"You have been there?"

"I have. I am returning from a trip to Prussia. My father died, and I had affairs to see to. But for the past eight years, I've made my home in the state of Wisconsin—"

"Wisconsin? Why, Wisconsin is our destination as well!" Rosina turned to face him. "My friends have arranged to buy a farm near Watertown."

"Milwaukee is my home." The man adjusted his collar against the wind. "I am no farmer. I am a Free Thinker."

Rosina wasn't sure what that meant—how did one earn a living as a Free Thinker?—but she didn't want to ask such a personal question. "What can you tell me about Wisconsin? Do people there play music? Are the birds much the same as ours, or quite different? And the trees, are they—"

"I think you must wait and see for yourself." He laughed. "You *do* have a curious mind. I thought so."

Rosina could not fathom his meaning. "You … thought so?"

"I have noticed you. When most are below, groaning with seasickness, you are often on deck."

"I am companion to Frau Sperber, who isn't well. I must bring up her bowl and pot quite frequently to empty and rinse."

"I did not mean to imply fault," he assured her. "I merely—"

"Rosina?" a familiar male voice called.

"Oh! I must go." Rosina realized she had lingered too long. "But I do hope we might talk again."

"I think that very likely. We've a long voyage on a small ship."

"Until next time, then." Rosina turned to take her leave.

"Wait! Will you not tell me your name?"

Cousin Maria would expect Rosina to answer primly. Introductions should be made through her traveling companions. But Maria was not there. "Rosina Lauterbach."

"A fitting name for such a pretty little rose."

She flushed. "And your name, sir?"

He bowed. "Leopold Zuehlsdorff, at your service." His words were sober, but his eyes crinkled at the corners, as if he'd shared some secret joke.

Rosina turned away, and saw Adolf Sperber searching among the immigrants crowded on deck. But as she joined him, the name echoed in her mind: *Leopold Zuehlsdorff. Leopold Zuehlsdorff…*

"There you are." Adolf looked relieved. "Will you look to Lottie? I was just below, and there are so many women in distress that I…" He made a helpless gesture with his rough, broad hands.

"Of course," Rosina said. "She was asleep when last I checked."

"She's never been strong," Adolf muttered. "Perhaps we should not have—"

"Everyone says the first days of the voyage are the hardest for those inclined to sea sickness." Rosina patted his arm. "Our Lottie will likely improve."

Below, two women were bickering shrilly about whose turn it was to use the tiny cook stove. Rosina edged through the dim labyrinth to the tiny space she, Adolf, and Lottie had been assigned for the voyage. Rosina widened her stance as the *Fair Wind* rolled.

"Lottie," she murmured to the pale woman sweating in the lower bunk, a crabbed affair with edges to help keep passengers from pitching to the floor when storms lashed the ship. "Would you care for a sip of water? And some *zwiebach*? Or I could fix some barley-groats—"

"No," Lottie moaned, and closed her eyes.

Rosina crouched and pulled her small trunk from beneath the bunk. She'd had little to pack: her Sunday dress and spare stockings, her mother's zither and *springerle* mold, sewing basket, sack of flax seeds and hackling combs and weaving shuttle. She found a clean towel and gently dabbed Lottie's face. "I know it's difficult, but you must eat. If not for yourself, for the baby."

Lottie managed to sip some water, and nibbled a bit of *zwiebach* too. "Thank you," she whispered. "You're so kind."

"It was kind of you and Adolf to pay my fare." Rosina's gratitude could swallow the Atlantic. "Will you come out on deck with me? It is truly a fine afternoon."

"I don't have the strength."

"I'll help you. The fresh breeze would do you good." The air below was sour with the odors of vomit, dirty diapers, stale sweat, and scorched peas.

But Lottie turned her head away. "I cannot," she whispered.

Rosina pinched her lips. Lottie was likely to deliver her first child before they reached America. Her feet and ankles were swollen, her cheeks hollow. Sweat plastered strands of brown hair to her forehead. Rosina did not doubt that Lottie felt wretched. But she also feared that Lottie had given up all hope of ever feeling better.

"Lottie," she began, but just then the ship dropped more deeply, prompting a moaning chorus of misery from the other immigrants huddled in their bunks. The wooden beams creaked.

Lottie rolled onto her side, facing the wall. "I'll try to sleep. You go on."

Rosina went back to the steep stairs leading to the deck and reported to Adolf, who'd been hovering nearby. He nodded glumly before returning to a group of men debating the political news—months old—from America.

After leaving Bremerhaven, one of the biggest ports in all the German states, the ship had detoured north, around Scotland. The captain said it was a safer route than the Channel, but the winds had been so piercingly cold that most of the immigrants had been no more comfortable on deck than they had been in the hold. Now they'd finally turned west, and the weather was fair. Women rocked their babies and jounced fidgety toddlers. Older children played dominoes. And ... Leopold Zuehlsdorff sat alone, leaning against the rail with knees bent like a schoolboy, reading a book.

It's just the blue of his coat that caught my eye, Rosina told herself. She hadn't looked for him in particular.

Paying particular mind to Leopold Zuehlsdorff would be most inappropriate for a young woman promised in marriage to someone else.

SIX

ROELKE'S SHIFT STARTED AT seven the next morning. Nothing urgent was waiting, so investigating the reenactor's death at Old World remained his top priority. Detective Goresko agreed that he should interview the interpreters in the Norwegian area to see if Steven Siggelkow's story could be confirmed. The historic site didn't open till ten, though.

Chief Naborski and Marie, the clerk, didn't usually arrive until eight, and Roelke loved this first hour. Few calls came in. Marie's radio, perpetually tuned to a pop station, was silent. He could drink coffee and collect his thoughts.

But Chief arrived while Roelke was scooping grounds into the coffee filter. He'd called Chief at home the evening before—standard operating procedure after any death, accidental or otherwise—so this early arrival was a surprise.

"Morning." Chief unlocked his office. "Got a minute?"

"Sure." Roelke started the percolator and followed the older man. He took a chair in front of the chief's desk, trying to figure out if he was in trouble.

"I saw the schedule change request," Chief began. "Fine by me."

"I'm trading shifts so I can work security for German Fest." Milwaukee had begun holding a series of ethnic festivals by the lakefront each summer. Lots of cops moonlighted.

Chief Naborski nodded absently and got down to business. "I got a call from Ralph Petty at six a.m. this morning. He is not happy."

"Oh?" Roelke's knee began to bounce.

"Not happy with Detective Goresko," Naborski clarified. "Petty said Goresko was, and I quote, 'rude, peremptory, and dismissive.' Did you witness any altercation?"

"No. And I've never known Goresko to be rude."

"Me either." Naborski tipped his chair back on two legs. He was a good chief—fair with his officers, fair with the public. The man had served in Korea, and while he wasn't an in-your-face kind of cop, he wasn't someone to mess with.

"I did have to restrain Mr. Petty from charging into the scene before Goresko and his crew had a chance to document it," Roelke mused. "I'm not surprised if he got mouthy with Goresko too."

The chief toyed with a paper clip. "Rumor has it that Petty is planning to run for the village board."

"He *is*?" Roelke's knee bounced faster. That would be bad. The Eagle police served at the board's pleasure. What if Petty got on the board? What if, having done that, he weaseled his way onto the Police Committee?

Holy toboggans, Roelke thought, Chloe and I could both end up answering to Petty. That would be *very* bad.

"Evidently Mr. Petty's political aspirations go even beyond Eagle, but he's willing to start here." Chief Naborski's tone was dry.

Very, very, *very* bad.

"Don't worry about it." Chief's chair banged down on the floor. "Just keep me posted. Petty's likely to try to get what he wants from me instead of going through the county guys."

Lucky you, Roelke thought, and went to pour them both a cup of coffee.

———

As Chloe drove to work, she brooded about the way the evening before had ended. She hated disappointing Roelke. And she had, big time, by not claiming the cabin for her personal retreat.

Chloe had begun sensing strong emotions that lingered in old buildings as a child, but the experiences were random and unpredictable. Happy vibes were a pleasant discovery. The bad stuff like anger, resentment, grief—those packed a wallop. She'd tried talking to whomever had left the emotional residue. She'd tried meeting negative energy with postive thoughts. Those strategies never worked. Once or twice she'd been able to make things right by sorting through some old problem, but that was unpredictable too.

This was the first time her dubious "gift" had impacted her personal life. The situation sucked. She needed space of her own. The cabin was perfect. Her inability to step inside—and the way it affected the man she loved—made her feel helpless.

And feeling helpless pissed her off. "I will find a way to fix this," she muttered, as she turned into the gravel drive that wound around to Ed House. Sure, she could turn a spare bedroom in the main house into her private space. But just seeing the cabin would remind them both, every day, that she'd picked up on something intensely negative in there. Her offer to search out Roelke family history was about more than documenting birth and death dates; she desperately wanted to discover whatever had left behind such bad energy.

Byron was, as usual, already at work in Ed House when Chloe got there. She and Byron each had desks in the open space that once had been a family's living and dining room. The building's only actual office, with an actual door, belonged to Marguerite, the curator of research. Sometimes Chloe envied the older woman's ability to shut out the noise and commotion. But she'd been given a private workspace of her own when she'd started—in a cramped trailer that had been pressed into service as temporary artifact storage. After a month or two of solitude she'd humbly approached Byron and begged for a corner.

"Hey," she said. "What's the word? Can we open the Schulz Farm today?"

"I figured you'd know."

"Sorry." Chloe did not feel obliged to explain that she had not slept in Roelke's bed last night, or eaten granola with him that morning, and did not know the status of police business.

With a melodramatic sigh, Byron reached for the phone. "I'll ask Petty."

The conversation was short and, it turned out, sweet. "We can open Schulz," Byron reported.

"Do you have time to run out there before morning briefing?" Chloe asked. "Knowing that the cops were still around when we left last night makes me anxious. I'd like to look things over before … "

Byron had grabbed his car keys and left the room.

"... the interpreters arrive." Chloe trotted after him and called, "I'll drive my own car." If anything at the farm needed to be cleaned or tidied, she'd stay.

She took care while winding through the museum grounds. Other than the trams used to transport visitors, no modern vehicles were permitted on site during open hours. Farmers, maintenance workers, or anyone else with modern business to conduct at one of the historic buildings or visitor rest stations knew their time was limited, and therefore sometimes drove fast on the twisting gravel roads.

Fortunately she made it to the hidden parking spot near the German area without incident. As she walked to the farm a crackle in the underbrush sent her heart skittering. Just some squirrel, she told herself. But Roelke's warning about the reenactor's death echoed in her mind: *Please don't wander around the site by yourself until we know whether we're looking at murder.*

I *hate* this, Chloe thought angrily, even as she quickened her pace. The unanswered questions had stalled over the historic site like a black cloud.

Chloe found Byron sitting on a bench, contemplating the farm. Cumulus clouds filled the sky. One of the oxen in the pasture lifted its head, then returned to grazing. The garden in front of the house was overflowing with mid-summer bounty. Chloe half expected Auguste Schulz to step onto the porch and beckon them inside.

"I love this farm," Byron said sadly. "I wish ... "

"Me too."

They went inside and checked through the house. "I don't see anything out of place," Chloe said with relief. Investigative police procedures and protective curatorial procedures were not always compatible.

They were in the workroom, devoted to spinning flax fibers into linen thread, and weaving that thread into cloth. "Schulz provides a great focal point for Civil War programming," Byron said.

"The 9th guys will be good partners for interpreting how immigrants from the German states reacted to the war."

"We can talk about women's activities too." Byron took his glasses off and polished them on his shirt.

Chloe contemplated the big two-harness loom, which was empty. "Aren't the interpreters weaving this summer?"

Byron looked glum. "The only person on staff who could warp this loom retired."

"That's too bad." Warping referred to the process of winding yards of threads along the back beam, then passing each end through eyelets on a harness, and through a reed for proper spacing, before weaving could begin.

He looked at her with sudden speculation. "Do you know how to warp a loom?"

"Ye-es," Chloe said warily. Before taking her current position as collections curator, she'd been employed on the education and programming side of museum work.

"Having this one idle frustrates the interpreters and disappoints the visitors."

Chloe studied the loom. The beater board was original, but the reed was new. The wood frame looked to be a bit off-kilter—hardly surprising in a century-old loom—but they could work around that.

"Linen is difficult to work with," she said, stalling to give herself time to think. "Every change in temperature and humidity affects thread tension."

"I know."

"I couldn't do it on work time. Not much, anyway. Petty would have a fit."

"I know."

"Someone would have to help me with parts of it."

"I know."

"Do you use what the interpreters spin for the warp threads?" That would be a deal-killer. Some of the women who worked Schulz were expert spinners; some were not. Warp threads were under constant pressure, and poorly spun thread would snap.

Byron shook his head. "No, I buy what's needed to dress the loom. Then we use what the interpreters spin for the weft."

Chloe sat at the loom and placed both palms against the front beam. She thought about all women who had settled on this very bench, touched this very wood. The idea of stepping into that continuum, getting the magnificent old loom working again, was appealing. It would be good to spend time in the Schulz house, getting back in touch—literally—with domestic work.

She swiveled back to Byron. "Okay. I'll do it."

"Really?" A grin lit his face. "That would be *so* great."

Byron did not grin often, and his reaction made her feel good. "My pleasure."

He turned toward the door. "I gotta head down to the inn and see who called in sick today." The interpretive staff began their day with a briefing in the basement of the restored inn in the village before scattering to the site's distant corners. The meeting lasted less than fifteen minutes, so once informed of last-minute absences, Byron needed to scramble.

Sometimes Chloe missed dabbling her creative toes in educational waters, but managing a big interpretive staff—remembering who knew what buildings, who fit the clothing available for different eras, who enjoyed moving from one house to another and who would sulk if assigned to a new area—was an aspect of museum work she did *not* miss. "Catch you later."

She needed to linger here. Before she could dress the loom, she had to calculate needed yardage. She always carried a clipboard, pad, and pen when she ventured on site. They were handy for jotting notes about artifacts needing attention. They also signaled to guests that she was a staff member, and therefore did indeed have every right to ask them *ever* so politely not to poke hogs with sticks, venture into barricaded rooms, leave their kids for interpreters to babysit, or otherwise earn a place in the Visitors' Book of Shame.

She was poking through some sewing supplies when footsteps sounded on the back step. Her pulse zoomed to Indy 500 speed.

"Hello?" a man called cautiously.

Chloe recognized Lee Hawkins's voice and put a hand over her racing heart. "It's just me," she called. Which was not particularly enlightening. "Chloe."

Lee poked his head around the door. Jenny was behind him, one hand was pressed to *her* chest. She put her basket on the kitchen table. "We didn't know what to think when we saw the back door open."

Chloe joined them. "Sorry. My car's hidden down the hill. Byron and I came out to make sure the police didn't leave any mess behind."

Jenny nodded. "I had the same idea." She planted hands on hips, surveying the room. She'd perfected the role of 1860s German *hausfrau*. Her round face was completely devoid of makeup, and the large headscarf covering her gray hair was knotted beneath her chin. An apron was pinned to her bodice and tied around her waist. Her workdress was made of a dark green print, now faded almost white at the shoulders. That happened quickly when tight budgets decreed that even full-time employees only be provided with one or two dresses. "Lee insisted on coming with me."

"Good man," Chloe told him. Roelke would surely approve.

Lee reached into his wife's basket and withdrew a small apple, which he presented to Chloe with a flourish. "In token thanks for all you did to keep things calm out here yesterday. I picked my first apples this morning."

She accepted it with delighted surprise. "So early?"

"Oxheart Pippins are summer apples," he explained with offhand pride. "An heirloom variety from England. Very juicy, good keepers, rich flavor."

The apple was ugly by conventional standards—small, a deep pinkish-red with yellow streaks and brown spots. But the gift lifted Chloe's spirits immeasurably. "Thank you, Lee. I didn't realize you had heirloom trees at home."

"It's become a retirement hobby." He smiled at Chloe, then kissed his wife's cheek. "I'll be outside."

As he left, Chloe turned to Jenny. "So. You know the building much better than me, of course, but I didn't see anything out of place. Now I'm just trying to figure out how much thread I need to warp your loom."

Jenny looked surprised. "You're going to warp our loom?"

"If that's okay with you." As German lead, Jenny was responsible, under Byron's supervision, for the day-to-day operations on the three working farms in the German area.

"I'm thrilled," Jenny assured her. "I just didn't expect the curator of collections to get involved in something like that."

"I spent a lot of time on the front lines myself over the years. I miss it sometimes."

Jenny leaned against the doorframe. "Alyssa will be delighted. She's already doing very well with the spinning wheel."

Chloe smiled, remembering how thrilled she'd been when she'd started her first job at a historic site. One of the best perks was *finally* getting hands-on experience with all the craft and baking and agricultural activities she'd been reading about all her life.

Then her smile faded. "I hope Alyssa's okay. She had quite a shock yesterday."

"I'm so glad you and Byron happened to show up when you did."

"As you probably know, Byron's planning some Civil War programming." Chloe clipped her pen to her notepad.

"Yes." Jenny looked pensive, her earlier pleasure gone.

Hmm. "Jenny, did I say something wrong?"

"It's nothing you said." Some of the tension left the older woman's shoulders. "I'm a bit concerned about Alyssa. Her father died in Vietnam."

Chloe closed her eyes for a moment. "I am *so* sorry to hear that."

"Interpreting a war—any war—might be a challenge for her." Jenny pulled a coffee can from her basket and pulled off the plastic lid to reveal a supply of flour. "She's a sensitive soul. We butchered a goose last week, and she didn't leave the spinning wheel all day."

Chloe nodded. Some new interpreters arrived at Old World with plenty of book smarts, but no practical experience; others had grown up on farms, and while they couldn't discuss academics at length, or assess visitors' cognitive development, they were natural storytellers with a wealth of practical knowledge. In Chloe's experience, such diversity within the interpretive ranks was a strength, allowing everyone to learn from others.

"Byron's not thinking about a battle," she explained. "Battle scenarios can be powerful, but we have a rare opportunity at Old World to interpret the homefront."

Jenny looked relieved. "That sounds much more like it." She dumped the flour into a reproduction crock and settled the crock lid in place to discourage mice, moths, or other critters. "Let me know how I can help with the loom. We only live a mile away, and I don't mind coming in early. Or staying late, if that works better."

"That's kind of you."

"I don't have any children or grandchildren waiting for me," Jenny said. "And Lee loves being on site during off-hours too. He helps Dellyn with the gardens."

"I figured I'd tackle the trickiest parts before or after hours, when we can concentrate, although ... " Chloe nibbled her lower lip. "Did you watch the news last night? I did not. If the media made a big deal of what happened, our visitor count might be lower than usual today."

"I never watch the news," Jenny admitted. "Or read newspapers, either. I've reached a point in life where I avoid getting depressed about current world affairs."

"I can relate," Chloe assured her. "Anyway, I'd hoped to figure my warp thread needs before scooting out of here. Do you know if there's a ruler or some other measure tucked away somewhere?"

Jenny rummaged in her basket. "Here you go. We have a homemade one for use around visitors, but this one's more accurate." She held out a rolled yellow plastic tape measure, and Chloe got busy.

———

Roelke waited until nine to phone Detective Goresko for a progress report. "No news," Goresko said. "None of the staff or visitors interviewed at the gate reported seeing anything. We've made no progress matching Private M to any missing persons reports, so we'll widen the search. The ME will do the autopsy today. I have no reason to expect evidence to emerge, but I'll check in with him."

"Gunter Diederich can likely get us in touch with other Wisconsin reenactment units," Roelke said. "Want me to follow up on that?"

"Already on it," Goresko said. "So far, no luck."

Marie arrived just as Roelke finished his call. "Morning," she said, stashing her purse in a drawer. Her desk was command central, where citations were typed and reports filed and everything prepared for court appearances.

Despite her deplorable taste in music, and despite the fact that she listened without compunction to any conversation taking place in the cramped office, Roelke's top professional goal was staying in Marie's good graces. She was a lifelong resident of Eagle, had worked at the EPD a *whole* lot longer than he had, and did much to make the officers' lives easier. If budgets got squeezed and Chief Naborski had to pick between his clerk and one of his officers, Roelke had no illusions about who he'd keep.

Marie turned her radio on just as the Bee Gees assured listeners that they were indeed still stayin' alive, stayin' alive. "Got a minute?"

"Sure." Roelke scooted his chair close to hers, trying to figure out—once again—if he was in trouble.

"I read about Skeet getting called out to the Geddings place," Marie said. "I know everybody's focused on identifying that poor man who died at Old World, but Maggie's all alone in that big place, and set back from the road like that . . . " Marie shook her head.

67

"I checked on Ms. Geddings yesterday," Roelke said. "I'll keep an eye on her place."

"I worry that whoever it was might come back." Marie's dark eyes didn't waver. "Her grandparents were friends, so I've been inside that house many times. All those antiques—it could be a temptation."

"I agree." Most thieves wanted quick and easy loot—wallets, jewelry, stereos, stuff like that. It was always possible, though, that someone knew more about the value of the heirlooms in Maggie's house than she did. "Do you know if Maggie's grandparents collected anything in particular? Something valuable that's small enough to grab? Maggie didn't notice anything missing, but it's possible she overlooked something."

Marie stared at the wall, thinking. "Ask Dellyn Burke," she said finally. "Maggie's grandparents were active in the Eagle Historical Society."

"Which Dellyn's parents ran for years." Roelke hadn't known Dellyn's folks, who'd died in a car crash. But he knew that Chloe's friend had inherited their house, and that some of the historical society's collections were stored in the attic there, waiting for the day when enough funds had been raised to open a small museum in the village.

"I can only think of one particular interest," Marie added thoughtfully. "Maggie's grandparents collected antiques from the 1860s."

An alarm pinged in Roelke's brain. "The 1860s?"

"Right." Marie nodded. "Bob Geddings was a huge Civil War buff."

SEVEN

Another week passed before Lottie felt well enough to venture, blinking, into the fresh air. With Rosina's help she lumbered up the steps.

Rosina inhaled greedily, purging fetid air from her lungs. The breeze was invigorating—a bit salty with whiffs of tar and smoke. "Shall we take a slow turn around the deck?"

Lottie actually smiled. "Now I see why so many rush up here each day."

One hundred and twenty immigrants were aboard, among them Saxons and Prussians, Württembergers and Hessians and Hanoverians. "The old people gather there," Rosina whispered, pointing to the worn men and women huddled beneath heavy shawls. "That family by the railing is always gloomy."

"Then I'm thankful not to be in close quarters with them," Lottie said. "You are always so cheerful."

"How could I be gloomy?" Rosina asked. "You and Adolf saved me from a life with Maria! I will be forever grateful."

Cousin Maria was unmarried and unhappy, ever focused on duty. "I took you in without complaint," she'd say, smoothing the faded black mourning dress she'd worn for a decade. "I cared for my dear parents in their old age, and now God has sent you to ease *my* years." Evidently Maria believed that God had caused Rosina's parents to die solely so the young orphan would be available as an unpaid servant.

Rosina hadn't dared hope that she would ever leave Maria's cottage, much less their little village. The blacksmith's son had once asked if he might walk Rosina home from church. Before Rosina had recovered from her surprise, Maria had sent the young man on his way. Rosina didn't really mind. He had dull eyes, and black grime perpetually beneath his fingernails. But she'd realized, with a sinking heart, that Maria would discourage any suitor.

Rosina was a skilled spinner—so skilled that Lottie, a neighbor, sometimes hired her to help clean and spin her flax into linen thread. Adolf was a farmer who'd learned the cobbler's trade from an uncle, and made shoes during winter months. He could afford to pay in coins instead of eggs or turnips. Rosina carefully saved her earnings, understanding that one day she'd be a true spinster, childless and alone. Lottie became a friend, and when Adolf decided to follow his brother to America, Rosina had grieved.

But one day Lottie had come to Maria's cottage and offered to pay Rosina's passage to America. "I have never been strong, and will need help when the baby comes," Lottie explained. "We can't pay wages, Rosina, but you may make a home with us in Wisconsin as long as you would like."

Cousin Maria shook her head. "Rosina—"

"I will go!" Rosina had exclaimed. And she'd soon moved in with Lottie and Adolf to help pack—and to avoid Maria's incessant and bitter complaints.

Now she squeezed Lottie's arm. "I feel like a hawk who's escaped the falconer's snare. Sometimes I imagine myself soaring above the waves toward America."

"You have such fancies!" Lottie said.

A tiny shiver rippled over Rosina's skin. Lottie had unknowingly summoned one of Maria's sharpest criticisms: *God did not intend girls to indulge in fancies. Attend your duties, and pray for guidance.*

But Lottie had spoken with affection, not contempt. "I do indeed," Rosina said lightly.

She spotted Adolf seated on a keg within a knot of men. As the women approached he jumped to his feet and settled the keg for Lottie a discreet distance away. Rosina sat on the deck. The scoured planks felt warm, and the ship's rocking was lulling. She pulled a piece of fine linen from her pocket—the sampler she'd begun as a child. It had been folded away for years.

Rosina had arrived at Maria's home clutching precious mementos of her mother: the gleaming zither, which evoked memories of musical evenings; the *springerle* cookie mold, which still smelled faintly of anise; and the sampler. She remembered watching her mother's calloused fingers carefully draw a length of red thread through her needle. "This is my favorite color," *Mutti* had confided. "Stitching with this is like seeing a red bird in the snow." She'd shown Rosina how to knot the thread, and how to fill the letters she'd penciled on a piece of linen.

Soon after, Maria had found Rosina huddled on a chair near the hearth, filling the elaborate capital P with red satin stitch. "You are in mourning, you wicked girl!" Maria grabbed a wooden spoon and smacked Rosina with it. "You disgrace your parents' memory with that scarlet."

Maria's anger had hurt as much as the blow. Bewildered, Rosina clutched the cloth to her chest. "But *Mutti*—"

"My cousin was a fool to marry your mother. A local girl wasn't good enough for him, oh no. Well, you'll have no need of such fripperies here, my girl." Maria reached for the sampler. But Rosina screamed so fiercely that Maria had retreated.

Now, on the ship, Rosina loved having the sampler to keep her hands busy. She opened her needle book and chose one threaded with a length of fine crimson wool. Somewhere behind her a baby squalled, and women chattered in a dialect she didn't understand.

Among the Prussian men a single voice rose, silencing the others. Leaders were emerging within this shipboard village—men the others instinctively turned to, leaning closer to hear their opinion, just as they would to a landowner or minister or military officer. Leopold Zuehlsdorff was one of those. Perhaps it was his experience in America; perhaps it was because he was not a peasant. Rosina suspected the men especially admired Herr Zuehlsdorff's natural ability to argue without offending.

They had not met any ships traveling from America, so they endlessly debated old news: Had the Southern States been right to secede? Should America go to war with itself? And if that happened, what part should German immigrants play?

"…want no share of it," one ruddy-cheeked farmer insisted. "I am forsaking my home, casting my lot to the unknown so I couldn't be forced into the Prussian army! Why would I enlist in a strange land?"

"It makes perfect sense to flee a state that *forces* men into service," Leopold said. "And therein lies the difference. If war commences in America, many German men will choose to fight."

"Why should we fight to free African slaves?" another man objected. "Most of us are heading to Northern states. Slavery in the South has nothing to do with us."

"Because slavery should be abhorrent to all who cherish freedom!" Leopold spoke eagerly, with no hint of anger or disdain, like a teacher encouraging students to understand something important.

"Perhaps war will not come," Adolf said hopefully.

"It will come," Leopold predicted. "And when war is declared, I will fight for the Union."

Rosina felt as if a cloud had sailed before the sun. She could hardly bear to think of Leopold Zuehlsdorff donning a uniform and marching off to fight in this American war.

"It's an easy choice for you," the red-cheeked man said. His long sidewhiskers did not conceal the belligerent set to his jaw. "Most of us have families! We can't leave them alone in a strange place."

"In St. Louis, Milwaukee—in any place where many German immigrants have settled—you'll find strong communities," Leopold said. "Good neighbors will provide help and comfort to those left at home."

"And who will plow my new fields?" a dark-haired young man fretted. "My wife can't slash and grub a new farm from the wilderness by herself."

Even with my help, Rosina thought, it would be impossible for Lottie to create a new home in America without Adolf.

"It would be a sacrifice," Leopold admitted soberly. "I don't pretend to know what is best for any other man. But I do know this: We left behind a society where democracy remains a dream. The rich get richer, and the poor get hungrier no matter how hard they labor. We left behind a society where honest men may not exercise their free will and improve their lot. I have lived in America, my friends. It's not a perfect place. It is not easy to start fresh there. But it is *possible*. In America a man may find failure or success by virtue of his own efforts. America is a democracy, and the land of the free. America has opened its shores to us. I will fight to defend it."

No one spoke. Several of the men exchanged uneasy glances. Lottie reached for Rosina's hand, quickly squeezed. Rosina prayed that she and Lottie and Adolf would be able to start their new life in a peaceful place.

Suddenly Leopold grinned. "Thank you, my friends, for forcing me to clarify my thoughts! We've had a stimulating discussion, but that's enough heavy talk for today. Perhaps it is time for a game of cards...?"

The tension disappeared like steam on the breeze. Several men pulled playing cards from their pockets. Leopold knocked old ash from his pipe, fished out a tobacco pouch, and began to refill the bowl.

Rosina bit her lip. Wisconsin was a strange name for a strange place she could not imagine. A civil war in America was even more difficult to picture. Leopold Zuehlsdorff's declaration—*When war is declared, I will fight for the Union*—made the war as real as a hot stone dropped onto her lap.

I shall not think about a war while we're at sea, she decided, and leaned over her sewing. Despite sleeping in a stinking hold, drinking stale water, and suffering occasional rough seas, she recognized this time on the Atlantic as a pleasant interlude between Cousin Maria's gloomy cottage in Prussia and Wisconsin's unknown challenges. She was determined to enjoy what delights the voyage had to offer: the extraordinary sight of whales breaching, the fascination of meeting fellow travelers from distant towns and villages, musical evenings beneath an ocean of stars.

But just as she counted threads and began her next stitch, a young boy chasing a ball stumbled into her. "Oh!" she gasped, as a drop of blood welled where she'd pricked her finger. She stuck it into her mouth quickly, but—yes, there. A spot of color bloomed on the linen. It may have been fanciful, but it seemed to Rosina that the tiny bloodstain marring the fine cloth was shaped like a tear.

EIGHT

No INTRUDERS PRESENTED THEMSELVES while Chloe calculated the yardage needed for the warp. She'd finished by the time Alyssa got off the tram in front of the Schulz house.

"Good morning!" Chloe met her in the drive. "Are you by yourself again today?"

"That stomach bug is still going around." Alyssa shrugged. "It's okay. I can handle it, and Jenny will spend time here when she can. At the moment she's waiting for a big tour group at Koepsell."

"I'm going to spend some time here this week, getting the loom up and going—"

"Jenny told me!" Alyssa beamed. "Can I help?"

The younger woman didn't look *too* traumatized by what had happened the afternoon before. And for that, Chloe was truly thankful. "I'd welcome your help. Now, I better let you get ready for the day."

Alyssa turned toward the house, but stopped. "Not again." She pointed toward a huge pasture in the distance, part of the Schottler Farm.

"What?" The empty field looked peaceful.

"Look at the fence. See? A couple of rails are down."

Chloe squinted at the zigzag split-rail fence around the empty pasture. Then she caught on. This particular pasture wasn't *supposed* to be empty.

"The Belgian horses spent the winter at the modern barn down by the Administration building," Alyssa explained. "For a while the farmers just brought them out during the day for field work. Now they're supposed to live at Schottler, but they don't seem to like it there, so..."

"So they walk through the fence." Storm and Sky were gorgeous draft horses—chestnut coats, pale manes and tails—and good workers. They were also enormous. Kicking through the fence would be like kicking through pick-up sticks.

"They always head back to the barn. The farmers will reinforce the fence when they have time." Alyssa looked over her shoulder. "I really can't leave the house, and there's only one interpreter at Schottler too, so could you—"

"I'll go after them." In Chloe's early outdoor museum years, when she'd been learning to spin linen thread and warp looms, she'd also wrangled her share of livestock.

"*Thank* you," Alyssa said, and hurried into the house.

Chloe walked to the Schottler Farm in search of Belgian horses on the lam. Historic site work, she thought, is never boring. After a few moments of searching the crushed grass she found the spot where the Belgians had entered the woods. From there the trail remained faint but unmistakable.

An image of Roelke's disapproving frown presented itself.

This isn't even a real trail, she argued silently. Out of Old World's 576 acres, within the state forest's 22,000 acres, the chances of her running into a homicidal maniac seemed slim. She was *not* going to start jumping at her own shadow.

She wound through underbrush, pushing aside low branches, waving away mosquitoes. Ten minutes later she emerged into a clearing at the base of a hill, and there they were, munching grass that was, evidently, much sweeter and greener than that in the Schottler pasture.

"Hey, boys," Chloe called.

Storm—he had a lightning blaze on his nose—gave her a quizzical look: *What on earth are you doing here?* Sky didn't stop grazing: *Human, you do not interest me.*

Chloe approached slowly, making nonsense conversation in a calm voice. Reaching up to pat Storm's satiny neck, she was reminded in a more visceral way just how big these horses were: at least 17 hands tall—in other words, taller than her—and likely a good 2,000 pounds apiece.

Sky seemed least open to interference. If I can get him moving, Chloe thought, Storm will follow. With any luck she could get the Belgians back to the modern barn in the Admin area. With a bit more luck one of the farmers would be there to help secure the blithe spirits.

"All right, Sky," Chloe said. "Time to go."

Sky gobbled more grass.

Chloe grabbed his halter and tried to raise the massive head.

Sky flicked his tail—possibly aimed at an annoying fly, possibly aimed at the annoying woman.

"Time to go!" Chloe kept tugging.

Sky took a step toward the woods, still munching.

Chloe planted her feet and curled her left hand around the halter leather beside her right. "Sky, buddy, help me out. It's time, to, *go.*"

Sky took several steps this time, walking as if unencumbered.

Chloe leaned back with bent knees, putting her body weight into the struggle, but found herself skidding over dead leaves and grass. "Sky!" she scolded. "Don't make me go for help. You'll embarrass us both."

Sky tossed his head. Chloe's hands slipped from the halter and she fell on her butt. Really hard. "Ow! You—"

She broke off as something glinted in her peripheral vision. Something metallic was lodged beneath a huge fallen log where nothing metallic should be.

After regaining her composure she crawled to the log. The glinting thing became recognizable as a tin cup-shaped boiler, strapped to the front of a black knapsack. The kind of black knapsack Civil War reenactors carried.

Chloe scrambled to her feet. The skin between her shoulder blades itched as she scanned her surroundings. Nothing.

Then she regarded the knapsack with dismay. So much for her statistical analysis regarding the near impossibility of her running into anyone—or anything—related to the dead reenactor.

Roelke and Detective Goresko would probably rather she not handle the dratted thing. She dusted off her hands and rear end. "Okay, you win," she called to Sky. "I gotta go for help."

———

Roelke sat up straight as he digested Marie's little revelation. "Bob Geddings was a Civil War buff?"

"Yeah," Marie said. "Why? Does that make a difference?"

"I don't know. Here's what I do know. Someone broke into the Geddings house, which probably held some Civil War–era antiques.

The next day a man wearing a Civil War uniform was found dead at the historic site."

"The man who died at Old World was a reenactor?"

"Apparently. Can you think of anyone else in Eagle who's a Civil War buff?"

"Gerald and Marjorie Ostermann."

Roelke ran the name through his mental Rolodex. Nothing.

"They live outside the village, in the township," Marie explained. "Left Milwaukee and retired out near Ottawa Lake. They're both reenactors, and—" The phone shrilled, and she broke off. "Eagle Police Department … Oh, hi, Chloe."

Roelke's gut clenched.

"He's right here. Hang on."

Roelke snatched the phone. "Chloe? What's wrong?"

"Nothing's wrong. But I found something on site that you'll want to see."

———

Chloe met Roelke at the Admin building. She'd already told the receptionist why a police officer would be leaving a squad car in the parking lot. "Hey," she said, when he got out of the car. She started to lean in for a kiss, then remembered where they were. "Up for a little walk? I'd like to get out of here before Petty shows up."

Roelke got his camera bag from the trunk, and she explained her discovery in more detail. He looked concerned. "Did you leave the horses in the woods with the knapsack?"

"Actually, they followed me here, and are safely stabled."

Chloe and Roelke followed the faint path made by the Belgians' frequent jaunts. In the little clearing, sunlight filtered through the trees and cast lacy patterns. She pointed. "It's hidden under that fallen tree. I'd never have noticed it if Sky hadn't knocked me on my ass."

Roelke crouched and peered under the log. He took pictures. Finally he put on a pair of latex gloves and pulled the bag into the open. "This is a reenacting thing?"

"Definitely. It's a reproduction US Army double-bag knapsack, made of heavy canvas, but tarred to make it waterproof."

He studied the pack. "That's one big tin cup strapped on the outside."

"It's a boiler. One utensil for cooking or drinking."

Roelke unbuckled the strap holding the knapsack closed and gingerly looked inside.

He was making her edgy. "What's in there?"

"Looks like a bunch of clothes. And a piece of heavy black cloth."

"Probably a gum blanket," Chloe said. "Guys roll up in them at night to keep dry."

Roelke closed the pack. "I still have to interview the Norwegian area interpreters, but I need to take this up to Goresko first."

"Okay." Chloe nibbled her lower lip. "The knapsack must belong to the dead man, don't you think?"

"It might. And it may shed light on how the guy entered the historic site." Roelke straightened. "Yesterday, Goresko theorized that the man likely got to that German farm either from the main gate, where all the visitors arrive, or the German gate on Highway S, which is closest. With limited manpower, he focused the search in those two directions last night. But this suggests that Private M may have entered the site through the Administration gate."

"If he was quick, and lucky, and hit the woods right away, it wouldn't have been that hard to escape notice," Chloe said pensively. "But why?"

Roelke hefted the knapsack in one hand. "I do not know."

———

After Roelke left, Chloe walked back to the German area, retrieved her car, and drove to Ed House. Byron was on the phone. She sat down at her desk and contemplated her calendar. Between checking the Schulz house, agreeing to warp the loom, and finding the knapsack, she'd lost half the day.

Byron smacked his phone down and turned to her. "Have you been at Schulz all this time?"

"No." Chloe filled him in.

Byron looked baffled. "I have no idea what to make of that."

"Me either." She pulled the clipboard from her tote bag. "I've got the warp planned out."

He glanced at her yardage calculations. "No problem. I've got plenty of thread stashed in the Schulz supply cupboard."

"Alyssa wants to learn, and Jenny volunteered to help too."

Byron looked at Chloe hopefully. "It would be nice to get that going before we do any special Civil War programming at Schulz."

"Are you ready to confirm something with Gunter? I wasn't sure, after our meeting yesterday was … you know. Cut short."

"I am." Byron picked up a phone message someone had left on his desk, sighed, and put it aside. It was very difficult to get his full attention, ever. "I'd like to get them out next weekend for a trial event focused on homefront issues, especially the response of German immigrants."

"Seriously? Next weekend?" That gave them just one measly week to prepare.

"It'll be low-key," Byron promised.

Sure it would. "Okay," she said weakly.

"Are there any artifacts in storage to support a homefront scenario?"

She gave him a pointed look. "Gee, I don't know. I'll give it some thought while I'm warping the Schulz loom."

"Sorry." Byron had the grace to look chagrined. "Speaking of Schulz... I half expected Alyssa to call in sick today."

"She seemed fine when I saw her." Chloe picked up a button hook and toyed with it. "Did you know that her father was killed in Vietnam?"

Byron's eyebrows rose. "No. That's tough."

"Jenny told me. She expressed some concern about doing anything related to a war at Schulz for fear that it would upset Alyssa."

"Jenny's spent more time with her than I have, obviously, but I'd be surprised if Alyssa had a problem. She's majoring in American History, so she can't be too squeamish."

"I'm sure you're right."

"Petty cornered me this morning." Byron picked up several papers on his desk, tapped the edges, and stapled them together with more force than necessary. "He wants me to contact another reenactment group."

"If we can pull off a strong trial run event with just the 9th Wisconsin, and get good visitor feedback, maybe we can talk Petty out of scheduling a big battle."

"I doubt it," Byron said glumly. "We've done low-key special events this year, so the events pendulum is due to swing."

Chloe sighed. In the historic sites world, administrators often came, preached their personal theories of museum programming, and moved on. Middle-managers like Byron, committed long-term to a particular site, routinely found themselves reacting to "new" ideas that really weren't. If a museum like Old World Wisconsin put a lot of energy into pulling off a big, elaborate special event and then suffered through a weekend of storms and low attendance, someone—usually the director, or the director's boss—was sure to demand that *next* year's special event calendar be filled with a series of small-scale weekend programs. After a season or two, when those small-scale programs didn't produce big numbers at the ticket booth, someone else was sure to demand that *next* year's special event calendar be filled with fewer and bigger programs.

She looked at Byron. "That damn events pendulum."

"Yeah."

Chloe grabbed her sack lunch—carrot sticks and a sandwich of Jarlsburg cheese, heirloom tomato, and baby lettuce—and spent the next hour typing up her notes regarding a recent home visit. A widow wanted to donate her family china to Old World. Chloe studied her Polaroids of the dishes. Final decisions about proposed donations were not up to her, but since her artifact storage facilities could euphemistically be described as "limited," Chloe could not recommend acquiring the dinnerware.

"What's with all the sighs?" Byron asked.

"Oh, sorry. I have to break a sweet old lady's heart. Her heirloom china—" The phone rang. She held up an apologetic finger and reached for the receiver. "Old World Wisconsin, Chloe Ellefson speaking."

"Hey," Roelke said.

"What's up? Did you find ID in the knapsack?"

"Nope."

"Damn.

"I'm headed back. I still need to talk to the interpreters who were working in the Norwegian farm where Siggelkow said he was yesterday afternoon—"

"Hold on. Let me see if, and where, they're working today." She explained Roelke's mission to Byron, who checked the staff schedule. "You're in luck," Chloe told Roelke. "Everyone who worked Norwegian yesterday is working today as well."

"Can you come out with me? They might feel more comfortable talking to a cop if you're there."

"Hold on." She put the receiver down again, and updated Byron. "Maybe it should be you who goes," she said to her colleague. The interpreters reported to him, after all.

But Byron shook his head. "No, you go ahead. I'm due to meet the Village lead in ten minutes. My to-do list is overflowing." He shoved back his chair.

My to-do list is overflowing too, Chloe thought. She wouldn't mind leaving Byron to deal with the police investigation stuff. No artifacts had been involved, so she should get a reprieve, right? Besides, her intern would be arriving any minute, looking for direction.

She sighed, watching a jay pounce on a sunflower seed at the feeder she maintained at the forest's edge. The truth was, Roelke would probably prefer her company on this task, not Byron's. She knew the interpreters, the site, and *him*. Not to mention the reenacting world. She could probably serve as go-between more effectively than Byron.

She picked up the phone again. "I'm expecting my intern any minute. But after I get her started, I'll go with you."

NINE

JULY 1861

"We must have music!" a Bavarian man wearing a patched coat declared. "Tonight we will shiver in our blankets, so now we should dance!" The sun was sinking into the western sea. June had faded to July, and the sky was clear, but the temperature was falling.

"Rosina?" Adolf nudged her. "Would you like me to fetch your zither?" He sometimes coaxed her to join in when musicians began playing tunes. Rosina liked settling the instrument on her lap, liked fingering the strings her mother had once fingered, liked playing as part of a group. Some songs were familiar, some were not; and when the couples danced some steps were familiar, and some not. It was all great fun.

Tonight, though, for reasons she couldn't define, she did not wish to play. "Thank you, no. I would prefer to listen this evening."

Others were not so reserved. An accordion player launched into a jolly tune, and two guitarists joined in. Soon the young peoples' shoes were clattering against the deck. A few children mimicked the steps. Lottie leaned against Adolf's shoulder, looking content.

Rosina was acutely aware of Leopold Zuehlsdorff, chatting with another man nearby. You should *not* be so aware of Herr Zuehlsdorff, she scolded herself. But how did one keep from noticing a fellow traveler? She tried by keeping her gaze on the dancers, clapping along. But after a particularly fast jig the young man who was lightest on his feet held up both palms in surrender. "Enough!" he gasped, chest heaving. The others cheered as he found a seat, fanning himself.

Rosina thought the entertainment was over. Then a guitarist started a new tune, much softer and slower, and began to sing:

Sah ein Knab' ein Röslein stehn,
Röslein auf der Heiden,
War so jung und morgenschön,
Lief er schnell es nah zu sehn,
Sah's mit vielen Freuden.
Röslein, Röslein, Röslein rot,
Röslein auf der Heiden

Once a boy a Rosebud spied,
Heathrose fair and tender,
All array'd in youthful pride—
Quickly to the spot he hied,
Ravished by her splendour.
Rosebud, rosebud, rosebud red,
Heathrose fair and tender!

The song was a bittersweet lament, not merry at all. "Excuse me," Rosina murmured. She slipped away and found a quiet spot where she could watch the sea. She felt strangely unsettled, as if a storm brewed on the horizon. But the sky was clear.

She was leaning over the rail when she sensed him approaching. "Frauelein Rosina, should I be worried now?" Leopold Zuehlsdorff joined her.

"There is no reason for alarm," she assured him. "I was watching for porpoises." Sometimes they surfaced right beside the ship, riding the bow waves.

"They are astonishing creatures, are they not?" Herr Zuehlsdorff looked over the restless water. "It is a fine evening."

"Do you ever wish our journey would never end?" she asked. Heat immediately flooded her cheeks. What a foolish thing to say! She was surely the only person aboard who—despite the high times on deck—didn't ache to reach America.

But Herr Zuehlsdorff did not laugh, or speak of dwindling supplies and cramped quarters and winds that sometimes sulked, sometimes howled. "Do you wish that?" he asked softly.

"Oh, perhaps at moments." She strove for a light tone.

"Moments…like this one?"

"Yes," she murmured, because it was true and she couldn't help it. "Have you ever watched the waves rushing against the ship? Sometimes I wonder where each drop has been. What shores it might have touched."

"I've never thought of it that way. But I will now."

Rosina didn't dare glance at him. "When I lean well over the railing, I feel as if I can almost peer into the sea itself. It would be most astonishing, don't you think? I've seen the hogfish that sometimes swim near the ship, and one of the sailors caught a nautilus, did you see it? I can't imagine what fish are darting about below us, right this moment." She held on with both hands and leaned as far over the water as she could.

"I must look for myself." He removed his hat, and steadied himself with the other hand. But instead of leaning over, he paused. "Oh," he said softly.

Rosina felt the feather touch of a finger tracing one of the scars on her neck. She jerked upright, quickly pulling up her shawl.

"My dear girl." He sounded stricken. "You have been beaten...?"

"Not often."

"Who could do this?"

"My father's cousin, who raised me." Rosina watched the first streaks of pink and orange tint the clouds.

"*Why?*"

Rosina shrugged. "Because I lingered to see storm clouds grow instead of hurrying home. Because potatoes scorched while I watched red birds in the snow. Because I asked questions, and indulged in—in childish fancies."

"Such things are signs of a quick and curious mind. You must never, *ever* let anyone tell you otherwise."

She met his gaze at last. The world seemed to shrink. There were no other people on board—no sailors shouting from the rigging, no plaintive chords as men tuned guitars, no squalling babies. There was nothing left but Leopold Zuehlsdorff's kind, sea-colored eyes.

"Has no one ever shown you kindness?" he asked. "Or tenderness?"

Faint whispers—perhaps Cousin Maria's voice, perhaps her own—echoed in her mind: He is so much older... he is a thinker, well educated... you are *promised*.

Her throat thickened. "I—I must see to Lottie," she managed, and hurried away.

Rosina lay in her bunk, staring at the darkness. Midnight was surely long past, but there was no quiet time in the hold. Adolf mumbled in his sleep from the bunk below, and dozens of other passengers added their own snorts and snuffs and snores. Babies cried and children whimpered and mothers murmured. The tall woman across the way was weeping into her blanket, as she did every night. Behind it all was the endless *creak-creak* of straining timbers, and *clink-clink* of tin basins and cups and coffeepots swinging on their nails as the ship rose and fell.

But in truth, it wasn't the noise that kept her wakeful. *Has no one ever shown you kindness?*

Yes, she answered firmly—as she should have said earlier. Lottie and Adolf are kind.

Or tenderness?

She did not know how to answer that question.

I must sleep! she thought, trying to find a comfortable position on the wooden bunk. Lottie's time was approaching. She must be prepared to hearten her friend through what would likely be a difficult labor and delivery. There were older, experienced women on board to help, of course. But Lottie would depend on *her*, and—

A whisper sounded from the far side of the blanket she'd hung for privacy. "Come up on deck."

Rosina's eyes went wide. She lay motionless, straining to hear.

Another whisper: "The northern lights are out." Then a board creaked as he moved away.

Was the whisper meant for *her?* Leopold Zuehlsdorff didn't even bunk in steerage, although she'd seen him there once or twice, playing chess with some of the men on rainy days. Surely even Herr Zuehlsdorff wouldn't dare creep close and whisper an invitation to an unmarried girl in the dark.

But … she'd never seen the northern lights.

Rosina eased from the bunk, suddenly grateful for the ever-present nighttime chorus. She needed only to slip her feet into her shoes. She pulled her woolen shawl over her head and tiptoed across the room. Holding the railing for guidance, she crept up the steps, and—"*Oh.*"

Shimmering ribbons of blue and green and yellow pulsed across the black sky. She barely noticed the few passengers clustered along the rail, and the wind's sharp sting. The heavens were on fire.

Someone touched her arm. "This way." He cocked his head and guided her to a sheltered spot away from the others.

It *had* been Leopold Zuehlsdorff down below, she thought numbly. She should be shocked … but fussy propriety seemed foolish right now. Conventions were insignificant. She and Leopold were insignificant. The night sky blazed with the chartreuse of tiny spring leaves, an azure brighter than cornflowers, fingers of robins' throat red.

"All the heavens are full of thy glory," Rosina whispered finally, because something strong and powerful was welling within her.

"Science can explain this phenomenon, I know," he murmured. "But some things are meant to be merely experienced. Look—do you see how the reflection glimmers on the water?"

She did. The sea shimmered like a thousand rippling mirrors. The night seemed dreamlike. Rosina felt dizzy with joy.

Once, soon after setting sail, the immigrants had experienced a violent storm. Huddled below, Rosina had been acutely aware of the ship ascending and falling over monstrous waves. At the height of each rise came a pause, as if time had stopped. She'd known that the gut-wrenching descent was inevitable, and so tried to somehow clutch that trembling moment when the ship hesitated at the crest of surging sea.

She felt that way now. The sky pulsed and the sea pulsed and something within her pulsed too. Some part of her knew a wretched descent was inevitable, but that seemed a far-distant thing, impossible to even consider. She watched a green streak flare across the sky. "I wish this moment would never end."

"*Meine Röslein.*" Leopold's breath was warm in her ear. He kissed the hollow of her throat. He fingered the top button on her bodice. "It doesn't have to."

TEN

CHLOE WAS FILING NOTES about the proposed donation when someone knocked on the screened door. "Hello?"

"Come on in, Belinda," Chloe called.

Chloe already had one intern, Tanika Austin. Nika was a dynamo destined to run the Smithsonian Institution one day. She was also working on her Ph.D., and wasn't able to work as many hours as she used to. Citing a tight budget, Ralph Petty had forbidden Chloe to hire another intern.

Then a social studies teacher from Palmyra-Eagle High School called. "Belinda Lansing is a top-notch student interested in museum work," he'd said. "I'm hoping you could give her a chance to peek behind the scenes. She'd volunteer her time, of course."

That had been all Chloe needed to hear. Her first meeting with Belinda had confirmed everything the teacher had said. The girl was smart, eager to learn, and a hard worker. She was also, like many extremely intelligent people, a bit socially awkward. She wore her honey-colored hair at shoulder length, with heavy bangs, and tended to hunch her shoulders. She reminded Chloe of a butterscotch turtle wary of poking its head from its shell.

Now Chloe gave the sixteen-year-old her warmest smile and gestured to an empty chair. "No need to knock."

"Oh." Belinda perched on the edge of the chair. "Sorry."

"No need to apologize."

"Oh. Sor—"

"I have a special project for you. We're hosting a new special event about the Civil War next weekend. I'd like you to help consider the impact the event will have on our collections. Start by visiting the three 1860s farms. Listen to the interpreters. Get a sense of important themes. Observe traffic flow."

"Okay." Belinda nodded. "I can—"

The door opened again, and Officer Roelke McKenna strode into the room. He looked focused and authoritative and, in Chloe's opinion, quite good in his uniform.

Belinda's tiny squeak was not in any way appreciative.

"Don't worry," Chloe told her. "He's here to see me." She cocked her head at Roelke, and they retreated back to the kitchen, which served now as a front hall.

She again resisted the impulse to lean in for a kiss. "I need a couple of minutes before I can leave," she told him instead, all professional. But she couldn't help from asking hopefully, "Has the dead man been identified?"

"Nope," Roelke muttered. "Goresko's widening the search to include neighboring states. Surely somebody's missing this guy, and will file a report. If that doesn't work, he might put photographs of the guy's belongings on the evening news."

"Good plan. Maybe someone will recognize the tintype, or the handkerchief." Chloe heard Belinda clear her throat, and dropped her voice to a whisper. "Listen, could you wait in the car? You're freaking out my intern."

Belinda was waiting with erect spine and wide eyes. It occurred belatedly to Chloe that she should have made it clear that she wasn't about to be arrested or something. She bestowed her best all-is-well smile on Belinda and reached for an old book on her desk. "I'm sending this with you. *Wisconsin Women in the War Between the States*, written by Ethel Alice Hurn in 1911. Perhaps this weekend you can skim through the early chapters."

"That would be … This is *great*." Belinda's shoulders lowered at least an inch.

Crisis averted and intern empowered, Chloe thought. Sometimes she did okay at this supervisor thing. "You'll be back on Monday, right?"

"I could come in tomorrow, if you want," Belinda offered. "I don't mind putting in extra time. I mean … only if you'd like me to."

Their original agreement had called for Belinda to work twenty hours a week—reasonable for an unpaid intern, and all Chloe felt *she* could handle. But based on Belinda's eagerness … and considering everything else that had recently been dumped on *her* shoulders … Chloe was happy to accept help.

"That would be wonderful," she told Belinda. "I'll be working this weekend too."

Once Belinda was on her way, Chloe locked up and joined Roelke in the squad car. "Thanks for your patience."

"No problem," Roelke said, as they drove to the Norwegian gate. "Um … I'm hoping you'll do me a favor."

"Isn't *this* a favor?"

"Another one. Goresko and I looked at what was in the knapsack you found, and honestly, we aren't entirely sure what we're looking at. After we stop in the Norwegian area can you go take a look?"

"Oh geez, I don't know." Chloe hesitated. Waukesha was half an hour away, and her calendar was full. Besides, she didn't *want* to talk to Detective Goresko again. She wanted Roelke and his fellow professionals to figure this out. She was busy with looms and china and special events, thanks all the same.

Still, she felt a certain responsibility to the poor man who'd died at the Schulz Farm. "All right," she said, trying to sound only a little martyred. "I'm glad to help if I can."

He reached an intersection, flicked on his blinker, checked for traffic. "Are you stopping at the farm after work?"

His question made her prickle. "Maybe. I'll probably have to work late, thanks to these little unexpected excursions. I agreed to warp a loom, and Byron's going ahead with a trial-run Civil War event next weekend."

"If you've got boxes in your car, I can drop them off for you."

She tried not to squirm. "What with everything that happened yesterday, I didn't get anything packed."

Roelke slowed as they neared the Norwegian gate. "Is something going on? You haven't brought anything over."

"I have so!"

"Not much."

She hugged her arms across her chest. "I brought the dishes, and some garden things…" Her voice trailed away. She knew how lame that sounded. She'd *said* she would bring a carload of stuff over every day. The farm was sorta-kinda on the way between Old World and her house. Dropping off boxes every day made sense. Except she hadn't done it.

"Are you having second thoughts about moving in?"

"No!" she lied. She'd already hurt Roelke's feelings about the farm by admitting that she couldn't bear to enter his grandma's cabin. She didn't have it in her to do it again.

"Then what's going on, Chloe?"

She squirmed on the seat. "I *do* want to move in. But I … I guess I'm just sorting through what that really means. My track record on relationships isn't the greatest." She didn't feel like reminding Roelke that her only other adventure in cohabitation had ended in utter disaster. And she didn't feel like reminding him that she needed private space, because he'd *offered* private space in the cabin, and that really wasn't working out so well. "I guess I have to figure out where I fit into this place that's all about your family."

"The place is about you and me now." Roelke pulled off the road.

"I know." She jumped out to unlock the Norwegian area gate, grateful for the reprieve. Somehow the Roelke farm just didn't feel like home.

After he parked it seemed reasonable to change the subject. "We're in luck." She pointed to a woman in period clothing eating lunch at a picnic table. "That's Delores, the Norwegian lead." She couldn't take a police officer into the area without informing the lead interpreter.

Delores's eyes widened as her visitors approached, but she gestured at the opposite bench. "I assume your visit has something to do with the man's death at Schulz yesterday. How can I help you?" She was a cheerful woman in her mid-forties wearing a faded farm dress with stained apron. Her hair was long enough to coil behind her head. Chloe knew her to be conscientious and generally unflappable, both good qualities in a lead interpreter.

"I need to ask you, and the interpreters working in the Norwegian buildings, a few questions," Roelke explained. "Did you see a man dressed as a Yankee soldier yesterday?"

Delores nodded. "Oh, yes. I was in Fossebrekke yesterday afternoon when he arrived."

Roelke pulled a notebook from his pocket. "Can you estimate what time that was?"

"I know exactly what time it was." Delores touched the small watch case hanging on a chain around her neck. It wasn't old, but the design was so reminiscent of antique styles that Chloe had approved it for wear. "Kyle Fassbender was working Fossebrekke, and he likes to have a late lunch. I gave breaks at Kvaale from noon to one, at the school from one-fifteen to one forty-five, and arrived at Fossebrekke at ten minutes before two."

"This is very helpful," Roelke murmured, scribbling.

"Kyle had visitors, so I waited outside until they left. Then I told Kyle he was free to leave, and checked my watch." Delores smiled ruefully. "I learned long ago to be specific about breaks, so I said, 'I'll see you at two thirty.' As Kyle left, the reenactor walked into the yard. Kyle seemed delighted to see him. I got the impression they knew each other well. They walked off together."

"Did you see where they went?" Chloe asked.

Delores speared a chunk of cucumber and munched thoughtfully. "No. Is it important?" Her forehead wrinkled, and she put down her fork. "Is Kyle in some kind of trouble?"

"Not at all," Roelke said. "We're just trying to learn as much as we can about what happened yesterday, and his friend's whereabouts hadn't been confirmed. Can you describe the reenactor?"

The older woman hesitated. "I didn't get a good look at him. Dark hair and beard, but with some gray, I think. Tall."

Sounds like Steven Siggelkow, Chloe thought.

Roelke turned a page in his notebook. "Was the reenactor with Kyle when he returned from his lunch break?"

"No, I didn't see him again. Kyle came back right on time, though."

"Officer McKenna needs to talk with Kyle," Chloe told Delores. "And the other interpreters as well. We'll try to keep the disturbance to a minimum."

Delores snapped the lid of her salad container into place. "I'll come with you," she said firmly. "I'll cover the buildings so you can speak with the interpreters outside, away from visitors." She lifted the cloth covering her big basket and slid the modern container away. "Let's go."

They stopped first at the Raspberry School. The interpreter there, an elderly woman named Marge, shook her head. "No, sorry. I didn't seen anyone dressed like a Civil War reenactor yesterday."

"Not surprising," Chloe told Roelke as they left her. "The school is from a later time period."

Two interpreters were working at the 1865 Kvaale Farm. Both were summer hires, one a young woman attending Ripon College and the other a thirty-ish woman who taught, if Chloe remembered correctly, high school art. Roelke spoke with them separately, and heard the same story. Yes, a Union reenactor had visited the afternoon before. Yes, they'd been making *krumkakke*. Yes, he hung around for a while. "He was really impressed with the *krumkakke*," the younger woman said proudly.

"It's tricky to make on a woodstove," Chloe added, in case Roelke didn't get that.

"I'm sure it is," he said politely. "Thank you."

The last exhibit in the Norwegian area was the Fossebrekke Farm, a single cabin in a small clearing. An enormous Ossabaw hog was snoozing in a muddy patch beneath an oak tree. Chloe eyed the animal warily—she had a dubious history with hogs—but this one didn't deign to open an eye.

Kyle Fassbender was an earnest young man with such an engaging grin that probably half the college women had set their bonnets for him. He parted his hair on the side in obvious homage to period style, and copper glinted in his longish brown curls. If the sight of a policeman in the farmyard was alarming, he gave no hint. "God, what happened yesterday was *awful*," he said. "Do you know who fell?"

"Not yet," Roelke told him. "We're trying to get a better understanding of who was on the grounds yesterday. Did you see any reenactors?"

"Just my friend Steven Siggelkow. He happened to show up right when Delores gave me my lunch break."

"Where did you go during your break?" Roelke asked.

Kyle shrugged. "We just took a walk."

"Did you see anyone while on your walk?"

The young man considered. "I don't think so. We went into the woods"—he gestured vaguely toward the trees beyond the farm—"because if visitors see you, your whole break can get spent answering questions and stuff."

Roelke nodded. "How long have you known Mr. Siggelkow?"

"A couple of years. We're both members of the 9th Wisconsin. He's been reenacting a lot longer than me, though. He's helped me a lot."

"Reenacting seems like an interesting hobby," Roelke said, in a congenial *Tell me more* tone most unlike him.

"Oh my gosh, it's awesome! Big events, small events—I like it all. Our unit decided not to officially do any national events this year, but Steven and I went to Gettysburg for the big 120th anniversary. There were units from all over the country, even some from Europe." Kyle's face filled with remembered awe. "When we did the battle I saw this enormous line of Rebels coming at us ... and then another line appeared over the hill ... and then another ... It was a bubble moment for sure. Just—just awesome."

His description reminded Chloe of big events she'd attended. It had been staggering to think that the thousands of reenactors taking the field were only a small percentage of the actual number of men who'd once fought and bled and died there. Critics accused reenactors of playing, of romanticizing a ghastly and bloody conflict, but a thoughtful reenactment could help onlookers move past abstract dates and figures. Roelke simply couldn't understand how it felt to be in the moment at a well-done event.

Kyle answered a few more questions without shedding any lamplight on Private M's identity. Roelke thanked the young man, and he and Chloe left.

"Steven Siggelkow was here yesterday afternoon," Roelke murmured. "But we have no way to verify where he and Kyle were during that half-hour lunch break."

Chloe stopped walking. "Surely you don't think Kyle had anything to do with what happened at Schulz."

"How long would it take to walk to the German farms from here?"

"Maybe ... twenty minutes? That's if you take one of the trails through the forest, and really book it. A lot longer if you walked the main site road."

"So the two couldn't have gotten to the Schulz Farm and back during Kyle's lunch break." Roelke stared toward the woods, brooding.

"No. And I believe Delores when she says she knows exactly when the interpreters come and go on their lunch breaks."

Roelke glanced back to the Fossebrekke cabin. "Okay."

"Kyle really is a nice kid, Roelke."

"What's a 'bubble moment?'"

She hesitated. "Well, it refers to moments at reenactments when everything looks so good, feels so right—no modern intrusions in sight—that for a second or two you forget that you're not really in the nineteenth century."

"Oh, come on."

"Hey," Chloe protested. "It can happen, whether it makes sense to you or not."

"Okay."

Chloe couldn't tell if she'd convinced him or not. "*What?*"

"I just … " His voice trailed away. "Nothing. Let's go."

ELEVEN

JULY 1861

Lottie Sperber went into labor the next day, and Rosina barely noted the excitement when the captain announced that they would soon reach New York City. She spent most of her final two days at sea behind the blankets hung around the bunk. Lottie groaned and shrieked and strained for seventeen hours before, with the help of a toothless Bavarian midwife, delivering a son.

Rosina let go of her friend's hands long enough to take the baby. "You have a fine boy. Lottie? Open your eyes." Rosina felt a cold hand close around her heart. Lottie was too still. Too white.

Another woman appeared at her shoulder. "Rosina?" she whispered. "Herr Zuehlsdorff asks if you would please join him on deck for a moment."

"Lottie is bleeding too much," the midwife muttered. "Find another towel."

"Is something wrong?" Adolf called anxiously.

"Please tell Herr Zuehlsdorff that I cannot come now, nor any time soon," Rosina hissed to the message-bearer, who nodded.

The next hours were terrifying. But the midwife knew her business, and she finally announced that Lottie would live. Rosina washed the linens and prepared broth while a woman from Hamburg with red-rimmed eyes, who'd delivered a stillborn days earlier, held the baby to her breast.

When the *Fair Wind* reached the harbor, Rosina left the Sperbers and wearily climbed to the deck. She was so exhausted, so overwhelmed, that her first glimpse of America hardly seemed real. But she did have something important to do. She persevered against the jostling throng of eager passengers, searching for... *there*. She recognized Leopold's ringing laugh.

She fought her way closer. I'm here! she called silently, happily. But Leopold did not see her.

Rosina felt lightheaded, inundated with the sun and chatter and shoving. In desperation she cried, "Herr Zuehlsdorff!"

Leopold turned his head, looking puzzled. Then his companions surged toward the rail, carrying Leopold with them.

Rosina elbowed into a gap and saw two men approaching in a small boat. One was rowing. Another man with wild red hair was in the bow, leaning forward like a figurehead. He shouted, but the wind carried his words away.

"*Quiet!*" someone bellowed.

Excited conversation died as the boat drew near. The man in the bow cupped his hands and tried again. "Hail *Fair Wind!*"

"What's the news?" That was Leopold, splendid in his blue coat, leaning over the rail.

"Confederates fired upon a Federal fort in South Carolina! The Union was dissolved in April!" The other man waved both arms. "It's war!"

———

The immigrants disembarked the next day. Adolf supported his wife as they crept down the gangway. Rosina clutched baby Gerhard, fighting dizziness and the odd sensation of ground still and solid beneath her feet.

"I must see to our belongings," Adolf muttered. "Stay with Lottie."

"Of course." Gerhard was a tiny weight in Rosina's left arm, and she used her right to support her friend. But all the while she scanned the milling crowd for a tall man in a blue coat. She still hadn't had a chance to speak with Leopold. To make plans.

When war is declared, I will fight for the Union.

Adolf returned first with the small trunk and Rosina's box. "I'll be back when they've unloaded the storage hold," he reported. "It will take time."

"Here, Lottie. Sit." Rosina helped ease her friend down on the sturdy trunk.

"Thank you." Lottie settled gratefully. She drew up her knees and rested her head on her arms.

Rosina hummed to Gerhard and watched anxiously for Leopold. Above, sailors shouted names as they hauled huge trunks from the hold. Immigrants milled about on the dock. Runners from nearby hotels shouted the virtues of *their* establishments, and men in tall hats and fine clothes shouted the virtues of *their* coach service to the Erie Canal. Mothers gripped their toddlers' wrists. Babies cried. Seagulls shrieked. Rosina despaired.

Suddenly there he was, striding past with several other men. "…but Wisconsin must raise a German regiment," one was saying—the man with red hair. "You'll join the fight, Leopold?"

"Of course!"

Rosina felt proud and afraid. "Herr Zuehlsdorff!"

Gerhard protested her shout with a fretful whimper, but this time Leopold heard her. *Saw* her. He murmured to his friends and broke away. Rosina hurried to meet him. "Herr Zuehlsdorff," she said breathlessly, weak with relief, rocking Gerhard. "The war—you're enlisting?"

"We Germans must do our part if we are to earn the respect of our new countrymen."

"But you and I … I thought we would … " Rosina's face flamed.

"*Röslein.*" Leopold stepped closer and touched her cheek with one gloved finger. "Surely you can see that now is not the time."

"But … " Rosina's voice faltered. After what they had done beneath the northern lights, was there any better time? "Are you leaving at once?"

"No, no. I am traveling on to Wisconsin as planned, to help recruit a German regiment. Good men are already petitioning the government, and—"

"But what about us?" Rosina didn't care how many men were petitioning the government. "Surely … we should wed." Yes, she was promised to someone else. But she knew things now that she hadn't known when Cousin Maria made that promise.

"Ah." Leopold paused, looking down at her, his eyes kind. "You are a special girl, a lovely smart girl—but *war* has been declared! I think we should wait to discuss our future until the Union has been preserved."

"Until the Union has been preserved?" Rosina echoed. Who knew how long this American war would last?

"Leopold!" one of his friends called impatiently.

"We will see each other again," Leopold promised. He looked as if he might kiss her goodbye, but seemed to think better of it. "Be happy, *Röslein.*"

Rosina watched Leopold walk away. She could not move. For the first time she understood why some of the immigrants faced the New World with glassy eyes and faltering steps. She had never felt so lonely.

Finally she plodded back to her friend. Lottie was sitting up straight, waiting. She glanced deliberately after Leopold Zuehlsdorff, then back to Rosina. "Careful, there."

It is too late for care, Rosina thought. Much too late.

TWELVE

As Roelke drove Chloe to the Waukesha County Administration Center, he stewed about a hobby that involved rifled muskets and "bubble moments" and wool coats in summer. He'd always given Chloe space for things he didn't understand, but he expected them to stay with *her*. He didn't like them intruding into his personal life, as they had at the old Roelke cabin. Now they were intruding into his professional life as well.

They ran into Goresko at the entrance to the Sherriff's Department's Detective Bureau. "I just checked in with the ME," he said.

Roelke was glad he had not been expected to visit the medical examiner. Some cops grew immune to the morgue, the pervasive smell, the work done there. He had not.

"He believes the man was malnourished," Goresko was saying, "but we'll know more when we get the full autopsy report." He turned to Chloe. "Thanks for coming in, Ms. Ellefson."

"Please, call me Chloe." She smiled but shoved her hands in her pants pockets, looking uncomfortable. "I don't know how much help I'll be."

"I'll take whatever help you can give me. Let's take a look." He led them to a meeting room that smelled faintly of wood smoke. The knapsack found that morning lay on a table, with its contents spread beside it—brownish pants and jacket, a dirty calico shirt, socks, the cup-thing she'd called a boiler, a few other odds and ends.

Chloe stepped closer. "This is the basic kit of a Confederate soldier—"

Roelke felt a sinking sensation in his chest. *Damn.* Another reenactor unaccounted for.

"Confederate?" Goresko repeated. "I thought Confederate uniforms were gray."

"When the war began, individual Confederate units left home in all kinds of attire," Chloe explained. "Including blue uniforms."

Goresko's eyebrows rose. "That can't have worked well."

"It did not," she agreed. "So the haphazard approach quickly evolved into standard gray uniforms for Southern troops. But by the end of the war, gray uniforms were faded and tattered, and soldiers wore whatever they could cobble together."

"So ... this was part of a reenactor's military uniform?"

"Almost certainly. It's dyed with butternut."

"Butternut?" Roelke asked. "Like the tree?"

"Yes. *Juglans cinerea*, also known as white walnut, produces a brownish dye. May I touch?" When Goresko nodded she fingered the coat. "This is linsey-woolsey, which means the warp threads are linen and the weft threads wool. Most commercial suppliers include a bit of polyester in their cloth. Some reenactors are willing to pay for handmade cloth."

"But the belt buckle says U.S.," Goresko objected. "Wouldn't that mean Yankee?"

"The buckle is federal issue," Chloe agreed, "*but*, Rebel reenactors sometimes wear them upside down to imply they'd taken the belt from a dead Union soldier, just as the original troops sometimes did. Same with the canteen." The canteen found inside the knapsack was held in a worn woolen sling with *U.S.* stenciled in black. "These are nice details for a late-war Southern impression."

Goresko's forehead furrowed. "So, it seems we have two mystery reenactors—the unidentified Yankee who died, and the unknown Confederate who stashed this knapsack and went on his way."

"Not necessarily." Chloe held up one graceful palm. "Experienced reenactors sometimes have to galvanize—"

"I don't follow." Goresko tapped his pencil against his pad. He'd hesitated when Roelke had suggested consulting Chloe, but Roelke was pretty sure that the detective had discarded his doubts.

"Sorry." Chloe paused. "Say you're organizing a major event somewhere in the South. Advance registrations show five times more Confederates than Yankees, but that makes no sense for the campaign you're featuring. *So*, some of the Confederate reenactors will have to galvanize—act the part of a Union soldier. That's most common, but Union reenactors are occasionally asked to portray Confederates."

"And everybody just goes along with that?" Roelke asked.

She shrugged. "Some men refuse. Others are willing if necessary. Some actually enjoy it. It gives them a chance to dig into a different persona."

Roelke turned all that over in his mind. "Well, hunh."

Chloe leaned over the table. "These wool socks are homespun and hand-knit, really nicely done. Tobacco pouch, pipe, matches, toothbrush and tooth powder, comb, playing cards … also reproductions."

"How about the stuff we found on the body?" Roelke gestured to another table.

Chloe studied the second display. "Ah—here's the cockade you mentioned." She indicated the bedraggled flowery thing made of red, yellow, and black ribbon. A metal button was in the center.

"What was the point of that?" Goresko asked.

"People wore cockades to express loyalty to one side or the other. Ladies' aid groups made special cockades for departing companies, or for each veteran wounded in a certain battle. Red, white, and blue were most common. These colors suggest Germanic heritage."

A German cockade on a reenactor who died at the German farm, Roelke thought. He couldn't decide if that made sense or complicated the mess further.

"There was no unified German country in 1861," Chloe said. "But these colors have a long history of importance among the German states. Maybe Private M had a German background, or maybe his unit portrays German-American soldiers. Or … " Chloe nibbled her lip. "It's also possible that Private M just participated in an event that featured a German unit. The identity of individual units gets set aside at big events."

Roelke frowned. That added up to … not a whole lot.

"This cockade is a reproduction, but very well done." She shook her head with admiration. "I've made a few cockades, but nothing that fancy. See how precise the folds are, and how tiny and even the stitches?"

Roelke and Goresko nodded obediently.

"The food is typical stuff. The uniform is standard for a Union soldier, with a few personal touches. The tintype is nice." She pointed at a small portrait of a young boy, maybe eight years old, staring earnestly toward the photographer.

Roelke pulled back one front of the blue uniform coat to expose a pocket. "The picture was in here."

"Some reenactors add pockets to their coats."

Goresko pointed to the handkerchief and a square of heavy glazed cloth. "He'd wrapped the tintype in those."

"For protection. The handkerchief with the satin-stitch *M* is also a beautiful reproduction." She fingered the heavier fabric. "I think this oilcloth is homemade, meaning someone coated heavy cotton with linseed oil. It's not a fun job, but modern oilcloth contains vinyl, so reenactors don't like it."

Roelke was getting a whole new understanding of the word *authentic*.

"What can you tell us about the photograph?" Goresko asked.

"Tintypes like that were made on thin iron plates. They were common during the Civil War because they were relatively inexpensive, and sturdier than CDVs."

Roelke raised his eyebrows: *Translate, please?*

"*Carte de visites.* Albumen prints, mounted on cards, two and a half by four inches."

Roelke didn't know what albumen prints were. It didn't sound relevant, so he let it go.

"Lots of reenactors carry photographs. I knew an officer who asked all of his guys to carry a civilian photo to help remind them that soldiers didn't magically spring to life the day they joined the army."

"Is that tintype an antique?" Goresko asked.

She hesitated. "I'm not an expert. I've seen old tintypes that look brand-new, and new ones that get beat up and look ancient. Most guys carry repros, but my best guess is that this one is actually from the period. See how the image doesn't go all the way to the edge of the metal plate? Originally, tintypes were clamped in wooden frames while the exposure was being made. That left a telltale black edge, like … " She pointed. "There." She contemplated the tintype sadly. "That sweet little boy might have been waiting for his daddy to come home."

"Was it likely that Private M was carrying a gun?" Roelke asked. He did not like the idea that a musket was hidden somewhere at Old World.

"Hard to say, since we don't know what he was doing there." Chloe poked a stray strand of hair behind one ear. "Is any of this helpful?"

"Everything is helpful at this point," Goresko assured her.

But Chloe seemed to have run out of observations. They stared at the items spread before them while a wall clock ticked noisily. A phone's shrill ring drifted down the corridor.

"Well, this is all very interesting." Goresko's mouth twisted wryly. "But I wish reenactors sewed those little name tapes in their clothes, like moms do when their kids go to camp."

"The very idea would make most reenactors cringe." Chloe shoved her hands into her pockets again.

Goresko closed his notebook, indicating an end to the interview. But Roelke sensed she had more to say. "Chloe, does the sum total of all this stuff suggest anything to you?"

"*Well…* everything here is authentic. This guy was hardcore."

"Hardcores are reenactors who want everything super-authentic," Roelke murmured.

Chloe nodded. "Right. This guy had been active in the hobby for years—"

"Or perhaps he just camped out during a storm," Goresko interjected.

"I don't think so. Some guys try to dirty up new stuff, but nothing compares to the look of a uniform that's been worn a *lot*. Also, beginners usually start with one basic uniform. Private M was interpreting a late-war impression, *and*—assuming the knapsack and Confederate uniform also belonged to him—he probably had at least three impressions."

Roelke wanted to be sure he was following. "New Yankee soldier, experienced Yankee soldier, and experienced Confederate soldier?"

"Right. Uniforms of any type are expensive, so it's no small thing to have two, much less three. And he'd added a lot of personal touches. That also takes time." She hesitated. "Instead of contacting just local reenactment units, you might want to reach out to units known for their high standards of authenticity. Ask the leaders of hardcore groups to check their membership, see if anyone's unaccounted for. There's no single governing organization, but I can give you some names."

Goresko pinched the bridge of his nose. "How many Civil War reenactors do you suppose there are?"

She thought for a moment. "The last figure I remember hearing was fifty thousand."

"Fifty *thousand*?" Goresko yelped. Actually yelped. "That can't be right."

"Something like that," Chloe insisted. "I'm sorry I can't tell you anything more."

"You've told us plenty," Goresko assured her. "Anyone would think you're an experienced profiler."

"It's what I do every day, actually." Chloe gave a tiny shrug. "Artifacts are clues to the people who left them behind. Sometimes I have only the tiniest scrap of information, and have to dig deeper to get a sense of the person who made or used the item, and how they felt about it. Analyzing a reenactor's belongings isn't much different."

The detective ushered Roelke and Chloe out. Chloe didn't speak until they were back in the car. "It's all so *sad*," she said with a sigh. "What if we never figure out who this guy was?"

"We will."

"What if we don't?"

"We *will*." Roelke started the engine. "Somebody knows who the dead man was. We'll find that somebody, sooner or later. You did great in there, by the way." He squeezed her hand.

She sighed and slid down on the seat. He thought she was going to prop her toes on the dashboard, but she seemed to remember that she was in a police car. She heaved a bigger sigh and straightened again. "So … what do you do next?"

"I'm going to go back to the spot where you found the knapsack, and widen the search," he said. "Maybe there's something else hidden away. If there's a musket out there somewhere, I want to find it."

———

After Roelke dropped off Chloe at Ed House, she glanced at her watch and groaned. Almost four thirty. When she walked inside, Byron turned from his desk with an *I've got bad news* look.

She groaned again. "What?"

"Petty's looking for you."

Chloe dropped into her desk chair with a muttered curse. "What for?"

"Didn't say. But he sounded … "

"Pissed?"

"Yeah."

"Lucky me." She reached for the phone.

Director Ralph Petty was, as Byron had suggested, not even a little bit happy. "Miss Ellefson? I've been trying to reach you for hours. Where have you been?"

"Helping the Eagle Police Department, mostly." Since she'd told the receptionist about finding the knapsack, that much shouldn't be a surprise. "The detective asked Officer McKenna to talk to the Norwegian interpreters, and I went along to—"

"To spend time with your boyfriend?"

Chloe's mouth opened, but it took a moment to find words. "*No-o*, I went along to keep disruption on the site to a minimum, and to help put interpreters and visitors at ease if—"

"Site matters are Byron's domain, Miss Ellefson."

"Byron had a meeting. I was helping out."

"Are your own duties well in hand?"

How was she supposed to answer *that*? Chloe had begun her tenure at Old World by inheriting thousands of artifacts housed in inadequate facilities, a mountain of programming-related needs, and a constant stream of proposed donations to contend with. Her duties would never be "well in hand."

"I'm doing my best," she said finally. "I met with Belinda Lansing earlier about—"

"I'm not interested in your charity project."

"Belinda is an *intern*, donating her time, and—"

"Have you completed the window inventory for the UV film project?"

She blinked, trying to keep up. "No, Mr. Petty, I have not. It's not due to Leila until the end of August." Leila was the curator who oversaw collections issues for all of the historic sites managed by the State Historical Society of Wisconsin.

"I want to see your inventory next week."

Chloe gritted her teeth. I need this job, she reminded herself. I need this job. I need this job. I need—

"Miss Ellefson?" The SOB's tone was decidedly smug.

I will not let him win, she vowed silently. "Then you'll have it next week. Is there anything else I can do for you?"

Evidently Petty hadn't expected acquiescence. "Not today," he snapped. "But next time, let someone know before you disappear."

"I did let someone know, you little prick," she muttered, because she was already speaking to a dial tone. She hung up and looked at Byron.

"What wasn't due to Leila until the end of August?" he asked.

"Leila's writing a grant for money to buy UV film for all the historic buildings at all of the sites. The film is almost invisible, but it will protect the artifacts on display from sun damage. I have to provide her with a list of windows and dimensions."

Byron looked stunned. "For all of our buildings?"

"Yep." Thinking about it made Chloe *feel* stunned. Measuring would be a huge job ... a job she now needed to complete very fast, while preparing for the Civil War event, and supervising Belinda, and warping the Schulz loom, and looking for reenactor information for Detective Goresko, and packing her belongings at home, and working at Roelke's farm, and—

"Forget I asked you to help with the Civil War stuff." Byron regarded her soberly. "And the loom."

Chloe hesitated. She really did need this job.

But ... she also didn't have it in her to cave to Petty. "No way," she said. "I said I'd help, and I'm going to help."

THIRTEEN

AFTER LEAVING CHLOE AT her office, Roelke stopped back at the station to make some calls. He wanted to search more of Old World Wisconsin's forested acres, and given just how many acres there were, some help would be nice.

But the DNR warden at the forest HQ had a missing swimmer at Ottawa Lake, and Deputy Sheriff Marge Bandacek was helping a stranded motorist. No one even answered the phone at Skeet Deardorff's house.

Well, hell, Roelke thought. He drove back to Old World's Administration lot, let the receptionist know why he was there, and walked back out to the spot where the knapsack had been found. He spent the next hour slapping mosquitoes, getting whacked in the face with branches, scratching his hands on brambles, and dirtying the knees of his uniform trousers as he searched for anything else Private M might have hidden.

Nothing. If the dead reenactor had hidden a musket anywhere near the knapsack, he'd hidden it well.

Roelke trudged back to his car. Well, he wasn't done yet. After stopping back at the PD to wash his face and change into a clean shirt, he headed north on Highway 67.

Gerald and Marjorie Ostermann lived on a sprawling, multi-acre lot bordered by six-foot hedges. "Just a little place in the country," Roelke muttered as he navigated the long, winding driveway. A new-but-old-timey mansion stood on a rise. Four white pillars graced the front, giving the place a vaguely plantation-ish look, although the attached three-car garage spoiled the effect. A huge grass lawn was cross-hatched with light and dark green, evidence of recent attention from someone on a riding mower.

A woman answered his knock. Her polite smile disappeared when she saw Roelke's uniform. "Oh God. Is it Mac?"

Roelke wondered who Mac was. "No, ma'am. Nothing's wrong. I'm Officer McKenna, Eagle PD. Are you Marjorie Ostermann?"

The woman's eyes remained wide. She was slightly overweight, in her early fifties, wearing dressy black jeans and a flowy red blouse with shoulder pads. She wore a lot of makeup, and the tips of her fingers were painted with crimson polish. Straight copper-colored hair was held back from her face with glittery barrettes.

"I'm Mrs. Ostermann," she said after a beat. "But—why are you here?"

"I'd just like to ask you a few questions. As you may have heard, an unidentified Civil War reenactor died at Old World Wisconsin yesterday. I've been told you and your husband are reenactors, and—"

"*Oh.*" Mrs. Ostermann's shoulders slumped with apparent relief and she stepped back, holding the door wide. "Please, come inside. May I offer you something to drink?"

Roelke admitted that a glass of unsweetened iced tea would be most welcome. While she was in the kitchen, he assessed the Ostermanns' living room. The furnishings were all glossy wood and flowered upholstery. They didn't look old. Still, he spotted a brochure for an antiques mall in North Point—one of Milwaukee's upscale neighborhoods—on an end table, so the Ostermanns must like some kind of heirlooms.

"Here you are." Marjorie Ostermann bustled back into the room with a glass and coaster.

Roelke thanked her. "So...you and your husband are reenactors?"

"Oh, yes." Mrs. Ostermann nodded. "We've been involved in the hobby for years. Gerald and I founded the 100th Infantry Regiment, and he commands the unit."

"Are you aware of any members who have gone missing?"

"No." She shook her head slowly. "Gerald isn't home, or you could ask him directly."

"Perhaps I can stop back later."

"Actually, he's away for the weekend. The 100th Infantry is participating at German Fest."

"At *German* Fest?"

"Is something wrong?"

He waved her concern aside. "I was startled because I happen to be working security at German Fest." And Chloe was working, right now, with a different reenactment unit to put on a German-focused Civil War event at Old World. "Is the 9th Wisconsin going to be there, do you know?"

"This is a big year because 1983 marks the 300th anniversary of the first Germans coming to America, so I'm sure the 9th Infantry will be there. Possibly one of the Iron Brigade units too, if they're willing to do the German thing, of course. You know how Iron Brigade people can be."

Actually, Roelke had no idea how Iron Brigade people could be.

"Some of them don't want to portray anyone else. We chose the 100th Regiment so we could be flexible. There was no real 100th Wisconsin, of course."

"Of course."

She pressed her lips into a line. "How did … perhaps I shouldn't ask this, but I was wondering … "

"It appears that the man fell from the second story of a stable."

Marjorie Ostermann winced. "How awful."

"If you do hear that one of your friends is missing, please contact us at once." Roelke gave her one of his cards.

"What did the man look like?"

"Dark hair streaked with gray, tall, thin, maybe fifty years old."

"I'll make a few calls." She rubbed her palms on her jeans. "That description could fit a number of our men, and I'd rather make sure everyone is accounted for."

"Thank you. Do all the members of your unit live in the area?"

"Mostly from Waukesha County and Milwaukee," she said. "We're all old friends."

"Just one more thing, ma'am. We also had a break-in in the village, and it's possible that the intruder was looking for Civil War antiques. Do you collect things from that period?"

"We do, but I doubt if anything is missing." She stood. "I'll show you."

Roelke followed Mrs. Ostermann down a hall to an interior door that was secured, oddly, with a padlock. She unlocked it, pushed the door open, and gestured for him to precede her.

Roelke stepped inside and stopped cold. "Holy toboggans." He felt as if he'd been ushered into another house. The windowless room had log walls and a fireplace with stone hearth. Almost everything in the room looked like an antique—desk and chair, a very small rocking chair, oil lamps, pictures on the walls, candlesticks and crockery on the mantel.

"This cabin was built in the 1860s." Mrs. Ostermann's voice held pride. "When we bought the property we couldn't bear to demolish it. This was our solution. It needed substantial restoration, but we're pleased with the result."

The old Roelke cabin could look like this, he thought wistfully. If Chloe lets me fix it up.

"We do collect, as you can see," Mrs. Ostermann was saying. "But the room is always locked when we're not here."

Roelke stepped to the mantel and peered at several photographs in fancy little cases. "Tintypes?"

"A couple of the early ones are actually daguerreotypes," Mrs. Ostermann said. "But that one you're looking at is a tintype. Isn't she sweet?"

The tintype showed a young woman seated in a chair with a child, maybe a year or so old, on her lap. The woman stared at the camera with an aura of sadness, or longing.

"Her clothing is definitely 1860s," Mrs. Ostermann said. "I'm a sucker for old photographs. And period jewelry." She opened a wooden box filled with fancy baubles. "I have a couple of original dresses too. Gerald focuses on anything military." She gestured to three swords hanging on one wall.

Roelke didn't understand the collector bug any more than he understood reenacting, but—to each his own.

Then a different type of picture at the end of the mantel caught his eye. He sidestepped and leaned close. "Is this … "

"A CDV."

"*Carte de visite*," Roelke said nonchalantly. "But I was looking at the people." He pointed at a woman in old-fashioned dress, sitting in a chair. A man in military uniform stood behind her, one hand on her shoulder. A boy—maybe fourteen—stood beside the chair. He also wore military garb and had posed with a drum. None of them were smiling. The composition and style were much like the other photographs he'd seen, but there was something … off about this one. "Isn't this you?"

"It is!" She smiled. "With Gerald and our son, McClellan, a few years ago."

Ah. So that's who Mac was. "Does your son still participate?"

"Mac grew up in the hobby. He portrayed a drummer boy for a while, and then a private." She picked up the CDV, her expression suddenly distant. "He's eighteen now, and he still participates, but he's sort of … grown out of reenacting with his dad. At least the military aspect."

And so it goes, Roelke thought. Naming the kid after a famous Civil War general seemed destined to end badly.

He looked at the next CDV. Something about the Yankee soldier caught his eye, but it took him a moment to figure it out. "Is this *you*?"

"Quite a few years ago now, but—yes." She lifted her chin. "I fell in with the boys a few times. Back in the day."

Roelke remembered Chloe talking about women's participation in uniform being controversial. No way was he bringing that up. He turned from the mantel. "Thank you for talking with me, Mrs. Ostermann. Will I see you at German Fest?"

"I'm afraid I have a family commitment and can't join Mac and Gerald at the festival." She led him from the room, carefully locking the door behind her. "I appreciate you stopping by."

As Roelke slowly drove back down the winding drive, he wondered again what prompted people to go hog-wild over a particular hobby. The Ostermanns had invested in restoring the cabin, in collecting Civil War–era antiques, in reenacting gear. Why did—

An engine's roar sliced the quiet. A red Harley slowed to turn in just as Roelke reached the foot of the drive. Roelke braked and eased over, but the biker swerved back onto the road and sped away.

Well, hunh. Roelke watched with narrowed eyes as the motorcycle disappeared. The rider had been signaling his intention to turn into the Ostermann drive. The hedge had hidden the police vehicle until the last moment, but Roelke had been driving very slowly, and there had been plenty of room.

Motorcycle Man's identity had been hidden beneath his helmet. There were surely plenty of red Harleys cruising Wisconsin. But Roelke knew of only one in Eagle … the one owned by site director Ralph Petty.

———

An hour later Roelke sat at the EPD officers' desk, brooding. Marie and Chief had gone home. Skeet Deardorff, who was on second shift, had come in, shot the breeze for ten minutes, and left when dispatch called in a traffic accident on Highway 59. I should head out too, Roelke thought.

But the death of the unidentified man gnawed at him. A whole day had gone by, and they were no closer to knowing who had died at the Schulz Farm.

Roelke didn't like things undone. He worked on problems until they were solved. The death at Old World presented two problems: the identity of the victim, and understanding whether his death had been accidental or otherwise.

Roelke grabbed some index cards—he always carried index cards—and spread them on the desk. He labeled one *Gunter Diederich, Leader of 9th WI reenactment unit.* He made two more "people" cards—one for Steven Siggelkow, and one for Kyle Fassbender.

Fassbender seemed like a nice kid. He couldn't verify how he'd spent his lunch break the day before, but Chloe didn't think he could have hoofed it to the German area and back in half an hour. Even if he'd run through the woods to rendezvous with the mystery man, it would have taken at least a few minutes to reach the stable, climb upstairs with the man, and shove him to his death.

That left Steven Siggelkow as prime suspect. Siggelkow admitted to wandering the site alone. His confirmed presence at the Norwegian area didn't preclude the possibility that he'd looped through the German area, killed Private M, and finished his afternoon conspicuously eating *krumkakke* at the Kvaale Farm. And the man had seemed nervous in the parking lot at the end of the day. But nothing tied Siggelkow to the Schulz Farm or the dead man.

Roelke frowned at his cards. It was difficult to investigate a suspicious death when he didn't know who the victim was.

Not that it was his investigation anyway. It had happened in his professional back yard, but the case belonged to Detective Goresko, who was liaising with the Capitol Police. Unless something else happened in the Village of Eagle, his involvement in the Private M case was about to end.

And that bugged him. He respected Goresko. Liked the man, even. And he didn't doubt that Goresko would let him know if the dead man was ID'd, or if anything major happened.

But something hinky had happened at Old World Wisconsin. Where *Chloe* worked. Leaving that unresolved was like having a popcorn hull stuck in his teeth. Which turned him back to investigating the death.

Go back to the basics, he told himself. He grabbed three more blank index cards and wrote *Opportunity* on the first, *Means* on the second, and *Motive* on the third.

Which helped not even a little bit. Opportunity? Lots of Old World staff could have been there—not just interpreters, but maintenance workers, the farmers and gardeners who were not assigned to any single farm, volunteers. Hundreds of visitors had toured the historic site the day Private M died too, and most had left before they could be questioned.

Means? If the man's death was *not* accidental, means meant only a hand or foot to shove the man from the rail. Again, not much to narrow things down.

That left motive. How the hell can I consider motive, Roelke thought, when the victim hasn't been identified? It was maddening.

With a growl he swiped up his cards, wrapped them with a rubber band, and slipped them into his pocket. He needed a break, and he had plenty to do at his own farm.

He was on his feet when the phone rang, but he reached for it. "Eagle Police Department, Officer McKenna speaking."

"Officer McKenna? It's Maggie Geddings."

"How can I help you, Ms. Geddings?"

"Well, I've been taking a harder look around the house, and I think a few things *were* stolen. Two for sure."

Roelke grabbed a pencil and notepad. "What were they?"

"Tintypes," she said. "One of a little boy, and one of a Wisconsin soldier who fought in the Civil War."

FOURTEEN

"I will not fight in this civil war," Adolf said quietly.

"Nor I," declared a man with bad teeth. "It is fine and good for the intellectuals to embrace war. They know nothing of life for the rest of us."

"We have sacrificed everything to make a new start in America," whined a cigar maker. "Everything would have been better if Stephen Douglas had been elected."

Rosina was reminded once again that not all of the Wisconsin-bound men wanted to fight in the Civil War. She'd become quite weary of the agitated discussions as the journey continued from the New York harbor. She and the Sperbers had traveled by coach to Albany, where Adolf arranged passage along the Erie Canal on a line boat carrying passengers and freight to Buffalo, 363 American miles distant. Many of the German-born farmers and mechanics on board believed President Lincoln was a poor choice to lead the nation.

Often Rosina and Lottie sat with baby Gerhard on the roof, watching towns and woodlands glide by, ducking every time the helmsman hollered "Low bridge," listening to the men dissect the news. An article by German-born Carl Schurz, a firebrand revolutionary who'd settled in Watertown, Wisconsin, and joined the new Republican Party, was read aloud over and over again. Rosina was sick of the talk.

This morning she and Lottie were struggling to wash Gerhard's linens on the tiny bow. "I pray Adolf never changes his mind about enlisting," Lottie murmured. "But the Republicans do want to abolish slavery of the Africans."

Which is part of why Leopold felt he must fight, Rosina thought, wringing out a tiny nightdress with reddened hands. She was proud of that. But oh, how she longed to hear his laugh, see his twinkling eyes, feel his fingers feather against her skin. She had not seen Leopold Zuehlsdorff since the day he'd said goodbye on the New York dock. He was surely traveling the canal too, but he and his friends would have paid the princely sum of four American cents per mile—twice what the Sperbers had paid—to ride on a smaller packet boat, which was faster and, people said, more pleasant.

At Buffalo, Rosina and the Sperbers left the canal boat and transferred immediately to a propeller steamship for passage through the Great Lakes. Rosina searched the wharves for a familiar figure in a blue coat. But he was likely far ahead of them—perhaps already striding the streets of Milwaukee with other educated men, or dining with the much-discussed Carl Schurz in Watertown.

Once, halfway across Lake Erie, she crept out on deck and stared at the night sky. The stars glittered, but no magical scarves of green and blue waved overhead. The engine's steady rumble replaced the gentle ripple of rainbow swells against the *Fair Wind*'s hull. No one whispered to her. But she closed her eyes and summoned the northern lights, and wrapped the memory of that precious night around her shoulders like a bright shawl. That night had hung suspended between past and future, and Rosina had wanted it to last forever.

Now she feared that it was going to … but not at all as she had thought. As the days passed it was harder to hope that she might have the luxury of waiting for Leopold Zuehlsdorff to march off to his war and march back again. Each night she fingered her undergarments, desperate to feel the stickiness of monthly blood. Each night she was disappointed.

———

The journey went on and on: down Lake Erie, up Lake Huron, across Lake Michigan. By the time they reached Wisconsin, Rosina knew that sometime in the spring, she'd provide Gerhard with an infant companion. Leopold lives in Milwaukee, she reminded herself. I must find a way to tell him.

She and the Sperbers spent a week in the city while Adolf sent word of their arrival to his brother Franz. They lodged in an area thick with settlers from the German states. Placards nailed to the gate of a *biergarten* advertised the local *Turnverein*, where men met for gymnastics. Draymen nudging heavy wagons through crowded streets shouted in Low German to their animals. Men in frock coats who gathered in the dining room spoke in High German of *freien Gemeinden*—Free Congregations.

"Those Free Thinkers have too much time on their hands," Adolf observed.

Lottie made little clicking noises with her tongue. "They do not believe in God."

They believe everyone should be free to choose what they want in life, Rosina thought. The notion of atheism was a bit shocking. But the only Free Thinker she'd ever met—Leopold—had made her feel that she was not a fool to take pleasure in God's creations.

Rosina walked and watched and listened. She even asked several men in the hotel lobby if they knew Herr Leopold Zuehlsdorff. Yes, they knew of him. No, they did not know where to find him.

Time ran out when Adolf's brother Franz arrived from Watertown with a newly painted wagon, muck-stained boots, and a wide grin. The two men embraced. Then Franz hugged Lottie, complimented the Sperbers on Gerhard's birth, and shook Rosina's hand with sincere welcome. "You have almost reached your new home!" he promised. "Just three days more of travel."

"Praise be," Lottie murmured.

Rosina tried to echo the sentiment, but her lips felt stiff. I have failed, she thought. Failed to find Leopold. Perhaps she should have confided in Lottie after all…

But it was too late. The two women and Gerhard were settled with the luggage in the back of the wagon. Soon they left the crowded streets behind and rumbled west along the Milwaukee-Watertown Plank Road. Rosina felt Leopold fading behind her with every turn of the wheel.

The men talked of what was waiting. "Your land butts against mine," Franz told Adolf, "and is but a half-morning's drive south of town. The house is small, but well built by a German carpenter. And twenty acres have already been cleared…"

Lottie leaned close to Rosina. "I scarcely dared believe I should live to see our new home," she murmured. "I would not have survived this journey without you. And perhaps Gerhard would have died as well."

"I did little," Rosina protested. "I will always be in your debt. You saved me from ... well. You saved me. You and Adolf."

And Leopold too? Rosina turned that over in her mind. No matter what comes, she thought, I have already experienced more than Cousin Maria ever will. I have seen the northern lights flare through a midnight sky. I have felt a man's tender touch. I have known joy.

"Our new farm will be your home as well, for as long as you wish," Lottie reminded her.

Rosina watched a barefoot girl walk by, herding a flock of geese. Franz was driving through beautiful country now—rolling hills, prairies of waving grass and flowers, wide fields green with hay or golden with ripening grains. They passed tiny log cabins and bigger homes too, some built of a queer cream-colored brick, a few constructed of stone. There was so much space here in Wisconsin. So much room.

"I hope it will be a *long* time," Lottie was saying.

Rosina buried her hands in the folds of her skirt and clenched her fists. "But you forget, I must send word to Herr Roelke as soon as we arrive in Watertown. Maria said that—"

"Maria should not have promised your hand without your knowledge." Lottie's voice held a rare edge of anger. "The tin peddler's wife's cousin, indeed! We should never have told her of our plans so early, and given her the whole winter to stew."

"Arranging the marriage was Maria's revenge, I think. For me leaving."

But the truth was, Maria's promise might yet be Rosina's salvation. If she moved quickly enough, and if this stranger—Herr Roelke— was still willing to welcome her to his farm.

FIFTEEN

Dᴇʟʟʏɴ Bᴜʀᴋᴇ ʜᴀᴅ sᴀɪᴅ that she'd come by the Roelke farm after work, so Chloe did stop on her way home that evening. She found a red bench gracing one corner of the garden. Dellyn was wrestling her rototiller through another neglected section. When she saw Chloe, she shut off the engine and waved.

"You," Chloe said humbly, "are a truly good and generous person."

Her friend flapped a hand. "You'd do the same for me. In fact you *have* done the same for me. Helped me, I mean."

"The bench is perfect."

"It's been sitting in the barn for years. All I did was dust it off and slap on a coat of paint." She smiled. "Every garden needs a bench."

Dellyn Burke was a thin woman in her late twenties. In addition to managing Old World's many gardens, she was a talented artist. She and Chloe had gotten to know each other when Dellyn was going through a bad time and Chloe was in need of a friend. Dellyn happily house-sat when Chloe traveled. The two women often kvetched about Petty atrocities and other site malarkey over coffee (provided by Dellyn) and pastry (provided by Chloe).

Now Dellyn tipped her head. "Are you okay? You look ... I don't know ... down."

"Ralph Petty wants to fire me."

"Ralph Petty has always wanted to fire you."

"Yes, but things have heated up again." Chloe stooped to pull bits of debris from the churned soil. "He scolded me for helping Byron with this Civil War programming. What Byron and I want doesn't mesh with Petty's vision, and he actually said—and I quote—that 'Anyone who *chooses* to invest time and resources in experimental programming does so at his, or her, own peril.'"

"Yikes."

"He also reamed me out for helping Roelke with the investigation into that poor man's death at Schulz yesterday."

"Seriously?"

"He accused me of wanting to, and I quote again, 'spend time with my boyfriend.'" That one was particularly disturbing. Chloe *hated* knowing that Ralph Petty knew anything about her personal life. Eagle was a small town; Petty lived there and Roelke worked there, and it was probably astonishing that Petty hadn't tossed this particular dart earlier. Still, she hated it.

Dellyn wrestled a wicked root from the clods of earth and pitched it toward the fence. "That's low, even for Petty."

"I'm trying not to freak out, but Dellyn, I can't lose my job! Not after promising Roelke ... " Chloe made a wide gesture that encompassed the farm. "Petty threatening me is *exactly* what I was afraid of. Roelke and I made a decision to do this, and before we even move in, I'm suddenly on very thin professional ice. I'd never find another museum job within commuting distance of this place, and—"

"Hold on," Dellyn said firmly. "Petty can't fire you without justification. Dating a local cop doesn't count. Neither does helping the police after a man falls to his death on the site. As for the programming thing… the Civil War stuff wasn't even your idea, right? All you're doing is helping Byron. Again, hard to justify any kind of disciplinary action under the circumstances."

"I suppose." Rational thought didn't always apply to Ralph Petty's machinations.

Dellyn pulled off one garden glove, examined a hole, and sighed. Chloe felt ashamed of her little pity party. Unlike *her*, Dellyn was officially a "limited-term employee," which basically meant that she worked as hard as anyone else but had no job security or benefits.

"I'm sorry for whining," Chloe said. Then she gestured to the patch she and Dellyn had bushwhacked earlier. "Did you see what's coming up? I know it's late, but I'm so glad we got some seeds in the ground."

Dellyn pulled a red bandana from her jeans' pocket and wiped sweat from her forehead. Her green tank top was blotchy-damp too. "And you can plant some cold-weather crops here when I'm done. Spinach and kale, maybe."

"I will." Chloe smiled. She obviously had some issues to resolve about settling into the farm, but growing food—especially heirloom varieties—made her happy.

"You should ask Lee Hawkins to look at the apple trees," Dellyn added. Several gnarled and ancient trees survived—barely—behind the barn.

"I will. I'd love to save them."

"Have you thought about flowers?" Dellyn asked. "I'll bet Roelke's grandma grew hollyhocks and daisies. And how about an heirloom rosebush by the garden gate? Or maybe even by the cabin door?"

Chloe's yo-yo of happiness began a descent. "Maybe next spring," she hedged. "I want to focus first on reclaiming the vegetable garden, and then on restoring some of the property to prairie. Roelke's renting out the fields, but there's still a lot of land we can restore with native grasses and flowers. Bit by bit, anyway."

"Sounds good." But Dellyn eyed Chloe again. "Are you sure you're okay?"

"Roelke thinks I'm having second thoughts about moving in here." The words popped out with no forethought.

"Are you?"

"Maybe a little," Chloe admitted. "The money thing is huge. I'll be contributing what I pay now in rent, but Roelke's the one who took on the big debt. And … he and Libby have so much history here. I'm not sure where I fit in." Not the cabin, certainly.

"It sounds like moving-in jitters to me. You'll work it out."

"I'm sure you're right," Chloe said, although she wasn't.

Dellyn got back to muscling the tiller through the neglected bed. Ten minutes later Chloe was on her knees, pulling weeds, when she became aware of someone leaning over the garden fence. "Oh!" she squawked, even as she recognized the man she loved, now dressed in jeans and a faded blue t-shirt. At the far end of the garden Dellyn turned to make another pass, saw Roelke, and cut the engine again. The mechanical roar faded.

"Didn't mean to startle you," Roelke said. "Hey, Dellyn. This is starting to look like a garden again, thanks to you. We sure appreciate it."

"My pleasure."

"Did Chloe tell you about the break-in at the Geddings place? Across the road from you?"

"She did." Dellyn nodded. "I'm being careful."

136

"Do you know if your parents had any Civil War antiques tucked away?"

Dellyn rubbed her nose, leaving a streak of dirt. "Do you remember anything, Chloe?"

Chloe thought back. She and Dellyn had been whittling away at the mountain of memorabilia packed into the house, cataloging everything with known Eagle provenance and selling or donating most of the rest elsewhere. "Nothing comes to mind, but there are still a lot of boxes we haven't even opened." She looked at Roelke. "Why?"

"Ms. Geddings called this evening. After taking a more careful look through her grandparents' stuff, she thinks a couple of things *are* missing. Two tintypes. One of a Wisconsin Civil War soldier."

"A Wisconsin Civil War soldier?" Chloe repeated slowly.

"And one of a little boy."

Chloe swallowed. "Private M was carrying…"

"We'll let Ms. Geddings take a look and see if the one in the dead man's pocket is the one taken from her house."

"But the dead man was *not* carrying a tintype of a soldier." Chloe rubbed her temples.

"Yeah." Roelke's expression suggested that his confusion equaled her own. "Ms. Geddings showed me a big box of photographs—tintypes and CDVs and stuff—that her grandparents had collected. She said when she was younger, as a treat, she'd be allowed to get them out. The box was in place, so it wasn't until she went through its contents that she realized those two tintypes were missing."

Chloe said, "This is getting *really* spooky."

"We don't know if this is in any way related to the reenactor's death at Old World," he reminded her, although he had to add, "but it is quite a coincidence."

"Is anything else missing?" Dellyn asked.

"Some little wooden disc things."

Chloe looked perplexed. "Disc things?"

"Ms. Geddings isn't sure what they were. But she remembers seeing them on earlier visits, and now they're gone. She said they had writing on them. Possibly names, but she didn't really pay attention. When she was a kid, she and her cousin used to play with them like tiddlywinks. Do you know what they might have been?"

Chloe tried to get past the image of kids playing tiddlywinks with antiques. "Um … tokens of some kind, maybe?"

"Tokens for what?"

"Well, sometimes storekeepers issued tokens instead of cash if people brought in eggs or butter or something. Or they even gave them out instead of making proper change."

"Why?"

"So the people had to keep on doing all their business there, instead of comparing prices at the shop down the road."

"Hunh." Roelke nodded thoughtfully. "What's the Iron Brigade?"

Chloe felt more secure on this one. "It was a famous unit during the Civil War, mostly Wisconsin men but also some from Michigan and Indiana. Some general watched them drive back a Confederate force—at South Mountain, I think it was—and gave them the nickname."

"I know nothing about the Iron Brigade," Dellyn said, "and I need to get going. Is it okay if I leave the tiller in the barn? I'm almost finished."

"Of course." Chloe hugged her friend.

Dellyn gave her an extra squeeze. "Don't let Petty get you down," she murmured.

Roelke stepped into the garden and watched as Dellyn slowly moved the tiller across the yard. "What was that about Petty?"

"Just Petty being … you know. *Petty*. I have a window inventory thing to turn in to Leila next month, and Petty announced that he wants it next week."

"Why?"

"He's annoyed about the Civil War event plans. And he was annoyed with me because I helped you."

Roelke turned, his gaze suddenly hard. "Are you *kidding* me?"

"Don't worry about it." Chloe understood Roelke's anger, even appreciated it. But she didn't want to deal with it right now.

Evidently he got that, because his next suggestion was totally unexpected. "Maybe you should call Ethan tonight. You know, talk stuff over with him."

Ethan, an old forestry school buddy, was Chloe's best friend. She was enormously touched that Roelke wasn't threatened by the fact that Ethan had been talking her through problems for years. "I'd do it if I didn't know that he's about halfway through a month-long backpacking trip."

"He's backpacking for a month?"

"Yep. He worked so many fires in the spring they told him he had to take leave." Ethan was a fire jumper in the Rockies. When he worked, he worked long, hard hours.

"Backpacking for a month. Wow."

"It sounds pretty good to me." She and Ethan had long kicked around the idea of doing a distance hike together. "At least he's got good boots and a down sleeping bag and lightweight pack. Some of my Civil War friends have done marches with only period gear. Not a month, just for a week or ten days, but that's long enough if all you've got is brogans and a shelter half."

"Marching for ten days in Civil War gear? Just … marching around? Wouldn't the spectators get bored?"

"There were no spectators. They did it because the real soldiers spent a lot more time marching than anything else. I actually did a three-day march, once. In Georgia. A few of us portrayed civilian refugees, fleeing from the Yankee army." She smiled at the memories. "It stormed one night, and we all got soaked. And I did worry a bit about copperheads deciding my blanket roll looked appealing. But it was a great experience."

"How come you never told me you used to be a reenactor?"

She shrugged. "It never came up. And … the hobby's difficult to explain to people who aren't involved. Once I got reamed out by a history professor for participating. Something about 'heinously contrived playacting.'"

Roelke opened his mouth, closed it again, evidently at a loss for words.

Okay, enough reenactment talk. Chloe turned to the garden. "Isn't it sweet of Dellyn to do this? I love having a little garden already underway."

"It looks great," he agreed. "Although if my grandma was here, she'd say the carrots need to be thinned."

Chloe gazed up at the clouds. "Yes, Mrs. Roelke."

"Did you decide what color you want me to get for the kitchen?"

Shit. She thought fast. "Why don't we paint it your grandma's favorite color? That would be nice, don't you think?"

He was silent for a moment, then changed the subject. "Want to come back to my place for the night?"

"I need to go home and dig out contact info for hardcore reenacting units to give Detective Goresko, remember?"

"Oh. Right."

"Want to come help me look, and spend the night at my place?"

"I'd like to, but … I have to be in Milwaukee early tomorrow for German Fest, remember?"

"Oh. Right." His walk-up was closer than her rented farmhouse. Although … not *that* much closer.

Shadows lengthened across the yard. Fireflies blinked up from the grass. A breeze riffled the stillness, and a whip-poor-will began to call. It should have been peaceful and soothing and perfect. But Chloe felt as if the Roelke cabin's shadow had come between them. And she knew that Roelke was still wound tight.

"Forget the case for the moment," she said softly.

"It's bugging me."

"I know. Me too. But there's nothing we can do about it tonight." He looked away.

"What?" she asked. She sensed his tension, taut as a wire.

"It's not just the case. Ever since we went to that tiny cabin at Old World today … "

"Fossebrekke?"

"Right." He hitched one shoulder up and down. "The people who lived there must have had a really hard life."

Well, *that* observation was unexpected. "The Fossebrekkes did have a lot of challenges," Chloe allowed. "But that farm is restored to its 1845 appearance. That's twenty years earlier than the Kvaale Farm— the bigger one, where the women made *krumkakke*. Fossebrekke gives visitors their earliest glimpse of life for Euro-Yankee settlers in pioneer Wisconsin."

"Hunh."

"Knud Fossebrekke arrived in Wisconsin with almost *nothing*. He spent his first winter in a shelter dug into the side of a hill. So for him and his wife, Gertrude, the cabin actually represented an enormous accomplishment. A farm of their own, four stout walls, windows with real glass, space to let newcomers stay while they got *their* feet on the ground, a hog…" She realized she was pontificating once again. "Sorry. I get defensive because I've seen visitors sneer when they visit the Fossebrekke Farm for the first time."

"I've seen those buildings before," Roelke acknowledged, "but I guess *now*, now that I own this place… it all makes me wonder how rough the first Roelkes had it when they arrived."

"Hopefully we can find out." Hopefully we can find out a whole lot of things, she added with silent fervor.

Roelke gathered her close. "Good thing we're moving in together. I feel as if—aside from work, right now—we hardly have time for each other."

"I know." Chloe nestled close, her head finding the little familiar hollow beneath his chin. Right that moment, she wanted nothing more than to spread a blanket on the ground and disappear into this man's arms.

But over his shoulder, the old cabin stood dark and brooding in the twilight.

SIXTEEN

As the cabin came into view, Rosina stared with dismay from the wagon seat. It is such a dark cabin, she thought. It seemed to brood.

"I'll add windows when I can," Klaus Roelke said, as if knowing her thoughts.

She nodded, not trusting her voice. The tiny cabin seemed as insignificant as the immigrant ship had seemed on the vast Atlantic Ocean. But the ship had bustled with life: with sailors' songs and old men's arguments, lullabies and the clatter of feet dancing on deck beneath the stars. Klaus Roelke's cabin was still and empty.

But she was a married woman now, and this was her home.

Lottie had urged her to wait. "Take time to be sure," she'd fretted. "There is no need to rush into marriage!"

Yes, Rosina had thought, there is.

Franz had driven the new arrivals from Milwaukee to Adolf and Lottie's tidy farm. A German carpenter had built the house in *fachwerk* style, as in the Old Country where trees were scarce. The beams and expanses of mortar had been plastered over and whitewashed, inside and out. It was a bright house, and cheerful. There was a shed too, and one big field was already cleared. The day they arrived Adolf began unpacking his lasts and awls and hammers, his hoarded leather and waxed thread, in the shed.

"He has several orders for shoes from fellow travelers, so we'll have some cash quickly!" Lottie exulted, as she and Rosina tidied the house. She pushed a damp tendril of hair back beneath the kerchief knotted over her head. "The journey took every coin we had."

Rosina was on her knees, scouring the plank floor with sand and hot water. "You should not have paid my passage."

"Don't say such things! I will always be grateful, Rosina. You are a good friend."

"As you have been to me." Rosina ducked her head to hide the glimmer in her eyes.

That evening she wrote her letter, and Adolf made arrangements to have it delivered to Herr Roelke's farm near Palmyra, some fifteen miles south. The reply came back the next day:

I rejoice to know that your long journey is over, and that you arrived in good health. May I meet you and your friends on Saturday? I am attending the Viehmarket in Watertown, for I wish to buy a piglet.

He wishes to buy a piglet, Rosina thought, and felt a bubble of laughter rising in her throat.

After consultation with Lottie and Adolf, who turned to Franz for advice, Rosina penned her reply:

My companions suggest we meet at the Exchange Hotel at eleven o'clock.

Five days later they all drove into Watertown, a community growing on the banks of the Rock River. "We started the monthly cattle fair last year," Franz explained proudly. "It's grown to a full market. People come from many miles."

"One would think that all of the German states have emptied due to immigration," Lottie observed.

"There are many others in Watertown," Franz said. "Irish especially, on the west side of the river, but also Yankees, and immigrants from Bohemia and Wales. Homes and businesses are going up at an astonishing rate because a railroad line has been built through the city. We have a Yankee mayor, although Carl Schurz was elected an alderman for the Fifth Ward—"

"Where does Mr. Schurz live?" Rosina's voice sounded rusty, and she licked dry lips.

Franz shot her a startled look over his shoulder before spitting deliberately into the street. "That Lincoln man moved to Milwaukee, and good riddance."

Rosina turned her head, pretending fascination as they passed a three-story building under construction. Milwaukee was behind her. Evidently the Free Thinkers were behind her as well.

Franz proudly pointed out schools and banks, a Daguerrean gallery and a toy shop, bakeries and lumberyards. They passed sawmills and gristmills along the river, and an oil mill and planing mills. They passed factories producing rakes and soap and woolens. They passed breweries and an iron foundry. Most of the homes and shops were built of sawn lumber. A few of the smaller ones were log, and some of the larger ones were constructed of the same golden-tan bricks she'd seen along the plank road.

Lottie and Adolf will find everything they need here, Rosina thought. Shops, a church, German merchants to buy Adolf's grain. For a moment she let herself long for what she could not have: a life with friends she knew. Her stomach felt fluttery as butterfly wings. Today I will meet my husband, she told herself, and the butterflies grew dizzy.

Franz found a place to park the wagon and they edged into the crowded market. Thrumming through the cacophony of braying cattle, ringing anvils, shouting farmwomen selling geese or cabbage or greasy fleeces, came the staccato rattle of a military drum. The Watertown Rifles, now known as Company A of the 3rd Wisconsin Infantry Regiment, had already marched away, Franz told them, wearing red, white, and blue cockades fashioned by local women. But flags hung from houses, recruitment posters in English and German were nailed to walls, and two old men were making their way through the crowds with drums and militant fervor.

"Do men here speak of enlisting in a German regiment?" Rosina asked. "We heard talk of such a thing."

"Some, perhaps." Franz clearly did not care.

They made their way to the Exchange Hotel. Rosina's heart hammered like the carpenters so busy outside. Please, *please*, she found herself thinking, although she couldn't define what she was asking for. The hotel lobby was jammed. She stood pressed against one wall, scanning the crowd, wondering which of these strangers might have traveled to Watertown that dewy morning to buy a piglet and meet his bride.

Then a man stepped forward. He was perhaps twice her age—thirty-two, thirty-three—with blond hair parted on the side and combed back from his brow, and a neatly trimmed beard. His gaze was direct, his shoulders square. He wore a farmer's boots, worn but polished, and a shirt, vest, and trousers that were mended but clean. There was a stillness about him. Only the tiny movement of his hands—slowly rotating the felt hat held before him—suggested that he might be nervous too.

Adolf asked, "Are you Klaus Roelke?"

"I am."

Adolf introduced himself, and the men shook hands. Then Adolf turned to Rosina. "And this is Fraulein Lauterbach."

"How do you do," Rosina murmured.

"Quite well," Herr Roelke said. "Quite well indeed."

Franz suggested they retire to a nearby *Sommergarten*. There, under the shade of an old oak, they sipped beer and nibbled little cakes while Adolf politely questioned Herr Roelke.

"I arrived in Wisconsin two years ago," Herr Roelke said. "I worked as a farmhand and slept in the hayloft while I saved money. A year ago I was able to purchase sixty acres. I don't own it outright but am steadily paying what I owe."

Rosina tried to pay attention but the moment felt unreal, as if she'd dozed off in the sun. He said he grew Yankee wheat as a cash crop, but raised good German rye too. He was buying a piglet now, when prices were lower than the spring. He hoped to purchase an ox or milk cow next year, but only after building a shed. "Some of these Yankees leave their cattle outside all winter," he added.

Franz shook his head with shared disgust.

When the glasses were empty Herr Roelke turned to Rosina. "I am a hard worker and a God-fearing Christian," he said simply. "If you accept my offer of marriage, I will do my best to provide a good home for you and any children who, God willing, bless our home."

Any children who, God willing, bless our home. God willing you truly mean those words, Rosina thought. "Do you plan to enlist in Mr. Lincoln's war?"

He looked startled, but answered readily. "I do not. I crossed the Atlantic to create a farm here in Wisconsin, and there is too much work to be done."

Everyone looked at Rosina. She tried to weigh the make of this man. If Klaus was not excited by ideas and learning and the role of Germans in America, as Leopold had been, he was also not a dull-eyed lump like the blacksmith's son in her old village. She could fare much worse.

"I am also a hard worker," she said. "I am not afraid of field-work. I know how to cook and garden, and excel at spinning and weaving and sewing." She did not mention fancies, or northern lights, or free thoughts. She would nurture those in her heart.

"Then we should get on well together." Klaus laced his fingers together. "When may I see you again? It's difficult to leave the farm at this time of year, but perhaps I could visit you next week?"

Rosina cleared her throat. "I think it would be best if we marry as soon as possible. I can help with the harvest."

Appreciation flared in Klaus's eyes. "I will speak with the minister today."

"It will take some time to prepare," Lottie protested.

Franz tapped one finger against his empty glass. "Not as much as you might expect. In the Old Country a man had to beg and coax for permission to marry. Here in America we may all do as we please."

The five of them strolled through the market, and the men conducted their business. Klaus, Franz, and Adolf shook hands. "Can't we offer you a ride out of town?" Franz asked. "At least a few miles to speed you on your way."

"I don't mind the walk, although I will borrow a neighbor's wagon for the wedding." Klaus briefly pressed Rosina's hand. "Goodbye." Then he swung the burlap sack holding the wriggling piglet over his shoulder, and walked away.

"He seems a steady man," Lottie had admitted. "God-fearing, a hard worker—those are good traits in a husband." She'd sucked in her lower lip. "But I wish you would take more time to get acquainted."

"If I am going to be a helpmeet, I may as well begin as soon as possible."

"It *is* a busy time. Still, I had thought we might sew a new nightdress together, and Adolf would gladly make you a new pair of shoes. There's no need for you to proceed in such a rush."

Rosina had regarded her friend over Gerhard's head. "Yes," she'd said. "There is." And she'd watched as understanding finally dawned in Lottie's eyes.

And so, earlier today, Rosina and Klaus had stood before the minister in his Watertown home, with Lottie and Adolf as witnesses. Lottie had made her a wreath of purple and yellow prairie flowers, and gifted the Roelkes with a beautiful wedding certificate. She and Rosina said goodbye with damp eyes.

"We'll see each other often," Lottie had promised.

"Yes," Rosina had agreed, clinging to that thought. "Fifteen miles is not so far."

Now, she had arrived at her new home with her new husband. An enormous oak stood sentinel by the wagon tracks leading into the yard. Prairie grasses stretched to the south and east, and dense woods curled beyond the farmyard to the west and north. Those things stouted Rosina's heart.

"The Yankees call land between forest and open prairie an 'oak opening,'" Klaus told her. "I was lucky to find these acres at a price I could afford. Yankees like the prairies best, but me, having lived in a place without trees … no. There is a spring in the woods, plenty of timber, and acres of prairie to turn to crops." He rubbed one calloused thumb over the leather lines. "It is good land, Rosina. We could not have dreamt of owning such land in the Old Country."

"You made a good choice."

"I had to build the cabin quickly."

"It looks sturdy."

"One day I shall dig a well, but for now … "

"I can carry water," Rosina assured him, but she ached with the missing of Lottie and Gerhard. And Leopold. Her Leopold.

"Perhaps you expected better." Klaus squinted at the landscape, as if seeing it with new eyes.

Rosina lifted her chin. The Sperbers were fifteen miles away. And her Leopold was gone.

"I can add a weaving shed. Perhaps next year."

She was truly alone on this raw farm with a man she'd only met twice. Klaus Roelke. Her husband.

"If my wheat crop is good, we shall have windows."

"We shall hope for good weather," Rosina said, thinking, Oh please, God, let us have windows before the snows come and I'm trapped inside.

"I know you'll want a proper bakeoven. I needed first to build a shelter for the pig." He gestured toward a thatched roof on poles that provided shade over a muddy wallow.

A part of Rosina wanted to resent Klaus, his fledgling farm, his precious pig. Most of all she wanted to resent him for not being Leopold Zuehlsdorff.

Another part knew that Klaus would do his best to be a good husband. *I* am the one, Rosina thought, who has brought secrets and lies to this marriage. She despised herself for having done so. But she hadn't done it for herself. If she'd been thinking only of herself, she would have stayed with Lottie and Adolf, waiting, living on the memory of color blazing against a black velvet sky.

But she was going to be a mother. She must make the best of things here, with the stranger sitting beside her with forearms on knees.

"I ... I planted a prairie rose." He pointed toward the cabin, and she saw the spindly bush staked beside the front door. "To welcome you home."

Rosina felt a flush of shame, and forced herself to meet Klaus's gaze for the first time since leaving Watertown. "It is a lovely little farm," she told him. "And I shall do my best to help it prosper."

SEVENTEEN

ALL CHLOE WANTED TO do when she got home from the farm was curl up with her cat. She'd just scooped Olympia into her arms when she heard a car in the driveway. She recognized Libby's Datsun and went to the door.

"Sorry to come by without calling, but I was running errands and had something to show you." Libby held up a box with the words CIVIL WAR written on the side. "Is this a bad time?"

"Nope," Chloe lied. Or maybe it wasn't really a lie, because Libby was a dear friend. Besides, she was intrigued.

They sat at the kitchen table. "You got me thinking about family history," Libby said. "My grandmother gave me a few things before she died. Roelke was in Milwaukee and Patrick was in trouble, so I got it all." She removed the box lid and pulled out a piece of parchment, folded in thirds so long ago that the creases were tearing.

Chloe winced. "Let me get a sleeve for that, okay?" She fetched an archival holder from her stash and slid the treasure inside.

"It's a wedding certificate," Libby said. "For the first Roelkes in Wisconsin."

Chloe bent over the lithograph, highly decorated with ornate floral borders, angels, children, flowing fountains—and, at the bottom, gravestones. "You gotta love the Victorians," she muttered. "But honestly, it's a beautiful piece."

"It really is."

The words *United In Holy Wedlock* were printed at the top. "*Klaus Roelke, b. 1829, and Rosina Lauterbach, b. 1845*," Chloe read slowly. "*Married September 12, 1861.* Wow." She did the math, surreptitiously counting on her fingers beneath the table. "Rosina was only sixteen."

"I waited until I was twenty-one, and I still didn't know what I was doing." Libby made a wry face. "Which is why I'm now a single mother."

"Your marriage might not have worked out, but it did give you Justin and Dierdre."

"I know. It's the ultimate paradox. I wish I'd never met their dad, but I can't imagine life without my children. Anyway, there's more." Libby pointed.

Chloe squinted at the faded script. "*John Roelke, born March 17, 1862.*"

"Evidently Klaus and Rosina were well acquainted by the time of their marriage," Libby observed dryly.

"It happens," Chloe murmured, and continued reading. "*Andreas Roelke, born April 27, 1863.*" She looked up again. "We'll have to figure out which son you and Roelke are descended from."

"I wish I'd asked my grandparents about family history before they died." Libby ran a hand through her hair. "But honestly, things between me and Dan were really bad by then. I had to focus on the essentials."

"Understandable."

Libby reached into the box again. "I think this is evidence that Klaus did serve." She produced a brittle envelope decorated with an American flag, a Union soldier, and a bald eagle, all printed in faded blue and red—now more pinkish, really—ink. The bald eagle held in its beak a flowing banner printed with *9th Wisconsin Infantry Regiment* in elaborate script. The letter had been addressed to *Rosina Lauterbach, Palmyra, Wisconsin.*

"The 9th Wisconsin!" Chloe tried to figure out the timeline. "Did Klaus enlist before they got married?"

"Presumably, but I have to warn you, there's no letter inside."

"Oh." That tempered Chloe's excitement. She grabbed another acid-free sleeve. "Well, it seems very likely. Once I confirm that Klaus served in the 9th, we can request his official military records from the National Archives."

"These things must go back to the Klaus and Rosina era too." Libby put a small roll of cotton on the table, tied with a satin ribbon.

Chloe sucked in a delighted breath. "It's a housewife!"

"A ... housewife?"

"A sewing kit. Women made them for their soldiers, who most likely had never sewn on a button or mended a tear before."

"Oh my." Libby looked half sympathetic and half amused.

"The fabric is classic Civil War–era. There are probably pockets inside, and little flaps for needles and pins. This one is in extremely good condition." It was odd, really. Most of the housewives she'd seen looked as if they'd been carried through battle—which of course they had.

"And this is the last thing." Libby plucked a ring from the box and placed it by the housewife. It was heavy and black, ornamented with a tiny silver motif of two clasped hands.

Chloe's eyes went wide. "*Ooh.*"

"Would Klaus have been able to buy something like that in Palmyra? Or would he have had to go to Watertown, or even Milwaukee?"

"For silverwork this fine, I'd guess one of the bigger towns." Chloe squinted. "I think the ring is made from gutta percha. An early form of hard rubber, sort of. Let me get cotton gloves and a towel, okay?" She wanted to take a better look at both artifacts, but she really shouldn't handle them here, on the kitchen table where—for all she knew—Olympia had spent her afternoon watching squirrels through the window and licking her butt.

"I've got to run." Libby pushed back her chair. "But you can keep it."

"Libby, no," Chloe protested.

"These things belong back at the farm," Libby said firmly. "I'll keep looking in my attic."

They walked out to the car together. "Don't forget about the next Wine and Whine," Libby said. "A week from Tuesday, my house. You coming?"

Chloe hesitated. Wine and Whine was a writers' group. She'd been a halfhearted member for a year, but honestly, she expected to get kicked out for nonproduction.

She did love to write, though. She was immersed in the business of people long dead. Research could only uncover so much, and historians could never truly know what lived in the heart and mind of someone long gone. And while historians could speculate, they could not fabricate. But fiction writers could fill in the gaps.

Chloe had started writing stories as a child after devouring the Little House books, *Caddie Woodlawn*, *The Witch of Blackbird Pond*, and every other tale of long ago she'd been able to find at the Stoughton Library. Once, when living in Switzerland, she'd even finished the first draft of a novel. Her relationship with a Swiss man had not survived, and neither had the manuscript.

But she'd been slowly working her way back toward writing again. The women of Wine and Whine critiqued each other's work, drank wine, and enjoyed whatever treat the hostess provided. And while they didn't often indulge in actual whining, they did commiserate with their scribe-sisters about the challenges of the difficult, ever-changing, and often nonsensical publishing industry.

Libby spoke into the silence. "Writers write, Chloe."

"I know." Chloe was toying with the idea of trying a historical mystery. "But Petty's on my case, and with all the packing at home and fixing up at the farm … " She squirmed. "And … I still haven't decided for sure what my next project is going to be."

"Decide soon."

"Will do," Chloe promised. "I'll be there next month for sure." Maybe.

After Libby was on her way Chloe thought again about indulging in a peaceful evening. Then she sighed. Obligations first. She'd promised Detective Goresko contact info for a few hardcore reenactment units.

In the spare bedroom she used for storage, it didn't take long to find the right carton, but excavating its contents did. She found drugstore envelopes holding pictures, with the negatives in their separate little sleeves. She found a reproduction dance card, several crisp ribbon cockades, and the antique jet earrings—what a splurge *those* had been—she'd worn with a mourning impression. She found period books, reproduction money, a pipe she'd carried when portraying a Kentucky refugee, a letter penned in browning ink entreating any sentries encountered to allow Miss Ingrid Ellefson to pass through the lines … Each find evoked a special memory.

"Good times," Chloe told Olympia, who yawned.

The reenacting magazines and newsletters she'd saved were, of course, at the bottom of the carton. Chloe found the names and contact info for three top-notch units, and called Roelke with the information. "It's old," she cautioned, "but hopefully at least one of these guys has the same phone number."

"Thanks. I'll pass this along to Goresko," Roelke said. "Listen, are you planning to drop a load off after work tomorrow?"

"Yes," Chloe said firmly, although she really hadn't given it any thought.

"Why don't you take Olympia over? I think we've got mice in the basement."

Chloe glanced at Olympia, who enjoyed playing with mice much more than killing them. "I want to wait until the painting's done. The fumes might not be good for her. Have a good day at German Fest, okay? It might even be fun. It's a big part of your heritage."

"I'm not going to think about my heritage," Roelke said, all cop-like. "More like drunks and pickpockets."

"I'm serious. Try to soak some of it in. Listen to music. Eat sauerbraten. Walk through the cultural exhibits. Maybe something will stir your soul."

"Right." Roelke clearly did not expect to have his soul stirred even a little.

Roelke's perspective on life—so different than her own—incomprehensibly made her heart overflow with love. "I look forward to hearing all about it," she told him, and they said good night.

Chloe went back to the spare room in search of something to take to the farm. A couple of cartons held battered spiral notebooks and miscellaneous projects from her college days. After the standard high school coursework, taking two semesters of dendrology—trees!—had seemed miraculous. Sitting cross-legged on the floor, she spent an hour skimming lecture notes and reminiscing about tramps through West Virginia's wooded hills.

"Those were good times too," she told Olympia, who had gone to sleep.

Well, she'd take these boxes over to the farm. She might need to look up something important about trees.

After hauling the boxes to the car it belatedly occurred to her that if she was going to work at the Schulz Farm the next day, she should work in period clothing; and if she was going to wear 1860s period clothing, it would be nice to actually wear her own instead of whatever she could scrounge from the interpreters' collection, like she usually did.

Chloe trudged back upstairs. Her favorite workdress was horribly wrinkled. With a martyred sigh she dusted off her ironing board. "You had to have pure cotton," she grumbled, although honestly, if she had to do it over, she'd make the same choice.

It took a *very* long time to press the dress, and when she ran out of steam—literally and figuratively—there were creases still in evidence. Maybe they'd hang out overnight.

She was refilling Olympia's water dish before bed when the Roelke artifacts caught her eye. She spread a clean towel on the table, and donned cotton gloves, before examining the ring. It was quite unusual, but she had no idea what to make of it.

Next, she gently loosened the sewing kit's ribbon tie and unrolled it on the towel. The housewife was made of several different cotton prints—probably scrounged from a scrap bag—but Rosina's stitches were tiny and even, the pockets square, the flaps of flannel embroidered with tiny roses. A padded tube was attached to one end to facilitate rolling. A thimble nested snugly in a socket perfectly constructed into the tube. Three pins and one needle were secured in one of the flaps, lined up with military precision.

Chloe eased open one of the pockets with a gentle finger and found several tin buttons. The second pocket held a bit of gray yarn and a darning needle. In the third she found two small squares of cardboard. White cotton thread had been wrapped smoothly around one, and the second was wound with linen thread.

"Is this handspun?" Chloe murmured. She found the end and unwrapped a length for examination. Linen was prone to little nubs, but this thread was extremely fine and even. Chloe had spun more than a few yards of linen thread in her day, but her best work didn't approach this. Rosina, she thought, if you spun this, my bonnet is off to you.

As she started to rewind the thread, something caught her eye. The length she'd unwound had revealed what looked like the edge of a piece of paper against the cardboard, almost hidden beneath the rest of the thread. What on earth ... ? She began unwinding more thread. Several yards of it were pooled in her lap before she could ease the folded scrap of paper free.

Chloe held her breath. She'd seen notes tucked into housewives before, along the lines of *My dear mother made this when I joined the 2nd Wisconsin Cavalry.* A similar note from one of Roelke's ancestors was more than she could have hoped for.

Time had given the paper a yellowish hue. She grimaced as the paper separated at the fold line into two pieces. Well, she'd want to store it flat from now on anyway.

Chloe grabbed a magnifying glass and studied the crabbed and faded lines. Some of the words were blurred, as if drops of water had marred the ink. One piece contained a single sentence, written in English:

Oh, my son, I have killed your father.

Chloe stared at the words for a long time before forcing herself to acknowledge that the individual letters were not likely to rearrange themselves into something more uplifting.

The second piece contained a single sentence in German. She'd picked up some *Suisse-Deutsch* while living in Switzerland, and turned to the second scrap hopefully. But when she parsed out the faded script, the same stark declaration emerged.

Chloe felt as if Rosina Roelke had reached from a cold, lonely grave to trace her spine with a fingernail. And it had to be Rosina, because Libby had said Klaus's parents died young and he immigrated alone. Something truly terrible had happened in the family during the Civil War—something that so tormented Rosina that she'd felt compelled to hide this note in the housewife. Had Klaus abused her? Had she murdered him?

No. Surely there was a better explanation. Perhaps Rosina felt responsible for some horrible accident that had taken Klaus's life. Or maybe she'd tried desperately to nurse Klaus through an illness that ultimately proved fatal. And... and maybe Klaus had been about to march off to war when he died, and in her grief, she'd scribbled the note and hidden it in the housewife she'd made for him.

Chloe sucked in a long breath, blew it out again. This note didn't directly explain the bad energy lingering in the old cabin, but—

The phone rang, and she almost jumped from her skin. She went into the living room to answer it. "Hello?"

"Hey." It was Roelke, sounding all husky and loving and sexy.

Now she really wished they'd been able to spend the night together. "Hey," she echoed. "Um... I thought we'd said good night."

"I wanted to hear your voice before I turn in."

"Oh. I love you."

"I love you too. And I'm sorry this has been a rough couple of days. You know, what happened at Old World, and a couple of disconnects about us moving to the farm."

Tell him about the housewife, a voice in her brain insisted. Tell him. Tell him. Tell him.

"I'm sorry too," she said instead. "Things will get better."

"I think so too. Listen, I'll likely be too late to call tomorrow night, so—have a good one. And be careful out at Old World."

After hanging up, Chloe buried her face in her hands. She should have told Roelke about the note she'd found. The people involved in *whatever* were long dead. Roelke wouldn't get upset. Besides, they had promised each other to not keep secrets.

But it's his *family*, she thought. The note involved the very first Roelkes to settle in Wisconsin. The people who had sacrificed so much to create the farm that he, Roelke McKenna, had sacrificed so much to purchase. All because it was his homeplace. A safe place for him, and Libby, and Libby's kids.

"Shit," Chloe whispered, rubbing her temples. Well, all she could do now was hope that research turned up something to explain the note—something tragic, but not criminal. She could decide how to tell Roelke about it after she knew more of the story.

Trying to pretend that she felt confident with that decision, Chloe carefully packed Rosina's letter and the housewife away. Then she picked up Olympia and plodded off to bed.

EIGHTEEN

ROELKE REACHED MILWAUKEE ON Saturday morning well before he was due. He hadn't been sure how he'd feel about returning. Before moving to Eagle he'd walked a beat in District 2, the Old South Side. Five months ago, his best friend Rick had died on duty there. The weeks that followed were the worst in Roelke's life.

He'd made arrangements to meet Dobry Banik, another friend from his Milwaukee PD days, at a diner. Roelke wasn't sure how he felt about that, either. Dobry, Rick, and Roelke had played in a cop band called The Blue Tones. Roelke had turned down several social invitations from Dobry in the past few months. The thought of playing music, or sitting in some tavern, had not appealed. But Dobry was working security at German Fest too, and getting together for breakfast at a George Webb's seemed like a good way to start reconnecting.

At the restaurant Roelke called Detective Goresko from a payphone and passed on the names of authentic reenactment unit leaders Chloe had provided. Then he claimed a booth, ordered a large OJ, and thought about the woman he loved. She wasn't a morning person.

When he daydreamed about the farm he sometimes pictured the two of them sitting outside at dawn, when the light was pearly and the birds just starting to sing. Honestly, that was not likely to happen.

But that was all right. He *could* look forward to seeing her asleep in bed—not his bed, or her bed, but *their* bed—when he rose early. He loved watching her sleep, loved seeing the curve of one white shoulder when she was curled on her side, loved seeing her long yellow hair fanned across the pillow. He loved—

"Hey, man." Dobry slid into the vinyl seat across the table. "Good to see you."

"It's good to see you too." With some surprise, Roelke realized that it was true. Yes, there was that expected twist in the gut that came from seeing Dobry and remembering who else should be there, but wasn't. But Dobry's freckled face didn't look as boyish as it used to. Rick's death had taken a toll on him too. Roelke hadn't realized how lonely he'd been until that loneliness eased, just a bit.

"Glad you could come in," Dobry said after the waitress took their order. "I worked Festa Italiana too, and I'm signed up for Irish Fest. It's about what you'd expect—drunks, lost kids, snatched wallets, that kind of thing."

"God knows I need the money." Roelke sipped his coffee.

"The farm is a done deal, right? You signed on the dotted line?"

"I did. And every time I go by the place, I get this anxious feeling inside."

"Buyer's remorse." Dobry nodded. "As soon as Tina and I bought our house, I was *sure* I'd made a mistake. I looked at the numbers and felt like somebody had dropped a giant boulder on my chest."

"That's a fair description."

"But it goes away. And coming in today was smart."

"I know, but I've got a thing dangling in Eagle. An unexplained death at the historic site where Chloe works. If I'd known..."

"What's going on?"

Roelke told Dobry about Private M. The waitress returned with a plate of steaming blueberry pancakes for Dobry and a Denver omelet for him.

Dobry poured a whole lot of maple syrup over his pancakes. "How's the detective on the case?"

"He's a good guy. Tries to keep me informed. But there hasn't been much to tell." Roelke shook out a napkin. "And in addition to not knowing the victim or exactly how he died, I don't know if the death is tied to the theft of a Civil War soldier's tintype that belongs to an Eagle woman."

"Well, there's nothing you can do about it today."

"Actually, some of the reenactors are going to be at German Fest. One unit in particular likes to portray German-American soldiers."

"I don't get the whole reenacting thing." Dobry used a bit of pancake to mop up a dribble of syrup. "A bunch of grown men running around with guns. If they ever dealt with the aftermath of real violence they wouldn't think it was so much fun."

"I'm extra edgy because this reenactor died where Chloe works," Roelke admitted. "She goes out on site before and after hours all the time. And now they're planning some special Civil War program for next weekend."

"I don't know Chloe well, but she seems like a smart lady."

"Oh, she is." Roelke stabbed a green pepper with his fork. "She's smart and capable. But she can get sort of... preoccupied. Caught up in her history stuff." Fanciful, even, as his grandma might have said. And that was not the best quality to have when a killer might be roaming Old World Wisconsin's prairies and wooded hills.

Chloe's alarm shrilled *way* too early on Saturday morning, and she slapped the radio several times before finding the off button. She'd had a terrible time getting to sleep, stewing about the disturbing note she'd found in the old housewife.

But she had promised to begin dressing the Schulz loom today. The first step involved winding and measuring the linen warp threads. Since she had to keep count, she wanted to get as much done as possible before visitors arrived.

Olympia was curled on Chloe's right shoulder. "Time to get up," Chloe mumbled. Olympia went all Gandhi-cat, limp with passive resistance. It took Chloe several tries to dislodge the feline and actually roll out of bed.

She squinted at the clock. Byron's no doubt already at work, she thought. And ... Roelke's already in Milwaukee. Good God. She padded into the kitchen, plugged in the coffeepot, and tried to face the day.

By the time she got to work, fortified by caffeine, OJ, and an English muffin, she felt marginally better. She parked out of sight near the German area and headed for the Schulz Farm. It felt good to be wearing her old 1860s workdress, a stained apron, and the appropriate undergarments. She'd pinned her long blond braid into a bun and laced up her reproduction shoes. She felt part of the cultural landscape, instead of a visitor.

Please don't wander around the site by yourself until we know whether we're looking at murder.

Chloe nibbled her lower lip. She didn't take Roelke's concern lightly, but right now, dressed in period clothing ... it was easy to conclude that Private M had gotten caught up in the magic of an 1860 farm, gone somewhere he shouldn't have gone, and paid the price. Had he been here before? Had he known about the rare architecture? Plenty of half-timbered structures had been preserved in European open-air museums, but not here. And unlike the house, some of the stable's original mortar had survived the move to Old World. The roof had been thatched by a European master.

Roelke didn't get it, but Chloe understood a reenactor wanting to visit the farmstead on his own terms—craving a quiet chance to simply *be* in the space. She imagined Private M climbing past the barriers to the stable walkway, knowing but not caring that it was off-limits. Maybe he'd even planned to spend the night up there. She'd known reenactors who'd broken rules and slipped onto battlefields because they felt compelled to sleep in Antietam's Bloody Lane or the Devil's Den at Gettysburg.

A tragic accident was *so* much better than Roelke's foul play scenario.

The Schulz house smelled of dill, vinegar, and wood smoke. Chloe made a slow circle through the rooms, imagining Auguste Schulz, wondering about her joys and sorrows. At first glance the house felt cold and spartan. But there was a good vibe here too. The unusual architecture, with its central walk-in chimney, would have been unpleasant to use by modern standards…but perhaps the *Schwarze-Küche*, like the half-timbered *fachwerk* construction, made Auguste feel at home in the New World.

In the still morning, Chloe felt *herself* settling into the house. It was a sensation she missed from her interpreter days. I think I'll use this house to anchor my new novel, she thought. She wouldn't write about the Schulz family, of course, and she'd fictionalize the setting. But this house was extremely wonderful. The whole farm was extremely wonderful.

In the workroom, Chloe was delighted to see that Alyssa had transferred the linen warp thread from modern spools to hand-wound balls. With two balls corralled in a tin basin on the floor, Chloe got busy. The warping board was a six-foot-square frame lined with pegs, and she measured the warp by winding it back and forth over the pegs. She let the threads flow loosely through her fingers. No one burst menacingly through the back door or otherwise prompted even a quiver of alarm.

Alyssa arrived at ten, and grinned when she saw Chloe. "Ooh! Can I help?"

"I was hoping you would."

Alyssa caught on fast. Most visitors explored the Crossroads Village before coming to the German area, and she'd made good progress by the time the first guests arrived. Chloe chatted with them about the life of a newly-arrived German family. *I do miss the front lines,* she thought wistfully as the family left, the children happily clutching souvenir bits of flax fiber.

It was past noon by the time Alyssa finished winding the warp. Chloe showed her how to put ties around the threads. "We'll leave it on the board for now," she decided. "Just don't let kids poke at it. Do you still want to help me wind it onto the loom?"

"Definitely!"

Chloe smiled. "How about eight a.m. tomorrow? It will take a while."

"No problem! I've wanted to learn how to dress a loom since— oops, gotta go." Alyssa darted away to greet an elderly couple.

Since she'd made arrangements to meet Belinda at the artifact trailers at one o'clock, Chloe slipped out the back door and headed for her car. During the short drive she ate a granola bar—one of the dry, tasteless ones she bought when feeling virtuous, and always regretted later—and got out of the car brushing crumbs from her bodice. No food allowed in collections storage.

Two ancient trailers were parked in a grove of pines behind the maintenance office. One had served as Wisconsin's "History Mobile" during the bicentennial celebrations in 1976. Chloe had no idea where the second, an ugly pinkish-gray monstrosity, had come from. During the whirlwind of work to open the first few buildings at Old World Wisconsin, these trailers had been commandeered and pressed into dubious service.

Belinda, smart girl, was waiting outside at a picnic table. Her notebook, the copy of *Wisconsin Women in the War Between the States*, and—unexpectedly—a J. C. Penney box were at the ready. Chloe slid onto the bench across from her young intern.

"Before we get started…" Belinda twisted her fingers together. "I was wondering…"

"Yes?"

"Could I ask you…"

"You can ask me anything."

"I've been thinking about my National History Day project, and—"

"Wait." Chloe held up a hand. "Isn't National History Day in March?"

Belinda flushed. "Yes, but I thought I might be able to do a project in conjunction with my summer internship."

"Ah. Okay, that makes sense."

"Would you be willing to, you know, sort of… mentor me?"

"Of course," Chloe said, wondering how much time that might take and where she was going to find it. "Do you have a project in mind?"

"I want to design a museum exhibit. You know, just on paper, but with photographs of artifacts and labels and everything."

"What will your exhibit be about?"

168

"Clocks."

"Clocks?"

Belinda's shoulders went up. "Is that a bad idea?"

"No, not if it interests you. Why clocks?"

"I saw a pretty china one in storage that day you gave me the orientation tour. I can go back through the accession ledgers to see what else there is."

"That's a great way to begin," Chloe agreed. "Have you thought about a theme for your exhibit?"

"A theme?" Belinda looked blank. "I guess I thought the theme would be … you know. Clocks."

"The clocks will *express* your theme."

Now Belinda looked worried.

"Consider it this way," Chloe said. "You could just write labels that say 'This clock was made in Milwaukee in 1878' or whatever, but that will make for a dry exhibit, don't you think? Look for human stories behind the clocks."

Worry turned to panic. "But … you said a lot of the donation forms don't have stories written on them. Just who donated the object, and when."

"You're right, and that's frustrating. But in some cases you might be able to dig a little deeper. If you find a hand-carved clock from Watertown, for example, you might be able to find some reference to a clockmaker in Watertown. An advertisement, maybe. Or if you find a clock dated 1914, you can think about what was happening in Wisconsin—and the world—when it was made. See what I mean?"

"Okay." Belinda's nod was unconvincing, but she seemed ready to move on. She opened a folder and extracted several pieces of paper. "I visited the 1860s farms, and last night I read the book you loaned me, and then I typed up some notes." She handed them over.

Chloe scanned Belinda's plan for integrating artifacts into the Civil War programming. "Good Lord."

"I'm sorry. I shouldn't have—"

"No, Belinda, this is fantastic." The girl had suggested themes for each Civil War–era building: Early war ladies' relief meeting at the Sanford Farm, political divisions within the German community at Schulz, wool production and the economic boon of US Army contracts at Kvaale.

Belinda's cheeks turned pink again. "It wasn't hard."

"The next step is to discover what artifacts we have in storage to support these themes. Remember where I keep the accession ledgers?"

Belinda nodded.

"I want you to go through the ledgers and list everything that's relevant." Chloe's predecessor, who'd originally furnished all the buildings at Old World, had filed each item's accession form into huge ledgers, arranged chronologically. There was no way to "sort by socks" or otherwise retrieve information thematically.

Belinda looked shocked. "You mean … all by myself?"

"I know it's a big job." Which is, Chloe added silently, why I'm asking you, as intern, to do it.

"It's just that … "

"Would you rather not?" Chloe asked, trying to think of a Plan B. She should have anticipated this. The trailers were in much better shape than they'd once been, but still, the workspace was cramped and solitary.

Belinda peered out from beneath her bangs. "I'm just surprised that you trust me to work there by myself."

"I absolutely trust you to work by yourself.

"Okay." Belinda slowly unhunched. "I'll start this afternoon. But … can I show you something first?" She slid the department store box closer and lifted the lid.

"Wow!" Chloe stared with astonishment at an antique homespun linen work shirt. "Is this a family heirloom?"

"No. My mom bought it at a garage sale in Palmyra."

A garage sale, Chloe marveled. The linen shirt, which easily might date to the 1860s, was in wonderful condition. Someone had embroidered two initials—*LZ*—in elaborate script on the yoke in scarlet thread. "This is an incredible piece."

"My mom said we could borrow it for the Civil War event. Only if you want."

"It's perfect for the Schulz Farm. There are loan forms in the top drawer in the trailer kitchen—just grab one and have your mom sign it. And grab some archival tissue too."

As Belinda scurried off, Chloe traced the embroidered letters with a fingertip. "And just what," she asked the shirt quietly, "is *your* story?"

NINETEEN

"This is a wonderful contribution." Lottie leaned closer to examine the linen shirt in Rosina's hands. "The weave is so fine!"

When the call for aid goods rippled through Wisconsin's German community, Rosina had sacrificed one of her best bed sheets. It would be a long while before she had new linen. "Thank you," she said. "But—I actually made this one as a gift." She unfolded the shirt.

Lottie's smile faded when she spotted the scarlet initials—*LZ*—worked in perfect satin stitch on the yoke. "*Rosina*. What have you—"

"I read in the newspaper that Herr Zuehlsdorff was commissioned a lieutenant in the 9th Wisconsin Infantry Regiment. Since we made his acquaintance on the *Fair Wind*, I thought a token of appreciation was appropriate." Rosina didn't mention that she'd slipped from bed the night before and settled on a low stool close to the hearth to add the embroidery while Klaus slept, exhausted from a day spent cutting and hauling timber.

In truth, she had struggled against the idea of embroidering the shirt for Leopold. She was married to Klaus. She was expecting a child. For their sakes, she must put Leopold from her mind. She tried. Every day she tried.

But she failed. Every single day she tried, and failed, to forget Leopold Zuehlsdorff. She saw his smile while kneading bread dough, heard his laugh while Klaus read from Scripture in the evening, felt his touch when the prairie breeze caressed her cheek. He'd become part of her.

Now Rosina implored her friend, "Please, Lottie. Will you deliver it to him?" The Sperbers planned to travel to Milwaukee to see the 9th Wisconsin officially mustered into service. Those German-born men who chose to serve would be honored.

Lottie glanced out the window. It was market day, and Adolf and Klaus were about to leave. "You should be thinking about Klaus, not Herr Zuehlsdorff."

"I *do* think of Klaus." Rosina bit back a sharper retort. She had buried her broken heart and faced her married life with all the strength and grace she could muster. Was this one favor so much to ask? "Klaus is a kind man, and hardworking. I have no complaints, and I believe he has none of me."

Lottie took her hand. "I know you did not love Klaus when you married. But love can come, in a marriage. If you let it. I believe with all my heart that in time, if you—*oh*." She looked out the window again. "There is the Muehlenberg wagon." Lottie was hosting the German women's aid society work party today.

Soon Lottie's sitting room was overflowing with the women who'd arrived with baskets of their own offerings for the German regiment: gleaming jellies, Testaments, roast chickens, chess boards, books.

The women had brought their sewing baskets too. "I purchased ribbon," Frau Muehlenberg announced. She wore an Old Country black skirt and shawl, and a big kerchief tied beneath her chin covered white hair. "We can make cockades for the men."

"Fripperies!" A middle-aged woman wearing a wine-colored dress over hooped petticoats waved a dismissive hand. "We should devote ourselves to practical items. I brought a pattern for havelocks." Havelocks were caps with neck protectors. "If the men must fight Southerners, they shouldn't have to suffer sunstroke as well."

After some debate the ladies sorted themselves into two groups, with the havelock makers moving to the kitchen where they could spread out on the table. "Rosina?" Frau Muehlenberg called. "You are handy with a needle. You will help me."

"Yes ma'am," Rosina said obediently, because she liked the image of a fancy cockade adorning Leopold Zuehlsdorff's fine uniform more than the unimaginable picture of him sweating through some southern swamp in the ridiculous-looking headgear.

Frau Muehlenberg produced red, black, and gold ribbon. "But—we should use American colors!" one of the women protested.

"German soldiers fought under these colors during the Napoleonic Wars," Frau Muehlenberg retorted. "And these colors are dear to those who struggled to create a unified country in 1848—"

"Struggled and failed," someone muttered.

In the end the women settled for the German colors because no one had brought red, white, and blue ribbon. Rosina obediently cut and folded and pinned and stitched. But Frau Muehlenberg is wrong, she thought. Leopold and his Free Thinking friends had turned their backs on the past.

———

When Klaus and Adolf returned from Watertown in the early afternoon, scraps of fabric littered the kitchen table and snips of ribbon dotted the sitting room floor. Klaus paused in the doorway, hat in hand, clearly overwhelmed by the women's energy. Rosina gathered her sewing things and said her goodbyes.

Lottie embraced her. "Please, *try*," she whispered.

"I *do*," Rosina whispered back, and turned away.

Outside, Klaus helped her up to the seat of the borrowed cart. He started to speak, paused, tried again. "I got something for you." He reached into his coat pocket and produced a length of ribbon.

It was much like what Rosina had been working with all day. "For a cockade? Have you decided to join the German regiment?"

"No." He looked away. "It's for your hair. I thought the color might please you."

Her cheeks burned as she accepted the ribbon. It was an unusual shade—not quite blue, not quite green. It was the color of the sea. She felt happiness and longing and shame, all braided together in her heart. "Thank you, Klaus. It is beautiful. You were kind to think of it."

Klaus looked pleased. "Are you warm enough?" He reached out and tugged the hood more snugly about her face. The October air was crisp as an autumn apple. "You must … we must take the best possible care of you." Now color rose in *his* cheeks. He clucked to the oxen, and they rumbled onto the road.

He knows, Rosina thought. She wasn't showing yet, and had good cause to wait as long as possible before speaking of her pregnancy. She hadn't thought Klaus would notice that she hadn't bled since their marriage, or that she sometimes—when her stomach was queasy—nibbled only dry toast in the mornings.

But he had. I am a wicked soul, Rosina thought. Klaus deserves better.

She touched his arm to acknowledge what he had tried to say, and his concern. And she vowed once again to turn her mind away from Leopold Zuehlsdorff and the 9th Wisconsin's camp in Milwaukee.

TWENTY

IN MILWAUKEE, ROELKE WAS eager to see the 9th Wisconsin's encampment. You're working, he reminded himself, as he and Dobry reported in at the Security Office by the festival ground's main entrance. On *duty*. First things first.

Sergeant McKulski, a heavyset man with dark eyes and a world-weary air, provided a brief orientation. Afterwards Roelke and Dobry checked their radios and shrugged into nylon vests with PO-LICE printed on the back, worn over their uniforms. The gig was straightforward: join other teams walking the beat.

Milwaukee's Henry Maier Festival Park occupied 75 acres of Lake Michigan shoreline, edged on the south by the confluence of the Milwaukee and Kinnickinnick Rivers. It was, thankfully, a fair distance from the Old South Side. The park was former home to an airport and, during the Cold War, a Nike antiaircraft missile site. But the city had made dogged progress since acquiring what most people now called "the Summerfest Grounds." Governor Maier had challenged the city's German-American population to create an ethnic festival, and German Fest was now in its third year.

"These festivals keep getting bigger," Dobry observed as he and Roelke began the business of Seeing and Being Seen. "I remember plywood-on-cinderblocks stages, with just a handful of food stalls."

"This whole anniversary thing is a big deal." Huge banners proclaimed GERMAN-AMERICAN TRICENTENNIAL, 1683–1983. Boisterous crowds were gathering beneath the banners, making Roelke surprisingly edgy. Well, hunh, he thought. Evidently he'd grown accustomed to small-town police work.

"These are your people, right? You should feel right at home."

"I'm only part German." Roelke put on his mirrored sunglasses, instantly upping his command presence mojo. "I think the Irish genes are dominant."

"It's all about *gemütlichkeit*." Dobry grinned. "Let's get the lay of the land."

Roelke and Dobry walked the main thoroughfare. Children tugged their parents toward carnival games. The heavy smell of roasting meat wafted from the *spanferkel* tent, where several dozen hogs turned slowly on spits and sweat-soaked women served plates of pork, sauerkraut, potato salad, and bread. People crowded into beer tents to buy souvenir steins filled with their favorite brew. A band's brassy *oompah* rang from one of the pavilions. Accordionist Myron Floren, of Lawrence Welk fame, dazzled a crowd at the next. At the third a man was crooning Neil Diamond's "Sweet Caroline." Roelke didn't get the connection but the crowd was into it, shouting, "So good! So good! So good!" at the appropriate moments.

"This event has a unique vibe," he observed. Lots of women wore dirndls and lots of men wore lederhosen. Some men had tucked astonishingly long feathers into their hats, and a few of the women displayed plunging necklines and high leather boots and short skirts in what appeared to be vague homage to the 1960s, or stereotypical buxom serving wenches. Seasoned visitors wore felt fedoras covered with pins that documented attendance at similar festivals.

Roelke paused to read a sign. "'The earliest of your ancestors left Krefeld, Germany, in 1683 and sailed to America to found Germantown, Pennsylvania. Thereafter, millions more crossed the ocean and many came to Wisconsin. Your parents, grandparents, or greatgrandparents had the courage to leave their German homeland. As you enjoy the fruits of the freest and richest land on earth, remember your forebears' sacrifices.'"

He thought about Klaus and Rosina Roelke. And he remembered Chloe's advice: *Try to soak some of it in. Listen to music. Eat sauerbraten. Walk through the cultural exhibits. Maybe something will stir your soul.* He knew such soul-stirring was serious stuff for her, so he tried. But honestly, he just didn't feel anything.

The crowd was upbeat, and for the most part well behaved. He and Dobry helped an overweight man with heat exhaustion, and an embarrassed and bleeding teenaged girl who'd tripped while exiting the Sky Glider, and a tearful six-year-old boy who'd gotten separated from his frantic mother. They escorted several underage drinkers to the gate, and edged through the jammed aisles of the souvenir tents. They assisted with crowd control during the afternoon's parade, when folk dancers, high school marching bands, people driving antique Volkswagens, and—also inexplicably, at least to Roelke—several Mardi Gras Societies streamed through the grounds.

The Civil War reenactors marched in the parade too. Roelke expected one of them to keel over any minute. Men of the 9th Wisconsin tramped by, red-faced and sweating, presumably keeping heat stroke at bay by dint of sheer will. Roelke spotted Gunter Diederich, the reenactor he'd met at the Schulz Farm, and Steven Siggelkow, the man who topped his suspect list, among the ranks.

"See that tall guy?" Roelke muttered to Dobry. "That's Siggelkow, who claimed to be wandering Old World Wisconsin alone last Thursday. Something about him bothers me."

The 100th Infantry Regiment was led by two soldiers carrying flags. Several hoop-skirted women holding parasols darted back and forth, spritzing their men from plastic spray bottles.

"That unit was started by a couple who live near Eagle," Roelke told Dobry. "I'm pretty sure that gray-bearded guy with gold epaulettes and scarlet sash is Gerald Ostermann, the commander."

"Does some guy in that group bother you?"

"I haven't met any of them, so—not yet."

"I'm sure it's just a matter of time." Dobry eyed them. "They look better than that first group."

They look…fancier, Roelke thought. And it wasn't just the women gussied up like Southern belles. Most of the men wore more elaborate uniforms than the guys in the 9th. But he'd been hanging around with Chloe long enough to know that in the living history world, "fancier" didn't necessarily mean "better."

Roelke and Dobry took their break at five. Dobry wolfed down a couple of brats. Roelke, out of respect for the woman he loved, searched out a vendor selling sauerbraten. Although the marinated pot roast didn't make his genes quiver, it proved tangy and rich and delicious. When he'd scraped the last smidgen of sauce from the paper plate, they checked in with Sergeant McKulski.

"Just do what you've been doing," he said. "Keep your eyes open and your radios on. The Civil War reenactors at the Cultural Tent will be doing some kind of drill at the lakeshore in about twenty minutes. If you're free, keep an eye on that. They're not using live ammo, of course, but the gunfire might startle some people."

They went back outside. "All right," Roelke said. "Let's go find the reenactors."

The Cultural Tent was at the south end of the grounds, beyond the main stages and beer halls. Roelke and Dobry passed exhibits for dance groups and music groups, genealogy associations and German clubs. They passed a woman spinning wool and a young man forging iron and an old man carving wood. Roelke was eeling through the aisle when a sudden snatch of music made him stop.

"What?" Dobry asked.

"Give me a minute." Roelke followed the sound to a small stage where five people in folk costumes—Pommersche Tanzdeel Freistadt, according to a sign—were performing. No spangles or exposed flesh here; the women's long skirts and aprons reminded him of the costumes interpreters wore at Old World Wisconsin. One played the accordion, and another a fiddle. The two men wore high black boots, loose white pants, red vests, and plain black hats. But it was the song itself that …

Dobry appeared at his elbow. "What?"

The musicians were performing the song Chloe said he'd been humming as they washed dishes at the farmhouse on Thursday evening. Roelke didn't remember ever having heard it before. He didn't understand the German lyrics. And yet it all seemed inexplicably familiar.

"*What?*" Dobry demanded.

"Nothing. Just a song."

"Come on." Dobry cocked his head. "The reenactors are outside."

The Civil War units were gathered on a strip of grass dotted by several small trees. The 100th was posing for a group photo near several big canvas tents—soldiers, women in hoopskirts, and a handful of adorable kids.

"Look at that camera!" Dobry sounded impressed.

Roelke followed his gaze. "Holy toboggans." Dozens of visitors were clicking away, but the chief photographer was a young man wearing a civilian costume who appeared to have an actual old-time camera on a tripod.

"How do you make pictures with that thing?" someone asked. "Is it real?"

"It's a reproduction," the photographer explained. "But I use the same process for making tintypes that photographers used during the Civil War." He yammered on about japanning, collodion, and silver nitrate, but Roelke stopped listening. There was something about the young man … Right. If Roelke wasn't mistaken, the photographer was Mac Ostermann, Gerald and Marjorie's son.

And he remembered Marjorie Ostermann's immediate assumption, upon seeing a cop at her door, that Mac was in trouble.

"That camera must have cost a pretty penny," Dobry observed.

"I've been to his parents' house. They're not hurting for cash."

Dobry checked his wristwatch. "The firing demonstration will start soon."

The 100th was still posing for the crowd. "It must be the 9th guys who're doing that."

Farther along, another group of reenactors had clustered by a few small—really small—canvas tents. Gunter Diederich was talking to a group of visitors. "…sentiments among the German community were divided," Diederich was saying. He, and the men with him, *still* wore their wool coats.

"Somebody's going to pass out," Dobry muttered.

"Many immigrants had left the German states in part to avoid military conscription," Diederich explained, "and they were overwhelmed with the demands of starting new lives here in Wisconsin. Those newcomers wanted no part of the war."

Seems reasonable, Roelke thought.

"But other immigrants believed that since America had given them a home after experiencing such misery in the Old Country, they *must* enlist in the Union Army. Fighting for the Union would prove their worth as new Americans. Some Germans joined local units. Our reenactment unit represents the 9th Wisconsin Infantry, the first regiment recruited exclusively from the state's German population."

Dobry leaned closer to Roelke. "Did any of your ancestors fight?"

"Somebody did. Chloe's going to look into it."

Diederich raised his voice as the crowd grew. "In October of 1861 the 9th Wisconsin Infantry mustered into service at a military camp just north of here. My unit is at German Fest this weekend to honor the farmers and clerks who trained to be soldiers right here in Milwaukee."

"What kind of gun did they carry?" a stocky man in a Green Bay Packers cap asked.

"*We* carry reproduction Springfield rifled muskets, but most men in the 9th were issued .58-caliber Saxon muskets, commonly called Dresden Rifles," Diederich said. "The US government was unable to completely equip their fast-growing army with American arms, and had to purchase guns from Europe."

Roelke eyed the Springfields, stacked nearby in little pyramids. He'd never fired a black powder weapon.

"The 9th Wisconsin did the state proud," Diederich said. "One observer noted that 'The Germans are entitled to great credit for their perseverance and energy, which has enabled them to overcome all obstacles and fill their regiment. Most of them, taken from the laboring classes, have been very badly embarrassed for want of means to support their families.'"

Dobry elbowed Roelke. "Maybe your great-whatever-grandfather joined the 9th."

"Maybe so." Roelke had to admit that it would be kind of cool if one of his ancestors had fought with Wisconsin's first German regiment.

"Aren't you going to shoot your guns?" a boy demanded.

Diederich pulled an old-fashioned watch from his pocket. "I believe it is time." Turning his back to the spectators he bellowed something in German, followed by, "Fall in!"

The two dozen or so reenactors who'd been lounging about jumped to their feet and scrambled to form two lines behind the stacked muskets.

"Right dress!"

The soldiers on the right end of the lines stood still. Everyone else jostled a bit as they came to stand shoulder to shoulder. Siggelkow, the tallest man, was on the left. Roelke also spotted Kyle Fassbender, the young interpreter.

"Front!"

The men moved smartly through each command—taking arms, removing bayonets, shouldering arms. These are the moves my ancestor learned, Roelke thought.

Diederich organized the ranks into a column of four to march to the waterfront. Roelke snapped out of observer mode and plunged into the crowd hemming in the column. "Make way! Clear a path!" There were too many people in the way, too many pushing in from behind. Too many children underfoot.

"Forward, march!"

The 9th Wisconsin guys managed to reach the water's edge without plowing down any tourists. Two other cops were placing temporary barricades to form three sides of a square. A tumble of huge boulders lining the lakeshore formed the fourth side. Beyond a narrow inlet, Lake Michigan stretched to the horizon.

The reenactors entered the square and reformed themselves into two ranks with their backs to the lake. Mac Ostermann had followed and set up his camera by the shoreline. Visitors pressed against the barricades, eager to see, eager to hear. Too many people, Roelke thought again.

Kyle Fassbender stepped out of rank to interpret. "We're about to demonstrate a firing drill. After months of practicing such drills, the 9th Wisconsin left for war on January 22, 1862. Thousands of cheering well-wishers turned out as the German Regiment marched to Lake Shore Depot. The soldiers boarded the train cars bound for Fort Leavenworth, Kansas."

Kansas? Roelke thought, as he grabbed a little boy trying to duck beneath a barrier, and returned him to his parents. Were Civil War battles fought in Kansas?

"The roster included 39 officers and 884 enlisted men," Fassbender continued, pacing back and forth. "Each bid a heart-wrenching farewell to his loved ones."

Roelke really wanted to find out if his soldier-ancestor had enlisted in the 9th. Had his great-whatever-grandmother been in Milwaukee that frigid day to say goodbye?

Diederich took over again. "We will load in nine times," he told the crowd.

"Load in nine times" proved to mean that nine different steps were needed to load a single round. Roelke tried to imagine doing that while being shot at.

"Shoulder arms!" Diederich bellowed. "About face!" His men faced the water.

Diederich first had the men fire by file, two by two, one man in the front rank and one man in the rear. "Company, fire by file! Commence firing!"

The explosions were precise. White smoke jetted from the muzzles. Babies cried. Excited kids bounced on their toes. Adults murmured with awe. The weapons boomed louder than modern guns. Roelke smelled black powder—pungent and faintly familiar. As if he'd smelled it before.

"Cease firing!" Diederich ordered, and had the men reload. "Company, fire by rank! Rear rank, ready … "

Each man in the back row positioned the barrel of his gun over the shoulder of the man in front of him. That's gotta be sobering, Roelke thought, as muskets were cocked with an audible "click."

"Aim … fire!"

Not to mention earsplitting. It couldn't be easy to train guys to fire in unison, but the volleys of both rear rank and front rank were crisp.

"Load!" Diederich ordered, then addressed the crowd again. "We're going to end with a single volley. This will be the loudest yet."

Some people covered their ears.

"Fire by company! Company, ready! … Aim! … *Fire!*"

The group volley was deafening. Perfect, Roelke thought—just as one laggard *pop* sounded.

The tardy shot was swallowed by the crowd's approving roar. The soldiers returned their muskets to their shoulders.

All except Siggelkow. Siggelkow fell against the man in front of him. Then he slumped to his knees.

A man behind Roelke brayed with laughter. "Looks like a Rebel snuck in and got one!"

Jesus. Roelke plunged between two barricades as Siggelkow crumpled to the ground. *This*—heat stroke? heart attack?—was not part of the show. "Get back!" he yelled to the reenactors clustering around their friend.

A woman screamed. Other people applauded.

Roelke grabbed his radio. "Male down. Possible heart attack. We need a med team at the lakeshore, south end."

Then he knelt by Siggelkow, and everything else disappeared. Roelke started to roll the reenactor over and felt something sticky against his hand. Oh, *fuck*. The dark coat had masked the gunshot wound, but now he saw the small hole. Blood pumped onto the grass and discarded paper cartridge wrappers. He was kneeling in blood. His hands were covered with blood.

"Give me a coat." When one appeared he packed it against the wound before rolling Siggelkow to his back.

Dobry was there too. He pressed two fingers against Siggelkow's skin, searching for a pulse—first the radial, then the carotid. "Come on. Come *on* . . . " He began CPR.

Roelke knew Dobry had to try. He also knew death had been instantaneous.

He grabbed the radio again. "Subject down with a gunshot wound. We've started CPR." Blood trickled from Siggelkow's mouth and nose as Dobry continued compressions.

Sensory overload roared back as Roelke leapt to his feet. "Stay where you are!" he bellowed to the crowd. Jesus God, there were people *everywhere*—some pushing in to see, some struggling to get away. He pulled his service revolver, barrel pointed to the ground, frantically searching the crowd for a shooter.

"Do something!" Someone scrabbled at Roelke's shirt—Kyle Fassbender, his lower lip black with gunpowder after tearing cartridges open with his teeth. "*Do something!*"

There was no time to explain. Roelke looked for a telltale trace of smoke among the onlookers, but a lake-born breeze had pushed the firing demonstration's haze back over the crowd. People surged, knocking over the portable barricades. A teenaged girl was sobbing. Children howled. Parents shrieked. Just north of the drill ground a crowd was belting "Ein Prosit," arms locked, swaying back and forth. Just west a band launched into "Roll Out the Barrel," and people began an impromptu polka. The Sky Glider flowed overhead. A grounds worker wrestled his trash cart toward the closest food stall. Two men on stilts made their way along the shoreline, tossing candy to excited children.

He's *here*, Roelke thought, his pulse pounding, hyper-focused. He heard the other cops yelling, and the wail of an approaching siren as the EMTs edged closer in their oversized golf cart. He smelled blood and burned gunpowder and the butter coating an ear of corn someone had dropped not far from his feet. But his vision blurred with the kaleidoscope of humanity surging forward and back. There were just too many people.

Hands. Roelke zoomed in on gnarled hands and fat hands and hands with painted fingertips; hands holding babies and bags of popcorn, hands gripping cameras and plastic steins.

But no hands clutching a gun. There were too many people. The shooter was gone.

TWENTY-ONE

JANUARY 1862

"There are too many people," Adolf said uneasily, his breath frosting white in the brittle air. Thousands had come to watch the 9th Wisconsin leave Milwaukee.

"There are," Lottie agreed. "I did not expect so many. Not in this weather." She turned to Rosina, huddled on the wagon seat beside her. "You should not be here."

Rosina felt overwhelmed by the crowds, and her toes and fingers were numb. But this was her last chance. "We've come all this way," she protested. "Please." She squeezed Lottie's mittened hand. "*Please.*"

Lottie pursed her mouth unhappily. Pedestrians, wagons, carts, and buggies clogged the street. She glanced at the parcel on Rosina's lap—the shirt made for Leopold Zuehlsdorff. Lottie had not passed it to him when the 9th was mustered in, as Rosina had asked. But Lottie had kept it, and when Rosina announced her desire to make the trip to Milwaukee with the Sperbers, Lottie had—with hesitation—given it back. "Perhaps you'll have a chance to give this to him," she'd murmured. "But if so, you *must* say goodbye. A true goodbye."

Now Lottie drew a deep breath. "Adolf, I think Rosina is right. We'll tell our children about this day. We should press on."

Looking dubious, Adolf clucked to the horse. They are such dear friends, Rosina thought. They edged forward.

Klaus, too, had been unhappy about the excursion. Since he had business in Watertown, they'd spent the night before with Lottie and Adolf. Rosina was six months pregnant now, and when they'd risen before dawn, Klaus's eyes had glimmered with concern in the candlelight. "It is so cold, *Spatzi*." Little sparrow—his pet name for her. "You should wait here. When my business is complete, I'll take you home."

"I'll be fine," Rosina demurred. "I've helped with the aid work, and I just—just *so* wish to see the German regiment off."

Klaus rubbed his chin, bemused. Rosina felt a familiar sickly twist of fear in her chest: Did Klaus know her secret? Did he suspect? But he often regarded her with such a look—when she played her zither under the Old Oak, or when she lingered by the springs instead of quickly returning with full buckets. In the early days of their marriage she had tried to explain: "I was trying to capture the red bird's tune," or "I saw three frogs swimming in the pool," or, "I was watching a cloud of butterflies feed on the purple prairie flowers."

If Klaus didn't understand her fancies, he never chastised her either. As he had not that morning, when he'd given in to her wishes. "Try not to get chilled," he'd said reluctantly.

Now Rosina leaned closer to Lottie, and slipped her hands beneath her wool cloak to shield her belly. Stay warm, little one, she whispered silently to her unborn child. We are going to say goodbye to your father.

Adolf managed to stable the horse and wagon several blocks away from the Lake Shore Depot. The women clung to his arms as they waded into the crush. On foot the crowds were more oppressive—pushing, crowding, trodding on toes. Their progress slowed, then halted. "This is as close as we can get," he said.

Rosina shifted from one icy foot to the other as they waited. She could see the depot's clock tower above the crowd, its sharp roof pointing to heaven. I *will* be a good wife to Klaus, she vowed. She just wanted to see Leopold one more time.

"Weren't they supposed to be here by eleven thirty?" a woman nearby complained.

A boy in front of them craned his neck. "I think I hear the band!"

Behind them a man spoke High German in a disapproving tone. "The German regiment formed with certain understandings. This reorganization is an unwelcome surprise."

"The 9th is headed to Fort Leavenworth to fight the Indians," his companion muttered, with equal disapproval. "Kansas!"

Rosina had heard similar complaints over the past few weeks—when their neighbors came to share dinner, after church in Palmyra. How did Leopold feel about going to Kansas? He'd dreamed of quelling the Southern states' rebellion, not marching off to the western prairies. She wished—

"I *do* hear the band!" the boy shrieked, jumping up and down.

The crowd surged, waving American flags, shouting. Rosina stood on tiptoe, but she couldn't *see*. "I'll be back," she gasped.

"Rosina, don't!" Lottie called, but Rosina was already elbowing her way forward. She *had* to see Leopold.

Constables stood with arms extended along the street. The parade approached just as Rosina struggled to the curb. Several civilian men on horseback led the column, followed by the Milwaukee Light

Infantry and a cavalry regiment. Finally the 9th Wisconsin Infantry Regiment marched into view. Two standard bearers bore flags, whipping in the lake-born wind—one American, one a blue regimental banner.

Rosina's heart thrummed with unexpected pride. The men wore splendid blue uniforms and marched in perfect step, staring straight ahead. They carried knapsacks and rifled muskets that gleamed in the sun.

As they approached the depot the ovation grew. Guns fired in salute. Men whistled. So many women waved handkerchiefs that the air itself seemed to flutter.

"Oh!" Rosina pressed her hands against her mouth. After months of separation, hours of anxiety—there was Leopold. He rode with the other officers, back straight, easily managing his prancing bay horse after a firecracker exploded almost underfoot.

"Leopold!" Rosina shrieked. Her voice disappeared in the din. She darted forward, carried along as the constables were overwhelmed by mothers, sweethearts, wives, fathers, children—all desperate for one last farewell before their men boarded the waiting Chicago and North Western Railway cars.

"Leopold! *Leopold!*"

He turned his head with an expression of surprise. He bent low from the saddle and said clearly, "Why, my dear girl!"

Rosina's heart overflowed. Her eyes welled with tears. The knot in her chest eased.

Then she saw the young woman in a stylish gray cape and silk bonnet thrusting a parcel of her own at Leopold. "It's a plum cake!" the girl cried. She spoke German, but looked American, as if her people had been part of Milwaukee society for a long time.

The crowd surged again, and the young woman in the silk bonnet was swept away on the tide. Rosina could not move. Blood pulsed at her temples. She thought she heard Adolf calling her name, but it didn't matter. Nothing mattered.

Then Leopold straightened, and his gaze met hers. And still she could not move.

Leopold shoved the cake at another man, swung from the saddle, grabbed the reins with one hand. Suddenly he stood before her, tall and grand in his uniform, both perfect stranger and the person she knew best of all. Everything else—the people, the military band, the cannon salutes, the sobs and shouts—faded away. Rosina felt as if they were back on the deck of the *Fair Wind* beneath a miraculous sky.

Finally Leopold spoke. "Oh, *Röslein*. I did not expect—"

"This is for you. I … " Rosina pushed her package at him. "I … I want you to remember me."

He glanced at the swell beneath her cloak, and his eyes went wide. "You are … "

"I am *married*—I had to—and settled near Palmyra. But … " She spread her hands helplessly. But it is you I love, she finished silently. In spite of everything, it is you.

He looked stunned. Bewildered, almost. Like a child. "I never intended … I just wanted to … "

"Mount up!" a man bellowed.

Leopold dropped the reins and seized Rosina by the shoulders. His eyes were full of emotions she couldn't read.

What did you expect me to do? Rosina asked him silently. Did it never occur to you that I might be in a family way?

After a long moment he kissed her cheek. Then he turned abruptly, swung back into the saddle, and disappeared.

Someone yelled, "Three cheers for the gallant 9th!"

And … who was that pretty young woman with the plum cake? Did that girl know Leopold, or had she simply picked a handsome officer for her gift?

"Huzzah!" the crowd responded. "Huzzah! Huzzah!"

Men shouted commands, and soldiers fired a perfect volley. Rosina flinched. She'd heard guns fire all of her life—men stalking rabbits or stags or quail. This volley was different—sharp and somehow vicious, and repeated again and again as company after company demonstrated its skill. These farmers and tailors and professors and Free Thinkers were soldiers now.

"*Rosina!*" A hand clamped on her arm like an iron band.

She roused herself. "I'm sorry, Adolf … "

But it wasn't Adolf.

Klaus's grip tightened. "Come away."

Rosina felt strangely empty, detached from the melee. You must think clearly, she told herself. It was time to think clearly, and act appropriately.

For Klaus was here, and Leopold was gone.

TWENTY-TWO

THE KILLER WAS GONE.

After Roelke's radio call, every guard converged at the scene. Roelke helped contain the crowd. The EMTs removed Siggelkow's body. Detectives arrived fast, and more cops. They interviewed everyone lingering in the area and asked photographers to relinquish their film. They shut down the festival.

Roelke was assigned to help interview the interminable lines of visitors leaving the grounds. "Did you see anyone suspicious?" he asked, over and over. "Did you see anyone with a gun?" No one had.

Hours later, Sergeant McKulski sent the security guards home. "It's up to the detectives now," he said.

Maybe so, but that didn't sit well.

Roelke had never watched someone get murdered right before his eyes. Never seen a man go down. Never knelt in blood and known it was already too late.

He was already frustrated about Private M. Steven Siggelkow's death was much, much worse. The detectives in Waukesha and

Milwaukee would do their thing. But no way, Roelke thought, am *I* going to sit on my hands.

———

At four that afternoon Chloe found Belinda in one of the trailers, at a tiny table in the tiny kitchen. At least it doesn't smell of mice anymore, Chloe thought. The trailers were cleaner, better organized, and less crowded than they'd once been. Nika, her first intern, had moved the textiles to a different space.

"Thanks for sticking it out this afternoon," Chloe said, taking the second chair at the table. "It's not the most pleasant place to work."

"It is a little … claustrophobic," Belinda agreed. "And this was supposed to be your office?"

"It was," Chloe confirmed. Evidently Petty had started hating her before she even began working at the site. "You can see why I moved over to Ed House. How's it going?" She nodded to the acquisitions ledgers. "Did you find anything that might be helpful for our Civil War event?"

"Well, I think so. Maybe." Belinda pushed a spiral notebook across the table. "Here."

Belinda's list identified artifacts with their accession numbers and dates of manufacture. All of the items—from wool socks to patchwork quilts to a map showing major military campaigns—dated from the 1860s or earlier.

Belinda twisted her fingers together. "Is that what you wanted?"

"This is *great*." Chloe turned a page and looked up, surprised by the next item. "We actually have a pattern for havelocks?" The odd muslin caps were fashioned after a style used by British soldiers sweating through India in the 1850s. Union women had made barrels of the things. The soldiers had no idea what to do with them, however, and the fad was short-lived.

"Yes. And as I understand it," Belinda said hesitantly, "it took women a while to figure out what men at the front really needed. So I thought that maybe … if you think it's a good idea … we could have some inappropriate things on display in the Sanford house. Glass tumblers of jelly that could easily break, chess boards, heavy books … things like that."

"That sounds perfect."

Belinda ducked her head. Chloe wished the girl wasn't so painfully shy. Petty's "charity case" remark rang in her memory. Screw you, Chloe thought. Part of the internship experience was gaining confidence.

"If you can come in tomorrow, I'd like you to join a meeting Byron scheduled at the Sanford Farm with the lead interpreter. We can talk specifics about programming before we start pulling artifacts."

"I can come in, but … " Belinda hesitated. "Byron always seems kind of impatient."

"He's just busy," Chloe assured her. "He'll be grateful for your good work, I promise."

———

After Belinda left, Chloe drove back to Ed House. The phone rang as she came in the door. She eyed it. It was after five, and she'd be perfectly within her rights to ignore it.

It rang again. She sighed melodramatically and grabbed the receiver. "Hello, this is Chloe Ellefson."

"Hey," Roelke said. "Did I catch you at a bad time?"

He must be calling from German Fest, she thought, and sat up straight. "Is everything okay?"

"No, it's not. And I didn't want you to hear it on the news."

"Hear *what*?"

"Steven Siggelkow is dead," Roelke told her tersely. "He was shot."

———

On Sunday morning, when Roelke and Dobry reported back to work, the mood at the festival park's security station was subdued.

A detective provided an update. "For those who were not here yesterday, here are the facts: A Civil War reenactment unit was performing a drill in a cordoned-off area against the breakwater. They fired reproduction muskets without live ammunition. Just as the last volley was fired, or perhaps a split second later, someone in the crowd fired what we believe was a single pistol shot." He glanced at Roelke.

Roelke nodded. He was certain he'd heard a pistol *pop* even as the musket volley's loud *crack* shivered in the air.

"The bullet hit reenactor Steven Siggelkow, who was in the rear of two rows, and struck his heart. Four officers were in the immediate vicinity, and the EMTs arrived in under a minute. Mr. Siggelkow died almost instantly. We did not identify the shooter, but we did find a pistol in a trash bin near the Cultural Tent."

Roelke felt a quiver of hope. This was new information.

"The gun is"—he looked at his notes—"a reproduction 1849 Colt pocket pistol with four-inch barrel. The five-shot revolver uses black powder to fire .31-caliber lead balls. "

Roelke frowned. That would fit a Civil War scenario. So … was the killer a reenactor?

"One cylinder had been fired."

Or was that just what the killer wanted the cops to think?

"We're waiting for the ballistics and ME's reports. Unfortunately, there were no fingerprints on the gun."

Damn. Gun shops registered weapons sold, but there was no nationwide database. And no requirements that individuals selling guns privately had to keep records. The shooter could have purchased the Colt at a flea market.

"At this time we believe that the shooting was an isolated incident," the detective continued.

Roelke shot Dobry a meaningful glance: *An isolated incident. Just like the reenactor's death at Old World.*

Dobry hitched his shoulders in a tiny shrug: *Forty miles away from the festival grounds.*

"We have already learned a few things that might bear on the killing," the detective said. "Mr. Siggelkow had been living apart from his wife for a month, and he filed for divorce two weeks ago. His wife claims he had an affair. The other woman involved is also married."

Oh, for God's sake, Roelke thought. Siggelkow had screwed himself right into a spot where all kinds of people—his wife, his wife's relatives, his lover's husband—might wish him dead. Statistically, it was likely that his killer was someone who knew him, or knew of him.

It might even be true that Steven Siggelkow *was* responsible for Private M's death, and that someone knew and had punished him for it.

Private M had died at Old World, which made that death personal. But Roelke was the one who'd watched Siggelkow get hit, fall, and die. Regardless of anything Siggelkow might have done, his death was personal too.

———

Chloe stumbled out of bed at an ungodly hour once again on Sunday because she planned to begin dressing the loom that morning with Jenny and Alyssa. After hearing about the murder at German Fest the day before, she'd considered canceling. In the end she decided that was not warranted.

Still, after letting herself into the old farmhouse, Chloe called to let the security guard on duty know that she was working at Schulz. She hung up scowling. She *hated* feeling anxious at Old World.

Jenny and Alyssa arrived together, promptly at eight o'clock. "Did you see the news last night?" Alyssa said as they joined Chloe in the workroom. "About that reenactor getting shot at German Fest?"

"It's a tragedy," Chloe murmured. "Honestly, I hate to think about it."

"Coffee?" Jenny pulled a Thermos and a Tupperware container from her copious basket. "And I brought sour cream doughnuts."

Chloe accepted a tin mug of coffee and a doughnut, which was fresh and moist and fabulous. "Where did you find the time?"

"Lee's been extra busy in the barn, getting ready for the harvest, and I hate having time on my hands."

"You are a wonderful human being."

Jenny scoffed. "You're doing us a huge favor with the loom."

Chloe licked her fingers. "I wanted to get started before any visitors were around because this step is the hardest part."

She showed them how to transfer the long bundle of linen threads to the loom and spread them evenly over the back beam. "The reed will keep the threads spaced evenly," she said. "Alyssa, you handle the crank as we wind the warp threads onto the beam. Add one of these wooden laths every revolution or so to keep the threads from piling onto each other. I'll handle the threads from here." She stepped to the front of the loom. "Jenny, you keep a careful eye on the warp as it passes. The trickiest thing is keeping the tension even among all the threads."

By nine thirty they'd made great progress. "It was fun!" Alyssa assured her. "But if we're done for now, I'm going to head down to the village."

Jenny watched through the window as Alyssa hurried away. "The college kids like to gather before the briefing. It gives them a chance to socialize before heading out to their buildings." She held out the plastic container. "One more for the road?"

"If you insist." Chloe didn't want to hurt Jenny's feelings.

"I think Alyssa and Kyle Fassbender have a romance brewing," Jenny confided.

Chloe thought, That's sweet.

Then she thought, Wait—Alyssa's in a relationship with Kyle? She could picture Roelke's eyes narrow as he scrutinized that tidbit.

"I got to know Kyle when he worked in the German area last year." Jenny hid the container away in a cupboard. "They're both good kids."

"You're a great lead," Chloe observed honestly.

"That's kind of you to say." Jenny turned away, checking the cheesecloth tied over a pickle crock. "I don't have a college degree in history, but I was raised on a farm. Five sisters, no brothers. I knew how to chop wood and butcher geese and most everything else before I started working here. I feel a kinship with Auguste Schulz." She shook her head. "That poor woman. After all the heartache and struggle of leaving Europe, coming all the way to Wisconsin, starting a farm … then her new country explodes in civil war."

"You can help visitors imagine all that next weekend."

Jenny checked her watch, pinned out of sight inside her apron pocket. "I need to get to the morning meeting. Are you going to change into period clothing and keep working?"

Chloe hesitated, nibbling her lower lip. On this beautiful Sunday a lot of visitors would likely wander through the site. The Schulz Farm was still short-staffed. And helping Alyssa here would sure be a lot more fun than crawling around guests while measuring every bloomin' pane in every bloomin' historic building.

But ... no. "Alas," she said, "I'm due at the Sanford Farm."

She retrieved her car, picked up Belinda at the artifact trailers, and drove to the Visitor Center. From there it was a short walk to the Sanford Farm. The beautiful Greek Revival house was once home to a well-to-do Yankee family. One interpreter had busied several children with reproduction watering pails in the huge garden.

Lee Hawkins—Jenny's husband—was talking to Byron on the porch. Chloe and Belinda joined them. "Belinda's done some great work preparing for the Civil War event," Chloe said.

"I want to talk to you about that." Lee looked from Chloe to Byron. "After what happened at Schulz, wouldn't it be best to cancel the event?"

"Cancel the event?" Byron repeated. "The police haven't found any reason to believe that the reenactor's death wasn't an isolated incident. An accident."

"It's not just that." Lee glanced over his shoulders—no one in earshot. "I think Civil War reenacting is a bad thing."

Chloe was clearly missing something, but she didn't know what. "Um ... why?"

"A bunch of men putting on reproduction uniforms is hardly a suitable way to interpret the Civil War."

"We do living history here at Old World," Byron said. "Reenactors do living history."

"It's different," Lee insisted. "We have temperance rallies, and talk about Yankee settlers' contributions, and demonstrate 1860s cooking and agriculture. The Civil War was carnage!"

"Yes it was," Chloe said evenly, "but—"

"Look, I used to teach high school history, so I do know something about pedagogy." He rubbed his hands together. "Sure, you'll get some kids who are excited by the chance to see men with guns. But to call what reenactors do 'living history' is offensive. We'd be glorifying violence!"

Chloe considered banging her head against one of the pretty Greek Revival columns supporting the porch roof.

"Let's talk through the plans in more detail," Byron suggested. "I think we'll be able to find common ground, and I welcome your suggestions."

Chloe smiled politely. "Since the lead interpreter seems to be running late, I think Belinda and I will head out." Calming down agitated interpreters was Byron's job.

She and Belinda walked back to the parking lot in silence. Belinda didn't find her voice until they were leaving the site. "I was kind of surprised by Lee's objections."

Chloe checked for traffic and pulled onto the road. "I value his point of view," she said carefully. "And certainly, there are challenges inherent in interpreting difficult topics like war and death. Or slavery, or the systematic genocide of Native Americans, or—" She checked herself. "But avoiding such issues is *not* the answer. We just have to be extra careful in planning our approach, and listen when people express concerns."

"I didn't realize how complicated museum work can be."

"All part of the internship experience," Chloe said. And it was true. Still, she didn't envy Byron. Petty wanted a battle; a top interpreter wanted to abandon Civil War programming altogether.

"Maybe Lee had some bad experience when he was teaching," Belinda suggested.

"Could be," Chloe agreed. "Or maybe he's just feeling protective of Jenny after what happened at Schulz." Jenny had worried about Alyssa, but Alyssa seemed fine; now Lee was worried.

And now Belinda looked worried too. "Byron will work things out with Lee," Chloe told her. "All this really means is that interpreters are, by and large, a sensitive and thoughtful bunch."

———

After the briefing, Roelke and Dobry made a point of visiting the little open area beyond the Cultural Tent. Only the 100th Wisconsin tents were still in place. A few visitors were chatting with members of the group.

Roelke approached the gray-haired man he'd noticed yesterday, looking splendid in a fancy uniform coat and sash. "Sir? Pardon me, but are you Gerald Ostermann?"

"Yes, but... oh God." The man's eyes widened, "Has there been another—"

"Nothing is wrong, sir," Roelke said quickly. "I'm Roelke McKenna. I just wanted to introduce myself because I'm with the Eagle PD."

"*Oh*." The tension lines around Ostermann's eyes and mouth eased, and he thrust out a hand. "You're the one who stopped by and talked with my wife."

"Yes, sir. She told me that you two founded the 100th Infantry unit."

"We did. Marjorie would be here this weekend if she didn't have to work." Ostermann lowered his voice. "I'm lucky that, unlike many reenactors, my wife shares my interest, and…" He paused, his attention diverted. "Mac? Mac! Come meet Officer McKenna."

The young man slouched forward with obvious reluctance, and mumbled a greeting. He was dressed as a civilian again.

"I thought your photographer impression yesterday was pretty cool." Roelke's thumb began to beat against his thigh as he remembered something. "Weren't you taking pictures yesterday just before the 9th Wisconsin did their firing demonstration?"

The teen paused, as if trying to think through any angle that might get him in trouble. Finally he shrugged. "Yeah. So?"

"For God's sake, Mac," Gerald Ostermann muttered. "Show some respect."

"The detectives investigating yesterday's shooting are trying to examine photographs taken by visitors during the demonstration," Roelke said. "Did they ask to see yours?"

"They interviewed all of us, of course," Gerald said. "But they didn't ask about the photos, did they, Mac?"

"Nope." Mac shrugged. "But I didn't see anything."

"You never know what might be helpful. Can I take a look?"

"They're at home."

"Well, how about I stop by tomorrow?" Roelke asked pleasantly. The kid's evasiveness only made him more curious.

Mac shrugged. His father frowned before turning back to Roelke. "That would be fine, Officer McKenna. I was not acquainted with Mr. Siggelkow, but that something like this would happen during a reenactment…" He shuddered. "We're happy to help in any way."

"Excuse me!" A woman in very short shorts interjected herself into the conversation, focused entirely on Gerald Ostermann. "May I take your picture?"

Roelke rejoined Dobry, who was scrutinizing the passing crowd. "Remember how yesterday you asked if anybody in the 100th Wisconsin reenactment group bothered me?"

"I believe I predicted that it was just a matter of time," Dobry said.

Roelke cocked his head toward Mac Ostermann. "That kid, Mac, doesn't like cops."

"I'd say Mac's been in trouble."

"That's what I'm thinking. When I stopped by the Ostermann house the other day, his mother assumed that I'd showed up because of her son, and … " He frowned as something nudged his memory. Marjorie Ostermann had said that a family obligation would keep her from German Fest, but her husband had just said she had to work.

It was probably nothing. Plans changed. Work schedules shifted. Still.

"I'm going to keep an eye on that kid," Roelke muttered. "And his parents too."

TWENTY-THREE

MARCH 1862

Rosina arched her spine like a cat. Back pain had become a constant as her pregnancy neared its term. The baby kicked, and she placed a palm over her belly.

"You are … unwell?" Klaus shifted uneasily in his chair. "Should I fetch the midwife?"

"I'm fine," Rosina told him. "I just—" A faint noise from beyond the cabin made her pause. "Is someone coming?"

Klaus went to the door and cracked it open. "It's Adolf and Lottie." He went outside to help with the horse. A few moments later Lottie burst through the door. Snow dusted her cloak.

"Come sit by the fire." Rosina lumbered to her feet and helped unknot the woolen shawl tied below Lottie's chin. Lottie's cheeks were red as apples. When she kissed Rosina's cheek, her lips felt like ice.

Rosina added wood to the fire, and water to the kettle so they could all have hot tea. Then she sank back down by Lottie. "I am so *very* glad to see you."

"How are you?" Lottie pulled off thick mittens and held her fingers toward the blaze.

"Oh Lottie, it's been so dreary! Sometimes I think this baby will never be born, and spring will never come, and I'll be trapped in this cabin forever." She spread her arms to indicate her world: windowless walls, bed in one corner, table and benches. Klaus's sickle and scythe, grub hoe and ax hung on one wall. A flour bin sat in one corner. Their few dishes were stacked neatly on the table. The room smelled of smoke and musty turnips.

Then Rosina thought of how hard Klaus had labored to accomplish this, never complaining, and she felt ashamed. "Please forgive me. I don't know what's wrong with me."

"Gracious, my mood was just as bleak before Gerhard was born. In a few weeks you'll cradle your own child. Sunshine will melt the snow."

"I've missed you," Rosina said. Even trips to church had become too difficult as snow drifted across the lanes. She'd only seen Lottie twice since the new year, and never alone.

"Is everything well between you and Klaus?" Lottie asked in a low tone. "He was so quiet that day in January… "

Rosina's cheeks flushed. She'd not soon forget the day the 9th Wisconsin had left Milwaukee, or the moment she'd turned away from Leopold to see Klaus standing behind her. "What—why—I didn't expect you!" she'd stammered, while her heart kicked against her ribs like a mule.

"I worried about you, out in this cold." His face had been inscrutable. So after a moment she'd tucked her hand in his arm and they'd slipped back through the crowd to join Adolf and Lottie.

Lottie took Rosina's hands. "Does he know?"

"I don't think so."

"Then you must never tell him. Do you understand me?"

"I do." Rosina's words came from the depths of her heart. "I *know* how fortunate I am. Klaus is a good husband. He'll be a fine father."

"And I trust you are not in communication with Herr Zuehlsdorff?"

"I am not." Part of her had hoped that he might write her a letter ... but no letter had come. Leopold was gone.

Something in Lottie's face eased. "*Good.* Then we shall never speak of this again." She reached for her basket. "I brought you two nightgowns that Gerhard's already outgrown."

"You're kind. I so wish ... I haven't been able to prepare properly."

Lottie nodded sympathetically. "You'll grow flax this summer. And I can loan you my spinning wheel."

"Klaus is building me a loom."

"That's wonderful! Soon you'll have new sheets and shirting."

But it isn't just shirting I need, Rosina thought. She needed to keep her hands busy on long, dark winter evenings while Klaus read the Bible—sometimes silently, sometimes aloud. After winter's damp cold had crept beneath the door and lodged in the walls, she'd been unable to keep her zither tuned. She'd had nothing to sew. Her mind insisted on conjuring images of Leopold riding into horrific battle.

Now, though, Lottie was here. Rosina was determined to do better. "Yes. Things will be much better when I have a flax crop. I want to hire out as I used to. Klaus works so hard, and we hope to buy a cow ... He's cut and sold fence rails this winter, but I want to earn some money too."

"It's no small thing to start a farm. But you mustn't work all the time." Lottie reached into her basket again, and produced small skeins of colored thread—yellow, orange, blue, green, and vivid crimson. "For you."

"Oh ... " Tears pricked Rosina's eyes as she gathered the bouquet. "Thank you."

Lottie smiled. "I knew you must be wanting." She leaned over to check the water. "Where do you keep your tea leaves? No—sit, I'll take care of it."

"That box on the mantel." Rosina stroked the colors with one finger.

Lottie sprinkled mint leaves into two mugs and added steaming water. "I won't pour for the men until they come inside. I expect they are discussing the war. The news is *so* troubling."

After reporting to Fort Leavenworth, the 9th Wisconsin had joined something called the "Southwestern Expedition" through Kansas and Oklahoma. Worrisome stories about incompetent leadership and harsh marches through Indian country were trickling through the German community. Rosina was desperate for news, but could hardly bear to listen.

But today Lottie had more bad news. "Adolf fears that the government will begin conscription."

Rosina was shocked. "Surely not! In America, men have free will." Leopold had said so.

"We shall see." Lottie clearly feared that America might not be *quite* so free as they'd been told.

The men came inside with a blast of frigid air, stamping their feet. Lottie poured two more mugs of hot tea, and Rosina held up the colored thread. "But I won't do any embroidery until I finish darning your socks," she promised Klaus. She was using fine wool thread, unraveled from her shawl, to fortify the heels and toes.

Klaus sipped his tea and smiled. "You do fine work, Rosina."

She wished she could darn Klaus's worn boots too. They'd run out of flour the week before, and Klaus had taken the last of their coins, hiked into Palmyra, and trudged home with a ten-pound sack. There was no money for new boots.

But spring was coming. If the wheat crop did well, by fall they'd have one window and a cow and a weaving shed. I *will* do better, Rosina promised herself. Then—

"Oh!" Her thighs were suddenly warm and wet. She looked at Lottie with wide eyes. "I think…I think my child is ready to be born."

———

The child was not, as it turned out, *quite* ready to be born. Since Rosina had attended to Lottie when Gerhard was born, she'd thought herself prepared. She was not. After many hours of labor, she was sure she was dying and she didn't even care.

And then—relief. "There, now," said the midwife. "It's a boy."

Lottie wiped Rosina's face with a damp towel. "Rest, my friend. You did well."

When Rosina woke next it was dark again. A warm bundle was nestled in her arm. Two precious candles burned on the table. Klaus was sitting on the edge of the bed.

He gripped her free hand. "We have a son," he said huskily. "Through God's grace you have given me a fine son."

Rosina felt something heavy and cold as old iron slip away, and only then realized how much she had feared all along that Klaus would reject Leopold's child. "What shall we name him?" she whispered.

He stroked her fingers. "My father's name was Johann. Do you like that?"

"Since our baby was born in America, we might call him John," she suggested. Leopold would like that best…

But Leopold had no place in Klaus's cabin. "Never mind," she said. "Johann is a good strong name."

"No, you're right. His name is John." Klaus cleared his throat. "Oh Rosina, there are so many things I want to give you. You and John."

"I have everything I need. *We* have everything we need."

"But you shall have fine things one day. I wish I could have given you a ring when we wed. I can't afford a ring—"

Rosina looked at his eyes, shining in the candlelight, and felt something in her heart shift, making more room for her husband. "Oh, Klaus. I don't need a ring."

"But one day," he promised, "you shall have one."

TWENTY-FOUR

CHLOE TURNED INTO THE Admin building parking lot on Monday
morning at a speed calculated to ju-ust barely avoid spewing gravel.
Moments later she slid into the lone empty chair in Ralph Petty's
office with fifteen seconds to spare. Weekly staff meetings at Old
World Wisconsin were the bane of her existence. She'd learned to
time her entrance precisely.

Petty looked at his watch.

"Morning, all," Chloe said. Beside her, Byron exhaled slowly.
He'd probably feared that she would worm out of the meeting, leaving him without moral support.

Petty moved through the first few items on his agenda quickly:
attendance and sales figures for the weekend, the ongoing efforts of
maintenance chief Stan Colontuono—AKA Stan the Man—to obtain
a new truck through the bewildering maze of state procurement
channels, technical problems with the slide projector used to provide
orientation in the Visitor Center. After chastising or otherwise

demoralizing everyone else, Petty turned his attention to Chloe and Byron.

"Next item," he announced. "The Civil War event planned for the coming weekend. Mr. Cooke, after the tragedy at German Fest, are you still prepared to hold the event?"

"I am," Byron said firmly. "I've spoken with Gunter Diederich, who leads the 9th Wisconsin. Everyone in the unit is shocked and grieving, of course. But the detectives involved suspect that the attack was personal. Everyone in the unit agrees that Steven would not want them to cancel."

"We've had posters up about the event," the Visitor Center manager put in. "There's been a lot of interest."

Stan the Man scowled. "Will I need to bring extra guys on? That's not in the budget."

"I don't think you'll need extra help." Byron passed around a two-page memo that provided an overview of the program goals, and how the event would impact the permanent staff, temporary employees, and volunteers. Chloe had reviewed the memo in advance. It was concise, but thorough.

The receptionist stepped in. "Pardon me," she murmured to the director. "Your guest is here."

"We will adjourn," Petty announced. Chloe was halfway to the door, right behind Byron, when Petty added, "Mr. Cooke, Miss Ellefson, please stay."

They settled back down reluctantly. Byron gave Chloe an uneasy glance: *What the hell?*

She returned the look: *Can't be good.*

The receptionist ushered in a young woman wearing a pink suit, pink high heels, and pink lipstick. She strode to Chloe and extended one slender hand adorned with pink nail polish. "Hello! I'm Kiki!"

"Kiki?" Chloe echoed, as the size-0 teen pumped her hand.

"Kiki!" the waif agreed happily, before turning her high-wattage smile on Byron. Byron greeted Kiki warily but Petty, last in line, returned her smile with more warmth than Chloe had thought biologically possible.

So this is what trips Petty's trigger, she thought. Kiki's brown hair was feathered around an oval face. Her lashes were weighted with mascara, her cheeks dusted with the same Pepto-Bismol shade as the rest of her ensemble. She looked like a little girl playing dress up.

Petty settled Kiki at the table before addressing Chloe and Byron. "Kiki is a tourism consultant."

Since when? Chloe thought. She had jeans older than Kiki.

"Given that you two are determined to rush into new programming—"

"We're not rushing," Chloe protested.

"—I decided it would be wise to hear what an *expert* has to say about trends and visitor preferences. Kiki kindly made room for us in her busy schedule. Kiki?"

Kiki produced three glossy red folders. "I'll let you read my report on your own—"

Thank God for small favors, Chloe thought.

"—and simply highlight the main conclusions. First: Wisconsinites like to spend leisure time with friends and family."

This is news? Chloe thought. Seriously, she was way too busy for this.

"Second: Wisconsinites like water features."

"Water features?" Byron echoed.

Chloe looked at him. "We could encourage visitors to wade in the kettle ponds."

"Or," he countered, "have the interpreters at Hafford do laundry more often." Mary Hafford had been a laundress.

Petty glared, but if Kiki realized that her audience was underwhelmed, she didn't show it. "And third, Wisconsinites like festivals. Big festivals."

Ah, Chloe thought. Now we're coming down to it.

"I understand that you're planning a Civil War reenactment." Kiki placed her palms on the table and leaned forward. "Here's my advice: Go big."

Byron looked as if he needed some Pepto. "Actually," he began, "we thought it might be best to test the water—"

Chloe sniggered. Petty glared. She stifled it.

"—on a small scale." Byron's cheeks had flushed a ruddy red. "Basing program elements on thorough research—"

"Big," Kiki repeated solemnly.

"—and thoughtful consideration of multiple learning styles," Byron finished doggedly.

"Big, is, *key*," Kiki said. "Think *fun*. Think *excitement*."

Chloe's hands, which were in her lap, clenched into fists. "But here's the thing, Kiki. Old World Wisconsin is not an amusement park. We have a mission to provide educational programming."

Petty folded his arms. "Miss Ellefson. Why are you so set against the idea of visitors having fun?"

Chloe managed to remain calm by extending one middle finger in his direction beneath the table. "I *do* want visitors to have fun. And as I have said before, repeatedly, there is nothing wrong with battle scenarios. But we have an unparalleled opportunity to create homefront programming, and the 9th Wisconsin can—"

"The 9th Wisconsin is no longer the only unit involved this weekend," Petty announced. "I have invited the 100th Wisconsin to participate as well."

Chloe and Byron shared a stunned look. That little *shit*, Chloe thought. This was the biggest Petty atrocity yet.

Byron said "You ... what?"

"I invited the 100th Wisconsin to participate. The leader assures me they enjoy presenting mock battles."

"Bigger is better," Kiki chirped.

Chloe clenched her fists again, because she truly wanted to smack somebody. She looked out the window to avoid seeing Petty looking all autocratic and smug. Think about the farm, she ordered herself. Think about Roelke. Think about how badly you need this job.

She couldn't speak truth to Petty. He *wanted* her to speak truth, and she couldn't, because he'd fire her for insubordination. And probably hire Kiki before the screen door slammed.

The situation was galling. And she couldn't do a damn thing about it.

A painful silence blanketed the room. Finally Byron shifted in his seat. His cheeks were white now. "Do you have contact information for the 100th?"

"Of course." Petty sent a slip of paper sailing across the table. "Gerald Ostermann lives just north of Eagle. In addition to adding manpower, involving his unit is good PR within the community."

Byron shoved the paper into his glossy red folder and stood. "Excuse me. I'm late for a meeting on site."

"I am too," Chloe said, which was a lie, but no way was she staying here alone with Petty and Kiki.

And Petty, having won this particular battle, let them go.

Roelke stood in the farm driveway on Monday morning, just taking it in: Birdsong. Farmhouse. Sunshine. Outbuildings. Fields. It had rained in the night, and the day quivered fresh and dewy. All of this was his.

The now-familiar ache bloomed in his chest. Despite Dobry's assurances, Roelke didn't think it was *all* buyer's remorse. He had no idea what caused his extra anxiety, though.

Or maybe … maybe he did.

Adam Bolitho was coming to help paint, and Roelke had arrived early to get as much prep work done as possible. That meant going inside. Spreading newspaper. Applying masking tape.

Instead, Roelke found himself walking inexorably to the old cabin. He put one palm against the closed door. What the hell did Chloe feel in there? Part of him wanted badly to know. Part of him did not.

He stepped inside. Sunlight slanted through the window, making a parallelogram on the floor. Roelke looked at the log walls, the wide floor boards, the empty space. All he felt was a flash of anger. There is nothing here, he growled silently. Nothing to see. Nothing to feel.

But aural memories overcame the stillness: a *thwack* of fist against skin and bone, a hard *thump* against one log wall, a sliding *shuush*, a softer *thud*.

Roelke's jaw clenched as he willed away memories of tears and curses, running feet and a racing car engine. And that most reprehensible emotion: profound, abiding shame.

The sound of tires on gravel—real this time—snapped him from the reverie. He shot from the cabin as Adam Bolitho climbed from his pickup. Roelke strode across the farmyard to greet him. "Adam, good to see you."

"Wow." Adam surveyed the farm. "This place is great."

"It needs a lot of work."

Adam shrugged. "Any old place does, but this one isn't bad. I hate it when people call me hoping to renovate a building that's beyond saving." He turned toward the truck bed. "I wasn't sure what we'd need today, so I just brought a bunch of stuff."

Roelke regarded the haul: tarps, paint brushes and rollers, an electric sander, impressive toolbox. Since he was too broke to hire help or buy tools, Adam's generosity was a *huge* boon. "I appreciate it," he said, because that was all a guy could say to a casual friend at a moment like this.

They started in the largest bedroom—the room he and Chloe would share. He'd picked out a sample card of ferny greens he thought she'd like. She'd chosen her favorite, and he'd selected a darker shade for accent details.

Adam moved with the efficient speed and economy of a professional. No blaring radio, thank God. No inane chatter about sports. Finally, when the tarps were spread and taping complete, Adam asked a question. "How well do you know Ralph Petty?"

"Not well." Roelke pried up a paint can lid. "I've heard a lot of stories from Chloe. I hadn't met him before that day at the Schulz Farm, though."

"Me either. But he complained to the fire chief that we—and I quote—'dawdled at our duties.'" Adam reached for a stir stick.

"*Dawdled?*" Roelke shook his head in disgust.

"He was pissed because we didn't remove the body. I explained that we had to wait for the ME, but … " Adam shrugged before pouring paint into a tray. "You want roller, or brush?"

"I'll do the brushwork." Roelke liked that—the precision work, just so. "Petty called my chief to complain about Goresko too, so don't feel like the Lone Ranger."

"Good to know. Fortunately my chief didn't seem to take the rant seriously. He knows we had to wait. He also said Petty wants a seat on the Village Board, and—"

"Oh, *hell.*" Roelke blew out a long, disgusted breath. "I was really hoping that rumor was unfounded."

"Afraid not. Apparently Petty's started throwing his weight around in the belief that acting like an asshole will win respect."

"It hasn't worked at Old World Wisconsin, so I don't know why he thinks it will work in the village," Roelke grumbled. He climbed onto a stepladder so he could reach the ceiling and began carefully dabbing paint against the tape. "But I think he's already sucking up to the wealthy and powerful. I was out at this big estate just south of Ottawa Lake last week, and Petty—"

"The Ostermann plantation?"

Roelke looked over his shoulder, surprised. "You know it?"

"The hedges, the pillars? Very la-dee-dah?" Adam studied his work and nodded, satisfied. "This is a good color for this room. Anyway, yeah, I do. We had a call out there...oh, two or three months ago, I guess."

"What happened?"

"Marjorie Ostermann overdosed," Adam said soberly. "Percocet with a whiskey chaser."

"Holy toboggans." Roelke thought of the photograph he'd seen of Marjorie with her husband and son, all wearing their Civil War costumes like a happy family. "Was it deliberate?"

"Who knows? Her husband said she was being treated for back pain, and once we got her to the ER..."

"Yeah." First responders met people in moments of deep personal crisis, and often didn't know how things turned out.

"What were you saying about Petty?"

"When I was leaving the Ostermann place, Petty was about to turn in, then veered off. It seemed odd. Maybe he's sucking up to one of the area's wealthiest families." Roelke climbed down and eased the ladder to the left. "Maybe he wants money for Old World. But *my* chief said he's heard that Petty's political plans go way beyond Village Board." Roelke blew out a gloomy sigh. Ralph Petty already had way too much power.

"That would suck."

"Yes it would."

They both paused to brood about the prospect of Ralph Petty, Village of Eagle Trustee; Ralph Petty, Waukesha County Supervisor; Ralph Petty, Wisconsin Assemblyman … Ugly.

"I don't even want to think about that," Roelke admitted. "Say, you're planning to stay for supper, right? Chloe's bringing a salad." He never knew what he might find hidden under a lettuce leaf—pumpkin seeds, dried currants, minced arugula, some weird unrecognizable heirloom vegetable—but Chloe's salads were always good.

"Thanks. I'd be glad to stay."

"And my cousin Libby is grilling trout. I don't know if you've met her."

"I have, actually. My nephew plays soccer with Libby's son." Adam loaded his roller again. "Is she seeing anybody?"

Roelke carefully stayed focused on his paintbrush. "Not that I know of. And I would. Know, I mean."

"Do you have any objections to me asking her out?"

Roelke considered for about three seconds. Maybe just two. "Nope."

"Okay." Adam put his roller down and backed into the center of the room to survey the wall. "Oh, yeah. This is going to look great."

"I think so," Roelke agreed absently. He was thinking about Libby. She'd been single for a while now, and she deserved a little fun and companionship. Honestly, though, what struck him most was that he'd never considered how lonely his cousin might be.

He and Libby were close. A good cousin would have been on the lookout for a compatible companion for her.

Roelke felt another flicker of shame. Sometimes, he thought, I really suck at taking care of the people I love.

———

Byron—who did not have a meeting on site—waited until he and Chloe were back at Ed House to explode about Petty's autocratic maneuver. "What are we going to do? The only thing I know about the 100th Infantry is that their name did *not* come up when I was making inquiries about reenactment units with high standards."

"This is bad," Chloe agreed. She sat at her desk and put her head down on her arms like an anxious kindergartener.

Instead of doing the kindergarten thing, Byron stalked back and forth. "It's ruined. Our event is *ruined*."

All right, Chloe told herself, that's enough defeatism for now. She sat up straight. "It's not ruined. We can salvage this situation."

"*How?*"

"Well ..." Chloe thought. "Okay, here's what we do. We keep the two units separate. I mean *completely* separate. The twain shall not meet."

Byron didn't stop pacing. "But how can ... "

"The 9th is setting up camp on site, right?"

"Yes. Near the Sanford Farm."

223

"Well, tell the 100th to set up their camp on the Visitor Center green."

"Petty won't go for that. Visitors don't have to buy tickets to see anything on the green."

"Petty won't know until it's too late. He already thinks he's won." Chloe wasn't entirely convinced, but that was her story and she was sticking with it. "Let the 100th do their battle thing at the Visitor Center, and the 9th can help us interpret the Wisconsin homefront on site."

Byron looked doubtful, but made an effort. "Maybe that will work."

And maybe, Chloe added silently, you and I can both get through the weekend without getting fired.

———

Byron soon left for the site. "I always feel better out there," he said. "And Petty can't find me."

Chloe considered going with him. Maybe they'd hear sandhill cranes. Maybe an interpreter at the Ketola Farm was baking *pulla* bread. *Pulla* bread, flavored with cardamom, made any day better. But Belinda was expecting a supervisory visit at the artifact storage trailers.

Ralph Petty sneered in her memory: *I'm not interested in your charity project.*

Chloe was used to Petty baiting *her*, but she hated him all over again for considering her intern with contempt. And all over *again* for tromping on Byron. She thought for a moment, then reached for her directory of state employees.

After making a couple of calls Chloe had two appointments scheduled for Wednesday. She took a few deep cleansing breaths, trying to rid herself of the last of Petty's bad energy. She spent two minutes trying to meditate at her desk, which was as long as she ever lasted. Then she locked up Ed House again, and headed out.

Belinda was waiting at the picnic table by the trailers. "I'm not finished going through the ledgers," she reported, "but I've found some good things." She turned her notebook around to display a growing list of artifacts that could support the Civil War program. "At least... I *think* there are some good things in here."

"Yikes." Chloe studied the report. Belinda had organized her notes into a table:

Location	Theme	Activities	Artifacts
Sanford Farm	Early War Excitement	Ladies' Aid Meeting—sewing housewives, havelocks; packing food in glass tumblers	Crocks, quilts, blankets, chess set, stationery, Bibles, patriotic cockade
Schulz Farm	German-American participation	Linen production, informal debate showing pro-war and anti-war sentiments	Linen shirt, anti-draft poster, German-language newspaper
Kvaale Farm	Economic boon	Wool production—spinning, knitting	Blankets, fleeces

"Is it too much?" Belinda twisted a strand of hair around one finger.

"It is not too much."

"I'll finish today, and then I can type it all up tonight."

"That would be *great*," Chloe said fervently, because Belinda's efforts were a godsend. "I'll meet you here tomorrow morning."

"Before you go, I—I had an idea for my History Day project. I don't know if it's any good."

"Lay it on me."

"*Well*, yesterday my grandfather came over for Sunday dinner, and I asked him about clocks, and he told me about when he had to leave the farm and find work in a factory during the Depression." Belinda's focus softened. "He said the hardest thing about factory work was having to punch a time clock. He thought it was insulting, like the bosses didn't trust the men to get their work done."

Chloe felt her Petty-prickles easing.

"I didn't even know he'd *had* to go work in a factory! But Grandpa said that a lot of the farmers around Palmyra had to get jobs. And for all of them, it was really hard to not be your own boss."

Screw Petty, Chloe thought. *This* was what museum work was all about.

"A time clock is ugly, but ... "

"It's a *perfect* thing to include," Chloe assured her. "It tells an important story about your grandfather, and about the community, and about what was going on in the nation. You've got a trifecta. Remember, an artifact's real power comes from the emotion it represents."

"It's sort of like ... archaeology, almost. Layers."

"That's it exactly."

Belinda headed back inside the trailer to continue scanning the collections ledgers. But something niggled at one corner of Chloe's brain. *Remember, an artifact's real power comes from the emotion it represents ...*

I, Chloe thought, am an idiot. She needed to talk to Roelke, because she'd overlooked something important.

———

Roelke's truck, Libby's car, and a pickup Chloe didn't recognize were in the drive when she arrived at the farm after work that afternoon. She parked and considered resting her forehead on the steering wheel for a while. She was tired, angry at Petty, sad about the two dead reenactors, anxious about the 100th Regiment's addition to the Civil War event, and worried that her job was in jeopardy. Seriously, she thought, I am not up for this.

Then the kitchen door slammed, Justin and Dierdre came running, and the day was suddenly brighter.

"Did you bring the stuff to make the butterfly house?" Justin asked anxiously.

Chloe got out and gestured toward the empty aquarium in the back seat. "We'll get it set up after supper, okay?"

Inside, the kitchen looked suddenly smaller due to the addition of a table and chairs, refrigerator, and stove. "Roelke said to leave everything in the middle until he paints the walls," Justin reported.

"Roelke won't let us help paint," Dierdre added grievously.

"Well, I could use your help. The ginger cream cookies I brought for dessert need to be frosted."

The kids were happily slathering away when Roelke came thumping down the stairs. He gave Chloe a quick kiss before introducing the tall man who'd followed him.

"Good to meet you, Adam," Chloe said. "Bolitho … is that Cornish?"

"It is!" A wide smile lit his face. It was a nice face—narrow but appealing in a rugged sort of way. Deeply tanned skin, and the tiny fan of crinkle lines at the corner of each eye, suggested many hours spent outside, and the muscles in his arms and shoulders suggested a man at ease with manual labor. He had a smudge of moss-green paint on his wrist.

Chloe liked him at once. "Were your ancestors miners?" she began, but caught herself before derailing the agenda with family stories. "Sorry. It's really nice of you to help us out."

More footsteps sounded on the stairs before Libby joined them. "I got the windows taped in the other bedrooms, so you guys can keep going," she said. "I have something to show Chloe."

"Another family heirloom?" Chloe asked hopefully.

"I think so." Libby picked up a flat rectangle wrapped in brown paper and handed it over. "This hung on the wall near my grand-ma's sewing machine."

Chloe loosened the tape, lifted the paper away... and her mouth opened with wonder. "A sampler! Look!" She held the framed piece up for Roelke to admire.

"Very pretty," he agreed politely, before escaping with Adam.

"It's astonishing," Chloe murmured. The obligatory alphabet took up only a narrow space at the top, and different colors of thread had been used for the letters—blue, green, yellow, white. Stitched flowers and birds, each unique, were scattered over the rest of the 18-inch linen square. The scale was off a bit in places, as if each motif had been created by whim, instead of considered as part of an overall design. The resulting piece of folk art was cheerful, inventive, and absolutely charming.

"I knew you'd like it." Libby sounded pleased.

"I *love* it. I just wish... often girls signed and dated their sam-plers. I don't see anything like that." She peered at the edges. "Do you mind if I take it out of the frame? I think it covers a bit of the stitching. We need to reframe this with archival materials anyway."

"Be my guest."

Chloe turned the frame over, gently tore away a layer of brown paper, moved the tiny hinges with her thumbs, and eased the sampler free. The edges folded over the cardboard backing were terribly crushed, and some of the embroidery threads had frayed.

"I think my grandma framed it," Libby said apologetically. "Not so good, hunh."

"There is some permanent damage." Chloe did her best to sound completely nonjudgmental. "I'll stabilize it as best I can. And … ooh, look, it is dated. *May 1862.*"

"Right in the middle of the Civil War."

"Yes, but … " Chloe rubbed her temples. "Samplers like this were generally made by children. Rosina Roelke was married and taking care of a baby by May of 1862."

"Maybe somebody else made it."

Chloe sighed. She wanted to believe that Rosina had made the sampler, so it would have personal meaning for Roelke and Libby and the kids. But she also suspected that Rosina had left the bad energy in the cabin. It broke her heart to think that the young woman who might have stitched this vibrant sampler ended up, it seemed, losing all hope in the future.

TWENTY-FIVE

MAY 1862

Rosina studied the rose petal she'd just completed on her sampler and smiled.

Earlier. that day she'd scraped and scrubbed John's diapers; boiled more water and scrubbed Klaus's spare shirt. She'd spread their bedding on the woven garden fence to air, and planted most of the garden. A little time spent with her embroidery did not seem so great a sin. She'd pulled a bench outside to enjoy this sweet spring afternoon. John cooed in his cradle. Pasque flowers bloomed in the prairie and bluebells bloomed in the woods. Just yesterday she and Klaus had heard the first warbling cries of returning cranes. The air smelled of damp loam and honeysuckle.

A shout came from the road. She waved at Klaus as he turned into the drive. "Papa is home from the neighbor's," she told John. Klaus had walked over to help raise a new stable.

"This is a fine sight to come home to," he called.

Rosina set the sewing aside. "You're home earlier than I'd expected."

"We finished everything but the roof. A thatcher's coming later this week." Klaus sat beside her and leaned against the cabin wall. "One day we'll have a work party here, and raise our own stable."

"That will be splendid," Rosina agreed.

Klaus looked over the farm: wheat field, rye patch, garden. Through the winter he'd girdled oaks and hickories, and once the frost left the ground she'd planted pumpkins and squash among the dying trees. Twice now their neighbor had come with his ox and breaking plow. The prairie sod turned with a great painful tearing sound as roots longer than Rosina was tall were wrenched from the soil. Their pig was now roaming the woods, and by fall would be fat from acorns and hickory nuts.

Rosina cast a sidelong glance at her husband. She'd become attuned to Klaus's stillness, and was thankful for it—more than ever these past weeks, as she'd struggled with motherhood's overwhelming demands. Now she reached up and brushed a lock of blond hair from his forehead.

He turned with a smile. "I brought home a newspaper too." He pulled the much creased and battered German-language paper from a pocket.

Rosina's mouth went dry as she took it.

"Well, there's still plenty of daylight left." Klaus touched John's cheek and left them alone.

Rosina quickly found another story about the Southwestern Expedition, which included the 9th Wisconsin. The correspondent bitterly condemned the leader, Colonel Weir, for "inflicting needless hardships on his men." Weir had marched the troops for many miles without supplies. They'd gone foraging into Indian territory.

He'd been careless with vital communications, allowing them to fall into enemy hands.

It made Rosina heartsick to think of Leopold—and all the other German men who'd left Milwaukee with such patriotic fervor—struggling against Indian attack and harsh terrain and incompetent leadership. "Is the war what you expected?" she whispered. "Are you proving yourself a good American?"

John began to fuss. Rosina gathered him up, unbuttoned her bodice, and held him close. The rhythmic blows of an ax rang through the afternoon as Klaus attacked one of the girdled and dead trees. "Don't worry," she whispered, stroking John's downy black curls. "Klaus isn't going to war. He will raise you to work hard and be industrious. And I will teach you to watch red birds in the snow, and to sing, and to think freely."

Perhaps it was only spring fever, but Rosina felt more hopeful than she had in a long time.

TWENTY-SIX

ROELKE WAS CONTENT WITH the progress they'd made by the time Libby called them down for supper. Adam seemed content too. He complimented Roelke on the work done so far, Libby on the seared trout and green beans, Chloe on the salad and cookies.

"Ginger creams were the Betty Crocker prize recipe in 1929," she told him. "But they wouldn't have been *any* good if Dierdre and Justin hadn't frosted them."

"But when are we going to look for monarch caterpillars?" Justin asked plaintively.

Chloe stood. "How about right now?"

The others watched them cross the yard, heading toward the wild border between woods and field. Dierdre held Chloe's hand. Justin bounded ahead.

Roelke's gut clenched. I can't default on my loan, he thought. It would break the kids' hearts.

Adam's pager buzzed just as Libby was refreshing the iced tea. "Damn," he said mildly. "Murphy's Law of first responders: most calls come at mealtime."

"At least take some cookies with you." Libby folded several into a napkin.

"Thanks!" Adam grinned. "Say goodbye to Chloe and the kids for me." He trotted toward his truck.

"He's a nice guy," Roelke observed.

"He is," Libby agreed. "Speaking of nice, it's terrific of Chloe to spend so much time with the kids."

"She loves them. And I don't think she wanted to help paint."

Libby rubbed at a spot of color on her fingernail. "Not everyone loves to paint."

"I think Chloe's having second thoughts about moving in."

Libby considered, then shook her head. "She wants to move in."

Except that Chloe won't step foot in the cabin, Roelke thought. And she hasn't brought hardly anything over from her own place. But the first thing wasn't his tale to tell, and he didn't feel like getting into the second.

"Talk to her," Libby urged. "Even good relationships take care and attention."

"Do you ever think about it?"

"Think about what?"

"A relationship. Or, you know, going on a date."

"No."

"I think Adam wants to ask you out."

She looked taken aback. "No!"

"He's a good guy, Libby."

"Maybe, but—no."

"You haven't been out since the divorce, have you?"

Libby put a hand on his arm, her gaze stern. "My children will be a *whole* lot older before I could even consider dating."

"That's ridiculous!" he protested. "You are a fantastic mom, but you deserve a life of your own too."

Libby's face settled into intractable lines. "I made a bad choice when I married their dad. How Dan acted, how he continues to act—it's been awful for them. Especially Justin."

Dan Raymo needed a good ass-kicking. If given the chance, Roelke would gladly do it. But he knew better than to say so.

"You are the dependable man in Justin and Dierdre's lives," Libby was saying. "I won't shake things up by bringing a guy around."

"But—"

"No buts. I mean it, Roelke. If Adam wants to ask me out, please tell him not to."

Well, hunh, Roelke thought, not sure how to tell Libby that he'd already encouraged Adam.

He backed out of the conversation instead. "Thanks for your help today," he said, and hugged her.

———

To Chloe's relief, she and the kids found a chrysalis and several caterpillars. They got the terrarium set up with stalks of milkweed before Libby announced it was time to head home.

"Clearly great progress was made today," Chloe said as she and Roelke waved Libby and the kids on their way. The dishes were washed and twilight was smoothing over the farm's rough edges. She loved this time of day. "This place is starting to look like a home."

"Do you really think so?"

Roelke's tone was odd. I should figure out what's bugging him, Chloe thought. And, she should show him the note she'd found in the old Roelke housewife. *Oh, my son, I have killed your father.* But she was tired, and stressed, and simply didn't know how to raise the topic.

Besides, she was also quivering with the suppressed need to talk to him about Private M.

"I do think so," she said lightly, and took his hand. "Do you mind if we talk cop stuff for a few minutes?"

"You want to talk cop stuff?" His eyebrows raised, but he made an open-ended gesture with his free hand. "I don't mind."

"Let's go sit by the Old Oak."

Chloe and Roelke settled down with roots below and limbs above and the ancient trunk at their backs, as if the wise old tree was embracing them, sharing its strength. There was something else here too—a sense of peace and contentment.

Roelke leaned against the trunk, and Chloe leaned against him, and felt ashamed of her petty insecurities. Fireflies blinked. Crickets chirped. A squirrel darted close, dashed off again.

Finally Roelke stirred. "So, what did you want to talk about?"

Right. "First, I need to say how sorry I am about what happened at German Fest." This was the first time they'd been alone together since Steven Siggelkow was killed.

"I've dealt with my share of dead bodies, but I *watched* Siggelkow go down." Roelke rubbed his hands over his face. "And to know that the shooter was there, right *there*, but not being able to spot the guy, and all this going down in the middle of thousands of people, kids ... *God.*"

Chloe couldn't imagine it, didn't want to even try. "It's horrible."

"And last I heard, no arrests had been made." He sucked in a long breath. "How are things at Old World?"

"I'll be glad when our reenactment event is over. Petty's being extra nasty. He invited a second unit to participate without even talking to Byron first. The 100th Wisconsin. Evidently the group has local ties."

"They do."

"How do you know?"

"The unit was started by Gerald and Marjorie Ostermann. Marie told me the Ostermanns were into the Civil War big-time, so I wanted to alert them after Maggie Geddings reported that those Civil War–era tintypes were stolen. I met Marjorie at their house, and Gerald at German Fest."

"Does he seem like a reasonable guy?" Please, she thought. Let him be a reasonable guy.

"He was pleasant enough," Roelke said cautiously.

"Pleasant is good," Chloe said, with equal caution because she was pretty sure Roelke wasn't telling all. "But Byron's furious with Petty for inviting them."

"I almost ran into Petty when I was leaving the Ostermann house. He slowed and signaled to turn into the drive, then veered off."

"That's strange."

"Rumor is that Petty has political aspirations."

Chloe made a disgusted noise. "What political aspirations?"

"Village of Eagle Board, for starters. Maybe County Board … who knows."

"He's got the hubris for anything."

"The Ostermanns are clearly loaded. They don't live in the village, but a lot of things the Board does affect the whole area."

"Petty blathered on at the staff meeting today about good community relations. I do get that, but … " Chloe sighed. "The 100th Wisconsin is not known for authenticity."

"They have a family focus. Some women and kids were at German Fest. The Ostermanns have a teenaged son, Mac, who grew up participating." Roelke pulled a stick from beneath one thigh and tossed it away. "Marjorie said reenacting had been a good thing for the family, but didn't you say the hardcores didn't like families getting involved?"

"I didn't mean to imply that. If there's a group of tents placed discreetly off to the side, no problem. But if the event scenario calls for men to be on campaign, with a battle imminent, it can be jarring to see women in ball gowns serving dinner from huge iron kettles to men lounging in Adirondack chairs. There are always other options."

"At German Fest Mac was pretending to be a photographer."

Chloe shrugged. "It's not surprising that he's developed multiple impressions. If you've done some really awesome national events, it's hard to get excited about camping on the local historical society's lawn during the annual ice cream social."

"So Mac doing his own thing doesn't necessarily reflect a conflict with dad?"

"Not at all. Maybe he got tired of saluting his dad, but he must still enjoy reenacting on some level." She tipped her head, trying to see Roelke's face in the growing shadows. "Why? Is there something wrong?"

"Not that I know of. Mac Ostermann can be surly, but that doesn't mean much. I'm just trying to get a handle on this whole thing. I'm going back to the house tomorrow to see if the photographs he took at German Fest might reveal something."

"How about the Private M case? Did Detective Goresko have any luck following up with the hardcore regiments?"

Roelke sighed. "He hasn't even had time to make the calls."

"How about giving photos to the media?"

"He said he'd wait a week or two. The truth is, things happen fast in Waukesha. Goresko's getting pulled into other investigations."

That didn't surprise Chloe, but it was depressing nonetheless. "Roelke?" She sat up straight and squirmed around to face him. "I think I screwed up."

"How did *you* screw up?"

"When I looked at all of the dead man's belongings, my instinct was to draw a single picture. I sent you guys looking for a hardcore reenactor."

"So?" Roelke rolled an acorn between his fingers.

"So, there are hundreds or even thousands of hardcore reenactors in this country. I was talking to Belinda about clocks today, and—"

"What does a dead reenactor have to do with Belinda and clocks?"

Chloe flapped a hand. "Forget Belinda and clocks. This point is, I think we should focus on specific things that make this particular reenactor unique. The details that suggest emotions."

"Like what?"

"Most of Private M's accoutrements were not unique, but the tintype, the cockade, and the handkerchief were. We need to look for the stories *they* can tell."

Roelke rubbed his chin with thumb and forefinger. "Okay, but … "

"In the Civil War, knapsacks often got left behind somewhere. Maybe with transport wagons while the men were rushed into battle. Occasionally haversacks got left behind too. Well, the same thing can happen at reenactments. In terms of belongings, there's sort of a tier. The man who died at Old World probably carried his least precious items in his knapsack."

Roelke nodded pensively. "Assuming the knapsack belonged to Private M, we know *it* got left behind."

"Right. The distinctive cockade was tucked into the haversack with the food, so keeping it close was more important than the fact that it would get crumpled and dirty."

"Do you have any suggestions for tracking down the person who made it?" Roelke asked.

"I'd like to talk to a couple of old friends who do really good civilian impressions. Would that be okay?"

"Sure."

"The other thing that intrigues me is the tintype. Private M added a pocket to his uniform so he could keep it close, and wrapped it in a special handkerchief."

"You said lots of guys carry photos."

"Yes, but if that tintype *is* an antique, it's the only original thing in his kit. Reproduction tintypes are easy to come by, so why carry an original? Most reenactors would never risk harming a period piece."

A long moment passed before Roelke responded. "I'm not sure how that helps us."

"I'm going to Madison on Wednesday. Do you think Detective Goresko would let me borrow the tintype and show it to an expert at the state historical society?"

"At this point I suspect he'll be glad for any lead you can supply," Roelke said. "I'm going to show it to Maggie Geddings tomorrow, and see if it's the one that disappeared from her house." He sighed.

All right, time to switch topics. "I haven't had a chance to ask about your time at German Fest before Steven Siggelkow got shot. Did anything call to you?"

He hesitated. Then, "No. But I'm glad you suggested sauerbraten. It was delicious."

Chloe couldn't tell if Roelke was still brooding about dead reenactors or if something at the festival had bothered him. "Anything else?"

"Well…"

Chloe waited, giving him time. A whip-poor-will began to call. The oak's limbs stood black against a deep blue sky.

"There was one thing," Roelke said. "I heard a folk group singing that song. The one you said I was humming the other night. I'd swear I never heard the words before, but…"

"But?"

He lifted his palms. "They seemed familiar. I have no idea what they meant, but they still seemed familiar."

Chloe sat up straight. "*Familiar?* Roelke, that's so cool!"

"What is?"

"Genetic memory! Maybe the song sounded familiar because your ancestors used to sing it!"

"Is that like what you experience sometimes? What you feel in certain places, like the cabin?"

"No. That's completely different."

"Is it like what you told me about reenactors? What did you call it… a bubble moment?"

"No. That's completely different too."

He made a frustrated noise, deep in his throat.

"I know it all must sound weird." Chloe snuggled against him, resting her head on his shoulder. "Genetic memory—some people call it ancestral memory—is all about inheriting certain memories. Scientists who study transgenerational epigenetics believe strong emotions can be passed down. Whatever I feel in the cabin didn't come from *my* ancestors, but your memory of that song might have come from yours."

He made another frustrated noise. More like a growl, this time.

"I think what you felt is very special."

"*I* think it's time to call it a day." He kissed the top of her head, displaced her gently, and stood.

Chloe scrambled to her feet too. "So," she said lightly as they headed back toward the house, "if I bought *lederhosen* for you, would you wear them?"

His strides grew longer. "I'd chain myself to the railroad tracks first."

"Okay, no *lederhosen*." Chloe grabbed his hand, tugging him to a stop. "Roelke? I know we're really different in lots of ways." She couldn't help glancing over his shoulder to the old cabin. "But we'll be okay. I really think so."

"I think so too," he said, and kissed her so wonderfully well that she *almost* forgot the doubt in his voice.

————

After she got home, Chloe began making calls. Cockades made in Germanic colors couldn't be *too* plentiful, right?

"I've never been to an event where the men wore red, black, and gold cockades," Lynn Kalil said.

"I remember reading about a period ball in Cincinnati with a German-American theme," Julie McKee said thoughtfully. "Or was it somewhere in Texas? I'm not sure."

"A lady in Pennsylvania commissioned a bonnet with a cockade in those colors once," Beth Turza mused. "I don't know if I can find contact information. That was years ago."

"Thanks," Chloe said, trying not to sound too dejected. Private M's cockade might have had great meaning, but she was no closer to discovering why.

She really wanted Private M to be identified, and Steven Siggel-kow's killer to be arrested, before Old World's Civil War event began. The detectives might not see any link between the deaths, but she felt something inside wind tighter and tighter as the days went by.

So far, Chloe thought, my contributions have added up to absolutely nothing. She hoped Roelke would have better luck with the tintypes.

TWENTY-SEVEN

ON TUESDAY MORNING, MAGGIE Geddings waved Roelke inside. "Glad you caught me before I left," she said. "I work at a bank in Pewaukee."

That meant a half-hour commute. Maybe forty minutes. Roelke got right to it. "The reenactor who died at Old World Wisconsin last Thursday was carrying a tintype of a little boy. I wanted to see if it's the one that was stolen from your home Wednesday night." He displayed the tintype that Private M had carried in his coat pocket.

Maggie needed only a glance. "No."

"You're sure?"

"Positive."

Roelke didn't doubt her. "Thank you," he said. He left with one more piece of information, but no more clarity.

———

Chloe had promised Byron to attend the interpreters' briefing that morning. "If we're going to get more dicey questions about the event," he'd said, "it would be nice if we can present a united front."

Happily, though, no one else questioned the program. Jenny and Lee Hawkins were there, but didn't speak. The other interpreters seemed excited about it.

Just to be sure, she trailed Jenny and Lee as they left the inn. "Got a minute?"

"Sure," Jenny said, although she glanced at the waiting tram.

"I just wanted to make sure you're both comfortable with the Civil War event."

Jenny glanced at Lee with exasperation and affection. "Lee told me about the conversation he had with you and Byron on Sunday."

"I got a bit more wound up than was necessary," Lee admitted.

"You're entitled to your concerns." Chloe paused as several chattering interpreters hurried by. "Especially with your classroom experience."

Jenny took Lee's hand. "It's not all about teaching. Or even the Civil War." She sounded subdued. "Young people like you and Byron remember Vietnam as it affected your peers. Lee and I... well, we remember it as parents. You have no idea how it feels to lose a son in a war that should never have been fought."

"I didn't know." Chloe put a hand on Jenny's arm. "I'm so sorry."

"Thank you. It happened a long time ago." Jenny patted Chloe's hand. "I really need to go." She kissed her husband before climbing onto the waiting tram.

"I'm so glad Jenny has you," Chloe told Lee. He had only a short walk to his building.

"I'm the lucky one." Lee watched the tram pull away. "After my own son died in the war I started hitting the bottle. Then my wife died in a car crash. I was driving."

His voice was flat, but Chloe could hardly bear the pain and grief in his eyes. "Oh, Lee. I'm terribly sorry."

"I sobered up after that. Started working here. That kept me going, but not by much. Then I met Jenny." He smiled and added simply, "She saved me."

Chloe didn't need to ask what Jenny had saved Lee from … depression, loneliness, emptiness, despair.

"Well," Lee said, "I better go open the Sanford house."

Chloe watched him walk away. The Hawkins's tale summoned bad memories of her own … but it also hinted at the power inherent in homefront programming. We can't hide from this stuff, Chloe thought. The Civil War was long past, but if a few visitors felt empowered to discuss their own struggles, she'd know they'd done something good.

———

Roelke drove next to the Ostermann estate. Gerald answered the door. "Officer McKenna! Is there news about Mr. Siggelkow?"

"No news, sir. But I'd still like to see the photographs your son took at German Fest the day Mr. Siggelkow was shot."

"Oh, yes. Of course." He waved Roelke inside before pausing at the foot of the stairs. "Mac?"

No response.

"McClellan!"

A voice drifted down the stairs. "*What?*"

"Come down here, please."

"Why?"

"Because Officer McKenna is here!"

Roelke took in the surroundings while they waited. Gleaming marble floor. Mirror on the wall. Flowers arranged in a ceramic bowl on a fancy little table. The only pedestrian detail was the same brochure he'd seen on his first visit, a trifold advertising an antiques mall—actually several of them, it looked like—printed on the color paper that copy shops called "goldenrod."

Then Mac slouched down the stairs. The young dapper Civil War photographer had been replaced by a sullen teen wearing shorts and a shapeless t-shirt that said *Homestead Highlanders.* His uncombed hair pointed in different directions. His eyes were bloodshot. His feet were bare.

"For God's sake, Mac," Gerald Ostermann hissed. "You look like you just got out of bed!"

Roelke stepped forward. "We're still looking for leads about Mr. Siggelkow's death. The pictures you took with your old-fashioned camera when the 9th was in formation might have caught something that everybody else missed."

"It takes time to capture an image using period methods," Mac said. "I only took one by the lake."

"I'd like to see it," Roelke said pleasantly.

"Of course," Gerald Ostermann said. "This way."

Roelke followed through the kitchen and to a workroom behind the garage. It was surprisingly tidy. A long counter had a sink at one end, and several empty tubs rested upside down. A dozen or more tintypes occupied a table. Books crowded a shelf mounted on one wall. A closed metal cabinet held whatever chemicals or tools were needed.

Mac gestured to a group of tintypes. "Those on the end are from German Fest."

A closer look extinguished Roelke's faint hope. Each picture was focused tight, with no modern intrusions. Which, Roelke realized, made perfect sense. Mac hadn't been taking the historical equivalent of snapshots. He'd been a participant, not a spectator.

"These are great," he said, by way of saving face. "Who taught you how to do this?"

Mac shrugged. "Nobody. We ordered the camera through the mail, and the chemicals and stuff. I did some reading and taught myself."

"My son is very intelligent," Gerald allowed grudgingly.

"Which picture did you take by the lake?" Roelke asked.

Mac stabbed a finger toward an image. "This one. Gunter Diederich was standing real still, looking out over the water, while Kyle talked to the crowd."

Roelke studied the picture. Diederich looked as if he had just staggered from a battlefield. Everything looked *right*. Diederich's expression didn't suggest a modern reenactor waiting for his buddy to stop yakking so he could fire his gun. His expression was ... grim.

Hunh. *Grim?*

Yes, the demonstration was serious business. Yes, discussing war—any war—was serious business. But did those things explain why the leader of the 9th Wisconsin looked so forbidding?

"Officer McKenna?"

Roelke realized the Ostermanns were waiting. "Thanks. I appreciate your help."

Back inside, Mac headed for the stairs as Gerald ushered Roelke to the foyer. "I understand your reenactment unit is participating in a special event at Old World Wisconsin this weekend," Roelke said.

Ostermann looked startled. "Why ... yes."

"Have you worked with Mr. Petty before?"

"Not really. His wife volunteers at the elementary school, and Marjorie and I visit each spring to discuss the Civil War. I suspect that's how he heard about our unit."

"Please give my regards to your wife. Is she at work today?"

"I don't think so."

"You mentioned that she didn't attend German Fest because she was working," Roelke said pleasantly. "She told me last week that she had a family obligation."

"Oh?" Ostermann looked genuinely surprised. It took him a moment to rally. "Well, it was both. I think she visited her sister after work."

"Where does she work?" Roelke asked, even more pleasantly.

Ostermann frowned. "I was under the impression that you came here to see my son's tintypes. Which you have done. Is there a reason you're still asking questions?"

"Just a policeman's habit, I'm afraid. My apologies."

Roelke thought through the exchange as he crept down the long driveway. The tintype of Gunter Diederich was intense. The Ostermann family was dysfunctional. But—once again—the visit had produced not one damn bit of solid information.

So far, Roelke thought, my contributions have added up to absolutely nothing. He hoped Chloe was making progress with the cockade thing. His mood soured as he drove south. It wasn't just cop stuff, it was Chloe stuff. The whole *I can't step into the old cabin* business annoyed him.

Actually, it pissed him off. It had never occurred to him that one of her strange encounters would affect *him*, or the home he was trying to create for the two of them.

And, it had never occurred to him that Chloe would declare that he, Officer Roelke McKenna, was experiencing some voodoo-y thing. That old folk song he'd heard at German Fest was still stuck in his head. Genetic memory, bubble moments, energy lingering through time—that kind of stuff was part of Chloe's world. None of it had anything to do with him.

The things that haunted *him* were actual memories. Buried deep, but all too real.

His radio crackled. "George 220. Are you available to serve a warrant?"

"Affirmative. I'm five minutes from the PD."

"Stop by for details," Marie instructed.

That meant the warrant was a juicy one, and Marie didn't want to enlighten anyone listening in on police scanners. "Will do. George 220 out."

He was grateful for the call. With any luck, he could actually go arrest a bad guy.

———

Chloe tiptoed into Old World Wisconsin's Admin building later that afternoon, hoping like crazy that she could grab her mail, tell the receptionist she'd be out the next day, and get the heck out of Dodge without interference. Instead, Ralph Petty stepped from his office with timing that suggested he'd hidden a surveillance camera over the front door.

Nothing to do but brazen it out. "Hello!" she said with a chipper smile.

He studied her. "Have you made progress on the window measurements?"

"Yes," she lied, without a shred of remorse. "Yes, I have."

"Will you be on site making more progress tomorrow?"

"I'm going to Madison tomorrow."

"Oh?" He smiled without humor. "The clock is ticking, Miss Ellefson."

I know the damn clock is ticking, Chloe growled silently. "I'm taking Belinda to—"

"You're taking the day off to entertain your little intern?"

"I'm taking Belinda to Madison to *help* me. The Veterans Museum is loaning us an artifact for the special event, and we're going to look at newspaper accounts from Palmyra and—"

"Why Palmyra?"

"Because I know that building good relationships with local communities is one of your priorities," she said, quoting what he'd said at the ambush/meeting with Kiki.

Petty failed to find a retort. Hard to argue with yourself, eh? Chloe asked him silently, and left him stewing.

————

Alone at the EPD, his shift long over, Roelke finished his paperwork. The warrant had been for a guy who refused to pay child support to his three ex-wives or ex-girlfriends and their collective seven—*seven*—children. Roelke had found the asshole at a friend's house. Asshole had fled out the back door. Roelke caught him with a flying tackle. Asshole obliged his mood by throwing a punch. Roelke had punched back, cuffed the guy, and hauled his sorry butt to jail.

Now Roelke pulled some index cards from his pocket. When working on an investigation he always used index cards to track details and people and hunches. They were easy to spread out on his desk, easy to rearrange as he played with ideas. He'd already begun making notes, and he shuffled through his *people* cards until he found the one he wanted.

Gunter Diederich
- *Leader of 9th Wisconsin*
- *German unit, hardcore*

Roelke tapped the card with his pen, seeing again Diederich's dark intensity just moments before Steven Siggelkow was killed. What had been going through Diederich's mind that afternoon? Could Diederich have been involved in … in whatever had led to Siggelkow's murder?

- *Connected to Siggelkow's wife in some way?*

Unlikely, Roelke thought. The Milwaukee detectives had quickly discovered Siggelkow's domestic mess. If Diederich had some tie to Siggelkow's wife, the cops would have been all over it.

Okay. Take a different angle. Roelke grabbed a clean card and began to write.

Problems among reenactors:
- *conflict between hardcore authentics and people who don't care about details*
- *conflict over role of women and families in the hobby*
- *anger about "galvanizing"—portraying the other side*

He thought for a moment before adding another line.

- *conflict between units who want to reenact specific groups (ex., Iron Brigade) and those who don't*

Everything he'd noted so far had to do with conflict *between* units. But Diederich and Siggelkow were—had been—members of the same unit. So...what would cause conflict *within* a unit? Two different visions for the group? Quibbles about how authentic was *too* authentic?

Roelke rubbed his temples. Civil War reenacting really was an incomprehensible hobby.

He shuffled until he found his three Ostermann cards: Gerald, Marjorie, and Mac. There was something hinky about that family. And Chloe had nothing positive to say about the Ostermanns' reenactment unit...

You better be very careful, buddy, Roelke warned himself. He could not consider area residents through his girlfriend's filter. That was *exactly* why Chief Naborski discouraged cops from dating locals.

Roelke shoved to his feet and began to pace. This investigation could blow up in his face six ways from Sunday. Ralph Petty had personally invited Gerald Ostermann to bring his reenactment unit to Old World Wisconsin. Petty had already complained about the investigation of Private M's death. Pissing off a potential board member could have repercussions for the entire PD.

Not to mention that Petty had never liked Chloe. Therefore, Roelke thought, Petty does not like me. If he pissed Petty off, the site director would take it out on Chloe. And if Chloe got fired...

But acknowledging Petty's power just pissed *him* off. "The hell with Petty," Roelke muttered. He dropped back into the chair, reached for the phone, and dialed. Dobry answered on the third ring.

"It's me," Roelke said. "Anything new on the Siggelkow murder?"

"Nope." Dobry spoke loudly to be heard over a television in the background.

"Can you do me a favor?"

"Wait a sec." The phone clunked down, and the TV volume went down a few notches. A Brewers game, it sounded like. They'd ended the 1982 season as American League Champions, and fans were psyched for a repeat this year.

"Okay," Dobry said. "What's going on?"

"Remember the Ostermanns from German Fest? See if you can find any record of McClellan Ostermann in Milwaukee. Parents Gerald and Marjorie. I—"

"Hold on ... hold on ... *Damn.* Foul ball."

Sometimes Roelke missed his friend Rick so much his gut ached.

"You there?" Dobry asked.

Roelke wiped a palm over his face. "My clerk said the Ostermanns retired out here from Milwaukee. Mac was wearing a shirt that said 'Homestead Highlanders' today. Does that ring a bell?"

"Nope, but that just means the school isn't in my district." Dobry's voice was almost drowned out by a roar—Roelke couldn't tell if it was of approval or disgust—from the television.

"Are you writing this down?" Roelke asked.

"I am," Dobry said dutifully. "I'll see what I can find."

———

Chloe stopped at the farm on her way home. She lugged two cartons of books and college notebooks inside, shoving them across the floor with one foot, and she hauled a suitcase filled with winter clothes upstairs. *There.* Her mountain dulcimer was the only thing left in the Pinto.

She went back outside just as late sun slanted through some clouds, as if blessing the landscape. "This is a sweet old place," she murmured. Maybe she could talk Roelke into getting a woodstove.

Maybe they could raise some chickens. Just a few. She liked Araucanas, which laid lovely blue eggs.

Chloe wandered to the garden. She admired her rows of carrots and onions, spoke encouragingly to the lone blossom on her lone cucumber plant, and spent twenty minutes pulling weeds.

But she couldn't ignore the cabin hunched just beyond the fence. She needed to discover the source of its dark energy.

The clock is ticking, Miss Ellefson.

She slapped her palms against her chinos and stood. Rehearsing what she wanted to say, she approached the cabin and opened the door.

"Rosina," she began, "I found the note you hid in the housewife." She widened her stance, bracing herself against waves of profound sadness. No, something much bleaker than that. Hopelessness.

Chloe clenched her fists. "Rosina, if there's some way I…" The hopelessness quivered in her chest, threatening to fill her. "*Dammit.*" She bolted and didn't look back as she retreated to her car. "I tried," she told Roelke, wherever he was.

She grabbed her dulcimer and retreated to the Old Oak. The instrument was a treasured memento from her West Virginia years, light and portable, with graceful curving lines. After settling it in her lap and checking the four strings' tuning, she played "Wayfaring Stranger" and "The Cuckoo," favorite folk tunes the Scots-Irish had brought to the Appalachians. The bad energy seeped away. A towhee called. The air held the sweet mustiness of new-cut hay.

Then, without conscious thought, her fingers found the notes of another folk tune—the German melody Roelke had hummed.

TWENTY-EIGHT

Rosina sat beneath the Old Oak, softly strumming "Heidenröslein" on her zither. The lyrics were melancholy, but the song transported her back to the *Fair Wind*.

> *Said the boy, "I'll pick thee,*
> *Heathrose fair and tender!"*
> *Said the rosebud, "I'll prick thee,*
> *So that thou'lt remember me,*
> *Ne'er will I surrender!"*
> *Rosebud, rosebud, rosebud red,*
> *Heathrose fair and tender!*

John, who'd been sleeping placidly on a folded quilt beside her, began to fret in his sleep—*eh, eh, eh*—as if he knew she was thinking of his father. "Hush, my son," she whispered. "Soon I must go make squirrel stew for supper, but it's so pleasant here. Let's linger."

John quieted. A towhee called. The air held the sweet mustiness of new-cut hay. A breeze stirred the prairie, and if she squinted her eyes, the rippling grasses almost looked like the sea.

She didn't try to stop thinking about Leopold anymore. Did he think of the voyage too? Had he counted the months and imagined her giving birth in another man's cabin? Or had he, after her surrender, plucked another flower?

Many would say that he'd taken advantage of her. But Rosina could not regret her hours with him. She treasured her memory of the night that northern lights danced across the sky. Now he'd given her John, a forever gift.

A wagon rattled into view, kicking up a cloud of dust. Rosina scrambled to her feet. Klaus, who'd been hauling deadwood from the field, joined her. Sweat soaked his linen shirt and slicked his hair to his forehead. "It's Adolf," he said, shielding his gaze with one hand.

Rosina felt a ripple of foreboding as the wagon pulled in. "I've come to fetch you," Adolf told Klaus. "The government is going to register men for a draft. My brother is organizing a meeting at his place."

Klaus looked away, across the prairie. Finally he nodded. "I'll wash up."

"I'll get my shawl," Rosina said. And spare linen for John, and—

Klaus put a hand on her arm. "You should stay here."

"*Please.*" Rosina kept her tone low, so as not to embarrass him in front of Adolf. But she needed to know what the German men were saying.

And her kind husband acquiesced, as he almost always did. "Very well," he said. "Fetch your things."

"This is an outrage!" Adolf's brother Franz strode back and forth on his threshing floor. His grain barn was the only space large enough to accommodate the crowd that had assembled by early evening. "Good German men can not respect this immoral edict."

Rosina, who'd crawled into the straw off to one side with the other women, took comfort from John's baby scent and the soft warmth of his skin. Lottie shifted so their shoulders touched, as she sought comfort too.

Herr Muehlenberg pounded his knee. "This is not the America we were promised!"

"I will not be sent to war like a hog to slaughter!" a young man declared. His sweetheart began to weep.

"I left my parents to face old age alone so I would *not* be forced into military service in my homeland," another farmer muttered.

Klaus stood leaning against one of the barn's massive support beams, arms folded. "There may not even *be* a draft," he reminded them. "If Wisconsin can meet its allotment with volunteers—"

"Forty-four thousand more men, by mid-August!" Adolf retorted. "The government officials must think that unlikely, or they wouldn't be demanding that Governor Salomon register every man between eighteen and forty-five."

And what will become of the wives and children left alone? Rosina wondered.

Good neighbors will provide help and comfort to those left at home.

The memory of Leopold's blithe assurance suddenly made her angry. What did Leopold know? He was not poor. He was not trying to create a farm from forest and prairie with little more than a grub hoe and axe. He had no family. For all of Leopold's worldliness, his experience, his years … he sometimes acted like a child.

A grumble rose from the men. "If an enrolling officer comes to my house, I shall refuse to give my name!"

"Well, *I* will run out the back door … "

"I'll register, but if drafted I will not go … "

A short man with dung-caked shoes waved his arms. "My cousin, who lives near Lake Michigan, says the German men of Port Washington and Manitowoc and nearby communities will respond to a draft with force."

"Heaven protect us," Lottie whispered. She rocked baby Gerhard.

A blond man stepped from the shadows. He wore a fine frock coat and brocaded vest, and did not have dung on his shoes. "My friends! I beg your indulgence to speak." He pulled a pipe from his pocket, as if intending to smoke while his friends decided whether to honor his request.

Franz muttered to the man, who quickly slid the pipe away. A Free Thinker? Rosina wondered. Farmers knew better than to strike a match in a grain barn.

"Herr Grünhagen is an attorney-at-law," Franz called. "I value his counsel. Let him speak."

Rosina wasn't feeling kindly toward well-educated men.

"I am thirty-nine years old," Herr Grünhagen began, "and ill prepared to survive the rigors of army life. If I am drafted, I will hire a substitute to serve in my place. The going price is three hundred dollars."

Rosina's mouth dropped open. Klaus met her gaze and slowly shook his head. Three hundred dollars was a fortune.

"You're the only man here who can afford that, Grünhagen," Herr Muehlenberg snapped.

"Perhaps so," Herr Grünhagen agreed. "Which is why we must act as a group."

Adolf stroked his beard. "What are you proposing?"

"That we create our own insurance company. Each man who participates will invest a small sum. If he is drafted, the insurance company will pay for a substitute."

"How much is 'a small sum'?" someone asked.

Herr Grünhagen spread his hands. "I can't say until we know if Wisconsin fails to meet its quota for new enlistments, and by how many men. Once we do know, I am willing to do the calculations, and prepare legal papers to form the company."

More talk surged through the group. "Seems fair … "

"That could work … "

"By God, it's the best chance we have."

"I'd like interested men to sign my ledger as a pledge of intent," the attorney continued. "If you know other men who wish to participate, send them to my office in Watertown."

He produced a leather-bound ledger, pen, and inkwell from a satchel. Franz lowered his wagon's backboard to serve as desk, and men jostled into line. Adolf and Franz were the first to sign Herr Grünhagen's book.

Klaus looked at Rosina with a helpless expression. This isn't fair, Rosina thought. Most of these men had arrived in Wisconsin with a few resources, as Adolf Sperber had; or been here longer, as Franz Sperber had. Klaus had arrived in America with nothing.

Klaus stayed where he was until almost all of the other men had signed the ledger. Finally he pushed himself erect and joined the line. He paused after gripping the pen, but signed his name. Then he came to join her.

"You chose to sign," she observed.

"I do not wish to fight," he said wearily.

America has opened its shores to us. When war is declared, I will fight to defend it.

Rosina didn't know what to think. She was terrified that Klaus might be drafted, but even now wished he spoke of this country's need. She was furious with Leopold for holding this American war more dear than anything else, but even now proud of him too.

"It is done, then," she told Klaus. He nodded.

Rosebud, rosebud, rosebud red,
Heathrose fair and tender...

TWENTY-NINE

CHLOE WAS STILL STRUMMING the German tune when Roelke turned into the drive. He met her with a grin. "You brought your dulcimer!"

"I did." She leaned in for a kiss and was breathless before he released her. "My dulcimer. Right."

"Do you want to hang it in the living room?"

"That would be nice."

In the newly painted living room, he pointed at a narrow space beside the front door. "How about there?" He got a hammer and nail, and did the deed.

Then they sat on the front steps. Chloe leaned against him and let his strength flow into her, and sent her own on to him, while shadows crept across the lawn.

For a while he seemed content too. Finally he stirred. "I showed Private M's tintype to Maggie Geddings, but she'd never seen it before. Also, Goresko said you can take it to the historical society tomorrow."

"Maybe we'll learn something." As unlikely as that seemed. She rubbed her thumb at a bit of peeling paint on the railing. "How was your day?"

"Frustrating," he admitted morosely. "As I'm sure *you* would have known, Mac did not snap half a dozen crowd shots, one of which miraculously included somebody pointing a gun at Steven Siggelkow."

Chloe took one of his hands in hers. It was strong and solid.

"Sorry." He rolled his shoulders. "Mac took just one photograph when the 9th was by the water, focused on Gunter Diederich. The look on Diederich's face was … I don't know … intense. Grim, even."

"Maybe he was just in character."

Roelke didn't look convinced. "I know different units don't always get along, but maybe we should look for trouble *within* the unit. Maybe whoever killed Steven Siggelkow was a member of the 9th—"

"No."

"—who didn't participate, and came to German Fest in modern clothes. Or maybe the killer was connected to somebody else in the 9th."

"I *really* don't think so."

"I have to consider it," he insisted. "What might cause conflict within a reenactment group?"

She let go of his hand. "All the usual stuff you see in any hobby group. Personality clashes." She thought back. "Sometimes guys get frustrated if they don't get promoted. There aren't a whole lot of opportunities for advancement in a company that can only field twenty guys."

"Siggelkow seemed nervous when Diederich and I met him in the parking lot," Roelke mused. "I thought it was because I was a cop, and because somebody had died, and because he'd missed an important meeting. But maybe he had some beef with Diederich."

"Then why would Gunter Diederich have invited Steven to attend the meeting in the first place? Gunter could have come alone, or invited somebody else."

Roelke tapped his thumbs against his knees. "Maybe Diederich was trying to keep an eye on him. If he's in charge, why invite anybody else at all?"

Chloe was liking this conversation less and less. "I don't know! Maybe … maybe he doesn't want to be seen as a little Napoleon, making all the decisions by himself."

"Which would be important if there was some resentment simmering within the unit. And if Siggelkow was part of a faction that resented Diederich, inviting him would be good strategy on Diederich's part."

"I think we're way off track here."

"You're the one who told me about all the politics that can crop up in reenacting."

"Yes, but … " She sighed. But I've met Gunter Diederich, she thought, and I like him.

"Can you sound out Kyle about friction in the unit?"

"*Me?*" Chloe stared at him. "I don't want to. Besides, don't you think the Milwaukee detectives already asked these questions after Steven was shot?"

"I'm sure they did, but I don't know if they got honest answers. The reenactors had just seen one of their own killed. They were in shock. Sometimes that makes people shut down—maybe to protect themselves, maybe to protect their friends."

"I suppose."

"Most of the detectives' attention will be focused on Siggelkow's marital mess. But if there are problems within the 9th, we need to know."

"You question Kyle, then."

"He'll be a lot more likely to confide in you."

"I don't want to," Chloe said again. She was tired of thinking about dead reenactors. Tired of trying to figure out how to do her job without antagonizing her lunatic boss. Tired of trying to navigate the complexities of moving into her boyfriend's family farm when she couldn't step foot into the original cabin without freaking *out*.

Roelke didn't say anything.

"Oh, all *right*," Chloe said grumpily. "I'll talk to Kyle before I go to Madison tomorrow."

———

Chloe still felt grumpy as she drove to work the next morning. She arrived at the Norwegian gate an hour before the site opened, but she'd decided she might as well measure a few windows. It was Wednesday; Petty was expecting her report by Friday. Fortunately there were only three exhibits in the Norwegian area—the Raspberry School, the Kvaale Farm, and the Fossebrekke Farm.

She'd finished the first two and had just let herself into Fossebrekke when the tram arrived with the Norwegian interpreters. Kyle walked into the yard with a cloth sack over one shoulder that probably held his lunch, and a dead squirrel in one hand.

Chloe stepped to the door. "Hey, Kyle."

"Hi." His smile was dimmer, but still engaging.

Lucky Alyssa. Chloe stepped inside, and he followed. "Squirrel stew today?" By 1845 Gertrude and Knud Fossebrekke had accomplished much, but game would still be a welcome addition to their diet. Nothing telegraphed "subsistence" to visitors like a small carcass in a big skillet.

"Yep." He put the squirrel and his bag down on the table.

"Well, I won't be in your way for long. I'm measuring windows because we hope to apply a film that filters UV light on the glass."

"Awesome." Kyle began sweeping the floor.

Chloe got busy with tape measure, clipboard, and pencil. "So, will you be working here this weekend? It would be a shame if you couldn't participate in the event with your 9th Wisconsin pards."

"I traded days so I can fall in with the guys this weekend."

"I'm *so* sorry about what happened at German Fest. I know you and Steven were friends."

"We were," Kyle said simply. "He was a great guy."

"Gunter seems like a good leader, so I imagine he's recruited good men." That sounded forced and awkward, and she hid a wince. She *hated* this.

"He has, yeah." Kyle stepped to the door and emptied the dust-pan outside.

"I used to do some reenacting. I loved everything but the politics." She stretched her measure across a pane of bubbled glass. "Does everybody in the 9th get along?"

"Yes! The cops in Milwaukee asked us that over and over, like they thought one of *us* shot Steven. But nobody in the 9th could have been involved. *Nobody.*"

Chloe was horrified to see tears streaming down Kyle's cheeks. She dropped the measure and folded the young man into a hug. "I'm so, so sorry."

After a moment of sniffling and snuffling, Kyle pulled away and swiped at his cheeks. "We'll do Steven proud this weekend."

"I know you will."

"The 9th is one of the best units around."

"That's what I've heard."

"I've only been involved for a couple of years, but my impression is improving. I've started collecting period images from the 1860s. Mostly I can only afford CDVs and tintypes, although I do have one daguerreotype in a really cool case."

Chloe wished Kyle hadn't mentioned his collection. This whole mess really was careening wildly out of control.

Kyle blew his nose. "I love old photos, don't you? We can learn so much from them." He was obviously struggling to meet her historian-to-historian. His grief, and his passion, wrenched her heart.

"There is indeed," Chloe said weakly. She finished her task quickly, and left the cabin just as Kyle began to skin the squirrel. A pox on Roelke for asking me to do this, she thought darkly. And a—a curse to hell on whoever killed Steven Siggelkow.

———

Chloe drove from the Norwegian area to the collections storage trailers. As she parked beneath the pines, Belinda stepped outside. "Can I show you something?"

Chloe couldn't tell if the girl was excited or distressed. "Um ... sure."

Belinda had been pulling the objects she'd identified for display during the Civil War event—no small task, given the disorganized state of the trailers. Tissue covered the counters and small table.

"Look at *this*." Belinda pointed at a flat bottle made of thick green glass, with an elaborate decorative design cut into the surface. A century of dust and grime had wedged a metal stopper into the neck. "A Wisconsin soldier carried this to war."

"*Very* cool."

"It still has something in it!" Belinda pulled on cotton gloves, gingerly picked up the bottle, and gave it a tiny shake. Liquid sloshed inside. "Do you suppose it might be quinine? Quinine was used to treat malaria. It came from the bark of the cinchona tree, which grows mostly in South America. During the Civil War the Confederacy was so desperate for quinine that agents tried to smuggle it across Union lines."

"I did not know that."

"And here's what it says in *Wisconsin Women in the War*." Belinda opened the book to a marked page. "'Occasionally some careful mother or wife would add a small bottle of cayenne pepper, or package of court-plaster, or perhaps a bottle of quinine, which was thought at that time to be a panacea for all the ills the flesh was heir to.' So I thought … we could maybe include a few medicinal things in the display at Sanford."

Chloe was growing more fond of her intern by the day. "That will be a perfect addition."

Belinda actually smiled.

"Now, though, grab your purse. We're going to Madison."

"We're … what?" Belinda's smile faded. "Don't we have to take these things out to the site?"

"We'll worry about that tomorrow," Chloe said. Evidently all this Civil War stuff had her channeling Scarlett O'Hara. "I'm grateful for all the extra hours you've been giving. You deserve a day out."

"But … " Belinda fretted her lower lip between her teeth. "I didn't get the car today, so my dad's coming to pick me up at five."

"We'll be back by five," Chloe promised, and cocked her head toward the door. "Let's go."

———

Roelke was recording the speeding ticket fee received from a sulky teen when the EPD phone rang. Marie took the call, then swiveled in her chair. "It's for you."

He punched the blinking light on his phone. "Officer McKenna."

"It's Dobry. I found something. Mac Ostermann was arrested for larceny in Milwaukee about eighteen months ago."

"What did he steal?"

"I haven't seen the report yet, just talked to a guy I know." Dobry snorted with disgust. "Probably something stupid, snatched by a rich kid who thinks he's entitled."

"Or maybe he was bored."

"Or both. Hold on."

Roelke heard a muffled conversation. Then Dobry came back on the line. "Gotta go. I'll call when I get more info." The line went dead.

Roelke replaced the receiver. Well, hunh. He was eager to learn more about McClellan Ostermann's arrest record. His fingers drummed a quick beat on the desk. *Very* eager.

Relax, he told himself. Dobry would call when he could.

Trouble was, Roelke was royally tired of waiting for the phone to ring. Milwaukee cops like Dobry never had downtime. Waukesha detectives like Goresko didn't have much downtime either.

Well, Roelke thought, I *do*. One benefit of being a village patrolman. There was no reason—no good reason, anyway—why he couldn't fly under the radar and do some legwork on his own.

THIRTY

THE STATE HISTORICAL SOCIETY of Wisconsin was located in the heart of Madison, Wisconsin's capital city. Chloe loved the society building—the worn marble stairs, the gleaming wood in the Reading Room, the immeasurable treasures held within. Incessant budget cuts had worn the staff to a collective frazzle, but the society's founders had created a collection of national importance, and erected a building worthy of housing it.

Belinda was in awe. Chloe took her to the microforms room and showed her how to thread reels of old newspapers on big readers. "Look for references from Palmyra and Watertown," Chloe said. "Watertown had a huge German population. If there's time we'll look at other communities too." Hey, they had to start somewhere. If something that illuminated Klaus and/or Rosina Roelke's experience happened to turn up, so much the better.

Once Belinda was happily scrolling away, Chloe climbed to the iconographic collections on the fourth floor. She gave her name to the student worker/gatekeeper. "Faye is expecting me."

Three minutes later she and Faye, one of the curators, sat at an empty worktable and donned gloves. Chloe removed Private M's tintype from its acid-free cocoon. "This is on loan," she said carefully. "It looks like an original to me, but I'd like your opinion."

Faye studied the tintype. She was forty-ish, with heavy black glasses, dark hair, and an air of intense scrutiny that made Chloe confident she'd come to the right place.

Finally Faye straightened. "I'm not sure."

So much for coming to the right place.

Faye pulled a small magnet from her pocket and let it click against the back of the tintype. "A lot of the forgers don't even realize that the images were processed on thin sheets of iron, not actually tin."

Score one for authenticity.

Faye squinted at the image through a loupe. "The kid's clothing and haircut look right."

"I thought so too."

"Contrast is good. Nice gradation between black and gray. All originals have a continuous tone." She turned the tintype over. "The back looks right. Almost every original tintype has a japanned black back, or occasionally darkish brown. But nothing over that. The fakes floating around often have some kind of shiny coating."

"Right," Chloe said, because she didn't want to sound like a rube.

"There's no bogus weathering. You know, the kind of thing you see when somebody scrapes the tin with sandpaper, or bangs it with a hammer."

The very thought of someone abusing this sweet image made Chloe's toes curl.

"*But*, my gut says it's new."

Chloe chewed that over. Although humbled by her own erroneous call, she decided she was glad Private M had not incorporated a precious original into his impression. Still, she was curious. "Why do you think it's a repro?"

"The tone is just a bit off. See this hint of blue?"

"Um … not really," Chloe admitted.

"After you study thousands of tintypes, you just get a sense of what they should look like. Photographers used potassium cyanide as a fixer to get a good tone, as light as possible. This tone is very good, but not *quite* what I'd expect. Still … " Faye took off her glasses, rubbed her eyes, replaced the glasses. "I could be wrong. The science of forgery is improving all the time."

"I don't think this was meant as a forgery," Chloe protested mildly. "It was originally owned by a reenactor. People in the hobby reproduce such things for educational purposes." She was well aware that many scholars and curators within these hallowed halls believed the good work done at historic sites—and, by extension, reenactments—was all pseudo-history. Their contempt made her crazy.

"Have you shown this to anyone at the Veterans Museum?" Faye asked.

"I'm going there this afternoon." Chloe repackaged the tintype. "Thanks for your help."

In the hall she paused, considering. She'd thought Private M had chosen an evocative original photograph to represent a child waiting for his soldier-father to come home from the war. But, now that she was focusing on the meaning of specific items, it seemed likely that Private M had his own earnest little boy. A son who, right this minute, was probably wondering why his papa hadn't come home.

That child had heartbreak in store, but he deserved to know the truth. We're trying, Chloe told him silently. We won't give up until we know who Private M, and *you*, are.

Before rejoining Belinda, Chloe trotted downstairs to the library stacks. She grabbed a fat Jefferson County history published in 1898, the kind paid for by stalwart local men who were rewarded with nice biographical sketches. Chloe found listings for Klaus and Rosina Roelke's sons: John, born March 17, 1862; and Andreas, born April 27, 1863. That confirmed what had been recorded on the wedding certificate.

There was no entry for Klaus, but that was not surprising. Based on the cryptic and disturbing note that had been hidden in the housewife—*Oh, my son, I have killed your father*—Chloe was pretty sure that Klaus had died during the Civil War. Whether he'd met his demise by a Confederate musket ball, a deadly case of measles, or a farm accident remained unknown.

John Roelke had been quite the proverbial community pillar: successful farmer, deputy sheriff, school board member. The same was true for Andreas: successful farmer, church trustee, etc., etc. But the old white guy/compiler had not even mentioned their wives or children.

Misogynistic biographers of the past also made Chloe crazy.

One of those sons had fathered the line that had led to the man she loved. But she was out of time today, so further investigation would have to wait.

She tugged a reluctant Belinda from the microforms room, and they grabbed a late lunch at one of the food carts on the library mall. Then they walked up State Street to the state capitol building, which housed the Wisconsin Veterans Museum. There Chloe introduced herself and Belinda to Richard, the museum director. "It's kind of you to meet with us."

"I'm working on the latest proposal for a museum proper," Richard said. "We desperately need more space"—he gestured around the cramped quarters—"and it looks like we might get a big new building on the capitol square, but the budget process is excruciating. I need distraction."

Chloe settled her heavy totebag on the floor. "As I explained on the phone, Old World Wisconsin is holding a Civil War event this weekend, which will include a special focus on German-American participation. We're working with the 9th Wisconsin reenactment unit."

Richard smiled. "Want to see the flag of the original 9th Wisconsin Infantry Regiment?"

Belinda's eyes went wide. Chloe tried to nod with professional decorum. It's rewarding to give Belinda this kind of experience, Chloe told herself—but honestly, the invitation made her woozy.

The flags were stored flat in a special cabinet. "Civil War flags are among our most precious artifacts," Richard said. "They represented everything the men were fighting and dying for." The 9th's regimental flag was a blue field with a state seal in the center, and *9th Wis. Vet. Vol. Infantry* inscribed in gold on a scarlet banner. Chloe and Belinda stared in hushed silence.

Finally Richard slid the drawer back into place. "I can't loan you the flag, but I do have the drum ready to go." He led them to a table crowded with artifacts presumably in the process of being accessioned, cleaned and stabilized, studied, or considered for donation. At one end sat a cylindrical tin drum, perhaps 16 inches tall, mounted upright on a wooden stand.

"That is simply *awesome*," Chloe exclaimed. "See, Belinda? It's a draft drum."

"By July of 1862, people realized that the war would not end quickly," Richard explained. "Wisconsin was told to supply an additional forty-four thousand troops. Most counties were able to meet their quotas with volunteers, but some German Democrats were vehemently opposed to military service."

"I've read about that." Belinda studied the drum. "How did this work?"

Richard opened an archival box and displayed a number of small wooden discs. "These served as ballots. Each was numbered, see? Provost marshals wrote the name of an eligible man on each. The discs went in the drum, and … "

Chloe flashed on Roelke's description of the small wooden "disc things," once used as stand-in tiddlywinks, recently stolen from Maggie Geddings's home. Not store tokens, as she, Chloe-the-curator, had suggested, but draft tokens. And if somebody made a point of stealing them, she thought, he or she is pretty damn knowledgeable about Civil War–era material culture …

She realized that Richard and Belinda were looking at her. "Sorry. May I take a picture of those?"

Once Chloe's Polaroid picture emerged from the camera she put it aside to develop. "I really appreciate you loaning the drum to us. I promise it will either be locked somewhere secure or in my sight." Taking responsibility for the draft drum made her queasy, but what it would add to the programming—not to mention the look on Byron's face when he saw the surprise—gave her the fortitude to sign the necessary paperwork.

"May I have another moment of your time?" Chloe asked, unwrapping Private M's tintype. "I'm trying to determine if this is an original. Even the society expert isn't sure. Anything about the boy's appearance look off to you?"

Richard took a close look before shaking his head. "No. I could tell you more if he was a drummer boy. I'm not an expert on civilian clothes."

Chloe glanced over her shoulder. Belinda had wandered away to gaze upon other treasures. "I also have a couple of artifacts that came down in a friend's family." Another small box, another unwrapping of archival tissue. "I've never seen a Civil War housewife in such good condition, have you? But the fabrics are definitely period."

"That is a nice one," Richard agreed. "I doubt it ever saw service."

"And then there's this." Chloe pushed back a corner of tissue paper and pointed at the ring.

Richard fetched a magnifier and pulled on gloves. He studied the ring, turning it this way and that. "This is a fabulous piece. The ring was carved from a hard rubber coat button. The inlay is likely German silver, and while the clasped hands are very nice, if you look closely you can see some inconsistencies. This might well have been made by a soldier."

The thought that Roelke's ancestor might have painstakingly *made* this lovely ring made Chloe shiver with delight. "Yikes."

"Do you have the soldier's name and unit?"

"Klaus Roelke, from Jefferson County. A patriotic envelope labeled *9th Wisconsin* was with the ring, but I haven't had a chance to check service records."

"Hold on." Richard disappeared into his office, and returned with an enormous old book. "*The Roster of Wisconsin Volunteers* was compiled in 1886. This volume covers the 9th Wisconsin."

Chloe quivered with anticipation as Richard ran his finger down the columns, page after page. Finally he shook his head. "Sorry. There's no Klaus Roelke in the 9th."

"Are you sure?" Chloe asked, which was a stupid thing to say to the director of the Wisconsin Veterans Museum, but she'd really expected a different outcome. My historical hunches are increasingly lousy, she thought.

"He may have joined the 26th Wisconsin," Richard mused. "*Unser Deutsches Regiment*—Our German Regiment. But he could have—"

"Richard?" A student worker leaned into the room. "Someone from the governor's office is on the phone."

"Obviously I need to take that," Richard said. "Good luck with your event. I've had the 9th guys here. They're good. And one of your interpreters has spent hours studying our Civil War photographs." Richard adjusted his glasses with one finger. "Kyle Fassbender. That young man has the makings of an expert iconographer."

"Isn't that nice?" Chloe managed.

But it wasn't nice, not at all. She *might* have chosen to "forget" mentioning what Kyle had said that morning about collecting period images. If Kyle had graduated from picking up cheap CDVs from rural antiques stores to studying the Veterans Museum collection, though ... that needed to be reported to Roelke. Who would instantly consider the nice young man a suspect for something. Shit.

And, instead of gaining even a hint of insight into what happened to Klaus and Rosina Roelke during the Civil War, she was more confused than ever. Why had an envelope from the 9th been passed down in the family if Klaus had not served in that unit?

THIRTY-ONE

SEPTEMBER 1862

"Thank goodness you're fast." Frau Muehlenberg took the flannel shirt from Rosina's hands. Lottie was hosting the German ladies' aid society meeting, but Frau Muehlenberg was a general at heart. "The cutters have outpaced the stitchers."

"Then I best start another."

The women working the shears had gathered in the kitchen. "…not fair of the Sanitary Commission to insist we send our aid supplies to them," one grumbled as Rosina approached. "I want to help *Unser Deutsches Regiment.*"

"The Commission gets supplies to whomever needs them most," another countered.

Rosina gathered pieces for another shirt and retreated to the front porch. She and Lottie had spent the afternoon sewing shirts from the yards of pale blue flannel donated by wealthy Watertown merchants. No one stitched foolish havelocks or fancy cockades now. The Watertown ladies hoped to complete five hundred shirts before winter, and the German women were doing their part.

"I'm eager to help with war work," Rosina murmured. "But ... after the gathering in Franz's barn last month, it seems strange."

"The men we're helping *chose* to enlist," Lottie reminded her. "Adolf and Klaus have every right to choose differently." She made a knot and snipped her thread. "They'll bring news back from the *Viehmarket.*"

The air held a tang, and Rosina snugged her shawl closer around her shoulders as she settled back to work. Autumn was well upon them. But this winter will be better, she thought. Klaus had finished her loom and weaving shed. *And* he'd purchased a glass window.

Rosina had gotten one arm set into her shirt by the time Adolf drove into view. Klaus sat beside him, hat pulled down against the sun. The women waved as their men turned into the drive and disappeared toward the barn.

Rosina finished her seam, folded the flannel pieces, and tucked them into her basket. "I'll see if John is awake. Klaus will be eager to start for home." They had a long walk ahead of them.

Adolf stepped onto the porch. "Rosina? Klaus wants to see you in the stable."

Rosina felt the afternoon pause, suspended at the crest of a wave rising between her past and her future. "What's wrong?"

Adolf shook his head, not meeting her gaze. Lottie was wide-eyed with alarm.

Rosina lifted her skirt and hurried to the stable. Klaus waited inside. Standing, just standing. In the dim light she could not read his expression. "What is it?" she cried. "Have they announced a draft?"

"You have mail."

"Mail?" Rosina echoed, bewildered. She never had mail.

Klaus pulled some folded linen cloth and an envelope from his satchel, and thrust them into her hands. The envelope was addressed to Rosina Lauterbach, Palmyra, Wisconsin. It was decorated with an American flag, a Union soldier, and a bald eagle, all printed in bright blue and red ink. The bald eagle held in its beak a flowing banner printed with *9th Wisconsin Infantry Regiment* in elaborate script.

Rosina's mouth went dry as flax tow. She became acutely aware of the mingled smells of sweaty horse and dried manure, the dust motes visible in the sun slanting in the door, the restless stomp of a hoof and a peal of childish laughter drifting from the yard. And her husband's utter, absolute stillness.

With shaking fingers she unfolded the linen, knowing even before she saw the letters—*LZ*, embroidered in scarlet—that she held the shirt she'd made for Leopold.

"I saw the mail carrier in Watertown. He was on his way to Palmyra, but since the only Rosina he knew was Rosina *Roelke*, he asked me about it." Klaus's voice was flat. "When I explained, he gave those things to me. The wrapping had been damaged."

"Klaus…"

"Read the letters."

The envelope's sealing wax was broken. Inside were two pieces of paper, each folded. She opened the first.

February 6th, 1862

My dear, sweet, Röslein,

She skipped to the signature: *Leopold.*

She couldn't bear to read Leopold's words in front of Klaus. After crushing the page back into the envelope, she removed the second letter.

July 17th, 1862

To Rosina Lauterbach,

It pains me greatly to introduce myself with grievous news.

Somewhere, a red bird stopped singing. Somewhere, a wild rose withered. Somewhere, the northern lights dimmed.

Leopold Zuehlsdorff, whom I believe was a special friend of yours, died of dysentery this morning...

Rosina's knees buckled. She sagged against the wall, then slid to the floor. *Dysentery.* A ragged sob came from some place deep, deep inside. Another came, and another, until she thought she might be sick.

Klaus stood silent.

Finally she managed to raise her head. "You—you read these."

"I did."

Another wagon rattled into the yard outside. Adolf's horse stamped one foot.

"So." Rosina licked her lips. "Now you know."

"I have always known." Klaus walked past her, and out the door.

————

Afternoon faded to evening. Rosina stayed in the stable, cradling the linen shirt.

Finally Lottie stepped inside. "Oh, *Rosina.*" She crouched. "Come to the house."

"Is Klaus there?"

"No. I'm sure he'll be back soon, though, and you can talk this through."

But there is nothing to talk through, Rosina thought. Leopold is dead. I've caused Klaus immeasurable pain, and shamed him before our friends.

Klaus did not return to the Sperbers' house that night, or the next morning. "He must be waiting at home," Adolf mumbled. "We'll drive you."

But as soon as they drove into the silent farmyard, Rosina knew. The sweet prairie rosebush Klause had planted by the cabin door had been hacked to bits. His heavy grub hoe lay a good distance away, as if hurled with frenzied force.

Inside the cabin, her husband's spare shirt was missing from its peg. The thick wool socks she'd darned were no longer neatly folded on the shelf. His Bible had disappeared from the mantel.

Klaus was gone.

————

Lottie begged Rosina to return with them.

"I can't," Rosina said fiercely. "I must be here when Klaus comes home."

The Sperbers finally left her alone. Rosina woodenly heated water. She changed and bathed John, let him nurse, held him over her shoulder until he burped, settled him down. Only then did she sit at the table and read the two letters.

July 17th, 1862

To Rosina Lauterbach,

It pains me greatly to introduce myself with grievous news. Leopold Zuehlsdorff, whom I believe was a special friend of yours, died of dysentery this morning. A sickness has swept among the men, and he grew ill last week. He was much admired, and all efforts were made to break the fever. But to no avail.

Leopold and I had become good friends over the past months. Please forgive any indelicacy on my part, but I had reason to know that he held you in high esteem, and worried much about your welfare. He wrote you a letter soon after we arrived at Fort Leavenworth. Many times I saw him remove the letter from his pocket, lose himself in thought, and then return it. Finally I asked what that was about. "It is for the girl who made me this shirt," he said, gesturing to the very shirt he was wearing. "But I don't know if I should send it."

After his death I found the letter, and thought perhaps it was time to send it to you, along with the shirt. I pray I have not done so in error.

Respectfully yours,

Heinrich Wittenberg

February 6th, 1862

My dear, sweet, Röslein,

It is difficult to put into words how great a shock you gave me that frigid day my regiment left Milwaukee. I had thought of you many times since our voyage ended. However, and I confess this with bitter shame, I also was swept along in the excitement of the times. If there must be blame, lay it squarely at my feet.

*I never intended you any harm. I wanted only to show
you that life is more than beatings and scoldings and dull
expectations. Your quick mind and interest in new experiences
attracted me. Our time on the Fair Wind seemed separate
from the responsibilities waiting for me in America. I let
myself behave most dishonorably.*

*You said you had married, but I do not know your
husband's name. I pray—and yes, Röslein, I do pray—that
he is a kind man and good husband. I pray you are happy. I
pray that the child will be healthy, and bring you great joy.*

*I pledge to not cause you concern or mortification, now or
in the future, but I will think of you and the child for the rest
of my days. I do not expect you to forgive me, but know
always that I hold you in highest esteem.*

Most sincerely,

Leopold

Rosina touched her lips to Leopold's letter before throwing it,
with the other letter, into the fire. At the last moment she hid the
envelope, and the linen shirt, away. Even now she needed some tangible
link to John's father.

THIRTY-TWO

ROELKE FOUND CHLOE SITTING in the garden that evening. She patted the bench. "Join me? It's quite peaceful."

Roelke sat. The oppressive heat was fading. A tiny bird—a wren, maybe?—was singing a mighty song from the fence. It *was* peaceful.

"You've made good progress in the garden," he observed.

"I'm determined to serve a homegrown salad."

"The carrots would do better if you thinned them."

"I know, but... I just *hate* thinning. I planted those seeds, and they germinated and grew in good faith, doing what seeds are supposed to do ... it's hard to just yank the plants out of the ground and toss them away."

Roelke had no idea what to say.

She sighed. "So. How was your day?"

"I got our telephone hooked up." That was a biggie, because he needed to be reachable. "As for work stuff, I got tired of waiting for news, so I called the contacts you gave me to pass on to Goresko. Nobody knew anything about a missing reenactor. *But,* when I mentioned a possible tie to German history, one guy remembered Gunter Diederich getting mouthy with another Yankee unit at an event in Illinois. Diederich lit into him about authenticity and standards, stuff like that."

"When was that?"

"He said five or six years ago."

"That's about the time Gunter started the 9th Wisconsin. He was probably proud of his own guys and feeling cocky. When we met, I didn't sense any bravado."

"I didn't either," Roelke admitted. "Anyway, each reenactor I called gave me a couple more names. I'm going to keep making calls until Private M is identified."

"I got nowhere with the German cockade," Chloe said, "but I did learn one thing at the Veterans Museum today. When drafts were held during the Civil War, the names of eligible men were put into a drum, and an official would give it a spin and then pull the names."

"They drafted guys back then? Hunh."

"The names were written on thin wooden discs." Chloe put her hand on his arm. "They look like what Maggie Geddings described."

"Yeah?" His spirits rose a notch.

"I took a picture for you."

"Great. I'll show it to Ms. Geddings." His knee began to jiggle. "Did you talk to Fassbender?"

"I did, and I made him cry." Chloe gave him a *Thanks a lot* look. "Kyle reported absolutely no conflicts or tension within the 9th Wisconsin. But … "

"What?"

"Promise me you won't make too much of this. Kyle, who happens to be dating Alyssa, mentioned that he collects images from the

1860s. And the director of the Wisconsin Veterans Museum told me that Kyle's come in to study photographs of Civil War soldiers."

Roelke fished his index cards from his pocket, found the one labeled *Kyle Fassbender*, and jotted a couple of notes.

"I wish you wouldn't do that," Chloe said. "I know Kyle."

"No, you don't. Not really."

"Okay, I don't know Kyle well, but I've known lots of kids like him. Once upon a time, I *was* a kid like him." Her gaze was imploring. "I simply can't believe he's involved in anything bad."

"Maybe he's not. But nice kids get sucked into bad situations all the time."

"I suppose." She sounded dejected.

"This is making me crazy." Roelke scrubbed his face with his palms. "One theft. Two deaths. I have no evidence to connect those things, and yet—the whole Civil War thing can't be a coincidence."

Chloe took his hand in hers. "This is probably a futile suggestion, but try to let it go for the evening."

He knew she was right. "Have you had supper?"

"I found a few ginger cream cookies left in the kitchen."

"Chloe—"

"Yeah, yeah. I'll have some fruit or something when I get home."

"And a salad."

"That is an *excellent* idea."

He narrowed his eyes. "You're going to make popcorn for supper, aren't you." It was not a question.

"Yes. Yes, I am."

"*Chloe—*"

"Hey, I've got more to tell you. Klaus Roelke isn't listed on the 9th Wisconsin Infantry roster. He must have served in a different regiment. Maybe the envelope came from a friend."

Roelke was surprisingly disappointed. He'd liked imagining his ancestor marching in the original 9th regiment. "How many Wisconsin men served in the Civil War?"

"Over ninety-one thousand. There is a record, and there's probably an index. I just ran out of time."

"Well, you'll track it down." In her own way, Chloe was a dogged detective.

"Um … Roelke?" She twined her fingers through his. "There is one more thing I need to tell you."

This couldn't be good. "What?"

"Libby gave me more Roelke family heirlooms that almost certainly date back to Klaus and Rosina. One was a little sewing kit, the kind women made for their husbands when they enlisted. When I was looking at it, I found a tiny note hidden inside." She sucked her lower lip between her teeth.

"What did the note say?"

"I haven't told Libby about this, but … " She took a deep breath. "It says 'Oh, my son, I have killed your father.'"

" … *What?*"

"I'm telling you, that's what it says. In English and in German."

He stared at the cabin just beyond the garden fence. "What the hell?"

"Maybe I can find record of an illness or farm accident. But *something* terrible happened, and the residue left behind is probably what I feel in the cabin."

Roelke massaged the back of his neck. I'm just starting to get interested in my ancestors, he thought, and *this* is what I learn?

"I'm really sorry, but I don't know how to get past this. Whatever happened between Rosina and Klaus happened over a century ago."

Or maybe, Roelke thought, the terrible thing freaking out my girlfriend is much more recent. *Thwack. Thump. Shuush. Thud.*

"Since the cabin has become such a problem for you," he said with surprising harshness, "maybe we should just burn the damn thing down."

Chloe jerked her hand from his. "We can't destroy the cabin!"

He knew he'd shocked her. Hell, he'd shocked himself. But he couldn't take the words back.

"Why would you say such a thing?" she demanded.

They stared at each other. The wren sang and sang and sang.

Finally Chloe swiped at her eyes, got to her feet, and left him there.

———

Chloe felt discombobulated as she drove home. Stunned? Hurt? Sad? All of the above. By the time she reached her own house, she added worried to the list. She'd seen Roelke angry before, but never at her. Not like that.

Inside, Chloe picked up Olympia and cuddled her close. "I've upset Roelke about his old family cabin, and I don't know what to do about it," she confided. "What if he decides he doesn't want us to move in?"

Olympia began to purr: *You still have me.*

"Call me selfish," Chloe said. "I want both of you."

She fed Olympia, popped some corn, drizzled it with melted butter and maple syrup, and fretted about the day. The whole Private M situation had become even more wretched with the knowledge that the tintype he'd been carrying was a reproduction—the kind of memento reenactors often had made at events. Somewhere, a real little boy might very well be waiting for his father.

We've got to narrow the search, Chloe thought as she nibbled popcorn. Most nineteenth-century German settlements fell within what historians called the "German triangle," anchored by Milwaukee, St. Louis, and Cincinnati. There were strong pockets of German settlement in Texas too. And of course Pennsylvania had attracted many Germans after those first arrivals in 1683.

It might be worth focusing investigative calls to units in those regions. I'll come up with a list of communities, she thought, and pass that on to Roelke…

Roelke. She really was worried about him.

———

The newly installed phone rang at about eight that evening. Roelke, sitting at the kitchen table in the fading light, ignored it. By the time he'd drained the Pabst Blue Ribbon, the ringing stopped. He put the bottle next to the first two and reached for another.

Fifteen minutes later he heard a car pull in, a door slam. He glanced out the window as Libby marched across the yard. Damn.

A moment later she banged on the back door. "Roelke?"

He didn't answer.

"I know you're in there, you nimrod." She tried the knob. Then a key rattled in the latch. She burst inside and flicked the light switch. "What is…" She froze, staring at the empty beer bottles on the table. "Jesus, Roelke, what are you doing?"

He winced at the flood of harsh light. "Drinking a beer in the privacy of my own kitchen."

"You're not drinking 'a beer,' you're drinking a six-pack." She crossed the room in two strides, snatched the bottle from his hand, and poured the contents down the sink. The two remaining bottles were emptied too. Then she dropped into a chair across the table from him. "Roelke, you do not do this."

"I am entitled to an occasional beer."

"You do not do *this*." She sent the empty beer carton to the floor with a swipe of her hand. "Not because I say so; because you chose a long time ago to limit yourself."

Roelke really wished his cousin would stop shouting. "Why are you here?"

"Because Chloe called me."

Great. Ju-ust great.

"She's worried about you."

"I had a bad day."

"Is it cop stuff?"

"Cop stuff pretty much sucks," he tried. "So I think I am entitled to—"

"Bullshit." Libby folded her arms. "What's really going on?"

Libby knew him better than anyone else. Right this minute, Roelke profoundly wished that wasn't true.

She ran both hands through her short hair so little spikes stood up in odd directions. "I thought you and Chloe were doing pretty well."

"I think I've changed my mind."

"About what?"

"Maybe we aren't meant to live together."

Her eyebrows shot up. "*What?* After everything you—"

"She's a vegetarian, you know."

"Yes, Roelke. Since I have shared many meals with Chloe, I do know that she's a vegetarian."

"She can't drive in reverse. I say, 'Just point it where you want to go and hold the wheel straight,' but *no*, she weaves all over the place."

Libby's expression suggested that he'd sprouted a second head. "Are you out of your mind?"

"She's part of this whole Civil War reenactment world, and I'm telling you, reenactors are from another planet."

Libby leaned forward, forearms on the table. "Roelke, I am fighting the urge to shake you silly."

Honestly, Roelke didn't blame her. But he couldn't tell even Libby what was really gnawing at his gut.

Still, she deserved at least some truth. "Chloe can't thin carrots."

Libby was starting to looked pissed. "You don't want to live with Chloe because she hasn't thinned—"

"I didn't say she hasn't. I said she *can't*. She said it's not fair because the seeds germinated in good faith."

" … Oh."

"Chloe won't watch *Rawhide* because she thinks the theme song is unkind to cattle. I've seen her cry because she read a sad book."

"Lots of people cry over sad books," Libby tried. "Chloe is a sensitive soul."

You have no idea just how sensitive Chloe is, Roelke thought. But he couldn't talk about what was going on in the old cabin. Instead he said, "I don't know if she really understands what it's like to live with a cop." He remembered kneeling in Siggelkow's blood, the blood on his shirt, the blood on his hands.

"I think she's got a pretty good idea."

Roelke's head was beginning to ache. "Chloe can't, thin, carrots! I don't know how to live with someone like that."

"You have a big heart, and—"

"But I need to keep her safe. I don't know how to protect her."

"I should not have drained that last beer," Libby muttered. She stood and began to pace. "Look, Roelke, Chloe doesn't expect you to protect her from the world, or even to give up hamburgers."

He shrugged. It was so damn complicated.

"Maybe instead of thinking about what you can't do for Chloe, you should think about what you *can* do for her. That will be plenty."

"Maybe."

"Have you had supper?"

"Chloe said there are some cookies around here someplace."

She picked up her car keys. "Come home with me."

Roelke followed her—partly because time with Dierdre and Justin was always good, partly because he really was getting hungry, and partly because obedience was the easiest course when Libby got that look in her eye.

But he'd put a barrier between them by not being completely honest with her. He had no idea how to get past that.

And she didn't even know that their great-whatever-grandmother may have killed their great-whatever-grandfather.

I really don't know why Chloe loves all this history stuff, he thought. Evidently there were things about Klaus and Rosina Roelke that he did not want to know.

THIRTY-THREE

"I do wish you and John would stay with us," Lottie said. "Just until..."

"Until Klaus comes home," Rosina said staunchly.

"Is there any news?"

"Just the one letter." She took the much-read letter from her basket and placed it on Lottie's kitchen table. "Would you read it?"

Lottie bent over the single page. Rosina recited it silently.

September 28, 1862

Wife,

It is difficult to know where to begin, and painful to revisit our last conversation. A better man would not have left as I did, but in that moment I could manage nothing more.

What I said is true: I had always known that there had been another before me. But I had not known that you still care for him. I had let myself believe that you had been ill used. I had let myself believe that you might grow to love me. Then I read that this man cared for you, and saw the anguish that his death brought you.

I am writing from a training camp in Milwaukee. I have enlisted in Company D, called the Salomon Rifles, of the 26th Wisconsin Infantry Regiment. There are several men from Watertown in the company, and almost every man in the regiment is of German birth or descent. We are scheduled to leave for the field in a few days. I do not know where we will be sent. Please do not try to visit me here.

It is essential that land payments are made monthly. I am to receive thirteen dollars a month, which I will send to you. As the wife of a Wisconsin soldier you are entitled to five dollars a month from the state, plus two extra dollars a month for John. Speak to the allotment commissioner if you encounter difficulties.

Know that I always have, and always will, treasure John as my own son. I hope you will agree that he should never know of this. I can not speak to the future in a time of such uncertainty. We must trust in God's mercy.

Klaus

Lottie straightened. "I hardly know what to say."

"Leopold's death did grieve me," Rosina admitted, "but not fully the way Klaus believes. I grieved because instead of saving the Union and proving the worth of German soldiers, Leopold suffered under a merciless commander and died of diarrhea. I grieved that Leopold believed that I might regret having met him, for I can not do that." She glanced at Lottie, daring her to demur. "But my tears were for Klaus as much as for Leopold."

"It's a dreadful situation."

"Do you think I should write to Klaus?"

"Yes." Lottie nodded. "I suspect he's already regretting his hasty actions."

Rosina pinched her lips together. Should she write honestly of her heart? Simply beg for forgiveness? Promise to protect the farm above all else? Or ... "Should I tell Klaus that I am carrying his child?"

Lottie nodded with more certainty. "Yes."

"I will, then." And maybe, Rosina thought, he will write back. What little she knew about *Unser Deutsches Regiment* came from newspaper reports. The regiment had been issued .58-caliber English-made Enfield rifled muskets and departed for Washington, D.C., in early October.

Lottie went to the window. "I do so wish Adolf hadn't gone with Franz."

"We must hope for the best," Rosina said, but the advice sounded hollow.

"You're right, of course." Lottie sat again. "Adolf and Franz will join the protest against the draft, and then they'll be back home with stories to tell."

Rosina hoped so. Adolf had fetched her and John to keep Lottie company while he and his brother were away.

Last summer Governor Salomon had pleaded with the government to postpone a draft, arguing that men would be more likely to volunteer after harvest. By November most counties had furnished the necessary recruits. But not all. Drafts had been scheduled, and some German settlers had organized protests. Adolf, Franz, and other local men had traveled to Port Washington to lend support.

"Forgive me." Lottie cast a sympathetic look across the table. "We shall hold off worries with work. I found a linen towel I can spare."

Rosina tucked her letter away. "I brought a tablecloth." It was her finest linen, made in the Old Country. Rosina would much prefer to make more shirts with it, but the Sanitary Commission had published a desperate appeal for the lint used to staunch soldiers' wounds in military hospitals.

Lottie fetched knives and teacups. She and Rosina held pieces of linen taut over the down-turned cups and commenced scraping the cloth to bits.

The chore broke Rosina's heart. It might be Klaus who needs lint after some battle, she reminded herself. But in more ways than one, it was hard to destroy linen.

THIRTY-FOUR

"It was hard to make linen," Alyssa told the visitors in the Schulz workroom. "German immigrant women planted flax seeds, grew and harvested the plants, and retted away the hulls. They crushed the stalks, scutched away the hard bits, hackled the fibers clean ... and *then* dressed the distaff, spun the thread, dressed the loom, and wove the cloth."

"Gracious," said an elderly woman in lilac shorts and white Keds.

"But during the Civil War, army surgeons needed absorbent material for bandages," Alyssa concluded solemnly. "Sometimes women destroyed their precious linen by scraping it to shreds."

The Keds lady put one hand over her heart. "Good Lord."

Alyssa is good, Chloe thought. She was quietly threading warp threads through string heddles.

"Did anyone from the Schulz family serve in the war?" a lady asked.

"Herman Schulz, the eldest son, was drafted in November of 1862," Alyssa said. "But a hired substitute served in his place."

"That was legal?" another visitor asked.

"Oh, yes," Alyssa assured her. "It was hard to spare a man of draft age from a farm. If you'll follow me outside, I can help you imagine the chores keeping Herman and his father busy … "

As Alyssa led her group out the back door, Jenny slipped in the front. "Progress!" she exclaimed, admiring Chloe's work.

"I'm determined to have you weaving by the weekend," Chloe said. "If you and Alyssa can finish threading the heddles, and the reed, I'll tie the warp ends on the front beam. Getting the tension even is tricky."

"We'll get it done," Jenny promised. "I can stay late if need be."

Chloe slid from the seat, considering the day ahead: prepping the 1860s houses for the Civil War event, finalizing the weekend's activities, and—with whatever time was left—measuring windows for Ralph Stupid Petty. "Belinda and I will be out later with a few extra artifacts for the weekend."

"I'm going to spend my time at the Koepsell Farm this weekend and let interpreters rotate here to enjoy the special activities. But I've got scraps of linen set aside to scrape for bandages."

Chloe was meeting Byron and Belinda, and so reluctantly left Jenny and Alyssa to the fun stuff. At Ed House she found Byron at his desk, typing with demonic speed. Belinda waited in what was obviously uncomfortable silence.

"Hey, guys," Chloe said. "Sorry to keep you waiting."

Byron pulled his missive from the platen and made two photocopies. "Here's the rundown."

Chloe scanned the agenda. Reenactors from the 9th and the 100th units would arrive after 5 p.m. the next day, Friday, and set up their respective camps. "Saturday," she read aloud. "Ten a.m.: Mock battle on the Visitor Center green." She glanced up. "The 100th is fighting themselves?"

"That's the plan." Byron pulled off his glasses and pinched the bridge of his nose.

Activities planned for the site included a recruitment rally at Harmony Town Hall, a dinner for new recruits at the Sanford Farm, and a reenacted draft at the Four Mile Inn. The 9th Wisconsin guys would also make several trips to the Schulz Farm.

"Kyle and I are planning some after-hours entertainment at the Koepsell Farm," Byron concluded. "That big back porch will work for a stage. The 100th is invited, although I doubt any of them will make the hike." He turned abruptly to Belinda. "Can you recite a poem? Or sing?"

Belinda made a visible effort to disappear into her blouse.

"Performing is probably best left to interpreters," Chloe said smoothly.

"But we still need to meet with the lead interpreter." Byron glanced at the clock. "Do you have time?"

Chloe fought the urge to check her watch. "Sure. But let's go over the collections stuff first."

Belinda produced the lists of artifacts to be moved from storage to the three 1860s houses, and Chloe reviewed their plans. "And please let the interpreters know that I'll be measuring windows tomorrow," she concluded. "I'd prefer to do it all after hours, but ... "

Byron nodded. "But the clock is ticking."

Something in Chloe's chest ratcheted tighter. The windows thing was the least of her worries. The reenactor deaths were *still* unresolved, Ralph Petty had launched an assault on programming integrity, and Roelke had threatened to burn his ancestors' cabin down. The ticking felt more like a time bomb.

———

"Coroner's summary on your John Doe got faxed down this morning." Marie handed a shiny piece of paper to Roelke.

"Thanks." Roelke anchored the top of the curling paper with a stapler and read the ME's conclusions. Bottom line: Private M had died of a broken neck consistent with the likely fall at the Schulz Farm. No signs of drugs or alcohol in his system, but the body showed signs of persistent malnourishment.

Roelke frowned. Why had someone with such expensive reenactment gear been half starved?

Chloe might have an idea. But she was pissed at him.

Oh, hell, he thought, and reached for the phone. He needed to clean that up anyway.

Chloe picked up on the second ring.

"Hey, it's me."

Silence.

"I just reviewed the autopsy results for Private M, and I'd like your opinion about something."

"I was about to head out on site," she said. "But I'll help if I can."

"He showed signs of chronic malnourishment. Considering the cost of all his clothing and gear, that makes no sense to me."

"Well ... " She sounded reluctant. "There are a few zealots in the hobby. Ultra-hardcores. The ultras go to extreme lengths to explore and interpret the soldier experience."

"I don't know what that means."

"It means they might try to exist on period rations."

"So … this guy could have been starving himself for the sake of authenticity?"

"I'm just speculating." She sounded defensive.

Roelke tapped a pen against the desk. He was running out of time. Private M had died at Old World Wisconsin. Where more reenactors were gathering this weekend. For an event that involved Chloe.

"I really need to go," Chloe said.

Roelke didn't want to mention last evening's debacle with Marie sitting three feet away. "Can you meet me at the farm after work?"

"I have to work late."

"You name the time."

"Um … eight o'clock."

"Thanks. I'll see you then."

After hanging up, Roelke tried to figure out what he was going to say to Chloe at eight o'clock. Just apologize, he decided. Nothing more was necessary.

What *was* necessary was figuring out this Civil War mess. He poured himself another cup of coffee. Then he sat back down, spread index cards and files on the desk, and started working the problem one more time.

———

Chloe tried to set personal problems aside in favor of professional ones as she and Belinda walked out to the Sanford Farm. "Tomorrow we'll find period clothes for you," Chloe promised.

"Me?" Belinda squeaked.

"Since we'll be working on site during open hours, absolutely."

"But…"

"I want you to set up the Sanford house parlor for the Ladies' Aid meeting," Chloe said.

"Me?" Belinda squeaked again. But this time she looked pleased.

"You've done the planning and identified the necessary artifacts. And don't worry, Lee and the other interpreters will talk with visitors while you work."

When they arrived at Sanford, Chloe heard Lee chatting with guests. "Many of Wisconsin's Yankee settlers cherished the ideals of a democratic government and were eager to defend the Union. Daniel Kenyon Sanford enlisted in the 28th Wisconsin Infantry Regiment in 1862. The governor had just begun instituting a draft, which was particularly unpopular in some German-American communities. Protests took place in Sheboygan and West Bend, and a riot broke out in Port Washington. Soldiers from the 28th Wisconsin were sent to restore order…"

Well, Chloe thought, Lee may think Civil War reenacting glorifies violence, but he's good at interpreting the topic. She *really* needed to spend more time with interpreters, and less with administrators.

She and Belinda joined Byron, who had of course beaten them to Sanford, and the area's lead interpreter in the front parlor. "Belinda's going to arrange the side parlor to suggest an aid group meeting in progress," Chloe explained. "Guests can look in from the doorway."

"And in *this* room, which will be open, we'll have some simple hands-on activities," Byron added. "Sacks that kids can fill with beans and peas and pack into boxes for the soldiers, that sort of thing."

"And guests can do some sewing if they wish," the lead added. "We're cutting pieces for housewives."

Oh, my son, I have killed your father.

303

Chloe felt an ache at the base of her skull. Maybe, she thought, I should let Roelke burn the damn cabin down.

————

When Roelke got to the farm that evening Chloe was waiting on the front step. "Thanks for coming," he said as he joined her. "I owe you an apology."

"Libby said you think I'm too sensitive. Something about carrots...?"

Roelke silently cursed Libby's eternal bluntness. "I had to say something."

"I know this is about the cabin." Chloe picked up a pebble, tossed it away. "I am who I am, Roelke. If you can't deal with that, you better figure it out now."

"I can't deny that your feelings about the cabin aren't... a problem. But I'm sorry I lost my temper. I didn't mean what I said about burning it down." He hoped that would do it.

But she shook her head. "We have a problem, and I don't know how to solve it. We may never know what happened to Klaus and Rosina that left such a bad resonance behind."

"Maybe the bad energy you feel in the cabin didn't come from Civil War times," Roelke heard himself say. "Maybe it's not nearly that old."

She turned to him. "What are you talking about?"

Roelke watched a bat swoop over the lawn and tried to figure out what in the hell was wrong with him.

"Roelke?"

"I—it's nothing. Just something stupid."

"Tell me anyway."

He exhaled slowly. "My parents used to fight a lot. Patrick and I hated it. My dad would get angry. Mom tried to stay calm, but she didn't cower. Once, when I was ten, Mom came upstairs late one night and told us to put some clothes and our schoolwork in a suitcase."

Chloe looked away, giving him space.

Roelke didn't want to describe how it felt to tiptoe past his father, who'd passed out on the sofa, and creep outside. "My mom drove us here. The next day was a Saturday. I went out to the cabin with a biography about George Washington Carver. My grandma had set some plywood on sawhorses for her gardening stuff, and I crawled underneath."

Chloe nodded.

"I was reading about peanut butter when my mom came looking for me. She'd just stepped inside when we heard a car pull in."

A second bat joined the first. Roelke watched them dart back and forth while he tried to detach himself from the boy in his story.

"My dad came in after her," he said finally. "He was furious at her for bringing me and Patrick here. He grabbed her wrist. I knew that was wrong, and I wanted to tell him so, but—but I didn't move. He tried to drag her outside, and she said she wasn't going anywhere with him."

Chloe nodded again.

"Then he hit her, really hard." The aural memories came again: the *thwack* of his father's fist against his mother's cheek, the hard *thump* as she fell against one log wall, the sliding *shuush* as her knees gave way, the softer *thud* as she fell.

Chloe reached for his hand. "And you think that terrible feeling in the cabin came from your mom?" she asked softly.

"No. Mom went from angry to unconscious. But it might have come from *me*. I was ashamed of my dad." He pulled away and shoved to his feet. "And I was even more ashamed of myself." Grandma had charged in, bellowing at Dad to get the hell out of there. She and Grandpa got his mom back to the house. All while he huddled silent in the corner.

"Oh, Roelke..."

"My dad threatened my mom, and I didn't even try to help her. Every time I looked at her split lip and black eye..." He felt hot with remembered shame. And it wasn't just the shame from not protecting his mom. He hadn't protected Libby, even though he knew her husband was an asshole. He hadn't protected Rick, even though they'd promised to always have each other's backs.

"You were just a kid!"

He shrugged angrily. "I will always regret—"

"You know what? I don't believe in regrets. I believe that we do the best we can in any given moment."

"That's a little simplistic."

"Not really. We should try to learn from mistakes, but investing energy in regret doesn't accomplish anything." She stood too. "I think it's time to forgive yourself, Roelke. Sometimes you just have to let go of the bad stuff. It doesn't mean the bad stuff didn't happen, only that you're not going to let it eat at you any longer."

Roelke couldn't find words.

She wrapped her arms around him. "Is this why you became a cop?"

"What? No. No, I don't think so."

"Oh, Roelke." She kissed his neck. "I love you, just the way you are."

Roelke felt the familiar tight pain in his chest. He didn't know if it came from confessing his worst secret or his growing suspicion that buying the old Roelke place was the worst decision of his life. Not only had he signed his soul over to the bank, he'd chained himself to his most terrible memory.

"I love you too," he managed. "And I better let you get going. I know you have a long day tomorrow." But for the first time, thinking about going in separate directions brought a sense of relief. That only tightened the vise around his ribs.

They walked to the driveway, and Chloe gave him the Polaroid photo she'd taken of the wooden draft discs. "I'll show this to Maggie Geddings," he said.

"I had another thought about Private M. If he had German ancestry, maybe he lived in an area of heavy German settlement." She handed him a piece of paper. "It's a long shot."

Roelke studied the list of cities in the fading light. "All I've got left are long shots."

———

On Friday morning Roelke drove to Gunter Diederich's Waukesha townhouse. Diederich's face lost some color when he saw who was waiting on the step. "Oh God. Did something else happen?"

"No," Roelke said quickly. "And I'm sorry to trouble you again, especially so early, but I haven't been able to reach you by phone."

The alarm faded, leaving Diederich looking simply tired. Haggard, really. Was it the grief and shock of Siggelkow's death? Or was there more to it than that?

"I haven't been answering," Diederich confessed. "Too many damn reporters calling to ask about Steven."

"Are you on your way to work?"

"I took the day off. I need to be at Old World Wisconsin before five this afternoon."

"We still haven't identified the man who died there. I hope to connect with some high-quality reenactors from these areas." He handed Diederich Chloe's list. "Maybe you've met people at big events...?"

"We did a top-notch event at a historic site near St. Louis a couple of years ago." Diederich stepped back, gesturing for Roelke to come inside. "I'll get the contact info."

In the living room, a bunch of Civil War stuff was already piled near the door—knapsack, haversack, blanket roll. The only antiques Roelke saw were two tintypes propped on the mantel. He stepped closer.

Diederich busied himself at his desk. "The one on the left is my great-grandfather," he said over his shoulder. "He'd been in the states for less than a year when he joined the original 9th Wisconsin."

"*Wow.*" The soldier looked like a teenager. For the first time Roelke understood what reenactors meant about honoring their ancestors.

"The other one is of me and a couple of pards. Mac Ostermann took that."

Roelke leaned closer. "I saw a photograph Mac took of you at German Fest last weekend. You looked like you stepped right off some battlefield."

"I try."

"Even your expression looked authentic. Stern, like you were worried about something. Did you have some premonition...?"

Diederich looked up sharply. "Of course not! I just had my campaigner face on."

Which was pretty much what Chloe had said. Roelke tried a different approach. "I've heard that the 9th Wisconsin and the 100th Wisconsin have different standards."

"That's an understatement." Diederich scribbled a name on a piece of paper. "But Mac's okay. He comes into our camp at events, just to take pictures or talk about improving his impression. It's awkward since his parents started the 100th. The Ostermanns would be apoplectic if Mac decided to fall in with us."

"It must have been tough at German Fest, with just your guys and the 100th Regiment participating," Roelke said. "Do your units just ignore each other, or what?"

"I got in some shouting matches when I was just starting out," Diederich admitted. "But honestly, there's no point in trying to change another unit's approach. These days I do my thing with my guys, and leave others to do theirs." He held out the paper. "Here's that name and number."

Back in the parking lot, Roelke considered all he'd seen and heard about Mac Ostermann. And Gerald. And Marjorie.

Roelke had very little to go on, but he was less inclined than ever to wait for someone to call with some scrap of information. He radioed Marie, then set out to get what he needed himself.

———

Belinda was waiting when Chloe got to work on Friday morning. "I've revised my outline for the clocks exhibit," she said without preamble, holding out several pages clipped together.

"Great!" Chloe said gamely, tucking the papers into her basket. "As soon as the special event is over, I'll take a look."

Top priority today involved prepping for the reenactment. The two of them took extra woolens from storage to add to the reproduction blankets and knitted goods on display at the Kvaale Farm, and a German-language recruitment poster and the linen shirt loaned by Belinda's mom to the Schulz Farm.

"The Sanford Farm interpreters know you'll be setting up the parlor display this afternoon," Chloe told Belinda. "I've got some windows to measure."

The church bell was ringing five o'clock by the time Chloe checked back at Sanford. Belinda had filled the look-in-only parlor with items enthusiastic citizens might wish to send off with their boys in the early weeks of war: medicinals, glass tumblers of jelly, bottles of wine, crocks of pickled meat, coats, blankets, coverlets, a chess board, Bibles.

"It looks fabulous," Chloe decreed.

Belinda flushed with pride. "It was fun. Did you get the window project done?"

"All but the Village buildings. I can still get the report into Director Petty's mailbox before Monday morning."

As Chloe and Belinda left the Sanford Farm, members of the 9th Wisconsin were already setting up camp with what they'd carried in a blanket roll or knapsack. At the Visitor Center, the 100th Regiment camp was also taking shape. Pickup trucks and vans were disgorging wall tents, cots, coolers, wooden Adirondack chairs, steamer trunks, suitcases, red graniteware kettles, garden hoses, and much more.

Belinda made haste for her car. Chloe tried to do the same, but Byron intercepted her. "Well," he said, "it has begun."

"At least things on the site look good."

"Byron!" Ralph Petty strode toward them.

"*Dammit*," Byron muttered.

"Mr. Ostermann needs to know what provisions have been made for supplying electricity to the camp," Petty barked. "Didn't you—"

"I'll go talk to him." Byron made his escape.

Which left Petty and Chloe staring at each other. "Miss Ellefson," Petty said, "it is Friday afternoon. Is the window survey complete?"

"Almost. I've gotten through everything but the Village." Chloe swiped a dribble of sweat from her forehead. "I can show you what I have—"

"I'm not interested in an incomplete report, Miss Ellefson."

"But..."

Ralph Petty smiled a tiny, mean smile. Then he walked away.

———

Chloe was still stewing about Petty's evil smile when she got back to Ed House. Surely that little prick couldn't fire her for not hitting a ridiculous artificial deadline.

But, by not hitting Petty's ridiculous artificial deadline, she'd given him ammunition for building a case: *Missed deadline... bad attitude... poor time management...* etc., etc., etc. "Shit," she muttered.

Her phone rang. It took effort to answer like a pleasant professional, but she did.

"This is Richard, from the Wisconsin Veterans Museum."

"I've got the draft drum under lock and key," she said quickly. Not that borrowing irreplaceable artifacts made her nervous or anything.

"Good," he said, "but I'm actually calling about that ring you showed me. Did you identify the soldier's regiment?"

Chloe lightly pounded her fist against her forehead. "Not yet."

"I'm going to have a work-study student pin him down."

"Great, but ... may I ask why you're making this a priority?" Involving a student seemed above-and-beyond.

"I've been collaborating with a distant colleague on a project, studying soldier art. Due to the nature of your piece, and the time needed to create such an elaborate ring ... " Richard hesitated. "I suspect it was made in a prison camp."

THIRTY-FIVE

JULY 1863

Rosina was pulling weeds from the flax patch when she realized that the afternoon was quiet … too quiet. Her three-month-old son Andreas was sleeping soundly on a blanket she'd spread in the shade. But where was John?

She whirled, shielding her eyes from the harsh sunlight—and there he was, staring transfixed at a black and orange butterfly on a milkweed plant. She snatched him close.

"*Mutti,*" John complained as the butterfly danced away.

Rosina kissed his cheek. "I must keep you safe," she murmured.

Klaus had been gone for almost a year. A day didn't pass without some worry … but she was coping. She'd done some spinning and weaving for hire, and managed to keep up with the land payments. People had stopped asking why Klaus had invested in the draft insurance company, only to enlist.

On the day Andreas was born the cranes had returned to the prairie. She'd heard their haunting cries as she lay in bed with the infant in her arms, the smell of damp earth drifting through the open cabin door. As Lottie bustled about, Rosina felt something she'd almost lost during the weeks of darkness and blizzards, precious and fragile as a new pasque flower pushing through the soil: hope.

"Surely now you'll come live with us?" Lottie had begged. "You can't stay here with two babies."

"Bless you, Lottie, but … we shall stay here."

She'd had to abandon the fields Klaus had grubbed from the prairie. Even if she'd had money for wages, there were no hired men to be had, with the war. But she'd planted a huge garden, and a bit of rye. Now her first flax crop was blooming blue. That, too, gave her hope.

John squirmed in her arms, breaking her reverie. "Let's sit under the Old Oak," she told him. "I'll fetch your brother."

It was cooler beneath the branches. John settled happily with a pile of pretty stones he'd gathered by the springs. Andreas kicked contentedly. Birds flitted about, and a drowsy breeze stirred the leaves. Rosina pulled her sewing from her apron pocket. She'd started stitching a housewife for Klaus.

She'd written him after Andreas was born. *We have a fine, beautiful, healthy son, and I have no dearer wish than to welcome his father safely home. I regret terribly the pain I caused. Perhaps one day I might earn your forgiveness.*

Klaus had not responded, but everyone said mail was difficult. Last spring the 26th Wisconsin had fought in a horrid battle at Chancellorsville, Virginia. She'd wept with relief when his name did not appear on the lists of casualties.

Then came tales of "German cowards" throwing their weapons aside and racing for the rear. Major General Carl Schurz, Leopold's old friend, hotly defended the 26th Wisconsin men. The whole business broke Rosina's heart—for both of the men she loved. How the taunts must hurt Klaus. How the accusations would have hurt Leopold.

Rosina had burned the newspapers. And with her newfound sense of hope, she'd decided to make the housewife.

She was pinning the first pieces together when she heard a faint *clippity-clop*. The Sperbers' wagon emerged around the bend. Both Lottie and Adolf were on the seat—unusual for midday. Rosina swallowed hard. "Come, John."

Adolf had halted the big bay horse in the drive by the time Rosina and her boys reached them. Lottie's eyes were red-rimmed. Adolf's jaw was tight, his eyes narrowed and grim.

A chill raced down Rosina's spine. "Tell me."

"There has been a terrible battle in Pennsylvania," Lottie said. "A place called Gettysburg."

Rosina took a step backwards. No. No, no, *no*. "Not Klaus."

"Klaus was not killed," Adolf said quietly, "but … here." He held out a folded newspaper, and pointed to a heading—TAKEN PRISONER—above a list of names.

John whimpered, and Rosina loosened her convulsive grip on his hand. "What does that mean, to be a prisoner? Where will they take him?"

"South." Lottie gathered them both in a gentle hug. "To a prison camp."

THIRTY-SIX

CHLOE, DRESSED AS AN 1860s farmwoman, arrived at Old World's Visitor Center on Saturday morning shortly before the mock battle was scheduled to begin. Visitors were already lining the green with lawn chairs. She found Byron in camp, talking to a sixty-ish reenactor dressed as Confederate General Robert E. Lee.

"Chloe, this is Gerald Ostermann, commander of the 100th Wisconsin," Byron said. "I was just explaining that it would be *really* helpful if members of his group made an effort to hide anachronisms."

"Really, *really* helpful," Chloe agreed. Gerald's tent flaps were open to reveal a Union general's uniform suspended from the tent pole on a hanger, shrouded in a dry cleaner's plastic bag. "We do strive to hide all modern conveniences here at Old World."

Gerald sipped coffee from a Styrofoam cup. "Of course, of course. We'll do what we can. But the real power is in the spirit we'll display on the field."

Whatever *that* meant. "The thing is—"

"It is ti-ime to mus-tah the men," Gerald drawled, evidently already channeling General Lee. He walked away.

Byron's cheeks were flushed a disconcerting brick-red. "This is worse than I could have imagined."

"Was Petty pissed to discover the 100th regiment out here, instead of on site?"

"Why, yes. Yes, he was. Since I'd already printed a thousand program sheets for visitors, however, I won that round." Byron stared bleakly at the reenactors shuffling into lines. "But this … "

"Maybe the mock battle won't be as bad as we think."

Astonishingly, it was even worse.

The Union force fielded three privates, three sergeants, four lieutenants, and a general emulating George B. McClellan. General Ostermann commanded a Confederate force of two privates, three sergeants, two lieutenants, and one colonel.

"A bit top-heavy," Chloe observed.

Byron steepled his hands in front of his chin. "Oh my God."

Ostermann strode onto the green with a sword held high. "Fo-wahd, sons of the South!" General McClellan marshaled his Yankees with equal zeal.

"Oh my God," Byron whispered. "Oh my *God*."

Orders were given, shots were fired, and men staggered to the ground with due melodrama. They writhed in apparent agony, or lay still as death, until boredom or some whispered command raised them miraculously to fight again. Two female reenactors cheered and wept from the sidelines as the tide of battle swept back and forth. One wore a zippered prom dress of sickly chartreuse. The second wore a frilled ball gown with hoops wide enough to hide a Volkswagen. Chloe made a mental note to steer clear lest she be knocked off her feet.

After an excruciating eternity—perhaps twenty minutes—the last fighting man fell. The two women rushed onto the field, dropped to their knees beside fallen heroes, and fake sobbed hysterically. Robert E. Lee and George B. McClellan strode to the center of the field, shook hands, and froze in a noble tableau.

"At least Lee Hawkins wasn't here to witness this," Chloe said. This little charade embodied everything Lee had railed against. "And the crowd has definitely dwindled."

Byron stood transfixed, like someone unable to look away from a train wreck. "Oh. My. God."

"Let's go out on site."

"*God.*"

Chloe grabbed Byron's arm and towed him away.

They headed to the 9th Wisconsin's small encampment of small tents near the Sanford house. There was nary an anachronism in sight, and Byron began speaking in complete sentences again. "I'll go check in at Schulz," she told him.

At the Schulz Farm, Alyssa was busy with visitors on the front porch. A second interpreter was explaining the *Schwartze-Küche* to another group. To Chloe's surprise, Jenny—who'd planned to spend the day at the Koepsell Farm—was bent over the loom. "I didn't expect to see you here today," Chloe said.

"I wasn't supposed to be here," Jenny retorted. She took a deep breath. "Sorry. Alyssa sent for me because of a problem." She pointed to a warp thread sagging below its brethren.

"Easily fixed," Chloe assured her. She weighted the wayward thread with a suspended pebble. "With linen thread, a century-old loom, no temperature or humidity control … " She shrugged. "It will probably happen again."

"I'll tell Alyssa she didn't ruin anything." Jenny sounded weary.

"Are you all right?"

"Just a bit tired. We're contributing sauerbraten and onion pies and rye bread for the dinner this afternoon, and Alyssa and I were here until dark last night—"

"Oh Jenny!" Chloe put a hand on her arm. "I think Lee was right when he said you needed to slow down."

"There's nothing worse than having time on my hands. How did the mock battle go?"

"Well, perhaps not quite as well as we would have liked," Chloe allowed. "The 100th Regiment's standards of authenticity are a bit ... um ... "

Jenny leaned closer. "Farby?" she whispered.

"*Exactly*. Byron was apoplectic. However, I have no doubt that all of the activities on site will go well."

"I sent the sauerbraten to the Sanford Farm on a tram, and I'm planning to take the onion pies down myself when they get out of the oven, but would you mind carrying some bread?"

Chloe helped Jenny load a basket with loaves of crusty rye bread. Gunter Diederich and several other reenactors arrived on a recruitment expedition. Some of the men had pinned small cockades of red, black, and yellow on their uniform coats, signal of their German heritage. "We have come to talk to Herman Schulz!" he informed Alyssa, while the visitors looked on with delighted interest. "All good German immigrants should fight to save the Union!"

Chloe felt a flicker of hope. They might just pull off a good event.

———

Roelke's morning began with another round of phone calls. He'd started with Diederich's St. Louis contact and branched out to friends of friends. His seventeenth call was to Frank Acker of Cape Girardeau.

"A missing reenactor?" Acker echoed. He was silent for a long moment. "I did hear something about a guy who went off the deep end a couple of years ago. He dropped out of his unit and went solo, disappearing into the woods for weeks at a time, that sort of thing."

Roelke's knee began to bounce. "What's his name?"

"I don't recall. But I can find out and call you back."

"Thanks," Roelke said, and provided several phone numbers.

It was almost ten, so Roelke drove to Old World Wisconsin. He was off-duty, dressed in jeans and a polo shirt. It was way too hot to wear even a light jacket. But his badge was in his pocket, and his off-duty weapon—a .38 Smith and Wesson revolver—was a reassuring weight in its ankle holster. He hadn't told Chloe he was coming. He had no authority here. But *somebody* needed to keep an eye on these reenactors.

He arrived in time to see the end of the hokey mock battle. Gerald was strutting around the field, and Marjorie was on the sidelines in a shiny dress. Mac Ostermann was doing his photographer thing again. A small wooden sign hung by his tent: *Tintype Artist.*

While in Milwaukee the previous afternoon Roelke had learned *where* Mac Ostermann had been arrested for larceny when he was fifteen. And there was more … But Roelke was still pondering the best way to act upon what he'd learned. Job one today was keeping the reenactors safe.

He was pleased to see that Marv Tenally was the security guard on duty. Marv was a retired accountant, not even a rent-a-cop, but he was smart and dependable. "Keep an eye on that kid, will you?" Roelke asked, cocking his head toward Mac Ostermann. "He's been in some trouble, so he's on my radar."

Roelke spent the morning wandering through the Crossroads Village, over to the Sanford Farm, through the 9th's encampment, and back again. He spotted Chloe bustling about several times. Blond strands had escaped the braids she'd wrapped around her head, her apron was stained, and she looked absolutely beautiful.

The special activities seemed to be going well. A rousing recruitment rally was held at eleven, and at noon the Village buildings all closed temporarily so visitors and interpreters could attend the reenactment of the 1863 draft. Kyle Fassbender made an impassioned speech opposing the vile act. A member of the 9th, dressed in an impressive coat and top hat, had the honor of pretending to spin the draft drum and reading names. The draftees reacted with groans, complaints, or flight. The visitors loved it.

Ralph Petty hovered on the periphery, stroking his beard. Roelke was tempted to go give the director an ever-so-friendly hello. Just to screw with him. But that could wait.

———

At two o'clock the grateful village women served an extravagant meal to the soldiers. Chloe helped the interpreters arrange kettles and pots and baskets on long tables set out in the Sanford Farm drive. A few of the 100th guys drifted in too, but at least they'd all donned blue uniforms for the occasion. The reenactors gazed in awe at the feast before digging in.

Chloe was piling dirty tin plates into a washbasin when one of the interpreters caught her sleeve. "Chloe? Something's wrong with Kyle."

She felt a flicker of unease. "With Kyle?"

"I took him behind the house."

They found Kyle leaning against the wall, head clutched between his hands. "What's going on, Kyle?" Chloe asked.

He raised his head slowly, eyes unfocused. "I can't ... " he mumbled. "I'm so tired."

She checked his forehead—no fever. "Do you have a headache?"

Kyle slid to the ground. His breathing grew more rapid.

"Call an ambulance," Chloe told the interpreter. "And find Byron." The young woman lifted her skirts and ran.

Chloe crouched and pressed her hand against Kyle's shirt. His heartbeat felt slow. Not Kyle, she begged the universe. *Please*. Not Kyle.

He peered at her. "Who ... are you?"

"I'm Chloe." She put a comforting hand on his. His skin felt clammy, so she grabbed the handkerchief peeking from his vest pocket and dabbed his face.

Footsteps sounded on gravel—Byron. "Oh, Christ." He dropped to his knees.

More footsteps, and Ralph Petty appeared. "What's wrong with him?"

Chloe didn't turn around. "I don't know."

"Is it food poisoning?"

"I don't know!"

An ambulance wailed in the distance. Thank *God*. A few moments later Old World's security car led the EMTs down the site road, driving *way* too damn slowly as visitors milled about. Every second ticked by like an eternity. Kyle began hyperventilating. Chloe swiped angrily at tears.

Then she heard a familiar, authoritative voice: "Clear the way! Medical emergency!"

Roelke's here, Chloe thought with profound relief. Then the EMTs arrived, Adam and Denise. Chloe stumbled aside.

Petty was reaming out Byron a few paces away. "…must be food poisoning!" Petty glared. "Somebody was careless."

"The interpreters are extremely careful—"

"This is a *disaster*," Petty muttered. "We could get sued!"

Adam and Denise got Kyle, now unconscious, on the gurney and into the truck. Adam's expression gave Chloe not one tiny bit of comfort.

Roelke joined her. "Talk to the interpreters," he ordered quietly. "Don't let anyone eat or drink anything, and make sure the interpreters don't throw anything away."

She stared at him. "You can't think that—"

"Just do it." He touched her hand. "Until we know for sure."

Lee Hawkins stood nearby, hands tented as if in prayer as the ambulance drove away. Chloe beckoned him over. "Go into the kitchen," she said. "Save all the food and beverages, but don't let anyone taste anything."

He looked stricken, but nodded. "Will do."

As Lee turned toward the house, Belinda plunged outside. "*Chloe!*" Tears streaked the girl's cheeks.

Chloe understood that this horrid afternoon was somehow about to get worse. "What's wrong?"

"The bottle is gone!"

Ralph Petty descended. "What bottle?"

"The green one with liquid inside! I displayed it in the closed-off parlor to represent medicinals. But it's not there!"

"Was it within reach of the doorway?" Petty demanded.

"I—I didn't *think* so," she quavered.

"Well, evidently you were wrong." Petty's voice rose. "What if the liquid in that bottle caused that young man's illness? You might have killed him, you foolish girl!"

Belinda's face went white, then crumpled. She backed away. Then, with a sob, she turned and ran, disappearing among the milling visitors.

The hot steam building in Chloe's chest exploded. "That theory is ridiculous," she hissed, leaning closer to Petty. "And Belinda did nothing wrong. For God's sake, she's an unpaid high school student. If you've got a problem with some collections matter, you take it up with *me*."

Petty drew himself up. "*Miss* Ellefson—"

"Shame on you." Chloe jabbed the air in front of Petty's face with one fierce finger. "We've got enough problems without your tantrums. So *knock* it off."

She turned ... and confronted a ring of shocked faces: Byron, an interpreter, two reenactors, a handful of visitors.

Roelke was there too.

The enormity of what she'd just done settled on her shoulders. And suddenly it was very hard to breath.

———

The look in Chloe's blue eyes—just before she whirled and hurried away—tore at Roelke like thorns. He swore a silent but mighty oath. This day was going to hell in a handbasket.

"Officer McKenna?" Petty's words were ice chips. "Do you have anything to add?"

Roelke looked at the SOB, expecting to see fury. Maybe some embarrassment. But Petty looked ... satisfied.

With an effort, Roelke found his calm cop voice. "Everyone needs to take a deep breath."

Petty walked away.

"I need to call Kyle's parents," Byron said. "And tell Alyssa what happened before I head to the hospital." He cocked his head. "I think Chloe went down to the basement of the inn. If you want to talk to her."

As they strode down the drive Gunter Diederich intercepted them, carrying a canteen. "One of my men brought a batch of homemade booze." He rubbed one hand over his face. "It should *not* have been opened during guest hours, but at least a couple of guys have it in their canteens. It's possible Kyle drank some. He's just a kid, probably not used to it. If I had known ... "

Roelke was dubious. Kyle had not presented as someone who'd had too much to drink. But God only knew what was in the homemade booze. He handed the illicit oh-be-joyful to Byron for transport to the hospital for analysis.

Byron pointed him through a side gate and downstairs to the inn's basement. Roelke passed first through the empty briefing room. The next room was dark, but Roelke heard a sniffle. He flicked the lights. The room was crammed with racks of costumes. There was also a single desk, but Chloe was sitting on the floor, knees drawn up.

"Hey," Roelke said. He shut the door and sat down on the floor beside her.

"Oh God, Roelke." She sounded dazed. "I just gave Petty cause to fire me. My career is—and *our* plans ... "

Roelke put one arm around her. "We'll figure it out."

"But Belinda is traumatized, and Kyle ... "

Kyle may be dead by now, Roelke thought. But speculation wouldn't help anything. "We can't jump to conclusions. And in the meantime, don't give Petty the pleasure of seeing you upset."

Chloe took a deep, shuddery breath. "Right now, what matters most is that Kyle's okay." She dabbed at her eyes with a handkerchief and smoothed the cloth in her hand.

Then her eyes went wide. "Roelke, this was in Kyle's pocket."

He looked at the handkerchief and his jaw slowly dropped. It was identical to the one Private M had carried: a square of linen, blue woven stripes on each side. Only the monogrammed initial—*F*, for Fassbender—was different.

"Holy toboggans," he said. "Surely the same person made both handkerchiefs. Does that mean Kyle Fassbender knew Private M all along?"

"Not necessarily. They might have bought them from the same vendor." Chloe pounded one knee. "*Dammit!* If only I'd spotted it earlier!"

"I doubt if Kyle will be able to tell us where it came from anytime soon." If ever. "But I'll get somebody over there."

"Someone in the 9th might know where Kyle got his handkerchief. Let's go ask."

"I need to use the phone first." He scrambled to his feet and extended a hand to Chloe. "Can you find me a clean plastic bag?"

Once the handkerchief was secure in a baggie, Roelke grabbed the desk phone and dialed 9 for an outside line. To his surprise, Detective Goresko was at his desk. Roelke told him about Fassbender's sudden illness, and the handkerchief. "You might want to get somebody local to the hospital to question Fassbender," Roelke said diplomatically.

"Absolutely."

"I can question the 9th guys. But if you think the site should be closed, it would be best if you call Director Petty."

Goresko paused. "We need to know more before we close the site," he said finally. "And I better talk to the reenactors myself. Petty called my boss yesterday, said I wasn't doing enough to identify the John Doe. In the name of good relations … Anyway. The reenactors are camping there tonight, right? I've got to finish some stuff here first, but I'll be down."

Roelke wanted to shut down the site, but he did understand Goresko's hesitation. Nothing suggested that Kyle's illness was not an isolated incident. And nothing suggested that Old World's staff or visitors were at risk.

He checked his watch and dialed again. "The ambulance should have reached Waukesha Memorial by now," he said to Chloe.

He identified himself, explained the situation, and drummed his fingers through a long wait on hold. Finally a different voice came on the line. "Officer McKenna? Kyle Fassbender is in critical condition and unable to communicate."

"Do you know what caused his illness?"

"Well … " She hesitated. "It appears to be a case of cyanide poisoning."

Jesus. "Are you sure?"

"No, not sure. Most of us have actually never seen this before. And frankly, cyanide victims usually die very quickly. But one of our docs once treated victims who inhaled cyanide fumes during some kind of industrial fire. He recognized the symptoms."

"Is there anything you can do?"

"We're administering antidotes to cyanide toxicity and waiting for confirmation from the lab."

Roelke hung up and met Chloe's gaze. "One of the ER docs thinks Kyle ingested cyanide."

She pressed one hand over her mouth. "*Cyanide?*"

"Do you know if any of the staff or reenactors has a chemistry background? Or works in a lab—something like that?"

"Byron and Gunter would know better than me. But…" She clutched his arm, horror growing in her eyes. "Roelke, Civil War photographers used potassium cyanide to develop their pictures."

He felt every muscle draw tight as a bowstring. "Have you seen Mac Ostermann lately?"

"He was at Sanford while we were serving the meal."

It would have been easy enough for Mac Ostermann to pour a tiny vial of the chemical into a tin cup of lemonade or a canteen of homebrew. Roelke strode toward the door.

Chloe scrambled after him. "Where are you going?"

"To find Mac Ostermann."

As they trotted toward the Visitor Center, Roelke tried to figure out his legal and moral authority. "I should probably call the sheriff's department, but I don't want to wait for somebody else." He pictured the 100th Regiment's camp as he'd seen it that morning. "Visitors sometimes go into the reenactors' tents, right? Is it fair to say that reenactors would have no expectation of privacy?"

"We don't spell it out, but… yes. That is a fair statement."

"So I don't need a search warrant to toss the kid's tent." Roelke slowed as they approached camp. If he and Chloe were wrong in suspecting that Ostermann junior had brought cyanide to Old World, Ostermann senior could cause a whole lot of trouble. "I don't want to make a scene, though—"

"I'll take care of it," Chloe said.

"You'll… what?"

She was already charging toward Gerald Ostermann, who was clad now in Yankee blue. Roelke's hands balled. What the hell was she doing?

"General?" Chloe called. "I have a sore grievance to discuss with you, sir!"

328

Ostermann looked momentarily flummoxed, but his dramatic inclinations triumphed. "What can I do for you, miss?"

Chloe planted hands on hips. "I live on the farm over the rise." She waved vaguely toward the woods. "I prepared a fine meal for several foragers this morning, and didn't ask a penny for it. But I soon discovered that one of them stole two silver spoons!"

A crowd of visitors was growing, delighted with the impromptu performance. The reenactors exchanged perplexed glances. Roelke kept his eye on Mac. Marv, the security guard, stood nearby. Ralph Petty was watching too, stroking his beard.

"Those spoons belonged to my mother!" Chloe overflowed with self-righteous anger. "I demand that you conduct a search!"

Roelke slid through the crowd, moving closer to Mac's tent.

General Ostermann assured Chloe—and the audience—that a swift punishment awaited any man caught with stolen goods. "You there!" he barked to a startled private. "Empty your knapsack!"

Chloe moved things along. "No, he wasn't there ... nor this one, sir ... but *he* was." She pointed to Mac.

The general marched over to his son, who backed up as far as the crowd allowed. "I must search your belongings."

"I'm a civilian," Mac protested. "You have no authority over me."

I do, Roelke growled silently, but he was willing to see how this played out.

"I have the authority of the Union Army behind me!" Gerald declared. He pointed to two of his subordinates. "You, and you— seize that man!"

Roelke thought Mac might make a break for it, but the soldiers stepped lively. Visitors snapped pictures as Gerald ducked into the tent. Chloe plunged in behind him. Roelke edged close, trying to figure out what he'd do if the search revealed only unlabeled bottles. He had no idea what cyanide looked or smelled like.

Gerald glanced inside a wooden crate. "Just the photographer's supplies, miss," he said. "No sign of your missing spoons."

Chloe was diverted by a carpetbag shoved suspiciously far back beneath Mac's cot. She hauled it out and began pawing through, then stopped abruptly. She held up a small, green bottle. "This was stolen."

"Now miss, it's too late to change your story," Ostermann senior said genially.

"I mean, this was *stolen!*" Chloe said sharply. "This is an Old World Wisconsin accession number!"

Roelke was close enough to see a tiny strip of white paint on the bottom, marked with teensy black numerals. Not what he'd expected, but all he needed. "Hang on to him," he barked to the two men holding Mac, and whipped out his badge.

"I'll call the sheriff's department," Marv said, and hurried away.

Gerald Ostermann's general's impression crumbled. Roelke watched him age a decade in mere moments. "Oh Mac. You *promised* us..."

Mac glared at the ground.

Marjorie Ostermann shoved through the crowd. She surveyed the tableau with a helpless expression. Her shoulders slumped. Then she turned away.

"All right, folks, the show is over," Roelke told the astonished visitors. "The camp is closed."

Chloe sidled close. "This is definitely the bottle taken from Sanford. And I can tell that it hasn't been opened."

"We'll hold him for the theft," Roelke said. "I'll secure any chemicals in Mac's tent. If there's cyanide in there, we'll find it."

"Okay. If you don't need me anymore, I'm going back out on site." Chloe started to walk away, then turned back. Worry darkened her blue eyes but she lifted her chin. "Kyle will survive being poisoned," she said, as if she couldn't allow for any other possibility. "He has to."

THIRTY-SEVEN

OCTOBER 1863

Klaus will survive being captured, Rosina told herself, because she couldn't allow for any other possibility. He had to.

There was nothing to do but keep stumbling through the days. She had an infant to tend, a toddler to mind, filthy linens to scrub. She had cucumbers to pickle and kohlrabi to pick, flax to pull and rett, wood to chop. She set hope like an anchor, and kept going.

In the days and weeks after Gettysburg, news arrived in Jefferson County like drips from an ash barrel, slow and acid. The 26th Wisconsin had made a forced march to the Pennsylvania town. The German men were ordered to help close a gap in the Union lines. They stood steady amidst canon and musket fire so brutal a brigade commander described the scene as "a portrait of hell." They stood too long.

Were they merely brave? Or had the *kameraden* vowed to shame their critics by proving their worth?

Klaus would tell her one day. But for now, Rosina only knew that the 26th had been almost encircled by advancing Confederates before they retreated, still under vicious fire. Every one of the regiment's field officers had fallen. A captain took command but he, too, was shot.

Rosina could hardly bear to imagine Klaus in that ghastly place of screams and smoke and blood. He had survived the field ... only to find himself trapped in a dead-end street during the chaotic retreat through Gettysburg.

"It's my fault your father was there," Rosina whispered to Andreas one afternoon as he finished nursing. She'd brought the boys outside to enjoy a warm day. Hickories glowed gold in October sun, geese stippled the sky, and winter was descending. "But he will survive, and come home."

When Andreas drifted off to sleep, she reached for her sewing. She'd almost finished Klaus's gift. Sleepless nights left her feeling dull and stupid, but she'd worked at it bit by bit. It represented what she had not been to Klaus—a good housewife. It had to be perfect.

The Confederate government listed Klaus among the soldiers held at a Georgia prison called Andersonville. Reports whispered of wretched conditions, but perhaps the guards would permit so small a thing as a sewing kit to be delivered. She had written letters to him at the camp as well and could only hope he'd received them.

Before the sun's warmth faded Rosina finished the housewife by tacking down the ribbon that would tie it. Pleased, she took the boys inside, settled Andreas on the bed, and gave John a supper of rye bread spread with goose grease.

"I'm going to write a letter to Papa," she told him. "Why don't you make a pretty design with your feathers?" John had collected dozens—red, blue, yellow, brown. She fetched a precious piece of paper, and lit a precious candle.

Before Rosina could settle, someone knocked on the door. She cracked it open, recognized a neighbor, and stepped back. "Come in."

The man shook his head. "I'm on my way home, Frau Roelke. But I picked up a parcel for you in Palmyra."

She took the palm-sized box with a foreboding of dread. After murmuring her thanks she shut the door. Then she sank onto the bed and studied the parcel. The handwriting was not familiar.

Finally she tore it open. A black ring was inside. A mourning ring.

She unfolded the single piece of paper enclosed and leaned toward the window. The letter was signed *Reverend Theodore Easley*. She had never heard of Reverend Theodore Easley.

Words and phrases jumped from the page … *working to verify records at Andersonville Prison … Klaus Roelke … regret to inform you of his death.*

The paper slipped from her fingers. Her heart pounded her ribs like a mallet. She looked helplessly at Andreas, sleeping sweetly on the patched quilt. "Oh, my son," she whispered. "I have killed your father."

THIRTY-EIGHT

IF I'M NOT CAREFUL, Roelke thought darkly, Chloe and I will *both* be unemployed. After Marv secured a sullen Mac Ostermann in Old World's security car, Roelke called Goresko. The detective wasn't at his desk this time, so Roelke left a message that would, he hoped, cover his butt.

Petty had been in the crowd when Chloe began her little charade, but the site director had disappeared. Roelke thought he knew why and was very glad he didn't have to deal with Petty's histrionics right now.

When Deputy Bandacek arrived Roelke filled her in. She transferred Mac to the back of her car.

Gerald and Marjorie Ostermann waited morosely at a picnic table. "Those are the parents," Roelke added, cocking his head. The 100th Regiment reenactors, still in costume, were hauling their coolers and junk toward the parking lot.

"This is kind of weird," Bandacek mused.

"You have no idea."

At the Sanford Farm, by the Crossroads Village, Chloe searched in vain for Belinda. She called Belinda's house but got no answer.

Home sounds pretty good right now, Chloe thought. But no way was she going to let Ralph Petty or Mac Ostermann send her scuttling home with her metaphorical tail between her legs. Besides, with Byron gone, she really needed to check on the German farms.

The church bell tolled five as she retrieved her own basket from the inn. Most of the interpreters were attending the entertainment, and Chloe joined the trudge up German hill, but her thoughts were too full to add to the conversation. While a guest at Old World, Mac Ostermann had stolen an artifact. It seemed likely the kid had poisoned Kyle, too, monstrous as that was. He did have access to cyanide.

But … something nagged her about that. *Cyanide* wasn't a word she heard every day, and she had the vague sense that she'd heard it more than once in the last week. But the memory eluded her.

Chloe had considered canceling the festivities, but at the Koepsell Farm, half a dozen interpreters were bustling about. "We're almost ready for the show," one reported. "Wait till you see the costumes we made for the tableaux."

"Great," Chloe said. "Is Jenny around?"

"I think she went to Schulz."

Chloe found Jenny and Lee Hawkins alone in the Schulz house. Lee, the prosperous Yankee farmer in a dandified brocaded vest, was carving a roast goose.

Jenny, in her kerchief and faded dress and stained apron, was piling the meat on a platter. She stopped, hand in midair, when she saw Chloe. "Is there news about Kyle?"

Lee caught Chloe's eye, gave the tiniest shake of his head. He'd seen Kyle, knew how bad it was, but he clearly hadn't shared all.

"I don't know how Kyle's doing," Chloe said truthfully. "I came to see if you need help."

"Fortunately Lee jumped on a tram so he could pitch in." Jenny patted her husband's hand.

Lee shrugged. "I wanted to help." He piled the final slices of goose onto a platter. "All set."

Jenny pulled plastic wrap from a hidden stash and covered the plate. "We roasted the goose in our bakeoven today, and I need to get it into the fridge so we can bring it out for show tomorrow." The German area's secluded restrooms had a refrigerator in the storage closet. "Oh—and before I forget, Chloe, we've got a few more dangling warp threads."

"I'll fix them and then join you," Chloe promised. Since everything here was under control, a few moments alone sounded heavenly.

Lee and Jenny headed out the back door. Chloe watched through the window as they crossed the yard. Lee is so good for Jenny, she thought. Just like Roelke is good for me.

Just like Kyle might be good for Alyssa. If they got the chance. Did people ever survive cyanide poison? Chloe desperately wanted Kyle and Alyssa to have a chance.

She swiped at her eyes and went into the workroom. Despite the crowds, Alyssa had managed to weave about six inches that day. The edges were even, the weave tight. But the sagging warp threads were a problem. Chloe frowned. Was the loom more off-kilter than she'd realized? It might need a shim. She'd have to take some measurements.

She found Jenny's big basket tucked into the narrow food pantry and set it on the table to look for the lead interpreter's modern tape measure. First-aid supplies in a plastic bag … empty Tupperware container … pad and pen … extra hairpins … hammer … scissors … *There.* The coiled yellow plastic had wiggled to the bottom.

As Chloe reached for it, something sharp poked her finger—one corner of a tintype, loosely wrapped in a lacey handkerchief. No, wait. There were two photographs.

Chloe drew them out. On top was a dog-eared, wallet-sized snapshot of a teen in an army uniform, posed in front of an American flag. This was surely Jenny's son, who'd died in Vietnam. He was so handsome, so damn young, that Chloe's heart clenched like a fist.

Then she looked at the tintype. The metal held the portrait of a small boy in period clothing, maybe eight years old, staring toward the photographer with an earnest expression.

Chloe's scalp tingled. "Oh my God," she whispered. The tintype was identical to the one found in Private M's pocket the day he died.

———

Marv Tenally stepped from the security office. "Officer McKenna? A Frank Acker is on the phone, asking for you."

"I'll check in with you later," Roelke told Deputy Bandacek. Then he followed Marv back to the security office.

"I've got the name," Acker told him. "Roy Metzger."

Private M, Roelke thought.

"He fell in with a Missouri unit for years, but like I said, he drifted away. Nobody in the unit has been in touch with him lately."

After hanging up, Roelke leaned back and tapped the desk with a pencil. He'd pass the name to Goresko when he arrived. Right now, confirming Private M's identity was less urgent than discovering who had poisoned Fassbender. *Cyanide*, he thought.

It was chilling to contemplate, but Mac Ostermann did look good for it. Means—check. Opportunity—absolutely. Motive ... well, if not check, at least maybe. Diederich had admitted to scolding sloppy units. Maybe one of those units had been the 100th Wisconsin Infantry Regiment. Maybe Kyle had joined in the taunts with the contempt that only a cocksure teen could muster.

And ... had Siggelkow chimed in?

Roelke frowned. No. Siggelkow's death didn't fit that tidy theory. Mac had been close to the water at German Fest, facing the 9th guys. Someone *behind* the reenactors had shot Siggelkow in the back.

Roelke felt as if answers were still dancing just out of reach. He pulled his index cards from a pocket and separated the three Ostermann cards. Mac was an antiques thief who displayed nothing but contempt for his father. Gerald was, as far as Roelke knew, a tired and embarrassed dad who just wanted to play soldier. And yet, father and son remained active in the same hobby, the same unit.

That was odd, but the real wild card was Marjorie. The day before, Roelke had visited the North Point antiques mall named on the brochures he'd seen at the Ostermann home. With the help of a few chatty dealers, he'd started stringing together Marjorie's hopscotch career buying and selling Civil War antiques. She'd once had a stall in a shop in Wauwatosa. After Mac was arrested for stealing an original cartridge box from another dealer, the family had moved to Cedarburg, and Marjorie had relocated her business.

Ten months later the family moved from Cedarburg to Eagle, and Marjorie shifted her business to the North Point mall. Not long after that, local EMTs had been summoned to the Ostermann plantation after Marjorie OD'd on, according to Adam Bolitho, *Percocet with a whiskey chaser.*

Did Marjorie still enjoy reenacting? Was she trying to keep an eye on her delinquent kid? Or had it all become business? Marjorie might have missed German Fest, but she'd come here, flouncing about in a huge wedding cake of a dress. Quite a change, Roelke thought, from the steely private he'd seen in that CDV at the Ostermann home. *I fell in with the boys a few times*, Marjorie had said with quiet pride. *Back in the day.*

Roelke went very still. Marjorie Ostermann had portrayed a soldier. Marjorie Ostermann knew how to shoot.

His knee bounced faster and faster as he imagined a new scenario. Marjorie could have easily slipped through the German Fest crowds incognito. Blue jeans, a baseball cap, sunglasses … She could have walked right by *me*, Roelke thought, and I wouldn't have looked twice.

Diederich claimed he had long since stopped hassling other units. But sometimes time, instead of healing all wounds, merely allowed them to fester. Maybe Marjorie hadn't wanted to forgive and forget. Maybe the whole damn Ostermann clan collaborated to kill Steven Siggelkow and Kyle Fassbender.

If that's the case, Roelke thought, Gunter Diederich is still in danger.

———

Chloe stared at Jenny's tintype. This was no coincidence. No case of two people purchasing identical knick-knacks at a sutler's booth. Jenny's tintype was an exact match for Private M's tintype.

What the hell? Chloe thought.

A memory surfaced. *I don't have any children or grandchildren waiting for me*, Jenny had said.

She'd also mentioned the son lost in Vietnam: *You have no idea how it feels to lose a son in a war that should never have been fought.*

Not "your only son," but "*a* son." And the boy in the tintype looked nothing like the teen in the color photograph. All of that suggested that Jenny had lost more than one boy.

Chloe touched a gentle finger to the metal. Private M had been about Jenny's age. Had he fathered her sons? Jenny had never seen the dead reenactor's body, so she wouldn't have had any reason to think she might have known the man.

Would she?

Chloe sucked in her lower lip, trying to retrieve scraps of recent conversations. Jenny had used the word *farby* that morning, a term that was not, in Chloe's experience, used in the historic sites world. Just the Civil War reenactment world. A world Jenny evidently knew.

Firecrackers were exploding in Chloe's brain. I really should carry index cards, she thought. She scrounged in her own basket for pen and paper, and tried to collect tumbling thoughts.

- *Kyle and Private M carried virtually identical handmade handkerchiefs*

Jenny likely made both—one for her reenactor-husband, one for Kyle years later. Private M's cockade suggested he was of German descent himself—maybe even descended from a German-American soldier. If so, he would have sought out other reenactors who portrayed German-American soldiers. How did reenactors meet other reenactors? At national events.

- *Kyle and Steven S. attended the big Gettysburg 120th anniversary event in early July—crossed paths with Private M?*

But why had Private M come to Old World Wisconsin? Did he simply want to see a German family's restored farm? Had he come to visit Kyle? Or … did he want to see Jenny?

Not enough information, Chloe thought, and switched to what she did know.

- *Jenny unhappy to learn the reenactment was being planned, tried to cover by fretting that Alyssa was too sensitive to cope*
- *Jenny's nerves frayed today*
- *Jenny spent most of the day at Koepsell, avoiding reenactors*

No, wait. Jenny had carried two onion pies down to the Sanford Farm herself that afternoon. Chloe had seen her.

Why hadn't Jenny sent one of the interpreters to Sanford? Jenny had put herself in the midst of the reenactors just as they settled down for their dinner …

"No," Chloe muttered. "No way." Jenny was too nice to hurt Kyle. Too fond of him. Where would she have gotten cyanide, anyway? Chloe couldn't wrap her brain around that theory.

And … dammit, what was it about cyanide that kept poking her memory? She just couldn't grasp it.

All right, set that aside too. Private M had not been poisoned. Private M had gone over the stable's second-story railing and fallen to his death.

How? *How*? Had he seen Jenny in the distance and leaned over too far? Had he sat on the railing, thinking to surprise his ex-wife, and lost his balance? Or …

No, no, no. Jenny was happily married to Lee now. Why would she want to kill her ex?

Two sons, both dead. Jenny's heart had broken twice, in the worst possible way. One son died in Vietnam, but the other ...

- *Was Private M somehow responsible for the little boy's death?*

Her scrawls had filled the page. She turned it over and realized she'd been scribbling on the back side of Belinda's clocks exhibit outline. The headings shouted in capital letters: ALL IN DUE TIME. TIME ON MY HANDS.

There's nothing worse than having time on my hands, Jenny had said.

BETTER LATE THAN NEVER. NO TIME LIKE THE PRESENT.

My sisters and I learned early that when life gets hard you just put your head down and do what needs doing, Jenny had said.

KILLING TIME. TIME HEALS ALL WOUNDS.

But time *doesn't* heal all wounds, Chloe thought. Sometimes time merely allowed them to fester.

Had Jenny pushed her ex from the railing? And ... had Kyle and Steven Siggelkow managed to reach the German farm on Kyle's lunch break that day after all? Had they seen Private M die? If so ...

But Jenny couldn't have killed Steven. She'd been at Old World last Saturday.

All right, Chloe thought, that's *it*. She was wasting time with speculation. She needed to talk with Roelke. She glanced up ... and her heart jack-rabbited. "Oh!"

Lee Hawkins was standing in the doorway.

Chloe pressed a hand over her chest. "You startled me."

"I came back to fetch Jenny's basket." He looked pointedly from the basket to the two photographs Chloe had left on the table. "But I see you already found it."

"Yes, I was looking for a tape measure, and … " Her voice died. Lee's eyes were filled with bleak despair. He looked ready to weep.

Then he took a deep breath, set his shoulders. Chloe's skin grew clammy as she watched anguish replaced by a flinty calm. He stepped forward.

She stepped back.

He slowly curled his fingers around the carving knife he'd left on the table.

"Lee," she protested, because this was the kindly white-haired husband, interpreter, and retired teacher she had come to admire. "You don't want to—"

"I'm sorry. But—but I *have* to."

She tried to scramble away. He darted forward with surprising speed, trapping her in a corner with a hutch on one side, a huge sauerkraut crock on the other, and the worktable hemming her in. Her heart was thudding.

He raised the knife. Chloe made an attempt to bore a hole in the wall behind her by sheer will. No luck, but something pressed into her legs—the heavy wooden tamp used to pound juices from sliced cabbage.

She grabbed it and raised it like a baseball bat. "*Stop!*"

Lee brought the knife down in a vicious slash.

Chloe swung with all her strength. The tamp hit Lee on the shoulder, deflecting his strike. The knife dug into the table. But her weapon flew from her sweaty palms. It sent a flour crock and coffeepot to the floor in a crash of breaking crockery and clattering tin.

Lee stumbled, but recovered and pulled the knife free before Chloe could grab it. Pain exploded in her cheek as—*thwack*—Lee back-handed her. She thumped against the wall and slid to the floor with a *shuushing* sound.

Lee loomed over her and raised the knife again—

Footsteps sounded behind him. He whirled, both hands clutching the knife now, arms held straight before him.

Roelke must have seen the blade. But with a wordless snarl, he threw himself at Lee Hawkins.

THIRTY-NINE

JANUARY 1864

"*Mutti.*" John tugged Rosina's hand.

She started, blinking in the gloom. The fire had died to embers. Ice crystals had clouded the window. "Oh *Schätzchen*, I didn't realize … " With a spurt of panic Rosina checked Andreas, nestled in quilts on the bed beside her. He was fine.

"*Mutti!*" John pointed at the door.

Someone was knocking. How long? Rosina felt addled. She stumbled to her feet and went to the door.

Lottie and Adolf waited on the step, well bundled against the cold. The brittle air stung Rosina's lungs. Sunshine glinting on crusted snow brought water to her eyes.

"May we come in?" Lottie swept inside with Adolf on her heels.

"I was about to warm some bean soup." Rosina busied herself at the fire, trying to gather her wits. Lottie had provided quiet comfort in the weeks after they'd learned of Klaus's death in Andersonville

Prison. But Adolf usually dropped Lottie off, or busied himself at the woodpile while the women talked.

Now he sat down and pulled John onto his lap. "I have something for you, John." He pulled from his pocket a little man astride a horse, carved from wood. John grasped it with delight.

Soon the fire was blazing, and bowls of soup steamed on the table. But something unspoken hovered in the air.

Adolf waited until supper was eaten before getting to it. "Rosina." His voice was heavy. "The man who sold Klaus this farm came to see me. He said you are three months behind on payments."

"Why speak to you?" she asked sharply.

"Because…" Adolf spread his hands. "He knows your situation. He knows we are friends."

And he was afraid to speak to me himself, Rosina thought.

Andreas began to fret. She changed his linens and dropped the soiled one into a lidded crock. Finally she sat back down with Klaus's son warm in her arms. "I don't have the money I owe," she admitted.

"You've done better than most could," Lottie said.

"However," Adolf began, then subsided, staring at his thumbs.

All I want to do is raise my boys right here, on this land Klaus chose, she thought. She wanted that for them. She wanted that for him.

But there was no hope left. Even if she had the money she owed, another payment would come due, and another, and another. Leopold was dead. Klaus was dead. And she had to sell the farm.

"We want to help," Lottie said quietly.

Rosina kissed Andreas. "I just want my sons cared for. I've heard that the County Poor Farm in Jefferson takes in destitute women and children, but—"

"No one's going to the Poor Farm!" Lottie looked shocked. "You will come live with us."

"It's too much," Rosina protested. "Three extra mouths to feed."

"We want you," Lottie insisted. "And it's not charity. I am expecting another child, you see. I need you."

Adolf cleared his throat. "You can use your widow's pension for living expenses, and set aside the money made from selling the farm for the boys' future."

It wouldn't be much, Rosina knew. But saving even a little for her sons…

"If you wish," Adolf added, "I'll handle the sale for you."

"*Please* come home with us," Lottie said.

Rosina looked around. Klaus had hauled those stones, built that chimney. He had felled those logs, skidded them from the woods, raised those walls. He had added a glass window to make her happy. He had been content, full of dreams. But now this was just a room, cramped and dark, smelling of smoke and urine and musty potatoes.

I'm sorry, she told Klaus silently. I'm sorry I caused you such heartache and suffering. I'm sorry I didn't realize that I'd come to love you after all. And I'm sorry I failed to keep this land for the boys and their children.

Finally she looked back at her friends. "Thank you," she whispered. "We will come."

There was little to pack. Adolf rolled out her barrels of potatoes and turnips and kohlrabi, her crock of sauerkraut, and placed planks so he could haul them into the wagon. Rosina took Klaus's grub hoe and axe from the wall to save for the boys. Lottie folded clothes into Klaus's old immigrant trunk, and Rosina added her seeds and dishes.

Then she knelt and retrieved her box from beneath the bed, wiped away dust, steeled herself, and opened the lid. She'd sold her mother's zither and *springerle* mold to a neighbor, along with the linen shirt she'd made for Leopold. "I can pick out the initials," she offered, forcing out the words.

But the woman had waved that offer aside. "It's just a work shirt. My husband won't mind."

That left little in her box. Her childhood sampler was folded on the bottom, and her wedding certificate, and the pretty 9th Wisconsin envelope she'd saved as a memento. She'd tucked away the sea-colored ribbon Klaus had given her, and the black ring sent from Andersonville.

And she'd saved the housewife she'd finished moments before learning that Klaus was dead. That day was blurred in her mind, but she remembered grief and remorse and wracking sobs. I should throw this away, she thought now, looking at the sewing kit in her hand.

But something made her put the housewife back in the box. She had a vague sense that it might one day be important.

FORTY

ROELKE AND LEE CRASHED to the floor in a frenzy of arms and legs. The men grunted, rolling back and forth. Crimson stained Roelke's shirt. Chloe's bones went cold.

"Stop!" someone screamed—Jenny Hawkins, standing in the doorway, eyes wide. "You're killing him!"

Roelke landed a fierce blow. The knife skidded across the floor. Chloe crawled after it, blood sticky-slick beneath her fingers when she snatched the hilt. She stumbled to her feet, knife clenched.

Roelke rose on his knees and slammed one fist against Lee's jaw. The older man's head banged against one of the table legs. He groaned.

"*Stop it!*" Jenny shrieked.

Roelke was on his feet. He suddenly held a gun, trained at Lee. "You move," Roelke growled, "and I shoot."

"You—you carried a gun?" Chloe stammered. A bit tangential, but he'd surprised her. "To Old World?"

"I pretty much always carry a gun, Chloe. Are you okay?"

Her ear was ringing from Lee's blow. Her cheek stung, and her eye was watering. She swallowed hard. "Yes, but—are you?" The blood splotch on his yellow shirt was growing larger.

He glanced down, grimaced, nodded. "Yeah."

Like hell you are, Chloe thought. She jerked the cupboard door open—the emergency phone was hidden in there—and dialed 911.

Roelke nudged Lee with one foot. "Get up."

Chloe asked for an ambulance and police assistance.

"What the hell is going *on*?" Jenny demanded.

"Jenny," Lee croaked, "get out of here." Wincing, gasping for breath, he rolled to hands and knees and looked at Roelke. "I'm the one, do you hear me? I killed Roy Metzger."

"*Roy Metzger?*" Jenny put a steadying hand against the wall.

Private M, Chloe thought. "Jenny, I think Roy is the unidentified reenactor who died by the stable last week."

Roelke shot her a glance: *You know about Roy Metzger?* She gave him a tiny shrug: *Still figuring things out.*

"That was … Roy?" Jenny faltered.

"I'm the one," Lee repeated. He stood like an old, old man—dull-eyed, shoulders slumped.

Jenny stared at her husband. "Lee, what are you talking about? You never even met Roy!"

Roelke gestured Lee into a chair with his gun. "Sit down, and do not move."

"You sit down too," Chloe told Roelke. She uncurled her fingers from the knife, and found a linen towel to press against the gash in his side. "Don't worry, it's a repro towel." As if it mattered.

"I killed Metzger," Lee repeated.

"That's ridiculous!" Jenny snapped. "You were at the Sanford Farm all day!"

Lee looked at Chloe. "I lost a son in Vietnam too. I know how Jenny has suffered. After Curtis…Jimmy didn't have to die, but he did. You can't blame her, not after what Metzger did. She's suffered enough."

"Oh my God." Horror dawned in Jenny's eyes. "You think *I* killed Roy."

Roelke had to be in pain, but his voice was all cop. "Start at the beginning."

"Metzger came to our place." Lee stared at his hands. "He said he'd been looking for Jenny for a long time."

"Roy was your husband, right?" Chloe asked Jenny.

"My first husband. But…how did you know?"

Chloe reached for the two photographs she'd dropped on the table, noticed the blood on her hands, and pointed instead. "Jenny, are those pictures of your sons?"

"Yes, but…"

"The reenactor who died by the stable last week was carrying a tintype identical to yours."

"Then…then it really was Roy." One tear trickled down Jenny's cheek. "I was seventeen when we married. Curtis was born two years later, in 1955. During the centennial observances of the Civil War in the mid-sixties, Roy got involved in reenacting. Curtis loved it too. We did a lot of events as a family."

Jenny's face eased as she remembered good times. Then it clouded again. "Curtis was fifteen when, out of the blue, I got pregnant again. Jimmy was only three when his older brother died in Vietnam."

Chloe watched blood appear on the folded towel she was pressing against Roelke's wound. Where was the damn ambulance?

"Everything fell apart." Jenny pleated her apron in her fingers. "Roy became…obsessive about reenacting. He disappeared for a week at a time with some of his hardcore friends. I lost interest, but sometimes Roy took Jimmy to reenactments. Jimmy had asthma, and I told Roy over and *over* that he had to be sensitive to that." Jenny's voice was hollow. "But when Jimmy was ten he had a terrible attack at a reenactment in rural Tennessee. He died."

Chloe put her free hand on Jenny's shoulder, squeezed.

"Roy quit his job—he'd inherited money and didn't need to work—and sort of disappeared into his reenactment world. Even his campaigner friends drifted away. Roy would go on solo marches for two or three weeks at a time in some national forest or wilderness area."

"Was this in Wisconsin?" Roelke asked.

Jenny shook her head. "No, Missouri. Roy ended up in a dark place. I tried to help him, but... I also blamed him for Jimmy's death. Finally I divorced Roy and left without telling anyone where I was going. I came to Wisconsin because I'd read about Old World. My ancestors immigrated from Germany—Roy's too, actually. Anyway, it was the change I needed. I made new friends here, and met Lee, and tried to leave the past behind."

Lee stirred in his chair. "Metzger said he met two Wisconsin reenactors at a big event in Gettysburg earlier this month, and figured out where Jenny was."

Steven and Kyle, Chloe thought. Maybe they'd met Roy Metzger by chance. Or maybe he'd noticed their little German cockades, and top-notch impressions, and struck up a conversation with kindred souls. In either case, after the Gettysburg event, Roy Metzger headed for Old World. He'd walked onto the site wearing Union blues and slipped to the 1860 Schulz Farm to wait for Jenny.

Chloe looked at the older woman. "Roy was also carrying an embroidered handkerchief just like one Kyle had in his pocket today."

"I made one for Roy years ago." Jenny still looked stunned. "I made Kyle's last year. He was *so* excited about reenacting … He reminds me of my sons."

"I wouldn't let Metzger see Jenny," Lee said. "But I never dreamed he'd come here! So I—I killed him."

Jenny rounded on her husband with sudden anger. "Lee, *stop* this. I didn't kill Roy, and you didn't kill Roy. Tell them!"

"It's too late." Lee sounded dazed. "When I heard that a reenactor had died here at the Schulz Farm, I knew it had to be Metzger. I hoped that would be the end of it. But Belinda said the cops might show pictures of Metzger's belongings on TV."

"*Belinda?*" Chloe echoed. Then she remembered the day she and Roelke had discussed that possibility in the Ed House kitchen, while Belinda waited in the next room.

"Jenny never watches the news," Lee said, "but … "

"But you were afraid Steven or Kyle would see Roy's handkerchief and spill the proverbial beans." Chloe sucked in a breath, trying to stop her brain from drawing the obvious conclusions. "They'd recognize Jenny's handiwork. Which would focus the cops' attention on her."

"Did you kill Steven Siggelkow?" Roelke demanded.

Lee nodded. "I bought the gun at a garage sale so I could show it to my students—"

"Show it to your *students*?" Chloe repeated. This from the man who'd spoken against the Civil War event with such conviction? But—Lee had never been worried about interpreting the war. He'd been trying to keep reenactors away from his wife, afraid she might discover that the dead man was her ex-husband. Afraid someone might mention meeting Roy at Gettysburg. Or—if she *had* killed Roy—afraid she might crack from the strain of carrying on.

Then—dear God, the cyanide. *That's* what she'd been trying to remember. "Roelke do you know where cyanide comes from? Fruit pits, like apple seeds."

"*What?*"

"I was reminded when I was packing stuff at home," she said, "and skimmed through my old forestry school notebooks. It would take a fair number of seeds to kill somebody, but Lee grows antique apples. He had access to all he needed."

"What does cyanide have to do with anything?" Jenny asked.

Chloe hated to tell her. "Kyle was poisoned with cyanide."

Jenny shook her head as if to clear it. "Lee, for God's sake," she begged. "Tell them this is all a mistake."

Lee dropped his chin.

"Metzger's death may well have been accidental," Roelke told Lee. "He was malnourished. Maybe he tried to sit on that beam, and got dizzy and fell. Everything could have stopped right there."

A low moan squeezed from Lee's throat.

"Shut him into the *Schartze-Küche*." Chloe couldn't bear to look at Lee anymore. Roelke nodded, waved his gun, and Lee went into the Black Kitchen without protest.

Roelke dropped heavily back into his chair, and looked at Jenny. "A warden told me about a man's daypack found near Ottawa Lake right after your ex-husband died. There was no ID in it, and the wardens thought someone had drowned. Is it possible that … ?"

"When Roy disappeared on really long marches," Jenny said slowly, "he'd sometimes carry some modern clothes, hidden in his knapsack. If he needed to be around people … he could change, not attract attention."

"Does it make sense that your ex-husband carried a Confederate uniform too?" Roelke asked.

Jenny nodded. "As far as I know, he's just drifted from event to event for the past couple of years. He didn't mind galvanizing if more Confederates were needed at a top-notch event."

"What about his musket?"

"He'd carry that along, I'd think."

"So there might still be a musket hidden somewhere in the Kettle Moraine Forest." Roelke shifted his weight, winced, went still. "I'm still not sure I'm following this. It's a long way from St. Louis to Gettysburg, and a long way from Gettysburg to Wisconsin. It's hard to believe Mr. Metzger walked the whole way."

"He would hitchhike when he had to," Jenny murmured. "But he probably walked as much as he could."

"The Ice Age Trail goes through the state forest, right past Old World," Chloe said.

Tears streamed down Jenny's cheeks. "This is all my fault! Roy wasn't well when I left him. I thought I'd go under myself if I didn't, and I was *so* angry at him ... I hated him for not taking care of Jimmy." Her voice broke. "But I've always felt guilty for abandoning Roy like I did."

Chloe felt like crying too, but struggled against it. "Jenny, this is *not* your fault."

Jenny looked from Roelke to Chloe. "You have to believe me—Lee's a gentle, loving soul."

That may be, Chloe thought. When Roy died at the Schulz Farm, Lee assumed Jenny had pushed him from the balcony. Everything that happened after that came out of Lee's efforts to protect Jenny.

The ache pulsed in Chloe's chest. Once, Lee had been drowning in grief and guilt—his son dead in Vietnam, his wife dead from a car crash when he was at the wheel. *Jenny saved me*, Lee had once said.

And sadly, he'd been willing to do *anything* to save her.

Roelke was glad to hear approaching sirens. He'd been hurt worse, but still, the gash throbbed, and Chloe hadn't been able to stop the blood flow. I'm going to need stitches because of that SOB, he thought. And probably a tetanus shot.

Within moments the Schulz kitchen got very crowded with EMTs—Denise and Adam again—and cops—Skeet Deardorff and Deputy Marge Bandacek. "Bad guy's in there," Roelke said, and jerked a thumb at the chimney door. And to Adam, "I can walk, dammit."

In the back of the EMT truck he let Adam clean and examine the wound. "Nasty," Adam observed. "But you'll live." He applied a clean dressing.

Roelke heard a distinct approaching roar, and reached for his shirt.

"No way," Adam protested. "You need stitches."

"There's something I've got to do first." Roelke eased the bloody shirt back over his head, waved Adam's protests aside, and climbed from the truck.

Ralph Petty parked his Harley in the drive. Skeet already had Lee in the squad. Chloe was standing off to one side with an arm around Jenny.

Roelke walked to the pasture fence on the far side of the drive. "Mr. Petty," he called, "a word, please." He thrust one palm in Chloe's direction: *Stay where you are.*

Petty had the grace to look startled when he saw the blood. "What on earth happened?"

"I was stabbed by one of your employees. After I prevented him from killing another of your employees. But right now, you and I have something else to discuss." Roelke leaned against the fence. "You treated that young woman, Belinda, quite badly this afternoon."

Petty's eyes narrowed. "How I discipline my employees is not your concern."

"But I'm sure you know by now that Mac Ostermann stole the artifact Belinda was worried about."

"That's a matter for the sheriff's department—"

"I'm sure you *also* know that Mac Ostermann already has a police record for stealing. From an antiques store."

Petty missed a beat. "Oh? Why, I—I had no idea."

"Actually, I think you did." Despite the pain in his side, Roelke was starting to enjoy himself. "Since Mac is your nephew."

Petty's face grew hard. "Officer McKenna, you have no right to dig into my personal business."

"I didn't dig into your personal business. I am investigating a crime in Eagle, and I suspect Mac stole a tintype and other Civil War antiques from a resident. And while tracking *that*, I discovered that his mother buys and sells Civil War antiques. She moved from one antiques mall to another soon after Mac was arrested for stealing from one of her colleagues."

Petty's face was the color of bricks.

"Marjorie must have been trying to distance herself from the scandal," Roelke continued. "Because instead of doing business as Marjorie Ostermann, she switched to her maiden name. Birth name, as Chloe would say. And lo and behold, what did I discover? That Marjorie's birth name is Petty. She's your sister. Which is something you all have obviously taken great care to conceal." Hell, Marie—EPD clerk and keeper of all local lore—didn't even know. It was actually quite impressive.

Growing anger emanated from Petty like heat waves.

"I also suspect that Mac makes tintypes so he, or his mom, or *both* of them, can sell them as originals." Maybe Marjorie had overdosed because of shame; maybe because of guilt. Either way, if reproduction tintypes were being sold as originals, the truth would come out.

The other man was rigid.

"But I digress." For the sake of those watching, Roelke smiled a friendly smile. "Here's the thing. I don't like bullies. You have some twisted need to make yourself feel important by grinding other people down. It's pathetic. And it pisses me off."

Petty clenched his fists. Roelke braced for a punch. Do it, he willed Petty, just as he had the day they met. Out of the corner of his eye Roelke saw Skeet start toward him, and waved him off.

But with an obvious struggle, Petty controlled himself. Then his expression changed—just as it had after Chloe told him off that afternoon. A satisfied smile replaced the rage. "Officer McKenna, you have made a grave mistake. I will lodge a complaint with Chief Naborski, and with the Village Board."

"That's your right," Roelke agreed. "But I can't help wondering how state historical society administrators would respond to the news that a site director personally invited a relative with a record of stealing Civil War antiques to participate in a special Civil War event. *Especially* since that relative stole an antique from the site's collection. If Chloe hadn't found that bottle, he would have gotten away with it."

Petty clearly had not, in the heat of the moment, thought that through.

"You took quite a risk, inviting the 100th to Old World," Roelke mused. "Did you honestly believe that Mac had seen the error of his ways? Did you really think you needed a battle to make visitors happy? Or did you just want to screw with Chloe and Byron's plans?"

Petty's face turned an interesting shade of purple.

"Anyway, your role in this wouldn't look good, do you think?" Roelke asked affably. "And it wouldn't look good to the people of

Eagle, especially if that director was interested in, say, running for the Village Board."

Petty opened his mouth, closed it again.

"Mac is an adult now, so future convictions will become public knowledge. I don't need to put extraneous details in *my* report. But you know how journalists are. They just love a good story."

A tic developed beneath Petty's left eye.

"Here's my advice." Roelke smiled pleasantly. "Apologize to Belinda. And get off Chloe's back. Or some eager young reporter might just get a juicy tip."

He started to turn away, then leaned closer to Petty. "And I might just beat the crap out of you."

FORTY-ONE

"Hurry, Tante Rosina!" Gesine stood beside her father's wagon, quivering with excitement. "We're ready to leave for your birthday picnic!" Gesine—Lottie and Adolf's youngest—was four, and graced with an impish smile and golden tangle of curls.

Rosina laughed as she set the last basket of food into the wagon bed and climbed aboard. "I'm ready too." She settled in the straw with Gesine, her sister, and her three brothers.

Lottie sat on the wagon seat. "How lovely that you were born in June, Rosina."

"I just wish the boys could have joined us."

"I know," Lottie said over her shoulder. "But we shall celebrate your thirty-fourth birthday in fine style nonetheless."

Rosina smiled, but she missed her sons. John and Andreas were seventeen and sixteen now. They'd hired out as farm labor that spring, leaving home before dawn, stumbling back at twilight. Their absence today reminded her that they were of an age to move on, make their own lives, wherever they wished. John was engaged to a sweet girl from a nearby farm. Andreas had begun walking a miller's pretty daughter home after church.

The wagon jolted down the drive and Rosina tried to take pleasure in the fine day, the landscape. Adolf's farm was thriving. After the wheat boom he had diversified and developed a fine dairy herd. Hayfields glowed emerald green beneath the sun. Half a dozen calves followed their mothers in a pasture behind the big dairy barn.

This is what Klaus dreamed of, Rosina thought wistfully, for the thousandth time. The Sperber farm had become her home, and she was content enough. But she would always grieve. Always feel guilty about what should have been.

Gesine crawled onto Rosina's lap and begged for a song. Even the children knew better than to suggest "Heidenröslein," or one of the war ballads. But they sang songs from the old country, and songs of America too.

Suddenly Rosina noticed they were heading south, toward Palmyra. "Where are we going?" she asked sharply. She hadn't traveled this road since that bitterly cold and wretched day in 1864 when she'd turned her back on Klaus's farm.

"It's a surprise," Lottie called. "Please. It's what the children wanted."

Rosina didn't feel like singing anymore. Her last hope for a *pleasant* surprise faded when Adolf turned onto Roelke Lane. As they approached the farm she stared at her hands, clenched in her lap. She had gladly let Adolf handle the sale, and never asked who'd purchased Klaus's dream.

The wagon turned into the drive and rumbled to a halt. "We're here!" Gesine cried joyfully. "We're here!"

Was the place overgrown and neglected? Or had someone transformed it into a prosperous showplace? Rosina steeled herself before looking around.

No new buildings had joined the little cabin and weaving shed. But the cabin had a new roof. A fresh woven fence surrounded the overgrown garden. And a small field—Klaus's first field—was green with new growth.

"*Mutti!*" John and Andreas strode toward the wagon, laughing.

Rosina caught her breath. "But I thought—"

"Surprise!" John lowered the backboard and lifted her to the ground.

"Surprise!" Andreas echoed, and kissed her on the cheek. "Happy birthday."

"But—I don't understand!"

"It's still our farm, *Mutti*," John said. "It was never sold. Andreas and I—with a lot of help from Gerhard—have been working here all spring. We'll get a bit of harvest this year, and more next."

"And we're going to build a proper brick house," Andreas said. "We've marked off the ground already. When it's finished, you'll have a room of your own."

Rosina looked from her sons to her friends. "How … Why … "

"We will miss you terribly," Lottie said softly. "But it's time for you to go back home."

———

They spread quilts beneath the Old Oak's mighty branches, and ate onion pie and wheat bread and baby radishes. Afterward the children raced about, squealing over garter snakes and butterflies. Gesine picked a bouquet of violets for Rosina.

The men leaned back on their hands, drinking beer, making plans. "Maybe we should burn down the cabin and enlarge the garden," John mused.

Andreas shook his head. "We can repurpose it for chickens, or a tool shed."

Rosina smiled at her two sons—John, dreaming big; and Andreas, more practical. Once they'd seemed as distinct as their fathers, but that had faded as they grew. Perhaps each had absorbed a bit of the other's temperament—as if each son had two fathers, and each father had two sons. There is need for industry *and* fancies here, she wanted to tell them. But they already knew.

Lottie suggested a walk, and Rosina waited until they were well away from the others before speaking. "You must tell me—how did this happen?"

"Adolf and I agreed from the beginning that the farm must be kept for your sons," Lottie said. "We made land payments until Klaus's original loan was satisfied."

"You've made the boys so happy. But ... it's *much* too generous."

Lottie walked in silence for a moment, her fingers brushing the tall grasses. "There's something I've never said. The day Gerhard was born, on the *Fair Wind* ... I heard someone tell you that Leopold Zuehlsdorff wanted to speak with you on deck. And I heard you say you couldn't leave me."

Rosina was still confused. "Of course not!" She remembered that moment too—the flowing blood, the midwife's worry, her dear friend's sunken cheeks.

"When we were on the ship, I didn't approve of Herr Zuehlsdorff. But over time, I saw how deeply you cared for him." Lottie stopped walking. "I've always felt terribly guilty. Had you gone up to speak with him, everything might have turned out differently. Perhaps you could have married the man you loved."

"I did love Leopold." Rosina looked over the rippling prairie. "But I also came to love Klaus. Please, Lottie, don't feel guilty. When I look at my sons, I can't possibly wish I had not met either of their fathers."

"Thank you for that." Lottie's eyes filled with tears. "Will you tell John the truth one day?"

"No," Rosina said firmly. "No good could come of it. That secret will die with you and me."

Lottie nodded. "And my dear friend, I hope that you can let go of your guilt as well. It is a hard load to carry."

But Klaus never forgave me for loving Leopold, Rosina thought. It was hopeless to think of absolution. That particular burden was hers to bear.

FORTY-TWO

CHLOE WAS ALONE IN Ed House a week later when someone knocked. "Come in," she called. The screened door opened and closed, but no one spoke. Chloe swiveled in her chair. "Belinda!"

"Is it okay for me to be here?"

"Of course. I'm glad to see you." Chloe knew Roelke was already waiting for her at the farm, but this was important. She'd tried calling Belinda after the disastrous Civil War weekend, but her mother had explained that the girl wasn't ready to talk to anyone from Old World. "She loved working with you, Chloe. But after what happened... well, I doubt she'll be back. And frankly, I don't want her there."

Now Belinda perched on the edge of a chair. Red spots flamed along her cheekbones. "Um... Chloe, I'm really sorry about the bottle."

"You have nothing to be sorry about," Chloe said firmly. "It was recovered. I'm just sorry that Mr. Petty let his... his frustration and worry spill over on you. It wasn't professional and it wasn't fair."

"I figured I was fired, but ... " Belinda twisted her fingers together. "Mr. Petty called my house last night and apologized."

Chloe almost fell off her chair. "He *apologized?*"

Belinda nodded. "He said he hoped I'd finish my internship here. So if that's okay with you ... "

"That's definitely okay. Truly."

"Oh, good." Belinda took a deep breath. "How is Kyle?"

"He's better," Chloe said, with profound relief. "He got a weak dose of cyanide, and the medical people administered antidotes right away. He'd also been drinking homemade wine, which might have helped. Something about alcohol neutralizing the acid."

"Thank *goodness.*" Belinda started to rise, then stopped. "There's just one more thing. My mom would like to donate that old linen shirt to Old World Wisconsin. If you want it."

Chloe almost clapped her hands with delight. "That would be fantastic! It can live at the Schulz house. I'm sure the collections committee will agree."

Belinda left with a smile on her face and a promise to return on Monday. Chloe replayed their conversation in her mind, shaking her head. Petty apologized? To a volunteer high school intern? "Hell has surely frozen over," she murmured. She could hardly wait to share that tidbit with Roelke.

Roelke. Who was already waiting for her at the farm. They were hosting a low-key housewarming party, and she *really* needed to get there.

She was on her feet when the phone rang. "Chloe? It's Richard, from the Veterans Museum, calling about Klaus Roelke."

"Oh?" Chloe had found the Roelke family genealogical records, but she hadn't had a chance to revisit Klaus's service record.

"Klaus definitely served in *Unser Deutsches Regiment*—the 26th Wisconsin Infantry," Richard said. "After being captured at Gettysburg he died in Andersonville Prison."

"He did?" Chloe tried to absorb both the news and its implications. It hurt her heart to think that Roelke's ancestor had died such a wretched, tragic, needless death.

But ... why on earth would Rosina have taken responsibility for that?

Richard broke her reverie. "I've been working with historians at Andersonville Prison National Historic Site. I've shared some letters and reminiscences that Wisconsin survivors wrote after the war, and they've identified a few Wisconsin records in their archives. Not much survived, obviously. But one thing that did was a letter written by Klaus Roelke before he died."

A tingle skittered over Chloe's skin. "*Really? What does it say?*"

"You'll want to read it for yourself. May I fax it down?"

"Please do." The site's shiny new fax machine was in the Admin building, which Chloe had been avoiding. Inexplicably, Petty had yet to fire her for telling him off in public, and she was lying low.

But a letter from Klaus? For that, she'd camp out in Petty's office.

Roelke was sweeping the front porch of his farmhouse when a car he didn't recognize pulled in and parked. He didn't recognize the woman who emerged, and went to meet her.

"Officer McKenna, forgive me for coming to your home," she said.

"Why—Ms. Hawkins!" Roelke tried to school the shock from his face. In worn jeans and a faded t-shirt, Jenny Hawkins was almost unrecognizeable. It was more than the clothing, though. Jenny

368

looked as if she'd lost five pounds in the past week. Her face was haggard, her eyes filled with an inexpressible grief.

"Chloe said it would be okay for me to come by." Jenny walked around the sedan and opened the car trunk. "I know I should have come to the police station, but I just … just couldn't."

She gestured inside. Roelke stepped closer and saw something long and thin, secured in a filthy canvas bag that had probably once been white.

"Please, take it." Jenny's voice was brittle. *She* was brittle, like an autumn leaf that might crumble at any moment, or just blow away.

"Is this … "

"I found it on my property this morning, quite by chance. Roy must have hidden it before he went to the house looking for me. After Lee sent him on his way, I guess he decided to leave it there before hiking on to Old World."

Makes sense, Roelke thought. Nobody would stop somebody in period clothes anywhere near the site, but a musket would have attracted notice. He picked up the gun. "What do you—"

"I don't care what you do with it." She slammed the trunk and slid back behind the wheel. When Roelke stepped back she did a three-point turn and drove back to the main road.

Roelke watched her drive away. He wanted to help Jenny Hawkins, but had no idea how. I'll talk to Chloe about that, he thought, and felt better. Chloe would know what to do.

He slowly undid the canvas ties and pulled the musket free, letting its protective sleeve fall to the ground. The reproduction Springfield rifled musket was about four and a half feet long and heavy, maybe eight or nine pounds. The wood gleamed. The metalwork did too. Roy Metzger might have been living on the edge, but he'd taken good care of his weapon.

One of my ancestors likely carried a gun just like this one, Roelke thought. He gripped the gun tight, taking the measure of it. It felt ... familiar, sort of. Like he had a memory, faint but real, of handling such a musket.

And to his surprise, the sensation did not annoy him. So be it, he thought. Chloe had her ways of connecting to the past. This was his.

He locked the gun in his trunk, pocketed the keys, and glanced toward the lane—still no sign of the woman he loved. Well, their guests weren't due for a while yet. Besides, he had one chore left on his to-do list.

In the garden, it took about five minutes to thin the carrots. He even buried the sacrificial seedlings in the compost pile. He did that for Chloe, and it felt good.

But when he stood, slapping his palms against his jeans, the old cabin loomed dark and dismal just beyond the fence.

"Dammit," he muttered. Learning even a little about his ancestors made them more than names on a wedding certificate. What Chloe perceived in the cabin, what she'd discovered on the note tucked into the housewife, mattered. He left the garden and went inside the cabin. What *happened* here?

Roelke didn't have it in him to talk to a dead person, but finally he took a deep breath and tried to think deliberate thoughts: *Um ... look, Chloe thinks regrets don't accomplish anything. That we do the best we can and should just try to learn from mistakes and move on. Sometimes we have to forgive ourselves.*

He paused. And to his astonishment, he thought that maybe— just maybe—he felt a tiny, indefinable hitch in the atmosphere.

Back outside, he saw the familiar Ford Pinto appear on the road. Chloe was home.

She jumped from the car and hurried to greet him. The black eye left from Lee Hawkins's backhanded smack still made Roelke wince, but it was fading.

"Guess what!" she said breathlessly. "I've got a letter from Klaus!"

"From Klaus?" After just handling the musket, that news was borderline eerie. "Klaus *Roelke?*"

"Yes. It's a sad story, though. I just learned that he served in the 26th Wisconsin, and was captured at Gettysburg and died in Andersonville Prison. An archivist in Georgia sent a copy to the Wisconsin Veterans Museum."

"My ancestor died in a prison camp?" Roelke repeated slowly. That was brutal.

"I'm afraid so," Chloe said sympathetically. "It was a real hellhole, and evidently the letter was never sent."

He almost wished she'd kept that to herself. "How can you do this stuff all the time? So much of it is sad."

"It can be," she agreed. "But one reason I do what I do is to honor the people who came before us. I don't want their stories to be forgotten."

He regretted sounding petulant. "I know."

"And Roelke, I'm confident that whatever happened, your ancestors did the best they could. They faced challenges we can't begin to imagine."

"I expect so," he allowed.

Chloe produced a piece of paper from her bag. "Here's the letter."

"Why don't you read it out loud?" For some reason, that seemed appropriate.

He followed Chloe to the cabin. She stopped on the doorstep. After squaring her shoulders she began to read.

October 1863,

My little Spatzi,

As I expect you know, I was captured and transported to a prison camp in Georgia. The human misery here is beyond my pen or will to describe. But God had a purpose in sending me to this place. It shocked me into realizing what a fool I have been. How thoughtless and small. I did not realize I was such a prideful man, but it was certainly pride that sent me to the army, and prevented me from answering your letters.

Dearest Rosina, I beg your forgiveness. You asked for mine, but in my heart I believe there is nothing to forgive. What was past, was past. We should have enjoyed a long life together with our beloved sons. I fear that is not to be, but God will decide.

It is difficult to get letters out of here. I have given a minister a ring I made for you. Not the pretty ring I had imagined, but the best I could manage. I carved it from a coat button, and with the help of a comrade, fashioned a tiny scrap of silver to add as a token of esteem. The same comrade will take possession of this letter if I die. If he survives, he will get it to you. If I do not live, know that my final thoughts will be of you, and our sons, and our farm.

Your loving husband,

Klaus

Chloe folded the page reverently and slipped it away. "Isn't that amazing?"

Roelke's throat felt thick. "It is," he said huskily. "What do you suppose they were forgiving each other for?"

"We'll probably never know. But they each felt guilty about *something.*"

Guilt, Roelke thought. He'd confronted too much of that lately. His guilt. Libby's guilt. Jenny and Lee Hawkins's guilt. And now Klaus and Rosina Roelke's too. Chloe was right—carrying guilt around did more harm than good.

"I hate knowing that Rosina never got that letter," he said.

"Maybe ... "

"What?"

Chloe stepped gingerly into the cabin, paused, took another step. He followed her. "Is it better?"

She hesitated. Then a slow smile lit her face. "Yes. It *is.*"

Roelke rubbed his chin, gazing around the room. Was the bad stuff gone because of what he'd mumbled before Chloe arrived? Because she'd read the letter from Klaus? Or had the whole mess been nothing but their collective imagination? Roelke didn't know, and didn't care.

Chloe smiled. "Let's hang Rosina's sampler in here, okay? I'm having it properly framed. And ... I think we should plant a prairie rose by the door."

―――――

If guests weren't on the way Chloe might have stayed in the cabin all evening, making plans for her personal retreat space. She felt as if an anvil had slid from her shoulders.

Back in the house, she began pulling plates and platters from the cupboard. "Did I tell you I love the kitchen walls?" she asked. A warm shade called Hubbard Squash had replaced the tired mint green. "Going with your grandmother's favorite color was a good plan." She'd dodged a bullet on that one.

373

"My grandma's favorite color was pink."

"It was?" So much for dodging a bullet.

"But you hate pink, so I picked out a color I thought you'd like." Roelke opened a can of mixed nuts. "It's not my grandma's kitchen anymore, Chloe. It's your kitchen."

Our kitchen, she wanted to say, since their cohabitation would not be defined by gender stereotypes. But, thank God, she stopped herself. "It's perfect," she told Roelke. "Absolutely perfect."

He was scrutinizing an almond. "So...there's cyanide in this?"

"That's a sweet almond, so just a trace amount," Chloe said patiently. They'd had several variations of this conversation in the past few days. "It's the bitter almonds you have to worry about."

"But—"

"Look!" she said. "Libby and the kids are here. And—there's Adam too."

The kids dragged out the croquet set, and the adults settled into lawn chairs. "Chloe, do you know how to make *springerle?*" Libby asked. "I happened to spot a cookie mold in an antiques store window last week. I'm not an impulse buyer, but it was the oddest thing—I just had to have it."

"I do know how to make *springerle*," Chloe said. "I've got a couple of old recipes. Next time you come over we'll try them out. And this Christmas we'll have *springerle* and marzipan pigs." She smiled at Roelke. He'd told her that his grandmother always made marzipan pigs in December.

"Chloe's learned some stuff about Klaus," Roelke told his cousin. "He died in a prison camp during the Civil War."

Libby sobered. "How horrid."

Chloe considered sharing Klaus's letter but decided that was better saved for another time. "I also found genealogical records in Jefferson County yesterday," she said instead.

"Do you know which brother we're descended from?" Roelke asked.

"I do. Your line comes down from Klaus and Rosina's oldest son, John."

"John." Roelke took that in. "Well, hunh."

Chloe was gratified that she'd been able to put her history skills to good use for once.

Adam helped himself to a cold beer from the ice chest, then turned to Roelke. "How's the gash?"

"Almost healed," Roelke said. Which wasn't quite true, Chloe thought. But it was getting better.

"Eagle's still buzzing about it all." Adam popped the top. "Sounds like Mac Ostermann had quite the scam going."

"Yeah." Roelke squeezed a lemon wedge into his iced tea. "We've identified at least a couple of reproduction tintypes that he sold as originals. And in addition to stealing the bottle at Old World, the antiques stolen from Maggie Geddings's house were traced back to him. Mac claims his mother had no knowledge of his activities, and nothing has surfaced to prove otherwise. But Mac's in serious trouble."

"I should have picked up on the clues," Chloe said, chagrined. "From what you told me, the kid didn't care much about reenacting or family bonding."

"No," Roelke agreed. "But he spent a lot of time perfecting the art of tintype photography."

"The curator I talked to in Madison used the word *fake* instead of *repro*," Chloe mused. "I got indignant, but it should have reminded me that for some people, artifacts represent money instead of education and heritage."

"But in the end, you guys figured everything out," Libby said.

Roelke looked disgusted. "Barely. I was on to Mac, but I thought his parents might have been involved in Siggelkow's murder."

"Well, I concluded that Jenny killed Private M," Chloe said. "Not my best deduction."

"Nothing further about that death?" Adam asked.

Roelke shook his head. "It's been ruled accidental."

A string of tragedies led to Roy Metzger's accidental death, Chloe thought. Which led to *another* string of tragedies. It was painful to think about.

She turned to Roelke. "Did I ever thank you for saving my life?" Those moments when Lee had threatened first her, then Roelke, with the carving knife were equally painful to think about. "How did you find us?"

"I'd decided that Gunter was in danger," Roelke said. "I went charging up to the Koepsell Farm, and there he was, just fine. But you weren't there, and that made me uneasy. So I went looking."

"Lee could have killed *you*."

"Nah," Roelke scoffed.

But Chloe was pretty sure she knew what was going on. As a child, Roelke hadn't helped his mom. As a teen, he hadn't kept his brother Patrick away from trouble. As a man, he hadn't saved his best friend Rick. He couldn't bear to lose me, she thought, and forever wonder if he might have stopped it.

But ... that wasn't entirely fair either. Chloe knew to her marrow that if Lee had been threatening a perfect stranger, Roelke would have launched at that knife just as readily. For whatever set of complicated reasons, that was who he was. It scared her a little. It also made her proud.

She was glad when Dellyn arrived. Her friend brought a hanging basket overflowing with petunias, fuchsia, and calibrachoa. "Hummingbird magnets," Dellyn said.

"You already gave us the garden bench," Chloe protested. "Not to mention hauling your tiller over here and fighting your way through years of neglect."

"That was to celebrate the farm," Dellyn said. "This is to celebrate your continued employment at Old World Wisconsin. If Petty was going to fire you, don't you think he'd have done it by now?"

"I hope so," Chloe said. "Honestly, I figured he'd punt my sorry butt off the site on Monday, but so far … nothing." She glanced at Roelke, who just shrugged. Well, his strategy is probably good, she thought. There was no point in making herself crazy. If Petty made a move, she'd deal with it then.

Tires crunched in the drive as a pickup pulled in—her sister, Kari, and brother-in-law, Trygvie. Chloe and Roelke went to meet them. Kari hugged Roelke—she was quite fond of him—before greeting Chloe.

"This place is *great*," Tryg added, gazing around with quiet appreciation. Roelke and Chloe had visited his family farm, but this was the first time he'd seen the Roelke place.

Kari pulled a tarp away from something in the truck bed. "And every old farm needs a porch swing."

———

Chloe brought her dulcimer outside after dinner. Roelke recognized the first tune she played with a twinge of panic. "Isn't that … "

"Gunter Diederich told me it's called 'Heidenröslein,'" she told him. "A German song seemed appropriate this evening."

I should have known Chloe wouldn't rat me out, Roelke thought. Maybe one day he'd try to tell Libby about the way hearing that tune, and smelling black powder, and handling that musket, had made him feel. But not tonight.

Since he hadn't done any of the cooking, he told the others to relax while he carried the dishes to the kitchen. By the time he rinsed plates and got leftovers in the fridge, the group had dispersed.

Tryg and Kari were sliding the swing from the back of their pickup. "We'll hang this for you," Tryg called. Roelke didn't object because Tryg and Kari were laughing together. They'd gone through a rough patch recently, so laughter was a good thing.

Chloe and Dellyn had taken the kids to the garden. "We need help making toad houses," Chloe had announced earlier. Now Justin's excited voice drifted over the yard. Sun glinted on Dierdre's rhinestone tiara as she darted about. Roelke hadn't known they needed toad houses in the garden, but clearly they did.

Libby and Adam were walking along the woodline. Each had hands in pockets, but they looked at ease. Content, even. Maybe, Roelke thought. Just maybe.

That ache came to his chest, stronger than ever. I can't lose this, he thought, as a band tightened around his ribs. He profoundly hoped he wasn't about to embarrass himself with a panic attack or something.

Chloe spotted him, and waved. He waved back but her distress meter somehow triggered, for she left the others and joined him. "Hey," she said softly. "You okay?"

"This is all I ever wanted," he said. "I didn't even know it, but it is. Me buying this place, you deciding to move in, Libby and the kids and our friends feeling at home here … " He exhaled slowly.

"Sometimes I get this—this tightness inside because I'm afraid I won't be able to hang on to it."

She considered. "But… maybe what you're feeling isn't fear. Maybe it's just happiness."

My fears are real, Roelke thought. He was a cop, and by virtue of training and experience, his brain would always look for possible calamity. He owed the bank an enormous amount of money.

And Petty had *both* of them in his sights now. Roelke had said a bit more than he'd planned, but he wasn't sorry he'd threatened the SOB. Still, he was acutely aware that the conversation might bite one or both of them in the ass one day.

"It's partly my fault." Chloe leaned back against him. "My experience in the cabin caused problems."

"It did." He glanced at the cabin. That problem seemed to be solved, though, even if he didn't understand exactly how.

And now that Chloe had found his full family history, he could trace a straight line back to Klaus and Rosina. Through John, the eldest son. Something about that pleased him.

But that didn't totally address the problems Chloe had been wrestling with. "It also seemed like you might have changed your mind about moving in with me."

"It's been hard," she conceded. "This will always be the old *Roelke* place. I've had moments of wondering if I could ever truly feel at home here. Kari struggled with that after moving to Trygvie's ancestral home, you know."

"I know."

"And I've worried about not contributing enough to the farm. Financially, and—"

"*Chloe.*" He had to interrupt. "I wanted to save my ancestors' farm. But I don't know anything about toad houses and elderberries and Christmas *springerle*. Don't you get it? My name may be on the mortgage, but you're the one who makes this place a home."

"Oh," she said in a tiny voice, and settled her head against his shoulder.

He wrapped both arms around her. To hell with financial worries, and with Ralph Petty's vindictive schemes too. Tonight, he thought, right here, Chloe and I have everything we need.

Wisconsin Veterans Museum

*1. Tintype of unidentified Union
soldier wearing a cockade.*

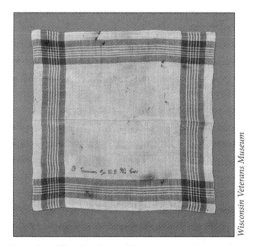

Wisconsin Veterans Museum

*2. Linen handkerchief with blue woven stripes and unit
embroidered on one side, used during the Civil War by
Fayette Cannon, Company E, 2nd Wisconsin Cavalry.*

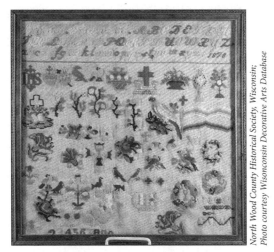

North Wood County Historical Society, Wisconsin;
Photo courtesy Wisonconsin Decorative Arts Database

3. Berlin woolwork sampler by Anna
Franzel Weigel (1859–1932), dated 1878.

Library of Congress

4. Family register, 1869.

Library of Congress

5. *Civil War envelope showing an eagle with American flag attacking a Confederate flag.*

Wisconsin Veterans Museum

6. *"Housewife" sewing kit, 1861–1865.*

Wisconsin Veterans Museum

*7. Draft drum and discs used
in Janesville, Wisconsin, in 1863.*

Wisconsin Veterans Museum

*8. Snuff container, a flat bottle of thick green glass with
elaborate cut surface, carried by Joseph Greiner, 45th
Wisconsin Volunteer Infantry Regiment during the Civil War.*

Wisconsin Veterans Museum

9. Ring, carved from a gutta-percha coat button with German silver inlay of two joined hands, made by John M. Pomeroy, 22nd Wisconsin Volunteer Infantry, while being held at Libby Prison in Richmond, Virginia, after being captured in 1863.

ACKNOWLEDGMENTS

I am indebted to the people who, back in the 1970s, conceptualized and developed Old World Wisconsin. The buildings now restored at the Schulz Farm, the Fossebrekke Farm, and the Sanford Farm are only a few of the architectural treasures that would have been lost without the efforts of historians and property owners. Many interpreters have brought those buildings to life over the decades.

Special thanks to Sgt. Gwen Bruckner and Lt. Steve Lesniewski of the Eagle Police Department. I wouldn't be able to write about Roelke McKenna without kind assistance from law enforcement professionals.

I am enormously grateful to Sgt. Jeff Diehl and his comrades in the 3rd Wisconsin Veteran Volunteer Infantry who provided wonderful special events at Old World in the 1980s and '90s. One of my favorite memories is of Jeff singing a German folk song at the Schulz Farm while looking for recruits. Thanks also to the 33rd Wisconsin for equally loyal and top-notch participation; bonus applause to John Wedeward and Michael Binder for help with photographs and details as this project came together. And thanks to my friends in The Mudsills as well, especially the women who worked so hard on civilian impressions.

I appreciate the help received from Russell Horton, Reference and Outreach Archivist at the Wisconsin Veterans Museum, and the North Wood County Historical Society Board. Their assistance made it possible to include photographs of key artifacts.

I'm fortunate to have guidance and help from Agent Fiona Kenshole, and everyone at Transatlantic Literary; and Terri Bischoff, Nicole Nugent, Amy Glaser, and the entire Midnight Ink team.

Special thanks to George Radtke, president of Pommersche Tanzdeel Freistad, who shared the music and lyrics of "Sah ein Knab, ein Röslein stehn" (also known as "Heidenröslein"). The folk song was adapted from a melody by Franz Schubert and a poem by Johann Wolfgang von Goethe.

I'd be lost without the help of Laurie Rosengren, Katie Mead and Robert Alexander, and Maddy Hunter. I'm also blessed with the support of my extended family; from Scott Meeker (AKA Mr. Ernst), my husband, partner, and former fellow reenactor; and from the reader-friends who make it possible for the series to continue. Thank you all.

If you are interested in experiencing a Civil War reenactment, opportunities range from tiny local events to huge national events that feature thousands of participants. Old World Wisconsin has included Civil War events on its calendar for many years, and the largest Civil War reenactment and encampment in the state takes place at sister site the Wade House every September.

Geri Gerold © Kathleen Ernst

ABOUT THE AUTHOR

Kathleen Ernst is an award-winning author, educator, and social historian. She has published thirty-one novels and two nonfiction books. Her books for young readers include the Caroline Abbott series for *American Girl*. Honors for her children's mysteries include Edgar and Agatha Award nominations. Kathleen worked as an interpreter and as curator of interpretation and collections at Old World Wisconsin, and her time at the historic site served as inspiration for the Chloe Ellefson mysteries. *The Heirloom Murders* won the Anne Powers Fiction Book Award from the Council for Wisconsin Writers, and *The Light Keeper's Legacy* won the Lovey Award for Best Traditional Mystery from Love Is Murder. Ernst served as project director/scriptwriter for several instructional television series, one of which earned her an Emmy Award. She lives in Middleton, Wisconsin. For more information, visit her online at http://www.kathleenernst.com.